THE *HARD* COUNT

ISBN: 0996873449
ISBN-13: 978-0-9968734-4-4

For my fellow IHS Patriots.
And for those of you who grew up knowing where O'Neil park was,
what Denton Lane meant, and who fed me way too much and cheered for
me just as loudly as your own daughters on the field. To the beautiful
families I grew up with, and to the beautiful family of my own.
And to the little boy, years ago, who watched me dance to oldies records in
my grandmother's South Phoenix front yard, then offered to share his
grapes with me when the sun went down.
I watched the lightning with you during the Monsoon.
My grandmother said you were sweet on me.
I think we were just good friends.
I can't remember your name, but I remember your dimple.
My Nico.

PROLOGUE

I look over my shoulder when I walk home from school. If the sun is setting, I run.

Mom says it's best for young boys like me not to be out on the streets at night. That's when the 57 comes out. I don't tell Mom, but they're out during the day, too. My older brother, Vincent, goes with them sometimes. I don't tell Momma that, either. I think, though, that maybe…she already knows.

I live on a quiet street. Me and my friends play football in the middle. The only time we have to stop our game is when one of them drives through. They drive slow. And they stare at me. Especially the one in the dark-blue car—his eyes look like the devil's, and there's always smoke coming from his mouth. My mom says it's drugs, and his brain is poisoned. But his brain seems to be working okay. He always looks like he's thinking. He's the one I watch for when I'm alone.

My best friend, Sasha, is moving. There's a sign in front of his house, and I heard his parents talking to my mom about how much the neighborhood has changed. I'm only ten, and it seems the same as it's always been to me. The grocery store still has my favorite pop in the freezer box right outside, Pete's Root Beer with vanilla. Marina and Paul still have the big orange house on the corner, and she always gives me tamales to take home any time I want. And Mr. and Mrs. Mendoza, who live across the street, still have the nicest yard I've ever seen. Vincent says boys aren't supposed to like flowers, but Mrs. Mendoza grows roses. They smell sweet, and I like to watch the bees eat from them. I don't care what Vincent says.

I like it here. And I don't want to move. But I think Sasha's parents have made my mom want to. She was looking at apartments in the paper yesterday morning during breakfast. I got angry and grabbed the newspaper from her hands and tore it into pieces when I ran out the back door. She caught me by the bottom of my Avengers T-shirt, and it ripped at the neck. She didn't hit my butt, but she made me run to the store and buy her a new paper. I tried to glue my shirt back together, but before I went to school this morning, I saw it in the trash.

I miss that shirt…

I'm going to miss Sasha. He says he's moving before they sell the house, but he won't be far. He's going to the other side of the freeway. We counted on a map, measuring with a piece of paper I ripped from Momma's Bible. It was one of the blank pages near the back, so I don't think she'll notice. Eleven miles. That's how far we measured. It costs less than three dollars to get to his new house by bus. Mom says I can go every two weeks. I asked Sasha if he would visit me on the weeks I can't go to his house, but his parents said *no*. I know they like me, though, so it must be our neighborhood. They must be tired of looking over their shoulders and hiding inside, too.

I'm tired of being scared.

I used to not be. Back before we had to sit on the ground and stay away from the windows to watch TV in the living room. Mom put that rule in place when a bullet came through our front wall. Vincent says it was an accident, and usually that means it's not going to happen again. It happened to Sasha's house a week later, though. I thought the hole was cool, but then my mom told me I could have died. That's when my headaches began, and I quit sleeping through the night.

That's also when Vincent started getting in the blue car with the Devil Man. My brother told me the bullets wouldn't hurt us now,

2

because we were protected.

But I don't feel protected.

I feel like I'm being hunted.

Every day.

I run home fast.

I don't play outside alone when the sky is orange.

I don't want to get in the blue car with the smoking man and his laughing friends.

I don't want to learn how to keep my fingerprints off a sawed-off rifle.

I don't want to sell drugs to "make some fast money" or "help my momma out."

Those are the things the Devil Man says when he waits for me and his engine rumbles in the street while I walk home from school. He always laughs when I run. But I'll always run. He'll never catch me.

I won't do any of it his way. I study hard. I get straight *As.* I run. I hide. I keep quiet. I stay out of trouble. I look at the tall rooftops and fancy cars on the other side of the freeway, and I wonder what they're like.

Momma says we can't afford the apartment. I don't care. I don't want any of it. I want my home with the sweet roses and tamales and music that plays loud on Saturdays.

I love my home.

I just hate what living here makes people do.

Nicolas "Nico" Medina
Journal entry
Fifth grade
Sunnyside Elementary at West End

CHAPTER 1

I can tell within a glance if someone hates me. Sometimes it only takes one word. Other times, it's those subtle nonverbal cues—a shift of the eyes or arms folded over a chest in an attempt to hide all of that hate inside that's dying to bore through their chest and grip mine until I choke or die.

Nico Medina is subtle about it. It's in the way he *doesn't* look at me, and how he breathes when I speak—the sound of air filling his chest so heavy I think it may just turn into fire and come back at me in flames.

It began our freshman year, when we partnered for peer grading on our first persuasive essay assignment. I spent hours on his, offering critique points in the margins, circling arguments he made that I felt were strong and jotting down my thoughts and ideas on ways he could make his points even stronger. I was impressed with him. Maybe a little enamored, too. I was fourteen and precocious, the twin sister of a jock football player and the daughter of our school's football coach and a socialite mother who spent every week planning the coming weekend's cocktail party at our house. I was dying to find someone willing to talk about politics with me, to debate classic literature themes, or maybe sit next to me in the school's editing bay working on video for the school's monthly announcement show, that nobody watched, but I put every ounce of my being into. I just wanted another nerd. And I thought I'd found one.

We exchanged papers, and my crush was *crushed* into a thousand tiny, sharp, jagged bits.

Nico gave me a B. He wrote WEAK on the top—and circled it.

In red.

I approached him after class, paper in my hand and finger pointing to his one-word review, and asked him "What is this supposed to be?"

His response: "It's a word. *Weak*. It describes your paper. You're bad at this…" he paused when he leaned forward to look at my essay, now wrinkled in my angry, rigid hands. His lips quirked just before he looked up at me again, "Reagan Prescott."

Every syllable sounded as if he had spit it on the ground. That was our first encounter. That was also our longest encounter, unless I count the times we debate in school. Somehow, our humanities class always turns into a session of point-counterpoint, and Nico is always quick to take up the opposite view of mine.

Because he hates me.

Right now—*hate*. I can hear him sucking in his breath through his nose, his shoulders rising like a shield against my voice. I'm talking. I'm…arguing. He *hates* that. The fire in his veins is waiting to burn me to the ground.

We've been debating over altruism—the idea of a truly selfless act. I believe they exist. Nico…not so much.

"I just feel like that perspective is too broad. It's a black-or-white kind of statement eliminating the gray. In this case, that gray area is an entire array of emotions that you've basically just boiled down into one category—"

"Yes, selfishness. You get it now. You're actually arguing my point exactly—that all acts are done out of self-interest. We are, by nature, ego-driven beings. We simply can't help it," Nico says, cutting me off and breaking the rules of decorum. Mr. Huffman insists we follow some basic rules of respect when discussions heat up in his classroom. He likes his students engaged, and even when we veer into taboo topics—

politics, religion, the weird place where they intersect—he never stops us. I'm fairly certain that's why he assigns reading subjects like Ayn Rand and topics that are so two-sided that a debate is inevitable.

"Go on," Mr. Huffman says, giving Nico a short glance in warning.

He meant for me to continue, but Nico, of course, talks over my words, reiterating his point. Most of the class is behind him now, half because he's a good arguer, and half because, despite his arrogance, he's mesmerizing to look at. Taller than most of the guys in our school, he has this one lock of dark hair that hangs over his right eye, and he smiles when he blows it out of his face. There's a dimple when he grins—the same dimple he gets when he speaks. That small dent in his bronze skin is deeper when he's sure he's right. His expressions are the kind that are bolstered by confidence, and as easy as it would be for me to chalk that up to his broad shoulders that seem to fill out every T-shirt he owns, I know it really comes from his beautiful mind—quick wit, nearly photographic memory, and a way with words that leaves me tongue-tied and slightly spellbound.

His perfection pisses me off.

I feel the enamel on my back teeth crackle with the harsh grinding motion while I clench so hard I may in fact break my jaw. After a two-second breath and pause to think, I open my mouth the second Nico stops talking and begin to speak just in time to halt Mr. Huffman mid-spin of the heels on his way to the board where he keeps notes during our classroom debates.

"That's not what I'm saying at all, though I do see your ego is in rare form today," I say. My remark gets a smirk from my teacher, and I catch Nico's shoulder lift with a single-breath chuckle. I bet he's smiling. I'm sure the dimple is there. I wouldn't know for certain. He doesn't turn to look at me. He never looks at me when he speaks—when we spar. That, more than anything, usually gets me so angry that I end up losing my train of thought. But there's enough time left today, and today— *today*…I'm not as angry as I usually am. I'm on point.

My lips part just enough for my tongue to slip through and wet the dry skin. I should probably take a drink from my water bottle, but I don't want anyone in here to see it as a sign of weakness. I'm right on this one. Not Nico Medina.

"You argue that we, as humans, only do kind things for others because of the pleasure it gives us," I say, pausing when I hear the noise of Nico's pencil tapping rapidly against his leg. He's like a snake coiled and ready to strike.

"We act because doing good makes us feel good," he blurts out, his voice full of that condescension I've come to expect every day from two fifteen to three o'clock. "We act in every way because it feels good. We seek thrills for pleasure. We avoid pain—*for pleasure!* And we do favors for others, we make donations, we give someone a piece of our body— an organ—because saving someone else makes us feel good. I'm not saying it isn't a good thing. I'm just saying we don't do it because we're good people. We do it because we like the feeling we get *when* we're good people."

"Not always," I swallow before continuing, my eyes firm on my opponent's form three rows across from me and one chair ahead. I lean forward, hoping to catch his periphery, and grip the edge of my desk. He doesn't turn a tick. "On occasion, we act because of duty. We self-sacrifice for the greater good of the community—even when it breaks our hearts to do so. I cannot believe that the pleasure from sacrifice is always part of the equation. I know it's not."

Nico's feet shuffle, crossing underneath his desk. His pencil has stopped moving, and the lines in his jaw flex. I've made him nervous. The dimple is gone.

Yes! I've erased the dimple!

I revel for a full three seconds, but my breath catches the moment my eyes are square with his. *He's turned around.* The deep brown is offset by flecks of gold, and they're wide at first, narrowing the instant he knows he has me caught—he's the sniper, and I'm on the run. He didn't face me out of weakness; this is a kill shot. His body is squared with mine as he turns in his seat, leaning forward slowly to settle his elbows on his denim-covered knees and rub his hands together as his smirk grows steadily along with his confidence.

I know exactly where he's going. He thinks he has me trapped—that I'll fall right in. My honesty is about to surprise him.

"Last year…" he begins, "we had a competition for our junior class. Our best debate team against the best team from St. Augustine."

The junior debate with our rival school is an annual event. It's a way to show off our academic prowess, which of course makes the parents who are writing ten-thousand-dollar checks to the school feel like they're getting their money's worth. It's also a way to show off scholarship kids—like Nico—and prove to those same boosters and parents that they're *making a difference.* I suppose Nico is right in one case—those checks aren't selfless acts. Those people want to feel good about helping kids from tax brackets well below their own, and they strut for compliments on debate night as if the scholarship kids were actually their flesh and blood.

"We won," I answer Nico, my voice strong and certain as I turn in my seat, mirroring him. His nostrils flare, but I'm sure only I notice.

"We did," he says, the left side of his mouth rising as his eyes lower more. The rest of the class has grown quiet to the point of breathless. I know most of them don't really care about our little point-counterpoint; they care about drama. They love it; it's what keeps life at Cornwall Prep going—a mini society fueled by rumors and innuendos, sex scandals and rivalries. Nico Medina and I are small time, but we're hot enough to fill the last two minutes of class. Our drama will do.

All I want to do is win.

Nico leans back in his seat, resting his back on the small curve of wood behind him, crossing his right leg over his left knee and folding his arms with satisfaction over his chest.

Conceited prick asshole.

"And why did we win?" he asks.

"Because I let you be captain," I say, my eyes blinking out the words slowly because, yes, they are painful to say. But I don't pause in saying them. I answer quickly.

"That's right. You made me captain, sacrificing your own desire to be a leader for the good of the team," he says, his words patronizing and dripping with condescension. "I'm pretty sure that falls into the category of *duty,* would you agree?"

"I'll agree," I say, my expression still flat as it was when he began. Nothing he's saying is surprising me. It won't.

"Then let me ask you this—your sacrifice…how did it make you feel?"

He's so sure he has me. I could cave so easily. I would look better if I caved, better in the eyes of my best friend Izzy who is sitting next to me. She's the one who asked me to let him be captain. She wanted to win, to carry home a heavy golden cup engraved with the word CHAMPION, to have a line on her resume that she was preparing for expensive colleges back East that said the same. Out of duty to my friend, I voted for Nico. Raising my hand felt like swallowing acid, and if I had it to do over, I would never make that mistake again.

"Well?" he prompts.

"It made me feel ashamed. It made me sick with regret. It's the worst mistake I've ever made, and I took absolutely zero pleasure from it."

The chuckles from the back of our classroom are faint, and Mr. Huffman's warning with the wave of his hand and finger-hush over his lips does little to quiet them. The bell rings, and our teacher begins to recite out page numbers for our next reading. Nico and I don't bother to write them down. I'm sure, like me, he's finished his already.

The rustling of papers and chatter—about the weekend's party, about tonight's game, about my quarterback brother and whoever he's dating—takes over the present, but Nico and I remain in our seats in the very-near past. We're locked in our duel. My stomach is twitching with the nervous patter of my racing heart. It isn't because of his eyes or smirk or tight T-shirt and somehow unbelievably-masculine seated position. I notice those things, but I dismiss them. It's because I've been in the ring with him, and I've come out victorious. I want to cheer! I want high fives. I want to whisper *yes*, and clutch my fist to my gut in celebration.

Neither of us moves or speaks until Mr. Huffman calls our names, stirring us from our locked positions as he kicks down the stop on his door, signaling he has hall duty. I'm the first to break. I tell myself it's because I have things to do. I need to get to the video room, to gather my equipment and make it to Dad's coaching office before the football team files in. I have a deadline that Nico doesn't have. But that's not why I'm moving. I'm moving because I know he won't. He'll just sit there and continue to stare, and no matter how right I believe I am, he'll make me think I'm wrong.

"I think I need to ask my question again, Reagan," he says, and my chest seizes under the rush of numbness pouring through both it and my veins like morphine. He's tapped into my nerves by just saying my name. He's trying to make me angry. He wants me to emote. But I won't. I won this time, and he's going to have to swallow that pill. I'm not going to play a war of words that doesn't matter.

My lips pursed, I raise my brows as I look at him and stand, my bags gathered over my shoulder and my books clutched against my chest. I look away when he doesn't speak immediately, moving to the opened doorway, ready to disappear into our crowded high school hallway. His voice at my shoulder slows me down.

"Your confession—just now—that you only admitted, for your own pleasure of beating me in some silly, meaningless, classroom debate over a book that's older than the bricks that built our school…" he slows, and I turn just enough to catch the dimple. "How did that make you feel?"

I part my lips to answer, ready to reject him, to refuse to walk down this path, but I can't. A small breath escapes me, and my heart beat slows into a steady, obnoxious drum. I close my mouth, because there's really no need for me to answer. Nico doesn't wait to hear one. He pushes his hair from his eyes and tugs his bag tight against his shoulder, tucking his long board against his side. His lip ticks up just enough to push the dimple even deeper as he takes three or four steps backward before turning away and becoming lost in the crowd before me, always a step ahead.

I wait for nearly a minute, leaned against the doorway, my mind retracing every word I said, looking for the flaw in his argument, until I realize just how obsessed I've become over the last hour, over beating him. I chuckle to myself, glancing at his seat and mine, then shake my head while my teeth saw at my lip.

I answer his question in my head as I begin my trek to the football locker rooms. Beating Nico in a debate felt great. It felt amazing in those small breaths of a moment where I thought I had. But I hadn't really.

Smug asshole was right all along.

Even worse, he doesn't care who knows.

CHAPTER 2

No matter how many times I hear the speech, I still get goosebumps.

The first time I went to the game early with my dad, I was maybe five or six. I crawled up on a training table in the back of the film room and pulled my legs in to make myself small so nobody would see me, but after a few of my dad's players mouthed some choice words, he was quick to point out that his baby girl was in attendance and all foul language would result in hours of running up and down the bleachers on Saturday morning. Mouths were glued shut after that, but I believe they would have been anyway, because the moment Chad Prescott turns into Coach Prescott, people are brought to attention.

It's always the same, yet somehow, each time, his words are unique, as if being said to virgin ears and being uttered without careful practice and memorization. Maybe it's the tradition of it all—the tradition he's at the heart of—that makes those words hit so hard.

My dad has coached the Cornwall Prep Tigers for twenty-two seasons, and he's brought them to the state playoffs for seventeen. The five missing years don't get discussed much. Four were early on, when he first took over the program from the beloved Michael Colson, who was my dad's coach when he played here. Colson's health was declining, and the transition of the team from him to my father was assumed to have rough spots. However, the other year—*last* year—is fresh on everyone's mind. Lips are sealed on the subject, at least when it's to my father's face, but the threat lives in everyone's eyes.

As much as Cornwall is built on tradition, it's also teeming with superstition. We don't talk about things that are broken. We eliminate them. We're not a religious institution. We're a private college prep riding on the wealth that pays for the best. Cornwall is all about the arts, the academics—a miniature college in many ways. And unlike our neighbor, nearby St. Augustine, our school was founded on one principle, and one principle only—we lead. And when we don't, we crush whatever is keeping us from being on top. Last year, we lost to a new contender—Great Vista High School, a newly-minted Division I public school with six times our population and a football team that decimated us on the field and left graffiti behind on our walls to rub it in.

The whispers started the moment the clock ticked down to zero and my father led fifty young men back into the locker room with their heads low and their hearts heavy. My father yelled. He threw things. He made boys cry. He blamed my twin brother, Noah, who my dad gave the starting quarterback position to over a senior. Words weren't spoken, but it's clear that's who everyone else blamed as well. My brother played hard, and against any other team, his effort might have been good enough. But Noah also likes to party and cut corners. Those small cracks in his work ethic became gaping chasms during last year's playoffs, and they've born an almost suffocating environment in our home.

That's what happens when you fail at Cornwall. You become the target. You become the thing that must be crushed. There aren't excuses, and my dad has one year to make things right. Noah—maybe less. I know they both will. And right now, their mouths are shut and their eyes unable to blink or look away from the man with graying sideburns and a permanent sunburn around his eyes, from where his sunglasses rest during practice; my father's team believes they'll right the ship, too.

I'm going to capture it all.

My camera began rolling seconds before my dad started *the* speech. In the sixty-year history of our school, nobody has ever documented the legacy of the Tiger Football Tradition. We don't call it a *team*, because teams are too fluid, rife with change. We're a tradition, one that once you're initiated into you have with you forever.

"This tradition is about your brothers," my dad says, his voice echoing off the concrete walls and floor. I stand, recognizing this part of the speech. I want to make sure my cameras are in the right position—one framing my father's face, the other in my hands to see the reaction of the boys who believe in him.

"Brothers," he continues, "are lifelong. And though you take that field tonight, you have also taken that field before, just as you will tomorrow, and the next day, and the next. That field is your home—*your* battlefield—and those other men are intruders. They don't respect it. They're trespassing—unwanted guests."

I check my arm and smile to myself when I see the small bumps resulting from chills. With my handheld steadied on my raised knee, my foot braced against the wall, I scan the room and capture those faces that look like they feel exactly as I do. My brother Noah is up front, rocking his weight from one foot to the other as he stands at attention. His hands grip at his shoulder pads around his neck, and his lips mutter along with the words he too knows by heart. His eyes crease, accented by the deep black lines smeared underneath.

Slowly, I pan down the row of familiar faces, and they're all rapt in the same way, their expression that of belief, of possibility. My brother's best friend, Travis, has his eyes closed for prayers to God, but in between he whispers the speech along with everyone else.

"They think they're better than you," my father says, mouths follow, pausing to let those words sink in.

The room pops with shaking heads and shuffling feet. Some of the guys respond with "no sir" and "hell no."

"We know they're not," my father shouts.

The room erupts in a deep round of voices that all chant, "Hoorah!"

"They think they've worked harder than you," my father says, his voice even louder.

Heads shake, and some of the guys chuckle, rubbing sore arms and bloodied and bandaged body parts that do not hurt in this moment, but rather remind them of what they went through to get here.

"I can assure you they didn't," my father says. Again, the room chants, "Hoorah!"

I hold my breath because this next part, more than anything that led up to it, is what I've been waiting for. I check the camera, my father still centered in my frame and his face as serious as I've ever seen it. Our team has won the first two games of the year, but he knows that two is not ten. A loss, at this point, will be unforgiveable.

"What's that word on your backs?" His question echoes, and the answer is swift.

"Honor, sir!" they all shout in unison. They always do. It's more than memorization, and it's always made me sit in awe of how it all plays out.

"Honor! That's right. There are no individuals in here. We all have one name. It isn't the mascot. It isn't your nickname or some fad that will be forgotten the second the yearbook is printed. It's a word that means *heart*, that means *drive* and *ambition*, that means giving your all and leaving the best of every goddamned thing you've got out there on that field. Turn to your right!"

They all do, seated in a circle on the benches, looking at the helmets and heads of their teammates. My dad should have been a preacher, or perhaps a general. He was born to stand before boys and make them believe that for two and a half hours, they are men.

"Turn to your left!"

All heads shift, the sound swift, but mouths quiet.

"Honor. Brotherhood. Tradition." He pauses, his team still sitting with heads angled and eyes wide on the dark blue sheen of the helmets and sweat-drenched heads next to them.

"Again…" he says, and this time they say it with him.

"Honor. Brotherhood. Tradition."

"Whose house is this?" my father asks, quiet and waiting for a roar.

"Our house!"

"Whose house is this?" He's louder now.

"Our house!"

"Whose house…" My dad's face is red and his voice is hoarse by the time he shouts the question painted above the door that the Cornwall Tradition runs through to the field. The final chant back is loud enough that it can be heard through the cinderblock walls. I know, because last week, I filmed the speech from outside.

With chests full, egos inflated, voices primed and muscles ready for abuse, this packed room of fifty—the number that always takes the field, even though less than half of them will play—stands, each putting a hand on the back of everyone in front of them. Everyone does this except for my brother, because he's in front.

I sprint with my camera to the front, kneeling low and turning my focus onto my brother's loud, clapping hands—the chalk dusting from them and the tape around his wrists tight against his skin, circulation choked just enough so pain is little and blood flow is maximized to his throwing arm. He's chanting—"honor…win."

They all chant with him, and without a sign, they know when it's time. The run through the tunnel is swift and loud, like inept thieves bursting through glass windows, and the thunderous sound of this year's Tiger squad is undeniable. Heads turn at the edge of the bleachers, watching the line rush over the track and into the end zone, through satin banners held by beautiful girls who dream of one of these boys taking them away when our time here is all done.

I set the camera on my tripod to capture the scene in focus, my father's form passing through my frame as he jogs behind, along with his coaching staff. They all seem like heroes—bigger than life, and juiced with aggression and desire for victory. They're made this way. My dad makes them this way.

It's beautiful.

It's also sad.

My video runs for nineteen minutes, mostly capturing warm-ups and the kickoff before the sun finally sets and I shut my recording off. I wanted to capture the drama of the performance so I could fast-forward it in editing and layer it with music.

I'm making a documentary on Cornwall. Mostly, it's on my dad and brother. They only half know that part, but they both like the attention—Noah more than anyone. My film is about the legacy of this program, but also about the pressure it puts on people—on families.

On my family.

The storyline is epic, and the potential for a fairytale or tragic ending is equal. This documentary is also my ticket into the film school at Prestige, a private art institution in the Northeast. My family lives football. My mom is queen bee of the social circle that comes with being a major donor and booster; my father is the man four wins away from setting a state record for the most wins ever with a single program. My brother is being courted by The Big Ten, and he's been interviewed by all of the big press that comes along with it.

All of that is the fairytale side of the story.

The dark side is the dysfunction we live with: my dad's blind eye to the rules my brother breaks. He drove his car into the river last season with six of his teammates packed inside, along with empty bottles and cans that somehow disappeared before any authorities showed up. It's also the pills my mom takes to keep the grin on her face, to stay in her marriage and not to sob herself to sleep when people write horrible things in chalk on our driveway about my dad losing his job.

It's the blood I know my father coughs up from ulcers.

The price of winning is steep, and sometimes it doesn't seem worth it. Yet, I adore my dad, and I root for my brother, and want to see my mom happy. I guess it's like Nico said; people don't make any decision unless they get some personal pleasure from the outcome. My family's success gives me pleasure—even when it's killing us.

I pull my camera from the tripod and close the screen, my eyes watching the end zone where my brother has just leapt over the Mountain Crest High defensive line to score six. The band kicks in, the drums beating hard and fast, gaining speed with the chants the crowd yells every time we score. They count to six, and fireworks will soon mark the extra point. I smile, because *this* is the fairytale stuff.

"Nice keeper," I fumble the camera and nearly drop it with my startle, but a swift, warm hand covers mine and pushes everything back into a cradle against my chest. I recognize the voice, but the touch is foreign, and it takes my mind a second longer to catch up to what my eyes see. Nico's shirtless, but still in his dark jeans that he wore to school, his T-shirt tucked into the waistband and his arm damp with sweat.

"Thanks," I say, peering at his bare skin, but quickly turning my attention over to my camera that I almost dropped on the asphalt. I'm sweating.

"For rescuing that fancy lens of yours?" he asks, taking a step or two away while he shuffles a football from one hand to the other. "Or for complimenting your brother?"

"Both, I guess," I stammer, my eyes unable to look away from the ball now clutched at the center of his chest. I force my gaze up, and I'm greeted by the dimple. That small trait of his kicks in my stubbornness. I open my mouth to speak, hoping something strong and independent will come out, but in a quick flash I recognize that Nico's not alone. Five or six guys are walking up behind him, all of them shirtless and out of breath, a few with gallons of water in their hands. I don't know why I'm overcome with nerves now; my brother's team is at the house swimming and running around half naked all the time.

"Yo, if you want to hit on baby girl, do it on your own time, Nico. Don't take the fuckin' game ball with you," one of them says.

His words stun my mouth shut instantly, and my brow pinches in an effort to ward off the red embarrassment I can already feel creeping up my ears as the rest of the guys snicker and call out "ooooh" while they high five. Nico Medina is *not* hitting on me. That's not our routine. In fact, talking outside of the one class we share is not part of the routine. He shouldn't be here, and...

"I'm nobody's baby girl," I say the instant his words truly register. My chest begins to pound, not from nerves, but with that same anger I get when I'm in a debate with Nico or trying to convince my parents that film school is the right place for me after graduation.

I bend down to set my camera in the bag at my feet, and take the opportunity to squeeze my eyes closed and calm my pounding heart and heavy breath.

"You're Coach's girl. That's just what we call you," he laughs out his words. Nico shoots him a hard stare that I catch, and I also notice his friend shrug his shoulders and mouth the word *what* in question-slash-apology. He rolls his eyes and looks back to me. "Sorry," he huffs. It's completely not genuine. "I'm mostly bustin' my boy because douchebag took the ball. Come on, Nic. We've got game," the guy says, brushing his hand forward until his fingers touch my arm. I fight the instinct to flinch and instead nod. He nods back with a wink, pushing Nico off balance as he runs back to the empty practice field lit only by the spill-off of light from the main field on the other side of the parking lot.

When I look back to Nico, I expect to see the hard face I'm used to in class, the one ready to argue, but instead his dimple is deep and his eyes are creased, his lips *almost* smiling, like he has more to say. I swallow. He sees it, and his lip quirks a hint higher. I hate that.

"You making a movie or something?" His eyes gesture to the equipment at my feet. I look down, too, then over my shoulder, remembering the camera I left behind in the film room.

"Uh, yeah. Something," I say, my mind ping-ponging between wondering if the room is unlocked still, and this conversation with Nico Medina, which is bizarre.

I snap back to attention when Nico's friend shouts something, and Nico tosses him the ball, underhand throwing a tight spiral that disappears briefly before falling back into the light.

"Right, well...you ever want to film a real game...instead of that *display* that happens over there; we'll be over here," he says, chuckling and jerking his head toward the dark field where his friends have started running and tackling one another.

I'm too tongue-tied to respond, but I manage to keep my nerves in check for the few seconds he's still close enough to hear me. When he turns to jog down the slope into the field, I let out the air I'd been holding hostage in my lungs.

I pick up my small camera bag and loop it over my shoulder, checking the scoreboard before walking quickly back to the locker room. The home score reads seven, and the air smells acrid, so I know the fireworks went off for the extra point. Somehow, though, I never noticed.

The film room is unlocked; I grab the rest of my things and make my way back to the main field in time for the second quarter. I hear a few mutters from the most-vocal critics as I walk up to the press box. They know who I am, and I know they only say those things in hopes that I'll repeat their concerns to my father.

"This is how our team started last year."

"Only up by a touchdown at the end of one. Maybe Coach isn't playing the right talent."

"I sure hope Jimmy's ready to step into the job."

That last comment comes up a lot, and I never repeat it to my dad. He hears it enough on his own. Jimmy O'Donahue is Dad's assistant. He was voted onto the staff by the board, and my father begrudgingly lets him handle the defense. Jimmy is the son of one of the board members, and he's alumni. While my father's alumni, too, his tradition stops there. He was the start of our family line. Jimmy's goes back to the day the school was founded, and there are a lot of people who would like to see him in that beloved head-coach role. Fortunately, my dad has enough friends on the board to keep him safe for now.

He just needs to keep winning.

Once my camera is set, I crawl out to the small section of bleachers on the rooftop of the press box and slide my notebook from my bag, where I write down the latest round of comments I've overheard. I know I need interviews to really make my documentary solid, but I can't seem to get the nerve to face the haters. I'm not sure what worries me more—if they'll pretend to love my dad to my face, or if they'll let me tape their honest opinions.

Instead, for now, I work things into my own narration script. I plan to catch their quips and jabs secretly with my recorder, and maybe that will be enough. It's probably not ethical, but neither are some of the threatening things they say.

Minutes pass with very little action, both sides trading punts and the ball never coming near an end zone until Travis intercepts a pass and runs it back forty yards with fifteen seconds left in the half. I stand along with everyone else, and I check my camera to make sure it's capturing game play while I pull out my handheld to get the other side of the story. My brother grabs his helmet and dashes to the line, and I zoom in as tight as I can on the huddle, wishing I had him miked to hear what he said, or at least to hear them all clap and yell "break!"

Katie, his girlfriend for at least the last few months, is standing on the first step at the front of the stands, her hands cupping her mouth; my mother is close behind her, holding hands with our neighbor, Travis's mom, Linda, as if her son was going off to battle. The clock begins, and as slow as everything feels, it all happens so quickly. My brother finds a receiver, he throws with a snap, the ball is caught, and the drums begin.

I bounce on my toes, and I feel my cheeks ache from smiling, but in the middle of it all, I think of Nico. The field is too far for me to hear them, but every now and then I catch a glimpse of their forms running in the dim lights, until the fireworks signal our field goal and the crowd erupts. Nico and his friends don't even pause—their own game far more important as the ball sails farther than any throw I've ever seen leave my brother's grip, landing easily into the hands of the boy who teased me several minutes ago.

"Some game, huh Reagan?" Jimmy says, headphones around his neck as he clears out of the press box area and walks down the bleachers to join the rest of the team and coaching staff in the locker room.

I rarely respond, mostly because I don't trust him. This is normally the time when I go find my friend Izzy and skim off her nachos and steal half of her drink that she's tried to hide—though not too well—on the small table right in front of the bleachers. Izzy's a cheerleader, but she went out of town for the weekend with her grandparents, leaving right after school. I climb down the few steps from the top of the press box and glance out at the crowd, most people making breaks for the restrooms and concession area. My mom is already on her phone, and her friends are all chatting around her. I could sit with these women, who I don't necessarily like, for twelve minutes, but instead, I find my feet carrying me down the back steps of the bleachers and out into the darkness where boys wearing nothing but muddied jeans and skin are still battling hard.

I walk along the far end, the action currently on the opposite side of the field, and slide to a sitting position on the cool, damp grass that slopes down. I bend my legs and wipe the pieces of cut crass from the backs of my thighs and test my denim shorts to see how wet they are. Satisfied it won't leave too much of a wet mark, I bring my arms around my knees and balance my camera on top, flipping open the viewfinder and zooming in as tight as I can. At first, I can't see much—the light too little—but as the action comes closer, my camera takes more in, and when the boys are yards away from me, I can clearly make out their faces.

Nico's friend—the talkative one—waves at me, but I don't wave back. I'm not part of the story. I hold my camera on him until I'm forgotten again, and the plays become all that matter. There are only eight of them down there, enough to play a small pickup game, to pass and run, but the longer I watch, the more I realize how very little Nico needs. He moves like Noah. His feet fall back naturally, and he glides out of the reach of his friend who dives at him, shaking off a tackle with no help from pads or a uniform. When his friend comes at him again, he shirks him off once more, twisting and sprinting to the opposite side, giving his receiver enough time to make it to the corner of their makeshift end zone marked with discarded shirts, skateboards, bikes and hats.

I watch through the safety of my camera lens, his arm coming back, his bicep coiling, his arm strong as it rushes forward, sending the ball racing into his receiver's waiting hands. I don't even notice I'm standing at first, but when I do, I stay on my feet, watching these eight boys celebrate together in a way that seems so much more important than what happens behind me. Under the lights, where a band plays and thousands cheer, hands get slapped and choreographed routines play out for attention while wealthy people keep tabs for bragging rights at weekend parties. Here, in the dark and forgotten field in a game that doesn't matter to anyone, something beautiful plays out.

Brotherhood. Honor. Tradition.

"You decide to cover the real story there, baby girl?"

Before I can stick up for myself, Nico slaps his friend in the chest, the smack knocking air from his lungs.

"Fuck, man," he coughs out.

"That's quite an arm you have," I say, deciding to ignore his friend.

"Thanks," Nico says, stepping closer to me. I press the STOP button on my camera and let it fall to my side, but not before Nico notices. He bends down to lift a nearby gallon of water from the ground, bringing it to his lips and tipping it back, guzzling until almost half of it is gone.

"So what kind of camera is this? Like a DSLR or whatever?" His friend is trying to be nice, so I indulge him, even though he has no idea what kind of camera I'm using.

"It's just a high-def handheld. It's easier to maneuver it, when you want to get action shots," I say, lifting it so he can see it more closely. He takes it in his hands, holding it with one while he pulls his hat from his head and runs his arm over his forehead, smoothing out his damp hair.

"Action shots, huh? You shoot a lot of porn?" he says, unable to get his jab out without laughing halfway through. Nico smacks him in the chest again, and I can't help but smile.

"Nobody wants to see a porn starring you, Sasha," Nico says, taking the camera from his friend's hand and returning it to me.

"I meant her, Nic…" Sasha says, stopping before finishing when Nico shoots him a warning glance.

"My boy's an asshole sometimes, but it's only because he isn't around girls a lot," Nico says, and his friends join in laughing while Sasha flips them off.

My fingers are tingling, so I busy them by opening and closing the lens on the camera, while Nico's friends all catch their breath and begin gathering their things from the field. Nico stays near me, and the longer we stand in silence, the stronger the urge is in me to fill the quiet.

"I'm making a film for my application to Prestige," I say, tucking my lip in between my teeth while my fingers flip the camera lens even faster. I don't know why I thought Nico was interested, and the longer it takes him to respond, the more desperate I am to escape this small dark patch of grass. I long for the press box, for the bleachers, for my mother's circle of friends. The game clock has started again, and my mind is actively searching for the right words to say goodbye, to leave without making it worse, to not be a complete ass.

"Like a documentary? On what? The team?" His questions come several seconds later, and I trip over my feet a little at the sound of his voice. He grabs my elbow, steadying me as we walk the few steps up the slant of the hill.

I hold my camera in one hand and pull the long, blonde braid around one side of my body so I can hook the strap over my other arm. Nico's eyes watch my hands, and my stomach rushes with a strange feeling that comes over me even more when his eyes snap to mine, catching me looking at him. I look down right away.

"It's on the team…sort of," I say, shaking my head and wondering how much sharing is too much. I don't know Nico well, and I don't really like him, but there's this odd, overwhelming desire pushing at my chest right now to tell him things.

"Is it on your brother?" he asks, and I flinch at how remarkably close to home his question hits. He grins, recognizing my tell, and I deflate seeing him look satisfied.

"It's on the team, mostly. On the legacy and history, but also on what the pressure of it all does to people," I say, sharing more than I planned. I hold my breath, digging in for an argument.

Nico looks back for his friends, and his eyes squint a little as his hand runs along the side of his neck. He stops walking, and I stop with him. Reaching for the shirt still tucked into his waistband, he pulls the dark gray tee loose, shaking it out and slipping it over his head and arms, fishing his black hat out when it gets stuck inside and putting it on backward. I expect the smirk and the dimple, and some response about how silly my idea is when he looks at me, but instead his mouth is a flat line, and his eyes bleed sympathy.

"I bet this sucks sometimes for your family, huh?" he says. His friends are still several feet away, and my family is still being judged out under the hot Friday lights.

I nod, just enough that he registers it and nods back, his eyes never leaving mine. Within seconds, his friends are close by, and Sasha hands him a backpack and longboard, the same ones he left the classroom with earlier.

"You've been here all afternoon?" I ask.

Nico drops his board to the ground and rolls it forward to the walkway, smirking on the side closest to me.

"So have you," he says.

"Yeah, but I drive home. It's dark out here, to ride a board..." I gesture to it. A few of his friends have already taken off on bikes, and two others are walking through the middle of the parking lot.

"I ride everywhere," he shrugs, looping his backpack over his shoulders and adjusting his hat.

I look back to his friend Sasha who is pushing his board forward and back with his foot, pretending not to be hanging on our every word.

"If you can wait until the end of the game, I could...I don't know...take you home?" I feel foolish the second I offer it, and the feeling only gets worse when I hear his friend let out a breathy laugh.

Nico chuckles, too, and I start to say something defensive, when he, per usual, cuts me off.

"You don't need to drive through my neighborhood, baby girl," he says, calling me the same condescending name he smacked his friends for using seconds before. I snap my head and take in a sharp breath that gets his attention. His smile falls quickly, the hard line once again on his mouth as he looks back into the dark parking lot. No apology follows, only more reasons why he doesn't need me, and why I never should have left the safety of the bleachers. "I'm staying at Sasha's. It's only two blocks away, so we'll be fine."

"Whatever," I mumble, a mixture of embarrassment and general pissed-offness brewing in my gut. I step up onto the walkway and begin my trek back into the spotlight, my fingers feeling for the comfort of the buttons on my camera at my side.

I want to turn around to see if he's watching me with every step I take, but I don't look until I get to the bottom of the bleachers and take the first few steps back to everything I was doing before—to the goals I never should have veered from. My film. My family. Screw Nico Medina. My hunch is confirmed when I look back to see him and Sasha rolling through the middle of the lot, stopping at the exit to the main road, bright red and blue lights flashing against their skin.

I'm so caught up in my head with Nico that I don't realize the crowd behind me has hushed and that the ambulance is being guided out onto the field. My instincts kick in, and I push the record button, stepping up through the breezeway to the second set of bleacher steps, my camera following the medics until I stop on the trainer and teammates all huddled near the thirty-yard line, my brother flat on his back, his fists at his head, his cheeks red and flushed with sheer pain as everyone works to lift his body to a board.

His hands are moving, so I know his spine is likely okay. But his leg seems to be facing the wrong direction. As a second splint is slid under his right leg and my father folds a towel in quarters, practically shoving the material into my brother's screaming mouth, I know it's a break. I know it's bad. I know that for my brother, this means his time on top—at least here at Cornwall—has come to a close. I also know that my father can't even mask his real feelings right now. His son is in pain, but even worse, his quarterback is out for the season. The two thousand people around me all want to know what he's going to do, and a few of them are rooting for him to fail.

I haven't stopped filming. I capture it all, because despite the rush of guilt I feel, I'm no better or worse than any of the others. I have the answer—*Nico Medina*. And the angle of my story just became amazing.

CHAPTER 3

The house has that eerie quiet about it. My mom has been pacing up and down the long hallway, first passing my bedroom, then my brother's. She walks from her and my dad's room back to the main living room, each time something different in her hands—a vase from there, moving to here, a new painting she picked up at the decorator store, better for the bedroom. She's redecorating, as if sprucing up our little suburban paradise will make people on the outside think we've got everything handled—that my *dad* has everything handled.

I've had my headphones on and my laptop propped on my legs for the last two hours, splicing video—watching Nico. My brother is in his room, in bed; his leg is propped up in a sling, a new rod holding everything in place. Broken tibias, snapped in the way Noah's did, take at least sixteen weeks to heal. Then comes rehab and a brutal schedule already mapped out with my brother's personal trainer to make sure he's ready for draft day. Two schools have already fallen off the radar, but luckily, the others see it as an edge—less competition to snag Noah later in the year.

My brother's worried. I can tell. And the fact that my father can't seem to talk to him isn't helping things.

"I'm heading to films," I hear my dad shout, the front door closing behind him. I pull my right headphone from my ear and listen to his engine pull away to leave. Nobody responded to his announcement, and my mom has started pulling down more things from the walls, setting them in rows in the hallway to evaluate their new homes. It's her way to be near my brother, but be just busy enough that she doesn't have to talk to him.

She doesn't know what to say.

I close my laptop and hop from my bed, sliding in my socks around my door and into his.

"I don't need your pep talk, Reagan," he says, his eyes intent on his phone. I step in and lean on the side of his bed, and he lets his hands fall flat, the screen down.

"Are you sexting?" I tease.

He pulls one hand up to pinch his brow.

"Get the fuck out of my room."

I don't leave right away. I stare at him until he looks at me, his eyes empty, but sad, until he purses his lips and raises his brow in warning letting me know he means it.

"It's just a broken leg, Noah. It happens a lot in sports, and the best always stay the best. You'll be fine," I say as I step away from his bed, wanting to bring a little of that light back into his face. I actually miss my cocky twin.

"I know I will; now get the fuck out," he says, sighing and returning to his phone. I don't linger, or push buttons. I know this version of Noah. I don't like him, but I understand him.

I go back to my room and slouch on the edge of my bed, dragging my laptop closer and flipping the screen open, Nico's smirk is dead center. The video is paused on the high five he's giving his friend Sasha after that perfect pass. Slowly dragging the PLAY icon back, I let the video play through again on the scene I've watched more than a dozen times now, zooming in on the footwork that I've come to recognize as perfection. It's better than Noah's. My only worry is can he do it more than once?

I shut the screen again and pull my backpack close, tucking my computer inside. After shoving my feet into a pair of running shoes, I grab my keys and twist my hair into a messy knot as I stop to kiss my mom on the cheek and let her know I'm leaving. She smiles, briefly, but never asks where I'm going. I'm not the child she's worried about right now; I rarely am. I'm okay with that role. I like being the easy one. My brother takes work.

I toss my bag into the passenger seat when I get in and buckle my seatbelt, taking a deep breath while I stare at myself in the rearview mirror. I blink at my reflection, sniffing once and crinkling my nose, running my fist over it like a boxer about to step inside the ring. I feel like that's exactly what I'm about to do. Convincing my father of things is impossible, but as his daughter, I've learned that the trick is making it all feel like his idea.

With one more deep breath and reassurance from the blue eyes looking back at me in the mirror, I turn my attention to the road over my shoulder, back out of our driveway, and make my way to my high school. I pull into the far lot, by the film room, taking the spot next to my dad's car. It's Sunday, and I know the rest of his staff will be showing up this afternoon to put their two cents in on the best game plan moving forward. That's why I had to come now.

I grab my bag, slam the door and hop up the curb to the heavy metal door, pulling it open rather than knocking. I can see my dad's feet up on his desk at the end of the long hallway. He has a small office, and it's where he goes to think. He spent most of the summer here after the team's big loss.

"You hiding?" I ask. His feet slide down to the ground, but his chair doesn't move.

"When am I not?" he chuckles.

I step through the doorway and he spins forward, his forearms on his desk that's covered in papers, data sheets, recruitment letters and empty coffee cups. I take the orange chair opposite him, letting the wheels glide back while I lift my feet up. My dad smiles, but only on one side.

"You'll always be that little girl," he says, his hands shuffling his strewn-about pile of papers into one sloppy stack. I scooch forward in my rolling chair to help him.

"I always did love coming to work with you," I say.

"You like looking at the boys," he says through a single punctuated laugh.

"Uhh, no thank you. No offense, Dad, but *these* are not my kind of boys," I say, my eyebrows raised.

My dad's gaze meets mine and he puffs out one more chuckle.

"Thank God," he says.

His hands rake over the smooth desktop, his mess all pushed to the sides, and he grips at the edge of the desk before scooting himself in close, folding his hands in front of his face, and leaning his unshaven cheek against his dry and cracked knuckles.

"I'm afraid I'm not much to watch at work today, kiddo," he says.

Kiddo. May I never stop being kiddo. Noah's never been kiddo. He's been sport, or a number, or QB-One and young man. Never kiddo. Sometimes it's easier being the girl.

"I actually came to help," I say, leaning forward where my bag rests between my knees. I slide the zipper open and slip out my computer, setting it on the desk in front of me and turning it sideways so my dad can see, too.

He pulls his hand from his head and rubs his weary eyes.

"Is it one of those funny late-night videos where they make people lip-sync to random songs? Because I could use a laugh right now," he says, looking on.

"No, but just...wait..." I say, my concentration on my video prompt.

I run the player back to the beginning, when I started recording Nico and his friends without them realizing it. It gets to the part where Sasha waves and my dad exhales heavily through his nose.

"Is this some artsy kid you have a crush on or something?" he says.

"Shhhhh," I hush him. "And no, just watch."

The video plays on, and Sasha turns his focus back over to the game.

I'm so glad I zoomed in on Nico at this point, because this…*this* is what I want my father to see. Nico steps back, feet crossing perfectly, out of the pocket, twisting, juking. He's so balanced it's impossible, yet we're both watching it. My dad notices, and I can tell he's interested by the way his hands have fallen to the desk and his eyes have squinted to study the screen more closely.

Nico sprints to the other side, his long strides impossible to keep up with. He could easily take the ball himself. Nobody would catch him. But he doesn't. I watched it Friday night live, and I've watched it nearly fifty times since. The ball releases, and the distance is the kind that gets people's attention—like, recruiter-type people with clipboards and cellphones that dial right into head coach's pockets for schools that play in bowl games. It's what happens when Noah throws, only…it's better.

My dad sees it. I know it. We won't say it, but it's better. Nico—he's better.

"Stop there. Play…rewind…or, how do you work this?" My dad is fumbling with the trackpad on my computer, and I giggle.

"Let me do it," I say, dragging back to the beginning of Nico's play. I pause on his footwork. I know what my dad wants.

He's quiet for several seconds, then nods and twirls his finger for me to play it forward again. The video goes and he jukes his friend, and my dad holds up a hand. I pause. He studies until he signals for me to continue. We watch it play out, and this time, without asking, I pause on his release—Nico's body strong, posture straight, shoulders square at his target, feet set. He's a poster child for proper technique.

My father lets out another heavy breath and pushes back from the desk, his hands folded behind his head and his eyes on the screen. I let it play through, all the way to the catch, through the celebration and then I cut it off before we get to Noah's injury.

I close the computer and slip it back in my bag, hugging it on my lap as I face my father. I look more like him. His eyes are blue like mine. Noah has his eyes too, but his features mirror my mom's. My dad and I are the ones cut from the same cloth.

His hand comes up to cup his mouth, and he scratches at his whiskers.

"What's his name?" he asks.

"Nico Medina," I say.

"Scholarship kid," my dad nods.

I nod back.

"Soccer?" my dad asks, his head tilted to one side.

I pause, a little thrown by his question. My brow pinched, I shake my head *no*.

"He's in honors. He's probably going to be our valedictorian," I say.

My dad nods, still lost to his thoughts before answering.

"Wow, good for him," he says.

My chest starts to tighten, but I don't let the words come out that I'm thinking. My dad isn't a racist, but I feel a little ashamed right now. My lips twitch with that defensive mechanism I feel in debate, and after a few more seconds of silence, I can't help myself.

"He's really smart. And not all Mexicans play soccer," I say, my heart thumping wildly. My dad laughs at my retort, but my breathing is still heavy.

"I know. You're right," my dad says finally. His eyes are soft when they meet mine, and I take his words and expression as an apology.

"His friend is pretty good, too," I say, shifting the focus back to the entire reason I came here.

My dad nods, but it's clear his focus is on Nico.

"Medina, huh?" he says, turning to the computer table behind him and logging into the school's database. It takes him a few minutes to pull up Nico's profile, and I wait patiently while my father's fingers drum on the desktop as he reads.

"He lives in West End," my dad says, not really to anyone. I don't respond.

After a few minutes of studying Nico's file, my dad flips the computer off and turns his chair back to face me. His expression appears conflicted.

"They want me to start Brandon," he says.

"Skaggs?" I say, my face twisted as if I've tasted something bitter. Brandon Skaggs is an asshole. He's also Coach O'Donahue's nephew.

My father nods.

"What would it take?" I ask.

My dad quirks his brow.

"For Nico? How does this work? Does he have to try out? Does the board have to accept him? Do you just have to invite him? Tell me what needs to happen," I say.

My father sucks in his top lip, leaning over his hands at his desk. He pulls in a paper from his stack and a pen from the cup on the other side and begins to draw swirls in the margin.

"If this Nico kid were to come out this week, preferably tomorrow, and ask for a walk-on tryout based on the open position on our roster, then I have the authority to grant him the time," my dad says, pen stopping abruptly as his eyes meet mine. "But he's going to have to impress more than just me, Reagan. If he's really this good, as good as that video you've got there, then I'll press for him. But I'm out of benefits of the doubt with everyone. And he's at-risk. They're not going to want to put someone like him on the team. They need to be convinced and want to let me take this shot."

I swallow, because I've known my dad was on a thin line, but hearing him hint at it makes me worry for him…*and us.*

"Okay," I nod.

"How well do you know this kid?"

I breathe in deeply through my nose because the truth won't give my dad that sense of relief he desperately needs, but I also don't want to lie and give him completely false expectations.

"Well enough," I say, standing and clutching my keys in my hands.

My dad nods, and looks back down at his doodle. He adds a few features and turns it into a smiley face, then spins it around for me to see.

"Maybe if this coaching thing falls through, they'll let me teach art," he jokes.

"I think you have a better shot at music," I laugh, "and I've heard you sing."

I sling my bag over my shoulder and blow my dad a kiss. He does the same, letting his hand fall to a slap on the desk. I watch him and walk backward a few steps before turning and exiting through the big metal door, skipping to my car, and tossing my things inside. I slump into the seat and smile at the possibility of seeing Nico out there on that field. I don't know why that thought makes me so happy, and I don't know why I want to see it happen so badly, but I can't deny that I do. It's more than making my documentary good. It's seeing something good happen for my dad and for Nico, and when the irony hits me, I laugh hard and start my car.

Damned Nico and Ayn Rand are right again.

I didn't want my dad to know I had no idea where I was going, but I've been driving through West End for ten minutes, and I've regretted not getting Nico's address for about nine and a half. The neighborhood is buzzing with activity, more than I thought it would. I'm not sure what I expected, really. Honestly, I've only driven through the area as a passenger during freeway closures and wrong turns when I was a kid. When I got my license, though, this was one of the places I was lectured about "not driving at night."

I'm out of place. My blonde hair, my freckles, my barely four-month-old sporty two-door—a glance around the streets I'm passing through shows how much I don't belong here.

I don't belong here.

I feel guilty thinking it.

I slow to a stop sign and wait several extra seconds while a small dog passes into the intersection, but grows frightened and backtracks twice before committing and sprinting to the other side of the road. He stops around a front gate of a house, the yard dirt except for a large tin water bowl and a few dog toys lying on a yellowed patch of grass, and I comfort myself with the thought that he probably lives there. I don't want him to get hit by a car.

With a heavy sigh, I turn down the last street. Just like the others, people are out on porches, and homes seem open, even as far as front doors propped wide open, welcoming strangers inside. The first thing we do in my neighborhood is lock the door when we step inside, yet here, in West End, where life is supposed to be scary, nobody seems to lock a thing, at least not during the middle of the day on Sunday.

I slow near the end of the street and take in the scene at one house where several kids are playing in the yard, splashing in one of those plastic baby pools. The lawn is immaculate—the edge of the grass trimmed perfectly, the color a deep green, the dirt freshly raked as if it's a Disney landscape. Rose bushes are trimmed back for the fall, but their color remains green and they're accented by seasonal flowers. I'm struck by the scene so much that I don't realize I'm blocking a car behind me while I idle in the middle of the road. The abrasive blaring of the horn shakes me back to life, though.

"Sorry," I mouth, waving in my mirror and pulling forward.

I'm about to double back to the beginning, not ready to give up, but a little less hopeful that I'll find Nico by randomly circling his neighborhood, when a woman catches my attention. She's stepping from an old, copper-colored Buick in the driveway of a house a few down from the one with the perfect yard, and she looks so familiar that I pull over and watch her in my mirror.

She's wearing a bright red blouse and black pants, her hair piled high on her head in a bun. She flips open the back-seat door and bends down, a little girl climbing out soon and grabbing her hand. The young girl is wearing a fluffy pink dress, and her hair is split into two ponytails. It's Sunday, and I'm sure they've just returned from church. My hunch is so strong that I wait for a few cars to pass and turn around, driving back into the neighborhood. I arrive at the house just in time for Nico to step from the passenger seat and walk toward the back of the car where he pulls open the trunk.

The woman eyes me as I slow my car, and she says something I can't hear, but it gets Nico's attention. He's holding a paper bag to his chest, but he sets it back inside the trunk, brushing his hands on his gray dress pants and saying something over his shoulder.

I kill the engine, and instantly begin to sweat.

Say something. Something smart. Be nice. Please don't be mad that I'm here.

"Hi," I say, bright and cheery as if they've been waiting for me to arrive. The woman, who I am pretty sure I recognize as Nico's mom from the few school activities I've seen her at, bunches her brow and smirks at me. She's pitying me. Because I'm an idiot. And I just took that whole looking-out-of-place thing to an entirely new level.

"Uh, hi," Nico says, his hand on his neck, one eye squinting more than the other as he looks at me sideways. "Are you...lost?"

"No," I answer quickly.

My heart is beating so hard that I feel it in my fingertips, so I flex one hand then switch my grip on my keys and flex the other. I step completely from my car, shutting the door, then walk up to the end of the driveway where Nico is standing with his hands in his pockets, a light-gray shirt on, and a thin black tie loosened around the neck.

I open my mouth to try to fix my first impression, but then quickly realize that this is more like my hundredth impression, and none of it is going to matter if he doesn't like the idea I'm about to throw out there on a prayer.

I exhale quickly and the rapid passage of air flaps my lips which makes the little girl still standing with Nico's mom giggle. Nico turns to look at her, and when he faces me again, his smile is less sympathetic and more amused.

"I'm sorry. I didn't really expect to find you, I guess," I say, shaking my hands before folding my arms over my chest.

"Mijo, we'll be inside. You talk to your friend, okay?" the woman says, leading the little girl through the front door, which she leaves open behind the screen. I laugh lightly at my thought about it, but shake it off quickly and step closer to the car trunk, which has several bags of produce inside.

"There's a farmer's market once a month, after church. My mom...she goes kind of nuts," Nico says. I catch how he runs his hand through his hair and his cheek reddens as if a trunkful of groceries is something to be ashamed of. I can't remember the last time my mom or dad brought a bag of any kind of food into the house that wasn't from a fast-food joint.

"She must cook a lot, huh?" I say, bending in and lifting a bag.

"She does, and you don't have to carry that. I've got them," he says. I hold up a hand quickly though and cock my brow.

"Don't make me argue with you over this, too," I say.

He breathes out a short laugh, then gives in, lifting two bags to my one before guiding me up the driveway into his house.

The difference between our two worlds is impossible not to notice the second my feet step onto the bare concrete floors of Nico's home. I look down to confirm, my eyes scanning the deep-gray floor still marred with marks from where carpet probably once stuck to the edges. This isn't some designer feature Nico's family decided to try after watching one of those home shows on cable. This is just what it is—a bare floor, cold and cracked, but swept immaculately clean.

I'm caught sliding my foot over one of the foundation cracks when Nico clears his throat, reaching for the bag in my arms.

"Oh, sorry," I say.

His smile is modest, maybe a little embarrassed.

"Makes it easy to clean. I can literally hose it off if I want," he says. I pinch my brow pretending not to follow, but he rolls his eyes. "I know you were wondering about the floor."

"Oh...yeah, it's just...different," I say.

"It's shit poor, but whatever," he says, walking past me and back through the front door to the car. His bluntness stuns me, so I fall a few paces behind.

I open my mouth once or twice, trying to find the words to make it better, but when Nico lifts the last bag from the car and shuts the trunk, I decide I should just let him have the last word on this topic. I jog back to the front door and hold the screen open for him and follow him back into his kitchen, where his mom is unloading the bags into the refrigerator.

"Thank you for helping," she says to me.

"My pleasure," I smile. She graces me with a smile that tugs her cheeks high and forces her eyes to squint. It's a real smile, different from the one my mom wears, and it makes me feel good to have earned it from her.

"I'm Valerie, by the way," she says, rubbing a towel over her hand, then taking mine.

"Nice to meet you. Reagan," I say. She nods with a tight smile, and her eyes squint like her son's do.

Nico grabs a soda from the fridge and holds one up for me. I shake my head no, but he tilts his head to the side and wiggles the can in his hand one more time.

"Okay, yeah. Thank you," I say.

He reaches in to grab another cola, handing it to me and shrugging me to follow him to the front room, away from his mom. The little girl, now free of her ponytails, barrels around the corner from a short hallway that I can tell leads to what looks like three small bedrooms.

"Is that your sister?" I ask.

"Niece," he corrects quickly.

I let that soak in, mentally working up to my next question, but Nico fills in the gaps for me.

"My mom watches her for my brother. She stays with us most of the time, but...sometimes...when he has a place," he trails off, sitting on the arm of an old sofa backed against the front wall and looking out the main window, his eyes careful not to meet mine as they dart around. I can tell he doesn't want me to ask what he means about his brother, so I let him have the last word on that topic, too.

"What's her name? Your niece."

Nico looks down at the soda in his hands, pulling the tab back and bringing it to his lips quickly to suck away the fizz. His eyes flit to mine for a second, just long enough for a half grin to dimple his cheek.

"Alyssa," he smiles, and it strikes me how much his looks like his mom's.

"She's cute. Is she in kindergarten?" I ask.

"Next year...maybe. She's a summer birthday," he says, taking another big drink.

I fill the pause by opening my own can and gulping down several swallows, enough that the carbonation burns my chest, and I wince. Nico chuckles, but his smile fades quickly.

"You were looking for me?" he asks.

I was. That's right. I'm here for Nico, to convince him. It seemed like such a cut-and-dry plan, and I felt so confident when I drove here half an hour ago. All audacity is gone now, though. I have a feeling, before too long, I'm going to end up begging.

"I'm here to tell you to try out for the football team tomorrow," I say, managing to hold in the swallow that is begging to slide down my throat in front of him. Nico's eyes don't blink for several seconds, and his expression remains void of any sign that he heard me at all. And then the laughter comes.

"Uhhh, not just no, but *hell* no," he says, laughing so hard that his mom peers around the corner to check on us.

"You okay out there? Can I get you guys something for lunch?" she asks.

"We're fine, Ma. Thanks, though," Nico says, dismissing her.

I never take my eyes from him, and I search for that last vestige of inner strength for me to be the girl who pitched this wild idea to her dad an hour ago.

"Why not?" I ask, setting the rest of my soda down on a small coffee table and standing with my arms folded in front and my posture as straight and rigid as I can hold it.

Nico laughs silently, locking his gaze with mine for a few seconds before blinking and glancing down. He sets his soda next to mine, then stands in the same pose as me, his smirk—his armor—in its place.

"For starters, I don't need the football team," he says.

"You're right. But we need you," I say, surprising myself. I practiced this on the way here, however short that rehearsal was. I knew I wouldn't be able to trick Nico. I'd have to appeal to his empathy—I'd have to ask, make him feel needed and wanted. Frankly, he is.

His smirk drops a little at my reply, which makes my chest loosen just a little. I breathe in long and deep, but the longer he looks at me without speaking, the more my fingers twitch and my feet grow restless until I break my folded arm pose and bring my hands to my eyes, rubbing while I pace a stride or two in either direction.

"My dad needs you. The team needs you," I say, opening my eyes to see him still staring at me, his smirk now gone completely.

I sigh, then tug my hair loose from the knot at my neck, scratching the sore spot where the band pulled it tight. Everything about me feels awful and uncomfortable right now, and I hate that Nico is looking at me. I'm already here, though, and I've already said the hard part, so I stare into his eyes and wait until his arms uncross, so I know he's feeling a little off his game, too.

"Friday night...when I watched you with your friends?" I wait for him to nod; to know he's willing to at least listen to me. "You guys were...you were really good," I say through a nervous laugh. I suck in my lip, needing something from him to encourage me to keep going.

"I'm sorry about your brother," he says, and my heartbeat kicks up at the mention of Noah.

My eyes fall to my feet, and I shift my balance, looping my thumbs in my pockets while I nod lightly.

"Thanks," I say.

When I look back up, Nico's gaze is now on the ground between us, and he's chewing at the inside of his cheek, which means he's thinking. I know he is, because I've seen him work through things in class—bide his time before he could speak and make a well-rounded, hard-to-argue-with point. I can't let him hit me with a foolproof defense before I get one last shot at this.

"He broke the tibia and fibula; he's going to be out for the season. My dad…" I stutter, my breath catching hard, because I know this move could be a defining moment for my father. Win or lose means in or out for Coach Prescott, and his fate is literally in the hands of his quarterback. "I know what I saw you do out on that field. I've watched my dad coach the best, and I know how they move. You…you look like my father's been working with you for years."

"Yeah, well, he hasn't," Nico snaps, his eyes still down and his mouth tight.

"No, I know," I say. "But I showed him…"

Nico's body jolts at my words, and I pause long enough for our eyes to meet. His are wide now, and I think maybe this is the only time I've ever seen him on edge, unsure of the next move or what side of the coin he needs to pick.

"I showed him the video I shot. And he can't ask you to come out, because of your scholarship. It can't be part of recruiting. But if you decided that football was maybe something you wanted to try…if you, say, stopped by his office hours in the morning and asked about a supplemental tryout…"

Nico doesn't blink. He also doesn't frown or smile or react in any way. But he hears me.

"Look, I'll understand. Or…well, no, I probably won't. Because…" My gaze falls down, and my lips push together tight, because, *gah*! This guy pushes my buttons, but damn it, I need him. And he's talented. And I can't deny that. My stubborn side does not want to pay him a compliment, but there's this other part of me, maybe a desperate part, that needs him to hear some good things about him.

"You have a gift," I say, my voice small. I can't look at him and admit any of this. My lips are actually quivering. "My dad would be good to you. I think maybe you'd like him. And…he won't say it, because…well…you get it, but you're better than my brother, Nico. You just are. It took me two minutes to tell. It took my dad ten seconds of video. So, please…just think about it. It might open some doors, is all. My dad…he has a way of getting people to pay attention."

Nearly ten seconds pass without a word, and when I sneak a look, Nico's attention is once again lost to the streets outside his window. Someone nearby has turned on loud music, and I can hear a few people laughing outside. I think he'd rather be there—anywhere but here, with me. I take it as a sign that my last effort probably wasn't good enough, and bend down to pick up my half-full soda, raising it even though nobody is watching.

"Thanks for the drink. I'll see you in class," I say, moving to the screen door, and counting in my head to fifteen as I open it, step through, and hear it slam closed behind me. The party at the house on the corner has grown. That's the music I heard, and more neighbors are gathering. People don't gather on my street.

"Hey!"

My eyes blink wide as I look over the top of my car to the busy yard a few houses away. My brain takes a few seconds to catch up to the fact that the voice I heard was Nico's, not just some neighbor late for the party. I turn and lean against my car to see him standing in his doorway, one arm holding the screen open completely, the other resting on the side of the doorframe, his body filling the space. Dressed for church, he looks years older than the eighteen I know him to be, and while I won't say *this* part out loud, I will at least whisper it to myself—Nico is handsome.

His hair falls forward just enough to cover one eye, and he flips it back casually. I breathe in quickly when he does, glad for this distance between us, and that he can't hear my response.

"Can Sasha tryout, too?" His eyes linger on mine, and I sense the slight crinkle in them over his hatched plan to get his best friend in on the action, too.

I bite the tip of my tongue with just enough force that I feel it to keep myself from smiling too big. I'm not sure how my father will handle it, but if it gets Nico out on that field tomorrow, I'm pretty sure my dad will be up for anything.

"I don't see why the same rules don't apply to him," I say loudly. Our eyes make a non-verbal agreement, and we both leave each other with the same nod and faint smile, like poker players each sure the other is bluffing.

Maybe we both are. But at this point, I'm all in. Nico's story as a part of the team is going to elevate my project to the kind of film that gets people to watch. My interest is selfish. It's for my dad, and for my future. I have a feeling, though, that Nico knows exactly what a run in the state playoffs with the Tradition can do for his college aspirations. And the one thing I'm sure of is that my father is going to love him.

CHAPTER 4

My father *hates* Nico Medina.

I could not have been more wrong, and the longer I watch practice from the bleachers, the more I consider scrapping my documentary all together and rushing home to begin searching for new coaching jobs for my dad.

Things started off okay, but when my dad began running drills—swapping Nico out every other squad with Brandon to see how he could throw—Nico's lack of true team experience became glaring. He can't take direction; and just like in class, he's defensive by default.

My father's frustrated, and they've faced off maybe a dozen times. Yet…neither has quit. My dad hasn't sent him packing, and Nico hasn't left. That's the only reason I'm still sitting here with my tripod between my feet and my eyes shifting from the version of the action on the screen and the real field on the other side of the lens. I watch as more plays run out, and my father finally throws his clipboard down and whistles for a water break.

I push PAUSE and slide around the camera, careful not to disturb the perfect position I've got it in, and jog down the bleacher steps to catch up to my dad. He sees me coming, and holds up a hand as he gets to his water jug.

"Not now, Rea," he says gruffly, twisting the lid from his jug and drinking down gulps.

"It just needs time, that's all," I say, ignoring his wishes. He rolls his eyes at me over the lid of his drink, then runs his arm over his chin as he tilts the thermos back and twists the lid in place.

"It just needs to be scrapped, I'm afraid. This...whatever I've spent the last hour doing—Reagan? This is a waste of time," he sighs, letting his water fall with a *clunk* onto the metal bench.

I open my mouth to put up a fight, but stop when my dad pinches the bridge of his nose and lets his head fall forward. He wanted this to work, too. He still does. He just doesn't know *how*.

"Scrimmage them," I say.

My dad's shoulders rise with his short chuckle.

"Why? So they can get slaughtered? So I can destroy that kid's confidence? Not that I could...I mean, hell, Reagan, that's half his damned problem! I don't know how to coach that! He doesn't hear a word I say. I keep telling him one thing, and he does exactly the opposite!"

My dad's hand moves to his neck now, and he rubs it. I follow his gaze to see him watching his players all watch the two new guys, all of them whispering or laughing at jokes that are likely about Nico and Sasha, feeding my dad's doubt more.

"You need to see him play *his* game," I say, my eyes watching the two boys *not* walking back to the field slowly with the others, but who are already on the fifty-yard line, waiting for more.

My dad sees them, too. He might not *think* Nico's listening, but a player doesn't hustle to be first on the field for more abuse unless he really wants to be here—unless he has something to prove. My dad needs to let him prove it.

I don't suggest it again, but I wait next to my father while he watches the rest of his team slowly amble back to the line of scrimmage along with his coaching staff. Nico's bullheaded, but he respects my father...maybe more than the others. My father sees that—he *has* to.

My dad pulls the whistle to his lips and blows loudly, and I take the sign to return to my camera. When I get to my seat, I watch everything play out through the viewing screen. I can't hear the words my dad is saying, but I can tell by the movements being made that he's breaking them up into squads.

Without pause, I lift my camera from the tripod and climb down to the field level, moving close to the small bench and medical kit near the trainer's table by the end zone. I don't want to be distracting, but I also don't want to miss any of this…in case my hunch is right.

It takes the squads a little time to figure out their positions, where everyone needs to be, and I notice Nico's team is flailing more than the other side—players arguing, everyone jockeying to be the leader.

Nico takes a few slow steps away from the group, a ball clutched between both hands and the white practice jersey loose over his borrowed pads. The arguing continues, but eventually, when Nico is several steps away, some of the players look up and watch him. Once he has their attention, he steps onto the field, taking his place on offense. He tosses the ball in one hand a few times, then bends down and sets it on the line, backing up a few more steps before folding his arms over is chest.

My father is watching, too. Sasha is the first player to walk over and take a spot several yards to Nico's right. They nod to one another, but still nobody says a word. The arguing seems to have stopped though, and slowly, one by one, the players on his squad walk toward him, filling in the gaps on the line, taking their positions.

"We're ready, Coach," Nico says, standing behind the guy playing center. That's Colton Wimsby, and he's one of my dad's favorite players. He's always the first to arrive and the last to leave. He's large, weighing about two-eighty, but nimble on his feet and quick with his hands. He's been my dad's starting center since his freshman year, and the fact that he gave him to Nico is telling. Colton twists back and says something to Nico, who nods, and they both pound their fists together.

The other team is lined up for defense, and Brandon is waiting on the sidelines, standing at attention. He's confident in a different kind of way. His feet are steady, and he doesn't even seem to be interested in the play about to happen on the field. It's as if this is all just a routine for him that he expects to fail, so he can get on with doing the real work.

My gut starts to twitch with my heartbeat, and the dose of adrenaline surprises me.

I'm rooting for Nico.

Colton sets up on the ball, crouching with his head down, until Nico shouts something that sounds like "Blue!" He says this a few more times, and Colton's head snaps up just as Sasha darts to the far right, almost out of bounds, and then…

It's beautiful. As if it's rehearsed. But there's no way. I know there isn't. My father knows there isn't. The other coaches doubt, I'm sure, and the team on defense is left trying to play catch up. They fail.

On the hard count, Nico switches the play, lining Sasha up against the other squad's weakest defender, sending him sprinting until he's almost twenty-five yards away. Nico gives him time, trusting Colton and his line, who hold the pocket as long as they can until Nico's feet take over, smooth and in charge. While he gains ground to the left, the defenders scramble to grab any piece of him their fingers can find. He slips out of every attempt, and just as Sasha hits the center of the field, Nico rockets the ball to him, hitting his hands while his feet are in full stride. His best friend's speed does the rest, and just like that—Nico's team is up by six.

Brandon no longer looks relaxed, his weight shifting from side-to-side, the cool and calm from before has now been jacked up to full-on anxious. He's so wired that he drops the ball when Sasha walks by and tosses it to him for his squad's turn to try to score.

I laugh, but cover my mouth with my fist, hiding the sound and expression.

Unlike Brandon's squad, Nico's is a man short, the rest of the defense, made up of the players that see less time, is at the other end of the field running drills. My dad notices and begins to pull his radio from his pocket to let the coach with them know he needs one more player, when Nico steps in and takes a position at corner.

"What the hell do you think you're doing? I'll get someone to step in there, go sit your ass down," my dad says, his typical tell-it-like-it-is tone he uses on the field.

Nico is unfazed by it, and just as my dad has the radio to his mouth, he sees his quarterback hopeful line up ready to sprint. Brandon doesn't waste any time, and the ball is snapped before my dad can step in and stop the play. My eyes work to take it all in—my father reaching for his whistle around his neck, Brandon sliding away from the safety of his offensive line, Nico seeing opportunity, tracking the receiver, until the ball leaves Brandon's hands and somehow ends up in his own.

He only makes it ten yards before someone tackles him, but he makes his point, tossing the ball end-over-end to Brandon as he walks by. Nico doesn't say anything to provoke him; his actions have done enough. Within a blink, Brandon has Nico flat on his face, his fingers gripping the collar of his pads from behind, his arm pushing Nico's mask into the grass, digging it into the ground.

"You piece of shit!" I hear him yell.

My father's whistle blares, and coaches and players run into the mix, yanking Brandon away while Sasha rushes to Nico, his hands flat on his friend's heaving chest. His jaw is rigid, and he's chewing at the inside of his mouth, his eyes narrow, and his mouth is ready to shout, rip, and tear down the guy who just blindsided him because he was embarrassed about being shown up.

"Fucking pussy!" Sasha yells, pulling on Brandon's jersey. My dad jerks Sasha's arm, spinning him until he can look him straight in the eye.

I tuck my knees in, wanting to be smaller, but I keep filming.

My dad points his finger at Sasha's face.

"Get off my field!"

"What about that dickhead?" Sasha shouts back to my father, shrugging his shoulders and losing the grip my dad has on his arm.

"You worry about your own ass. I'll worry about my team, which, right this moment, you are *not* a part of! Take your helmet, and sit your ass on the bench outside my office. I'll deal with you after practice," my dad says, his words still coming out angry and loud. The entire team has now circled around the scene, and I notice Sasha's eyes scan to see them all until he stops on his friend, still adjusting his pads and picking grass from the helmet he's just pulled from his own head.

Their eyes lock for a moment, and Sasha drops his arms to his side, leaving the helmet on the ground.

"Man, I don't need this shit. Fuck y'all," he says over his shoulder, his stride long, but slow—almost dramatic, like a child wanting to be asked to please stay.

He won't get begged from my dad. I just hope this doesn't mean Nico's gone now, too.

My father brings his hand to his face, running it over his eyes and cheek, dragging it to his neck while he turns slowly and takes in his broken team.

"That's it for today. Clean up, and tomorrow—come out here ready to work. Tomorrow won't be easy," he says.

The team breaks with a clap, everyone participating but Brandon and Nico. Both stand about a dozen feet apart, and my father's face moves from one to the other a few times before Coach O'Donahue puts a hand on my father's shoulder, whispering something and gesturing for his nephew to come closer.

My father nods once, but never looks him in the eyes. Brandon steps closer to his uncle, and the two walk toward the locker room together, his uncle playfully jabbing at his nephew's shoulder a few times before putting his arm around him when they get to the top of the hill. My dad sees it all play out, and he keeps his eyes on them until the locker room door slams shut behind them.

Nico hasn't moved a single step, but he has found me. His gaze is on mine, and I've now closed the view screen on my camera, shutting it off and setting it down next to my feet. I see him through my own eyes, and I wait for all of the familiar gestures, the expressions—I wait for the fight.

My father looks toward him, but he's slow to raise his eyes all the way. I think he's struggling to find the right words. I know I am. Nico is a wild stallion full of promise and gifts, and I'm not sure if he can be tamed.

I'm not sure if he should.

My father steps forward, pulling his hat from his head and running his fingers through his thinning hair, his mouth poised to speak as the authority, only Nico beats him to it.

"I want to apologize," he says, his hand out for my father. My dad puts his hat back in place, and holds his hands on his hips for a breath, clearly surprised. He doesn't take Nico's hand right away, instead looking him in the eyes first, forming a standoff.

"What for?" my dad asks.

I shift my weight and lean back on my palms, and they both turn to see me.

Nico's eyes stay on me, even when my father turns back to face him. He doesn't grin. There is no dimple. His jaw is relaxed and his eyes look almost scared.

He wants this.

"For not respecting your field, your rules. I apologize for that," he says, blinking his eyes shut and opening them on my dad.

My father takes in a short breath and lets out a small laugh.

"Fair enough," he says, taking Nico's hand. They hold their grip for a few long seconds, and Nico stares at their touch before they break.

"So is that it?" Nico's question lingers, and his eyes move from my dad to his right foot, which kicks at the dry grass. Eighteen, yet still such a young boy. All he wants is approval. He has no idea how to ask for it, though.

"You show up here tomorrow. Three. Sharp. Be ready to go hard. And—" my father pauses until Nico looks up, "be ready to listen."

The standoff continues long enough for me to dust the grass from my legs. When I look back, my father has his hand on Nico's shoulder, a hard pat that I know is his way of telling him he's impressed, but also reminding him who calls the shots.

I wait at the table, pushing myself up to sit on one end while my legs dangle out in front of me, swinging, so my toes can catch the tips of the grass. Nico walks toward me, expressionless, his eyes on my camera as he kneels down in front of me and picks it up, handing it to me.

"Thanks," I say, sucking in my top lip, and flipping open the viewing screen. I push the playback button and drag the icon to the middle of my film, stopping it on Nico's great play.

"So do I get any residuals or…how does this all work? You know, since I'm starring in your movie and all?"

His fingers tap at the top of my camera, and I adjust my hands to avoid his touch, my heartbeat picking up while I struggle to find a safer place to hold my gear, a place where his hand doesn't come near mine, where I don't react like this.

He's Nico. *We don't play nice.*

When I look up at him, the left side of his mouth is pulled into a grin. I give back a reserved smile to mask my nerves, then look down at my camera in my hands, turning it to show him the video I shot of him.

"You wanna see it?" I ask. My heart is still thumping wildly.

His eyes flit from mine to my hands and back, then his lip tugs up a little higher, and he nods *yes*. He leans closer to me, so I slide down the table, making room for him to sit beside me. He's wearing pads, and his bulky leg mashes up against mine, which only makes the heavy beating in my chest feel harder.

I'm sure my hands are trembling, so I lay the weight of the camera on my lap, paying close attention to my touch on the screen, willing my fingers to behave, not to shake, not to care that I'm sitting next to him. I don't want to care. That wasn't what any of this was about.

"I rewound it to the good part," I say, giggling nervously. I feel better when he laughs with me, until he speaks.

"So I'm the good part, huh?"

His leg nudges mine, and I react with a nervous sort of snort-laugh. I cover my mouth immediately and shut my eyes, my pulse now so loud that I'm sure I wouldn't be able to hear my own voice—*if* I could talk, that is.

Nico nudges me again, and I open an eyelid to look at him. He laughs once, snorting through his nose and pretending to push up glasses on his face.

"You're such a nerd," he says, leaning into me with his upper body now. There are no pads on his arms, so we touch—skin against skin— and I resolve myself to the fact that I feel it.

"You're a bigger nerd than me," I say back, my cheeks burning because I'm flirting, and while part of me wants to stuff my silly, girlish words back into my mouth, another part of me wants to dole out more.

"I am *so* not a bigger nerd than you. I mean, look…" Nico twists the view screen on my camera, his hand now basically in my lap. He laughs, then flips the screen closed before looking at me. "One of us is in the AV Club."

I do my best to narrow my gaze on him and hold my eyes squinted, my mouth hard, as if I'm really pissed, but I break character, and my mouth betrays me, bending at the corners first until my own laughter escapes.

"You're right. I am the bigger nerd," I say, jerking when I feel a tickle at my arm. I sigh in relief when I notice it's just the wave of my hair from my ponytail.

I tug the band loose and let my hair fall down before sweeping it back up and into a knot again. When I look back to Nico, his expression is softer, and I like that he watched me do that. Maybe that's why I let my hair down—to see if he'd notice.

"So what do I look like on film?" he asks, his attention back to the now-closed screen in my lap. I'm relieved at the change in subject.

I flip the screen open and prop the camera at an angle he can see, then press PLAY.

"You won't get any sound, not that you really need it, but this is that great play you did," I say, twisting my lips because I'm not sure if I should be feeding his ego. Nico was great. But he was also undisciplined and difficult.

I look up to watch his eyes as he watches himself. He doesn't look proud. Instead, his expression looks critical, and when the play runs out, he taps the icon on the screen to pause it.

"Can you rewind so I can see that again?"

I nod and play it again for him.

I watch with him this time, and I wonder what detail he is fixated on. I pay close attention to his feet, to the way he moves, and every step is as if it's choreographed—it's the same thing I saw the night I taped him and his friends. It's raw, but it's brimming with potential. Maybe it's even more, maybe it doesn't need to be touched. Maybe, Nico's style of play is just the thing my father needs.

"I'm too slow. Look," he says, pausing and dragging the player backward. He lifts his finger and looks to me to show him how to start it again. I press the button and he nods. "There, look. I know that guy—Garrett. I'm so much faster than he is. He shouldn't be that close to me, let alone close enough to get his hand on my jersey. I'm too slow. How do I fix that?"

I watch it again, and even though Nico makes the same remarks, this time in whispers, I ignore him and try only to see what he sees. I think we are looking at it differently, though. He's seeing his flaws, which are all things my dad can help him with. I'm seeing the things he does right. He does *so much* right.

"He has a head start on you. The line always will. But, look…here." When I stop the video this time, I drag it in so we can view the touch better, the way Nico instinctively bends and twists out of the defender's grasp. "You knew what to do."

"I don't know anything," Nico says quickly, lifting from the table and picking his helmet up from the ground. My leg is suddenly cold from his absence. He turns to face me, his eyes on the screen at first, then on my face. Even the air stops, the breeze taking a pause to fill the quiet between us with a little more urgency, until Nico's gaze breaks away.

"Tell your dad I'll see him tomorrow."

The video remains paused in my lap, and the boy on the screen walks away from me in real life, never once looking back. I watch it again when he's out of sight. I watch it through his eyes, and after the fifth time, I finally see it.

Nico doesn't want to get caught.

CHAPTER 5

Last night I dreamt about Nico. It was one of those odd sort of dreams, only partially making sense. He and I were partners in a game where we had to find a secret room in a house that somehow always had a hallway that led to more rooms and more secret doors and hallways. I slept for six hours last night, but my dream felt as if it lasted for twenty. The search went on forever, and the secret room that held some prize we needed never showed up. But in those few seconds—right before I awoke—Nico turned into me and kissed me on the lips.

I felt it.

It felt...*real.*

I jolted out of bed and froze, and it took me nearly fifteen minutes to convince myself that it was all just my weary head, the Cheetos I ate for dinner, or the super-sized Mountain Dew. It's probably due to the hours I spent last night watching my film footage. That's what I'm telling myself, anyhow.

But sitting here, only five or six bodies away from Nico, the side of his face in full view—the side that turned and kissed me in my dreams—is messing with my head. It's thrown me off my game, and I haven't spoken up at all while we discuss the excerpts we've read from Plato's *Republic.* For once, I honestly can't find fault with Nico's position and questions.

I blame the damned dream!

"Plato's concept doesn't allow for exceptions," Nico says. He's responding to one of our classmates, Megan, who just argued that Plato's *Republic* is a sound blueprint for peace. Megan's father is a Superior Court Judge. Nobody is surprised that she's arguing that class systems work and put people in place to succeed.

"Exceptions create chaos," Megan says.

My fingertips tingle, so I tap them on my notebook that I have folded to my chest, my eyes switching between Nico and Megan as if I'm watching a slow game of tennis. I want to join in, but I know I don't need to. Nico is saying everything that's in my head. We agree. My God, we agree on something.

"*Exceptions* are responsible for pivotal moments in history," Nico says. In typical fashion, his head is down, his chin tucked at his chest and his hands gripping the top of his desk, as if he's too disgusted by his opponent to look at her.

This is how he argues with me...

"Abraham Lincoln was born in a one-room cabin, the son of a carpenter. Are you saying our world would have been a better place if only he had stuck to his born position in life and built things out of wood?"

"Of course not. Lincoln is different, he's..." Megan stumbles, her words trailing off. She tries to mask it with a few *ums* and head-waggles, as if she's searching for the right words, but Nico doesn't let her off the hook.

"No, you want to apply it to our world, where guys like me work at Mountain Burger, slinging grease-slathered food into paper bags so we can make eight bucks an hour. While *you* pull through the drive-thru in your red convertible—Daddy bought for you when you were sixteen—on your way to some college class you only show up for half of the time, because it probably won't matter since Daddy's law firm has a spot held for you when you're done playing college."

My mouth hangs open. My eyes shift slightly to both sides to confirm that everyone else's mouth is in the same *WTF* mode mine is in. And then I realize something even more amazing. Nico's hand is on the back of his chair, his body twisted so he can look Megan in the eyes, leveling her with a heavy dose of reality—both his reality, and hers. He isn't wrong. But he is being unfair.

I don't enter the argument this time. For once I don't have a good counterpoint. I'm stumped completely. The awkward silence lingers in the room until Mr. Huffman fills it with his off-color humor, saying, "*Da da da*, and until next time…" just as the bell sounds and the quiet is covered with backpack zippers and the clatter of students rushing out at the end of the day.

For the second time in only a handful of days, Nico and I are the last to leave the room. I waited for him. Though now that we're alone, my mind is divided—the loud half wishing I hadn't stuck around. I stand at the closed door while he drags an overstuffed bag out from beneath his desk, swearing under his breath when one of the straps is caught on a chair leg, and when he finally pulls it free, his head tilts up and his eyes find me waiting.

"What?" he snaps.

I manage to keep my mouth shut. My eyes, on the other hand, can't hide my reaction, and they open wide, my brow lifting.

He's like an angry bull right now, his nostrils flared while he breathes, standing from his desk chair and tugging his heavy bag over his shoulder. He pulls his hat from his back pocket and smooths his hair back before sliding it in place. When he looks at me again, his rage isn't as obvious. He breathes in deeply, then releases it in a gust.

"Sorry," he says. "I shouldn't take that out on you. I just…sometimes it feels personal."

"I get it," I say.

"No, you really don't."

Head down again, Nico walks toward me, to the door. Just as he reaches for the handle, I grab it in my hand and step in front of it, clutching it behind my back in a move that brings my toes and Nico's only an inch apart.

I have nowhere to go, unless I decide to break down and let him leave with the final word. My fingers twitch, wanting to push the handle down and slide back into the hallway, releasing us both into the crowd. I squeeze the metal hard and hold my breath.

No.

Maybe because of the dream.

Or maybe because I don't want Nico to think he can sum me up that quickly, too, because I *do* get it. And the fact that he can dismiss my empathy so easily really pisses me off!

"You're being a jerk," I say.

"Am I?" His response is fast, and snarky.

"Why do you do that?" I ask, grateful when he takes a step back, giving us distance.

"Do what?" he sighs.

"That's your thing. You respond to every argument I ever give you with a question," I say.

His lip quirks up.

"Do I?" Amused by himself, his shoulders shake with his quiet laughter.

My head tilts, and I catch his eyes.

"Are you going to give me a real answer?"

Nico runs a hand down his face, holding it still after a few passes before cracking his fingers open over his eyes to look at me. My palms are sweating, and I can feel my pulse in my fingers that are still clutched around the door handle behind me. I'm in a room alone with Nico Medina, and he's just stared at me from two feet away, and his eyes match the ones on the version of him that kissed me in my subconscious. They're golden. They're so different. My dream got them just right.

"You know you just answered me with a question…right?" he says.

It takes me a few seconds to register his words and then replay my own in my head. My eyes look up while I think, and my head bobs slightly as I say my own words in my head, and in the end, all I can do is growl.

I growl. Like a petulant child mad that she didn't get the color she wanted from the crayon box. I'm one foot-stomp away from making this a truly spectacular display of my maturity. Add to it the burning feeling creeping up my chest, over my flesh, making me want to shut my eyes and maybe vomit a little. I don't like any of this.

My hand pushes down on the handle, releasing me from my prison, and I step to the side, my back against the now-open door as I wait for Nico to step through in front of me. He doesn't though. Instead, he leans on the closest desktop, his dimple deep and his smirk on the verge from dropping him into a fit of laughter—at my expense.

"You frustrate me," I say, my words sharp and a little louder than they probably need to be. The few people still walking in the hallway glance my way, and I hold up a hand to wave. They look away immediately because, frankly, I'm not that important.

The afterschool crowd thins quickly as lockers slam closed and people clear out for home or practice or special clubs. My shoulder aches from my equipment bag, which makes me think of Nico's, so I finally give in and turn to face him. When our eyes meet, he pushes up to a stand and steps closer.

"I'm glad I frustrate you. Good; we're even," he chuckles, walking past me, but stopping a foot outside the door. "Are you coming to practice again?"

I twist my lips, so completely rocked by everything he says. We're nowhere near even. And...I frustrate him? He's standing here, waiting to walk with me. I wonder if there's a pill I can take that will keep me from dreaming, because...he's waiting to walk with me. I like that, and *that*...that's all the damn dream's fault. I know it!

"Yeah, I'm coming to practice," I say, stepping away from the door and falling in next to him.

The door slams shut behind me, and we're now the only two people left in the hallway. When we get to the end, Nico holds the glass door

60

open for me, then stops with his hand out. I stare at it, my stomach actually swimming, unsure what he means by this gesture. I bunch my brow and look from his hand to his eyes, to his smirk which breaks quickly into a laugh.

"Can I help you carry some of that? Your bag always looks so heavy," he says.

"That's because it is," I snap.

"Wow," he responds quickly, eyebrows lifting with the single word.

I pull my mouth in tight and squint. I'm being short.

"Sorry," I say, not liking this emotional yo-yo I'm on.

"I get it," he shrugs, but can't hold in his laugh as he mocks what I said to him earlier.

"No, you really don't," I say back—just like he did. I'm unable to keep a straight face, and soon we're both laughing.

Nico reaches for my bag, his fingertips running along my shoulder as they sweep underneath the strap. The touch hits me with such surprise that I let him take my bag without any protest; whatever will get his fingers off my bare skin faster because…*holy*.

"Touché, Reagan Prescott. Touché," he says.

All I can think of while we walk across the main lawn is how Nico is carrying my bag along with his, and how they both look to weigh a good thirty or thirty-five pounds. I'm sure he's carrying his books along with his practice clothes and shoes, but then it hits me—something's missing.

"Where's your board?" I ask.

"Sasha's driving me home," he says.

I stop walking, but Nico continues on a few steps before his feet finally halt. His legs bend slightly and lift up quickly as he adjusts the weight on both shoulders before turning to face me.

"I need your advice," he says, his eyes making it to mine briefly before getting lost in the activity of the parking lot behind me. I know what he's going to ask, and part of me wants to make him go through the painful task of mustering up the words and having to make his case to me because I'm going to be a hell of a lot easier than my dad, but then again…*I'm going to be a hell of a lot easier than my dad.* He needs to save his strength.

"You want him to give Sasha another shot," I say.

Nico grimaces.

"My dad doesn't do that," I say.

"I figured," he says.

He leaves it at that, but he doesn't move. His eyes stay on mine, wearing away at me until I have to avert them. I pull my hair loose from the twist, my fingers pushing the band down around my wrist as I cross my arms over my chest, letting the breeze unwind my hair around me. I watch as players file one by one into the locker room door, some of them leaping to tap the metal sign on the way in that reads TRADITION OF BROTHERHOOD—the answer to the question on the other side— WHOSE HOUSE IS THIS? I think some of them believe it. *Some.* Not all, though. Definitely not all.

Nico and Sasha do. What I saw that night on the field. What I saw in practice yesterday. One leads, one follows—neither abandons.

"All you can do is ask," I say, not looking at him until I'm done talking, not expecting his eyes to be waiting for me. They're sincere and hopeful, and my small sliver of a boost pushes his mouth up on one side.

"A'right," he says, slipping my bag down his arm and holding it out for me to take. I grab it and pull it up on my shoulder, letting the weight of the tripod rest on my hip.

"Good luck," I say, my eyes squinting from the bright sun. I hold my hand up to my brow to shield my eyes, and Nico's are still looking at me just the same as they were before. My body reacts with an instant rush of chills, followed by a suffocating flash of heat.

"You should wear your hair down more often. It's pretty," he says. He's walking away before I can blink. And I stand on the bottom of the hill outside the boy's locker room stunned stupid, because I'm not sure if he really said those last words at all or if my crushing alter-ego made them up because of a damn dream.

Whatever the case, I tuck my hairband into my back pocket and move forward, planning to wear my hair down again tomorrow, and maybe the next day, too.

I've never really seen my father compromise. I've never really seen him give in. But Sasha is here. Granted, he's been running up and down bleachers for the last hour, but still—my dad let him put on a practice jersey and take the field...on his way to the bleachers.

Nico must have asked. My dad must really want Nico to feel comfortable.

The circle of wants, needs, and punishment is in full effect as Sasha's heavy feet clunk down the bleachers next to me. The team is on the opposite end of the field, and it's clear—even from where I sit—that they're a squad divided. Nico's half is smaller. It isn't even a half. It's...maybe six or seven guys.

"So how long do you think your dad will make me do this shit?"

Sasha's steps slow completely, and I turn just in time to see him taking a seat behind me.

"Probably a lot longer if he sees you taking a break," I say, craning my neck to look over my shoulder.

Sasha's eyes meet mine, and he smiles on one side of his mouth, running his arm over his forehead, clearing it of sweat.

"You're lucky you're not in full pads doing this," I say, just as he dips his head. He pauses and tilts his chin up enough to look me in the eyes. I nod to confirm I'm not kidding.

Sasha rolls his eyes along with his shoulders, adjusting his position and sinking more into the bleachers as he leans to one side and spits through the small opening to his left.

"Why are you even doing this?"

He doesn't look at me when I ask, his focus on the loose drawstring dangling from the waistband of his gray practice pants. He tugs the string between his thumb and forefinger, pushing the end in the elastic.

63

When his face comes up, he looks beyond me, out to the field. Leaning to his side again, squinting, he holds his finger out straight and points.

"That's my boy, right there. He's never quit on me. Not once." His gaze shifts to mine, his expression tired but hard—determined. "He asked me to be here. So I'm here."

I look from Sasha back out to the field, where my father is talking to Nico.

"You better get up, then, before my dad sees you," I say.

When I turn around, Sasha's already five steps up and climbing again. His pace is steady, and his legs look exhausted. But he's not quitting.

Sasha runs the entire practice. My dad calls him out to the center of the field when he dismisses everyone else, but Nico stays behind, walking over to me. I don't shut my camera off, and he's quiet when he sits next to me. We don't say a word as we watch my father speak with his best friend—both of them standing closed-off, their arms crossed over their chests. When my dad moves his hands to his hips finally, I hear Nico breathe in deeply. He doesn't exhale until his friend reaches a hand forward and shakes my father's.

I shut the camera off when they both walk out of the view from my frame, and as I'm packing up, Sasha and my dad are both at the bottom of the bleachers.

"We good?" Nico says, his feet tucked underneath the bleacher seat, and his hands gripping the metal front as he leans forward to make eye contact with his friend.

Sasha nods.

"Yeah, we all good," he says.

My dad twists the leather band of his watch on his wrist, repositioning it and checking the time. The sky is transitioning from orange to violet behind him. "I'll see you at home," he says, his eyebrows raised just a hint. I'm sure only I would notice the difference in his expression, but I know my dad means it's time for me to quit hanging out at dusk with two boys on the bleachers—two boys he's called *at-risk* at least a dozen times at home.

He's being protective. It's sweet. But it's also…I don't know…something more. I kind of want to stay. Maybe I feel like I owe it to Nico, because he walked over here to sit by me. I would be abandoning him. And maybe I want him *and* Sasha to think that I'm better than the eighty percent of the football team who doesn't seem to be on board with the idea of Nico taking the lead.

"I won't be far behind," I say to my dad, and the way his eyes level on mine, I get the subtle warning and nonverbal translation. I may be eighteen, but there will always be a curfew for me when boys are involved.

"A'right then," he says, pulling a pack of gum from his pocket and unwrapping a single piece. He pushes it into his mouth, chewing vigorously, and I smirk because he's being so very much a dad right now.

I watch my father walk around the end of the bleachers toward his office where, while I know he said he'd see me at home, I suspect he will be for the next several hours reviewing plays and thinking about how his offense *could* run if he really goes through with this.

When I turn back, Sasha has climbed the steps to sit on the rail near us. He pulls the tape from his ankles and balls it up, throwing it in the trash while he and Nico talk about meeting up with Colton.

"Dude, I need to get my ass home. My mom's already pissed that I'm getting a *C* in Government," Sasha says.

"That's because you keep *skipping*," Nico says, tilting his head toward his friend.

"Yo, I do. And it's worth it every time. Damn Brittany Shafer! Fuck, man…that girl is so fine," Sasha says as he brings his knuckles up to his mouth, biting them to show exactly how *fine* he thinks Brittany is.

"Pssshhh, dude, don't be like that in front of Reagan," Nico says, which only makes Sasha roll his eyes.

The entire exchange makes me suddenly aware of every inch of my skin, and I push my feet farther under my seat, tucking my hands under my thighs and looking down to notice the goosebumps raised on my pale white and freckled skin.

"No, it's fine. I get it. Brittany's pretty fine. I'm with him on this one," I say, mostly to deflect.

Sasha begins laughing instantly, holding his palm out for me to slap. I do, and as lame as my attempt to fit in probably is, it feels good to do this stupid little thing with him.

"Hey, just go with her," Sasha says when he leans back on the railing. "Reagan, you've got your car here, right? Can you take my boy to Charlie's?"

My mouth feels dry and fat all at once, but I manage to mutter out a "Sure."

At some point, Sasha tells me I'm, "Awesome," and we slap hands again, this time my palm numb and my head spinning, trying to figure out what I just agreed to. The longer it takes Sasha to leave, the more I realize that I'm going somewhere with Nico, together, and I start to work out the excuses in my head. I'll need to get him home, because that wouldn't be cool. But I could do that; take him home? I know my way in and out of West End now, and I could go now, and still get home way before my dad does, and nobody would need to know any of it…

"You don't have to go. Really. I can walk," Nico says, already standing and slinging the small gym bag, that I know is only a fraction of his things, over his shoulder.

"Oh…no, really. I don't mind. I was just going to go home, and I don't really have anything to do," I say, suddenly overwhelmed with the need to erase any evidence that excuses were ever floating through my mind. I stand nervously, and my bag tumbles open at my feet, my camera and several memory cards spilling out along the grated metal landing.

"Here," Nico says, dropping his bag and helping me pick up my pieces quickly. My heart is racing ridiculously, and my fingers can't seem to work right to flip open my camera and test it. Nico notices, and when his hands cover mine, squeezing them to calm down, it has the opposite effect, and everything starts to feel faster—the world brighter, my legs wobblier.

"I'm sorry, I…" I don't finish, instead just sitting down and giving over my camera to his steadier hands. I tuck my nervous ones back under my thighs and suck in both my top and bottom lip to quell my anxiety while my inner voice prays that my camera isn't broken.

Nico kneels in front of me, his lip raised without laughing, and his able fingers flip open my view screen easily. He doesn't know where the power button is, so I reach forward to show him, my hand still trembling with the jolt of adrenaline, and he nods. I pull my hands back in, this time pushing a few of the nails on the edge of my teeth. It's a bad habit, and it's the reason I don't have long, pretty fingernails. It's also the reason I can type wicked fast, though.

"Am I supposed to see you through this thing," Nico says, holding the camera up to face me. He stands when I reach for it, and then holds his arm out to stop me when I stretch forward again. "Oh no, it's your turn. Tell us, Miss Prescott. The academy wants to know why film is so important to you."

"Oh my God, stop. I don't like being on camera," I say through nervous laughter. My hand finally snares the sleeve of Nico's jersey, and he brings his left hand down, gripping mine tightly while he holds the camera steady on me with his right. "Nico, I'm serious!"

I *am* serious, but I'm also laughing hysterically, and I'm holding his hand…or rather, tug-of-warring with his hand. I battle with him, squealing and using my other palm to block my face when I finally give in and sigh, folding my arms over my chest before pushing my now-tangled hair out of my face, blowing the final strand out of my eyes before pursing my lips in the best pout-face I can make.

Nico keeps the camera on me for a few seconds, his face hidden behind it as his laughter subsides, until he lets it slide a few inches down, still recording though he's no longer viewing. His smile is sweet and simple, no dimple or bragger's rights painted on his expression. It makes my breath stop, but I hold my pose, praying I can bluff my way through this without giving anything away—without him realizing exactly what that look does…to me.

The heavy locker room door slams in the distance, and it breaks the strangeness we were both just living in. Nico looks down at the camera he's holding, turning it off and flipping the view screen back in its place. He puts it in my bag, zipping it and handing it to me. I clutch it tightly this time, and I stand as he takes a few paces back to his own bag.

"Really, I can walk," he says, looking up at me sideways as he lifts his bag back up to his arm.

I give myself exactly three seconds to consider my options, and I *do* consider them. I could go home, where my mom is sleeping thanks to her heavy prescription and my brother is locked in his room, pretending that he isn't feeling the pangs of disappointment. I could wait for my dad, like I usually do, only to have a short conversation with him in front of the refrigerator while he kicks off his shoes and drinks milk from the carton. Or I could take Nico to Charlie's Custard, and take him home when he's done, and maybe help him find a way to convince people other than my dad, Sasha, and Colton that he's just as good at leading as Noah.

He's better.

"I swear I really don't have anything to do. And I'd…" I stop for a breath. This part wasn't planned. "I'd like to come."

His lip ticks up as he winks, and there's absolutely nothing cocky or arrogant about it. His eyes avert, and his cheeks are either red on their own or the setting sun is painting them. Either way, he can't look at me when he says, "Thanks."

And I can't look at him while we both walk along the main path between the locker rooms and the parking lot.

"I'll wait for you at my car. It's the gray one with…"

"I know your car, Reagan. Remember, you stalked me at my house?"

The flush happens quick, and I crinkle my eyes and nose when I look at him guiltily.

"Maybe that was my stakeout car," I say, just needing to make this less about how odd I am and more about how clever and funny I am.

"Okay," he laughs, holding up a thumb as he turns toward the locker room, leaving me and my *oh-so-clever* self to walk toward my gray car. That is *not* a stakeout car; that he already knows, so I can spend a few more hours trying my damnedest not to superimpose scenes from my dream into every real-life moment I'm with him.

I march to my car, my feet picking up speed the closer I get, and I'm almost walk-jogging by the time I grab the handle and the sensors unlock, letting me in.

"Reagan Prescott, you should have said *no*," I say to myself in the safety of my two-door sedan. I let that thought sink in, but it's quickly clear that I don't mean it. Flipping my visor down, I raise the mirror, turning on the light so I can wipe away the streaks of dark brown eyeliner smudged under my eyes. I run my fingers quickly through my knotty hair, scratching my fingertips along my scalp to give my hair some sort of body. I pull the long waves over one shoulder and rake my fingers through, combing as quickly as I can, checking around the visor constantly to see if Nico's coming. As soon as I see the door open, I flip the visor up and pull the bottom of my plain, gray T-shirt up, rubbing it along my dry lips. I would give anything for a tube of ChapStick right now.

Nico walks toward me with his heavy bag from earlier on one shoulder, and the smaller duffle on the other. He changed into his faded jeans and a black T-shirt that has words on it that I would probably read if I weren't so freaked out about being caught looking at his chest. My mind flips back and forth from wishing I'd said *no* to affirming that I can do this, be his friend, support him, not…freaking fantasize about him, and then he tugs on the door, opening it just enough to lean in, and all of my senses go numb.

He showered. Quickly. His hair is wet, and he smells like that kind of body wash that guys use when they want the hint of cologne without actually wearing it. And it works for him. Because all I can focus on in the immediate are the beads of water somehow still on his forearms, the way his hair slicks back except for that long part up front, and the way he freaking smells.

"Trunk?" he says, and I think he's said the word twice. I don't know, because I'm having a neurological response to his goddamned soap.

"Right, hang on," I say, leaning down and pushing my teeth into my bottom lip hard enough to feel it, like pinching in a dream, though I doubt that really works.

I pull the lever for the trunk, and Nico drops his heaviest bag inside, closing it and coming back to his seat in seconds. As good as he smelled when he was outside, the effect is only multiplied by being enclosed in about one hundred cubic feet with him.

I flip the air on, despite the chill already brewing outside. Nico leans forward to press a few buttons on my stereo, and I fight my urge to be in control, wanting to be a good host—*not wanting to be a bitch*—when he stops on the jazz station. My brow pulls in quickly as he sits back, adjusting his seatbelt along his chest and relaxing into his seat, his arm resting along the base of his door and his fingers drumming to the beat.

I don't think my car has ever, not once, been on this station. I didn't know this *was* a station. And the music is soft, elevator-style, with some kind of xylophone and saxophone solo happening. I sigh, noticeably, and lean forward on instinct, but stop myself and push the air up one more notch instead. When I lean back in my seat, pulling up to the school exit, Nico begins to chuckle.

"How long were you going to let me listen to this shit?"

I stop hard at the light exiting the school, enough to jerk him forward, and he only laughs harder.

"I was trying to be nice! That's it; your deejay rights are revoked!" I say, pointing a finger at him.

He pulls his knees up and clutches his fists to his chest, laughing harder while I press my favorite stations until the indie rock channel comes on.

"Oh hell no," he says, leaning forward to press the stereo button. I grab his wrist, no longer thinking about how he smells, but instead thinking about how he's screwing with my stereo, and the cocky bastard laughs again, leaning back in his seat. I look over in time to catch him pushing his hand through his wet hair, and my chest fills up with what I think might be hope, and my arms and legs get tingly again, sending me right back to where I started. The light goes green, and Nico gestures for me to look forward and go, so I do.

"I was just kidding," he says. "I actually love this song."

I purse my lips, and a part of me waits for him to take that back, too—to keep messing with me. Instead, he sings the chorus, lightly, but loud enough that I can hear it. His voice is nice, even if it's a little off-key. I think about my damned dream again, and kissing him, and looking for secret rooms with him.

"Do you ever have those dreams where…" Shit! I'm telling him about my dream, my subconscious forcing my lips to talk even though this…*this* is the last thing I want to talk about, to say, to admit. I swallow and look out my window, check my mirrors, suddenly focusing on every aspect of driving my car the six blocks it takes to get to Charlie's. We stop at the next light, because the universe is cruel and wants this trip to take me forever.

"Dreams where what?" Nico asks, and I glance to my right. He's genuinely interested.

I draw in a deep breath and do my best to rest my palms on the steering wheel, to act natural and let myself get comfortable. I bunch my lips, stalling, looking for a graceful way to make this conversation now make sense.

"I've had the same dream the last three nights in a row," I lie. I don't need to tell him everything. And this conversation might be just right for this circumstance—just the right length, just the right depth. Polite. Interesting. Casual.

"Me and…" I stop myself, coughing to change my story before I slip and say Nico's name. "Me and my brother are in some house we've never been in, and we keep opening doors that lead to new hallways and rooms and parts of this house, and every time we do, it's like…it's like the house just keeps on getting bigger and bigger. Every room is bigger than the last, and there's always another doorway, or hallway, or whatever."

The light goes green, so I glance at Nico briefly before pulling forward. His forehead is knitted and his mouth is twisted in thought. "Maybe, yeah," he says. "It's never a house, and usually I'm with Sasha and we're somewhere kind of familiar, like the school. But I've had the door thing. Like...you're looking for a secret door? Or you've found it, but you can't open it?"

"Yes! Just like that!" I pound the steering wheel once, excited that my detour worked and that we have this weird, silly, pointless thing in common...*sort of.*

"I dreamt about you once, actually," he says.

My knuckles glow with the red of the stoplight that I've just pulled to a stop at, pressing on the brake a little too hard. Nico chuckles as he holds out his hand to grab the dash, and my eyes are frozen on the glowing red spheres dangling from a wire about twenty feet high in the intersection in front of us.

"Not that kind of dream; don't get all...all...girl freaked," he laughs, shifting in his seat. I can see from my periphery that he's adjusted enough to face me, and I suddenly feel as if every movement I make is on display.

"I'm not...*girl freaked,*" I say, scowling, and very much girl freaked indeed—whatever the hell girl freaked is. It might be the most genius description ever, come to think about it. I'm a girl, and I'm freaked. Nico is dead on with this.

"Whatever...you are. But don't be," he says, pulling one leg under the other, his long fingers wrapped around his shin, holding it in place. He has a silver ring around his thumb, and somehow it's the most masculine thing I've ever seen. If I were his girlfriend, I would touch it.

I look forward as the light turns green, my head snapping in place.

Girl freaked.

"It was last year, when we were practicing for the debate. I had a dream that you," he stops, letting a genuine laugh play out, and I grip my steering wheel hard, preparing myself for some sort of insult. "You punched me."

My eyes narrow, and I look him straight on this time.

"I…punched you?"

I'm kind of proud. Proud of this dream punch, that isn't real, and actually only happened because Nico's subconscious made up a version of me that did it, but I'm proud regardless.

I'm a girl-freaked, dream-puncher!

"You did," he says, and I glance over to catch the dimple.

"You probably deserved it," I say, looking back to the road quickly.

Nico shifts back the right way in his seat, chuckling. "I'm sure I did," he says. "I don't remember why, because I don't remember a lot of my dreams. But I remember you hitting me. My nose bled like a son of a bitch, and when I woke up, I rushed to the bathroom just in case."

A man speaks through my speakers selling insurance to veterans, followed by an ad for the weekend's "big sale at Big Al's Super Five Honda and Acura," and Nico and I both get lost in the mundane sounds of the radio.

"So you never remember your dreams, huh?"

I don't know why I speak when I do. I don't know why this is the question I ask. But the moment I say it, something shifts in the air— something shifts inside Nico. Somehow, his large frame feels smaller, and his confidence feels lost, a certain energy instantly zapped from the air we both breathe. I look over at the last light before Charlie's and catch a glimpse of his profile, his eyelashes moving with the tiny flickers of his eyes, his thumbnail lodged in his teeth while he thinks, his Adam's apple moving slowly with a labored swallow.

"I have a lot of nightmares," he says, his gaze seemingly caught on the bright Charlie's sign out in the distance. "Not really the kind of things you want to hold onto."

My instinct is to apologize, but the moment I open my mouth to do so, I can tell that's not what Nico wants me to do at all. He shifts to sit taller, bends forward to tug his hat from the small duffle bag he kept at his feet, and slides it on his head, tilting his neck to the right and cracking it once.

As we pull into the lot for Charlie's, Colton is sitting on the tailgate of his truck, waiting for us. I shift into park, and we both look out the front window as Colton hops down, holding a hand up to get Nico's attention.

I scan the lot and recognize many of the cars, including my brother's friend Travis's Jeep. I've never been the girl who dates the football players. Maybe it was always just too close to home. Not that any of the players ever really had a thing for me. I was always Coach's daughter—even when the boys were young and playing Pop Warner. Even so, for most of my life, I did harbor a sort of crush on Travis. It's probably just because I knew him the longest, because we took him with us on family vacations when we were kids, and he lived next door. When I was little, I always thought he looked just like my Ken doll. Light brown hair and blue eyes, Travis is built more like Ken now, too. But as high school went on, Travis and my brother grew into boys who snuck out to house parties and didn't come home in the morning, while I became the girl who begged her parents to sign her up for tech camp and take her to readings by her favorite authors.

That said, Travis and I are still close. And as much as my brother was an anchor for this team, Travis was his right hand. If he's here, Nico needs to win his confidence. I don't think walking in with Coach's daughter is going to do him many favors.

"I don't think I should go in there with you," I say, my eyes still scanning the parking lot and patio of my school's favorite hangout. One by one, I recognize more of the players here.

Colton is standing about a dozen feet in front of my car, paused with his phone in his hands, texting. Nico doesn't shift to look at me when I speak, and we both keep our eyes on the only player other than Sasha he can really count on right now. I can tell he knows it, too.

"Thanks for the ride," he says, pulling in a deep breath before pushing open the passenger door. "I'll get home fine, really."

"You understand…it's not that I don't want to be here with you, I just…" I lean forward, hoping to catch his eyes. He doesn't look at me, but nods, and I can tell he knows why I'm backing out.

"Hey, man!" I hear him shout as my passenger door slams to a close, drowning out the sounds of traffic and the rest of his conversation with Colton.

They both slap hands and pull in for a half hug before walking toward the patio area, a few heads turn and watch them walk up. They're all judging him—right now. Nico stops halfway, turning back to me, then holding up a finger to Colton and jogging over to my side of the car. I roll the window down as he leans down to speak.

"Can you just keep my things in your car? I don't need any of it until tomorrow," he says.

I nod *yes*, and his mouth curves into a slight smile as his hand comes down to pat the base of my window.

I watch him jog back to Colton, and I think of the dozen things more I should have said. I should have told him not to worry, that he could do this—that they would all warm up to him quickly, love him— just like they love my brother.

But I just didn't want to lie. I can't promise him any of that. But I know one thing—Travis better have his back. Otherwise, I'm digging out my Ken doll and feeding him to the blender.

CHAPTER 6

"Nico. Nico, get up!"

My brother pushes down several times on my mattress, shaking the springs until my head moves enough that my eyes startle open. His eyes hit mine, and he stands up from the floor where my mattress lies, moving close to the window, pulling my curtains to the side, but not enough to really look out my window.

"What is it, Vincent?" I sit up in my pool of covers, my hands fists that I ball and rub into my eyes. I'm so tired, and I can tell it's still nighttime. He hasn't been home in days. Mom is going to be so happy. "Are you coming home?"

"Shhhhh," my brother says, rushing back to me, but still looking out the barely-exposed window. He pulls me into his arms, and I hug him tightly.

"Sorry," I whisper.

Vincent pushes my shoulders square with his, then rubs his right eye, which is swollen and bruised. He's been fighting, and I swallow hard because it scares me, and I don't like looking at his face when it looks like this.

"I need your help," he says, his grip on my arms tight.

I've grown a lot over the last year. I'm almost twelve, and I'm nearly five inches taller than I was last summer. Vincent has grown, too. He's seventeen. He stopped going to school a few months ago. He also has a lot of numbers and strange symbols tattooed on his arm, and he tells me they don't mean anything when I ask. My mom always makes him put on a long-sleeved shirt to cover them. I heard her tell him he should be ashamed of them. He doesn't say anything to her face, but when she walks away, he calls her bad things. I don't like it when he does that, and I tell myself he doesn't mean it.

I miss how he used to be, when we were little. I liked it when we built forts out of Mom's sheets in the living room. He was home every night, and some nights, he let me sleep in his room with him. That was before he started hanging out with Cruz. Before the smoke poisoned him. My mom threatens to kick him out of the house when she finds it. He always leaves first.

"I don't want you to be scared," Vincent says, reaching to the back of his jeans, pulling a gun from inside the waistband. I stiffen and try to push away from him, my heart racing.

"Shhhh, Nico. It's okay. Look, here," he says, flipping the gun open in his palm, showing me an empty chamber, clicking it closed. My heart slows, but not much. I've never been this close to a gun. I lied once and told my friends I saw one when Cruz drove by our playground nice and slow. I needed an excuse for running home. I didn't want them to know I was just afraid.

"It isn't loaded," Vincent says. He sounds out of breath. I think he ran here. "Someone might be looking for it. They can't find it. I need to hide it."

My mouth is watering, the way it does right before I throw up. I pull my hand to my eye and wipe away the tear forming in the corner.

"Nobody will look here, Nico. I need to hide it here, okay?" he says, and I nod, because he's Vincent, and I just want him to come home. I don't want anyone to find it, to find him.

"And you can't tell Mom," he whispers, his right hand back on my shoulder, the gun in his grip between us. I nod again, but this time shake a little with my cry.

Vincent pulls me in close, holding me tightly to his chest, and I fall into him, watching as he slides the gun inside a beanie that he pushes under my mattress, against the cold concrete floor.

"I love you, Nico. No matter what. Know that I love you," he says into the small space below my ear, his lips pressing on the top of my head. His hands shake where they grip my back, and I cling to his sweaty T-shirt, holding tightly but losing the battle as it slips through my fingers and my brother flees my dark bedroom.

I hear the back door slide open and closed again, and after several minutes, I sneak out of my bedroom, taking quiet steps to the sliding glass door. I get on my knees, and feel for the small pin that locks the door completely, and I put it in place, hoping I'll remember to pull the pin free before my mother notices in the morning.

I won't sleep. I'm too afraid. Whoever wants Vincent, wants his gun—they might come looking for me.

I want him to come home.

Home.

CHAPTER 7

Friday pep rallies at Cornwall are kind of a big deal. We pack the gym, and parents and boosters come; so seating is always tight. Certain people get a special section with padded leather seats lined up behind the podium. I always sit on the floor, next to the cheerleaders, but in the far corner. I usually walk in carrying Izzy's extra pom-poms, but since I've started my film project, I haven't had to lean on my best-friend's cheer connection to get a good reserved spot. I just go wherever I need to go—carrying a camera gets me an odd pass into a lot of places.

"The football team is lame. You should change your subject to cheer," Izzy says, leaning into me to talk louder than the deafening blast from the marching band. Izzy is *literally* the perfect girl. She's a genius in math and science; she's built like an Olympic swimmer, and has auburn hair that always curls in one giant wave as if she's a cartoon and her hair is just drawn that way. I'd hate her, except she's an exceptional friend. She never dated Travis when I had a crush on him, and she put him *off limits* when I was over him, simply on principle. She also let me hide at her house during most of the summer, when the Cornwall football spotlight-and-gossip mill was in overdrive around and about our household.

"Your cheer team would make a really boring movie. Not enough drama. You need to be one of those cheer squads where moms plot murder and bribe competition judges with sexual favors to warrant a documentary. You guys don't even really dance," I say, offering half a smile.

"Are you saying this…is not a dance?" Izzy drops her pom-poms on the floor, and begins to twist her feet and pump her arms in a pattern I *think* is supposed to be the running man. She stops the minute I hold up my camera, wrapping her palm over my lens.

"My bad—you're right. We can't dance. Don't you *dare* film me doing that," she says, her hand still on my camera, but her mouth laughing.

I move to my normal spot, resting my back against the wall and sliding my gear bag from my shoulder. Most of the students are slowly making their way in now, so I scoot to the side just enough to get a wide-angled shot along the floor, but showing the expanse of the gym. I zoom in when the big spenders show up, including Brian Hawthorne, the guy who wrote an eight-thousand-dollar check to the team at last year's awards ceremony so they wouldn't have to wear the *losing uniforms* this season. Brian owns several carwashes across seven states, and apparently there's a lot of money to be made in dirty rims and windshields.

I let my frame capture the high kicks Izzy and the other cheerleaders are doing while the drums pound behind me, but I keep my focus on their feet, fading them to the forefront and bringing the background in crisp and clear when the team starts to walk in.

Nico isn't first. He isn't even second, third, or fourth. He walks in with Colton and the rest of the line—in the middle. He doesn't sit up front. Brandon does. My stomach sinks.

My dad isn't going to start him.

I let my video continue to roll while I sit up to my knees and lean back on my heels. The cheer squad spreads out, and as the final few students filter in, the doors shut and Izzy flips her way across the gym floor. One at a time, each member of the squad goes until they all meet in the middle and shout words nobody can really hear or understand other than the occasional over enunciated "Go!" and "Fight to Win!"

"Thank you, guys! Thank you, Tiger Cheer!" Principal Locket says, his voice squealing the mic. He turns it to the side as if there's something he can do with the volume. It squeals every time we have one of these.

"So, what's up with Nico sitting in the middle?" Izzy whispers as she slides down the wall until she's sitting next to me, carefully pushing her short skirt under her straight legs, palms on her lap. There are a good twenty minutes of announcements and thank-yous to major donors before the real *pep* part starts for tonight's game, so Izzy always comes to sit by me.

"I don't know. I was so sure my dad was settled on starting him," I say, and just saying it out loud makes my stomach tighten again. I'm invested in Nico's success, and part of that is the fact that this documentary on the team is a whole lot more interesting with Nico at quarterback. But I also want this for him. He wants it. Badly. I can tell.

I want it for him…more…

I've kept Izzy up to date on most of the football drama. She came to our house to visit Noah as soon as she got back into town on Wednesday. Her family believes in life experiences more than school attendance, so she misses a lot of class for trips. Her grandparents took her with them to visit a new exhibit opening in L.A., and Izzy paints, so this trip held a little more academic relevancy than most. Her dad is on the board, though, so she's almost always excused, and her assignments are done on the road.

The mic is passed to a few different people. Everyone *thinks* they want to hear their voice at one of these things, but then they don't really know what to say. It's a lot of the same stuff—"I love this team!" Every single one of them has been a member of The Tradition. Now bald, fat, divorced, but usually rich, they all relive their best moments right here in the middle of our gym they helped pay for.

They all want to see Brandon. They don't want to see some "scholarship kid." That's why my dad isn't going to go through with it.

He's bending…caving.

"I've never noticed how hot Nico is," Izzy whispers. I stiffen, half because I'd gotten lost in the background noise of the presentation, and half because of the words she just said.

"Yeah?" I say, my lips barely parting. They're so dry. My throat…dry.

"Maybe because he's usually so…I don't know, argumentative? You know how he is in our class. And you don't have calculus with him, but he's that way in there, too. He's always sighing—frustrated when Mr. Talbot has to go through a formula again. But I don't know, there's something about him in that jersey…"

"You're just smitten with football players," I say, smiling on one side of my face—the side she can see.

"Maybe," she giggles. "But I don't know…"

Izzy winks at me as she stands with her bright-gold pom-poms. For the first time ever, I hate her perfect legs when they walk by me in the deep-blue skirt, her white shoes topped with blue bows, glitter on her cheeks, and the perfect swirl of her ponytail resting on her bare shoulders. I stretch my own legs out, tugging the roll of my denim shorts down my thighs, but the fit still so snug that my leg indents where the fold rests. Freckles spill out down my knees and all the way to my ankles, where my feet slip into my Vans without socks. Everyone always says they love my freckles. They say they're like stars—like a map to the universe. The people who say that are all old. Boys here want curvy, smooth, golden—they want the fantasy because there are so many of them. I move to my knees and tug my shorts down one more time, pulling so hard that they slide down my hips a little. I decide that as uncomfortable as this is, it's better than the tight fit around my thighs. There isn't anything I can do about the freckles.

"I think we'd all like to get a report on how Noah Prescott is doing, right?"

I stand as Principal Locket begins to rile the crowd up about my brother. I know Noah is here. I saw him outside the gym when I walked over with Izzy. It was the first time I'd seen him smile since the break.

My brother's leg is bound in a cast that covers his knee, so walking on crutches is slow, but he ambles to the mic with the help of his girlfriend, Katie, who takes one crutch from him so he can lean into the other as she moves to the background.

I move to the small space between both sections of bleachers so I'm centered in front of the team and my brother. I want to get the best view of everything, and as much as I don't like people watching me work, I also don't give a damn if it makes my video better. Folding my legs up, I rest the camera on the small tripod stand and lean forward to watch my brother through my screen.

Everyone around me has stood by now, screaming and cheering for the same guy they were ready to hang for not doing enough to win a playoff game last year. My brother thrives off their fickle love, though. His cheeks are red—the same way mine turn—and he clutches the mic in his hand while he rests it on the top of his head. Sometimes I can't tell if his humility is earnest or well-rehearsed. I think both forms are okay today, though.

He brings both hands forward, his left arm unable to stretch completely due to the crutch, and gestures downward, urging everyone to quiet and take their seats. Everyone ignores him, though, still cheering until he turns to his team with laughter—his smile real this time for certain. The crowd finally settles when his voice booms in the mic. Of the two of us—Noah is the loud one.

"Seriously, thank you guys!" he says, garnering a few more chants of his name and whistles. "Thank you, so much. That means a lot!"

After several more seconds, the chatter grows more manageable. I zoom in close on Noah's face, and my chest fills because he looks like himself—the smile in the right place, and real. The scowl he's worn for the last week as he's kept us all out of his room is as if it never was. I miss this Noah—and I realize now that I see him this way—I was worried he wouldn't come back.

"This team...you guys," Noah says, turning enough to look at the boys he's known for years—*his* brotherhood. "Being a part of The

Tradition has been everything to me. Last week..."

My brother stops midsentence, bringing the mic down along his leg, his eyes falling forward with his swallow. The clapping begins again, and the crowd cheers for him to go on. He nods.

"Last week was both one of my greatest moments on that field...and my lowest."

Everyone is rapt, and silence comes fast and evident. I force myself to notice just how quiet it is—so much so that I can hear the crackles of the heavy air conditioning units pushing cold air through the ductwork. The only other time I can hear that is when I'm in here alone.

"Winning with these guys...it's...it's everything. And getting to lead them on that field is an honor I don't know that I will ever know the equal to again. You know, a lot of people like to gun for us. We're easy targets—private school...amazing fans..."

Noah pauses for another round of loud cheers. He's planned this—thought it out. My brother is an inspiring speaker, and if I could push him, I'd make him love politics. But I know that I can't, and I know his heart is in sports and an environment just like this.

"We're winners. Just look up there! Look at that wall!" He turns enough to point with the mic to the several banners that hang above the rows of stands where our team currently sits. The display is impressive, and the succession in recent years is even more so. But I wonder about the glaring banner missing from that display.

"I wanted to put one up there for you. I wanted it," he pauses to rap the mic against his heart twice. His head hangs low, and fewer whistles pull him out of it this time. "I want it this year. And I would like to think I got things started."

His head comes up again, his eyes determined and his face matching as his bottom lip tucks in his teeth while he nods *yes*. Yes. This year, yes. I scoot forward so I can pan to the faces nearby, everyone sitting on edge. Boosters nodding. Their poster boy is doing good.

"I'm not quitting just because of some cast. I'll be there tonight—on the sidelines. I'll be there at practice. I'll be there with these guys—my brothers. I'm not going to stop until I put one more banner on that wall!"

The gym erupts, and the "No-ah" chants come in quickly. My mouth hurts from my smile, and I look at everyone, all smiling just the same. Everyone except two people.

When my eyes fall to my father, I notice two things. His eyes are forward, to a spot on the floor somewhere between where the tips of his shoes end and the back of my brother's heels begin. And his mind is not on the words my brother is saying. My dad is conflicted. I see it, just as I've seen in on his face for the last year, since the big loss. I saw it during every cruel prank phone call with threats in the middle of the night, and I see it now. And then it hits me.

My dad wants to start Nico.

"I might not be QB-One, but I will always lead this team. That's what you do when you're a part of The Tradition! You step up! You step up and lead no matter what your role is, what your jersey says, where you are on the field. I'll lead! We lead! Whose house is this?"

"Our house!" The team shouts behind my brother.

He only does it once, because it will be said a lot today. That chant will echo on through the night. I just hope that it gets said in about five minutes, when the guy who I've long thought to be the cockiest person I've ever met stands up in front of a team that does not yet trust him and asks them that very question.

Nico's legs are bouncing. First it was the right. Then the left. Now both bob with tremors that I see easily between the row of muscular bodies all sitting still and relaxed in front of him. Too nervous to sit any more, I hold my camera steady against my chest, tilting the screen up so I can watch comfortably when I need to. I keep my eyes forward, on Nico's legs, on my father's mouth—the hard line still there to match the deep divot above his brow, a wrinkle from fear and what I am guessing was also probably another sleepless night.

Noah turns to where my father sits, and my dad stands, walking over and taking the mic from him, shaking his hand and squeezing his shoulder. Only a split second passes where their eyes meet, and in that tiny sliver I see how unhappy both of them really are. My brother was supposed to finish this. My dad wanted that for him.

Plans fell apart. Plans are shit. A person can't count on anything except their gut.

Instincts.

Those are what my father has always rode—his instincts. I shut my eyes, but hold my body still. I don't pray often. We aren't the kind of family that goes to church unless there's a social reason we're expected to. But I do pray. I don't talk about it. I do it for me. I do it when I need to escape being a Prescott. I do it when I need to know I'm not crazy, when I'm worried things aren't going to be okay. I do it for others.

I do it now—for my dad and for Nico.

The cheers are heavy again as I open my eyes to watch my father walk with the mic to stand in front of his team. His coaching staff sits in the first row just behind him—deep-blue shirts, whistles, low-slung hats, and khakis. I could flip through more than two decades of team photos and those men, though different people, would always look the same. Behind them, his team is silent. Their eyes on their coach, all of them waiting to know who to follow. Only a handful of them are truly prepared.

"With great adversity comes great opportunity," my father begins as chatter subsides. He glances to his team, looking at them for several long seconds without speaking again. A few of the guys shift their weight under his scrutiny, but most of them hold their position—both feet flat on the floor, hands on their knees, eyes on their coach.

"Football is a dangerous sport. I'm not saying anything earthshattering or new to any of you. We all know the risks. We've all seen the injuries. Hell, this isn't even the first bone football has broken on Noah's body. I..." My father's head falls forward as he chuckles. "I remember when he was eight, the first time he broke his wrist. My wife, Lauren—oh she was pissed. She was ready to pull him."

The audience responds with a mix of laughter and "noooooo!"

chants.

My dad holds up a hand.

"Clearly...I prevailed in that argument," my dad says, and the laughter grows.

"Noah has broken his wrist twice. He's lost a tooth—one permanently—had a few concussions, had some pretty deep bruises, including one that bulged out of his thigh for what...seven weeks?"

My brother shouts "eight!"

"Eight, yeah...right," my dad says, his laughter quieter now. "He's had more stitches than the clothes I'm wearing. And he's just one of more than three dozen of our state's finest gentlemen sitting up there who can point to countless body parts and spout off injury reports."

"Yet they all come back. They show up every summer, for training. They show up for first practice...for second practice...for fiftieth practice. They show up under the hot lights, under our high expectations. And they perform!"

There's a wave of cheers for this part, and my dad expected it, so he lets it die out. He's never been one to take away from the praise his boys earn. But he does not milk it.

"They show up. And they respect. And they follow. They follow each other because inside of each of them is someone who can lead. These men are all leaders. And they are going to take what they learn out here on the field and bring it forward...into their lives. They are going to lead in life. Through commitment. Through promises they make to each other. Through the strength of their brotherhood."

The quiet is back. I'm holding my breath, and I realize how much I'm probably moving so I turn my focus back to my camera, watching the next part play out through the screen.

"As a father, it breaks my heart to see my son have to miss experiencing this the way I know his heart truly wanted to. I'm devastated for him, but so proud to see him here today. I know Noah is a man of his word, and I know he will continue to do whatever he can to help his brothers be better...stronger. But as a coach, I need to make a decision that will help that spirit flourish out there on that field."

My eyes glance from the camera view to real life and back again while my father's neck muscles tense in preparation.

"Tigers…I'd like to introduce you to your new QB-One, who I know in my gut will take you to the end this season—who will get that banner, who will take Noah's direction, who will guide and lead in a way you need right now, in a way you probably need more than ever. Please give me a *hoo-rah*…for Nicolas Medina."

"Hoo-rah!"

The chant happens fast, because it's programmed that way. My father requests it and it gets said, no matter if it's heartfelt. And this time, it is not. The word is loud, but the quiet that follows is suffocating. There are not cheers. There is polite applause, and slow handclaps while elbows rest on knees of expensive slacks in the booster row.

My brother's eyes are lasers on Nico as he works his way through the middle of the stands, his thumbs looped in the top of his pockets, his jersey number eleven, unworn since my father wore it years ago. My brother wanted to be his own man. He wanted to be number one, both literally and in life. Nico wants approval.

The exchange of the mic is slow, and my father says something in Nico's ear, and I stare as he listens and nods. He grips the mic fully in his hand, his back to me as he watches my father move to the only open seat in the coach's row. Nico knows the drill. He's the last one to speak. His job is to set a tone—to make them believe.

His task feels impossible.

His wrist twists with the mic, tapping the live end along his thigh, making a few *pop* sounds through the speakers. He stops as soon as he realizes, but doesn't lift the mic to his lips just yet. He takes in his audience, gazing down the row of linemen, many who are nodding, but several who refuse to look up, and then he sees his receivers, his offense, and Brandon, who many thought would be the one standing here in his place. He pivots slowly, eyes scanning over the crowd, a tight smile and nod to acknowledge boosters and the school's faculty. His eyes never really seem to settle as they make their way to the student body, even when they pass over me several times.

I've never seen him lost. He's always so sure, always right. If there was a task Nico was born to handle, this was it. But my heart isn't sure this time, and it pounds so loudly that my ears dull.

"Noah," he says finally, and I hold my breath. "Dude. You're a really hard speech to follow."

My lips twitch with hope, and there are a few giggles in the crowd. My brother offers a one-sided smile and shrug, and I let my shoulders drop from the tense hold I had on them.

"Thank you, Coach. Thank you, Tradition…guys. I know what kind of opportunity this is. It's the kind that, as Coach just said, comes from adversity. And I know that means it's not necessarily the kind everyone wanted…wants."

His eyes fall forward to his feet, and he kicks at the free-throw line on the gym floor, his mouth raised on the side nearest to me, and I smile, too. I don't know why, but seeing him do so just brings it out.

"For those of you who don't know me, I prefer to be called *Nico*. It's what my Nana called me when I was a little boy, and it's what I answer to. I live eleven miles from here. Eleven miles south of here. In West End."

His eyes are still down at the tip of his toe, where his shoe is digging at the embedded line as if one of these times it will actually move from his touch. He's nervous, and I realize that he does this when we debate in class—he focuses somewhere else, almost as if his mind needs the distraction so doubt and fear won't get in the way of his words.

His words. They are always so brilliant. Even when I hate them. I breathe deeper, and my muscles relax more. Nico…he's got this.

"My boy Sasha," Nico stops to look up as Sasha yells. He holds up a fist and Sasha does the same. "He's crazy. Sorry about that. Sorry, Coach."

My father holds up a hand and encourages him to go on. The students near me chuckle.

"Sasha and me grew up together, until he moved. He's still West End though. You see our neighborhood, it's a lot like this team. Tradition is such a good word for it, ya know? The first time I heard Coach say that at practice, it settled in my chest. Right here."

Nico pats his chest. His eyes close when he does.

"I know a lot of you guys probably don't drive around in West End. I get it," he says through laughter. "Believe me. There are times *I* don't drive through West End."

The audience laughs with him this time. I laugh with him. He's winning. He's closing.

He has them.

"But…let me tell you about that world on the other side of the freeway. Where I come from, we don't have a lot of extra anything. We're short on things. Ha…we're short on *everything!*"

"Damn straight!" Sasha yells.

Nico turns to his friend and tilts his head, and Sasha sinks down slightly in his chair.

"Sorry," Nico says, excusing his friend. Nobody seems to mind, though. People are listening. The boosters are even listening. Players heads that were seconds ago looking down are now looking up—eyes focused on their new leader. A few are holding out, but Nico will win them over. He'll own them, too.

"There's this great thing that happens, though, when you don't have everything. You find something deeper. In the locker room…out here today…we call it brotherhood. I like that. Family—that's what we call it at home. It doesn't have to be blood. It's my neighbors down the street. It's the time Carlos Mendoza closed down his shop to drive me to school because someone stole my board. It's how his wife went out and bought me a new one. It's how my mother's fridge was filled with food when we were hungry; how my brother's daughter always has the prettiest dress for Sunday school; how my boy Sasha, even though he moved away when we were kids, remained and will always be the best friend I'll ever have."

"Family. Brotherhood." Nico looks to his team, most of them meeting his eyes now as he says this. He turns enough to glance my way next; his eyes find me, this time stopping, his lip raising, his confidence building on itself so quickly before my eyes, I feel like this may be his superpower.

"Adversity. Opportunity."

The room is silent, filled only with the sounds of the rushing air and crackling building again.

"I understand this. I take this job. I take this role. And I will be what you need because I know what it's like to need…to need someone. To need to believe again. I believe…"

He swallows, his eyes still on me, the intensity so strong that I bend my head forward to peer at him through the lens. Even there, in black and white, he owns me in a way that makes my palms sweat and my nerve endings fire in anticipation. He's made me want to act, to be better. In a little more than a minute, Nico Medina has made me believe—he's made *most* of us believe.

"I *know* we are going to win tonight. I know it. I feel it. Right here," he says, fist to his chest as he turns toward his team, taking steps forward until he's close enough to reach their hands. "I feel it! Do you feel it?"

"Hoorah!" They yell, Colton standing and clapping, others following. My father stands and begins to clap with them, his mouth still a hard line, not ready to accept that any of this could be so simple, but relieved to see them willing to try, to go along with his crazy plan.

"Whose house is this?" Nico says, his voice strong, the words tinged with energy. He's amped. His legs are steady, and his muscles are flexed.

"Our house!" They yell.

"Whose house is this?" His question comes out louder this time.

"Our house!"

The response matches.

"Whose. House. Is. This?"

It's always done in threes. This is tradition. And they respond just as loud.

"Our house!"

Nico reaches forward grabbing Colton's hand, their chests crushing together as he makes his way down the line, celebrating and fueling the mass adrenaline with fist bumps, hand embracing, and chants. He reaches Sasha, and they both roar, their smiles large and the worry that was almost dragging Nico into the claws of dread is nowhere to be seen.

My feet move automatically, and I film it all—my footage a messy scene of chaos, unbalanced shots and unsteady filming. I smile through it all. The scene is brilliant. The story is set. We have to win. Losing is not an option. We all believe.

I stop the moment my camera focuses on Nico and my brother. Nico's hand held out, my brother looks around, his eyes working fast to see who is watching, and without a second thought, Noah pushes by Nico, moving his hand aside as he works his arm over his crutch and slings his body forward to catch up to Travis. The two of them walk out through the side door into the locker room, not once looking back, and never acknowledging the power of the celebration they left behind.

"It's going to take time," I say to Nico. He isn't facing me, but I know he knows I was standing near him. He nods without speaking at first, smiling and shaking hands with more of the guys as they slowly exit the makeshift platform at the back of the gym. My dad is long gone, not one to press flesh with boosters who all have opinions. Nico knew his role, though, so he stayed. I stand with him, and I hold the camera up under the guise that all of this is for my film. I'm not even rolling by the end of it, though. I stayed because I didn't want to leave.

I didn't want to leave him.

Sasha and Colton are the last to head to the locker room, and Nico lingers behind.

"I'll catch up," he says. Colton smirks at him, and I flush at the way his eyes take me in, assuming I'm something more than I really am to Nico.

"Yeah, I gotcha," Colton says.

I let my camera dangle in my hand, wanting to keep the focus on everything in the small space between Nico's eyes and mine.

"How'd I do?" he asks, and I laugh on reflex.

"Have you ever lost a debate?"

Nico chuckles and his head dips down, pulling one side of his mouth in for a smile before leveling me with the gold in his eyes.

"Do you always answer questions with questions?" he says.

I smirk at him, tilting my head in response.

"Sorry. You just left me that opening," he says, swinging his hand forward into mine. My free hand moves without my permission when he does, catching the tips of his fingers in my own, and the sudden touch forces a jolt of air from my lungs, my mouth parting, a sharp exhale audible to both of us.

Nico's eyes haze as they focus on our flirting fingertips. He doesn't dismiss me, but he doesn't grasp my hand for certain, either. He lets our touch remain in this fleeting, awkward place where I completely submit and let him decide how hard we touch, how long and, most importantly, why.

I glance from our hands to his mouth, to his jaw—my breath held as I watch his muscles work, his teeth holding his tongue at the front of his lips as they fight against smiling, fight against speaking.

They just fight.

They battle until they close, and his eyes flit open to mine with a hard swallow, our fingers still feathers dancing and barely holding on.

"I'm scared of failing," he says.

I can feel his fear—it radiates; it's in his touch and reflected in the way his eyes tilt with worry. He doesn't blink, and I hold his stare and force my eyes to remain open, too. I don't want to breathe too hard. I don't want to startle him. I want to give him what he needs.

Seconds pass, and every pass of his thumb and forefinger against mine pushes me forward, each press from one part of his hand on mine like a slow ballad being tapped out on a fragile piano. When his fingers stop moving, my breath hitches, and I react—clinging, my fingers wrapping around his, threading and squeezing tightly. The force is like when two magnets come together in just the right way, and I feel his arm grow stronger as mine falls apart, and when I can no longer squeeze and hold, he takes over—he takes my strength.

"You won't fail," I say, our eyes not once leaving one another, my hand now gripped in his between us. My mouth whimpers a sound that is part cry and part laugh, the product of all of my fears and reservations mixing with confidence in this boy who has invaded me without warning—without asking.

"You never do," I say, the nerves that I've held in my chest pushing out, making my lips tremble with my words. I want my camera. I want the safety of living this part through the lens. I don't want to be part of the story, but I am.

I'm a part of Nico's story. And he's a part of mine. I believe in him. More than I've believed in anything, and the enormity of it makes my chest hurt. I ache, and I want to escape, my fingers numbed by his tight hold, my face hot under the reflection of his rapidly-growing smile. His dimple. His confidence.

His power.

"Nico."

The sound of his name. My father's voice. Our hands drop, and when I shift to the side I see my father's eyes down at the floor, his hands on his hips. I ball my fingers into a fist, savoring the feeling they had seconds ago, ashamed my dad caught us. Nico does the same, and when I see him flex his fingers, I worry he's trying to rid himself of the memory.

"Sorry sir. I'll be right there," he says. My father nods, and Nico looks to me, mouthing "thanks" before jogging to the door held open by my father's foot. My dad pushes it open wider as Nico jogs through, then catches it with his hand before it closes, his eyes coming to meet mine for only a beat.

My dad looks at me just long enough for me to know that he's going to pretend he didn't see us holding hands. He also looks at me in a way that lets me know he doesn't approve. He's gone behind the heavy blue door in a blink, and I open my hand wide again, brushing the tips of my fingers along the top of my other hand just to see if it feels anywhere close to the same.

It doesn't.

Not even close.

CHAPTER 8

The hype Nico infused in the team at the pep rally carried through the third quarter of the game. I have never seen the team look so gelled, so together as one on the field—at least on offense. The score, unfortunately, also tells a story about our defense, and with about four minutes to go, The Tradition sits at forty-six, while St. Margaret's Prep trails only by four.

I leave my camera posted on top of the press box and climb down the small set of steps to the bleachers, weaving through the crowd of students all standing with their arms raised—as they have for the last three minutes—until I get to the bottom, to Izzy. I just can't handle watching the game alone any more. Even though I'm surrounded by coaches, it's still lonely in the press box. And Coach O'Donahue has kept his mouth shut tight—I think inwardly rooting for Nico to fail. Every time I felt him make a wish for something to go wrong, I made two for something outstanding to happen. My wishes must carry more weight.

"Hold that line, Tradition! H-O-L-D!"

The cheer squad is shouting, and I can tell Izzy's voice is hoarse. Even my best friend is more invested in this game than she's ever been.

I sit on edge of the bleachers, poking my legs through the front by the railing and resting my arms on the bar in the middle. I'm just high enough to see the play on the field, and the pass from St. Margaret's quarterback is almost caught, broken up in the last minute by Sasha. I scream when it works, bumping my elbows on the metal bars—forgetting where I am.

Nico is standing a few steps behind my father, his helmet on, but tipped so his face is exposed. He's chewing on his mouthpiece nervously, his hands gripping at the pads by his neck while he sways with the countdown of the clock. On the far end of the field, near Travis, my brother is doing the same, his weight held by two crutches. They're both almost in sync, the way they look to the clock, then to the field, over and over again as if they're hoping to somehow speed it up.

I'm watching them when it happens, I don't have to look at the field to know that St. Margaret's completed a pass. Their faces both look pained, and the roar from the other side of the field grows until it absolutely swallows us whole—our fans falling silent.

"Block it, block it!"

The guys all shuffle down the field as St. Margaret's sets up to kick the extra point. Arms waving as those not on the field leap—including Nico—as if somehow they can jump and make a difference from here.

They don't. The ball sails through the uprights, and this game shifts into that precarious place with a minute and fifteen seconds on the clock. We can either win—or we lose or tie; despite those options, there's really only one that anyone cares about at Cornwall. We win. Ties are losses. And no matter how great Nico was tonight, it won't matter if that scoreboard doesn't fall in our favor.

He'll lose the starting position.

My father will lose control.

And we'll all slip deeper into the cesspool of whispers and snide remarks when we run into families from the school off campus.

My father is holding Nico's face close to his, his hands gripping both sides of his quarterback's helmet, his jaw hard, veins exposed, his face red as he yells over the cacophony of screams, drums, and whistles from the refs who want to finish this game, and finish it now.

I can't hear him, and I wish I could because not once did I ever see him talk to my brother this way. He isn't mad. He's passionate right now. He's...begging. Willing Nico to go out there and give him one more miracle, on a night that he's thrown for three hundred yards.

Nico jogs out to the guys waiting in the huddle, and the cheering around me grows even louder. My brother looks on, standing alone, at least a dozen feet away from the rest of the team. My heart breaks for him because he's helpless. All he can do is watch. All any of us can do is watch.

Nico's hands gesture, moving to both ends of the field, up the middle, then coming to the center of the huddle in fists. He looks each of his teammates in the eyes, then, hands in the center, they all chant "break." The Tradition all filter to their positions, Sasha and Travis both lining up on the far right side of the field. They are the speed, and if we have any shot at all, Nico is going to need to hit one of them.

Nico begins to shout, raising his knee once on the count. He repeats everything again, his eyes on his opponents, assessing them and every tiny move they make. He moves in closer to Colton, his hands ready, then shouts something different, his line shifting maybe a second before the ball is snapped, never once offsides, but on the edge enough to force St. Margaret's to scramble to play catch-up. The move buys Nico a precious extra second, his feet falling into step, his legs carrying the defense to the opposite end while Travis and Sasha divide and sprint forty yards out.

The clock is at fifty-six seconds; Nico stops hard, changing direction and shirking two defenders, one gripping his pads and nearly pulling him off balance. His feet recover quickly, and his speed only grows with the close call. He works his way back to the center, the ball clutched in both hands as he pumps once...twice...getting his timing just right, waiting just long enough until he lets it go right before a defender's hands find the center of his chest, shoving him to the ground so hard he bounces and skids. Nico pushes his tackler off him so he can get to his knees to watch as his best friend runs as fast as he can, his right hand out as the ball begins its decent. My head works to calculate the angle, and it seems so impossible.

Tradition players crowd down the field, running in step with him, bodies low and crouched with hope until they explode in leaps, arms pumping as they all chant "Go! Go! Go!"

I can't see Sasha through the bodies, but I do see Nico. He's on his feet in a blink, his arms over his head as he rushes toward the rest of his team, the crowd behind me the loudest they've been tonight. I know he pulled it off. I don't need to see the scoreboard. I only need to see the sheer elation exuded in every step Nico takes until his chest collides with his best friend's, the ball that a breath ago passed into the end zone still clutched in Sasha's hand. Sasha lifts Nico, who hugs his friend's helmeted head, his palm patting it in pride. This is what makes football great. The moments when impossible happens; the boys who make impossible happen.

My eyes scan the field while our team kicks an extra point, and as I trail down the sidelines to where my brother stands, I see a different emotion. His hand runs over his face, and his jaw hangs open. Travis runs up, raising a hand that Noah takes, clutching it as they come together to bump chests. My brother smiles when Travis celebrates, but he doesn't give him everything. He holds something back.

Envy.

I get lost watching it—not really coming out of the scene my eyes can't seem to tear themselves away from until I feel a tug on my dangling feet. I startle and look to see the top of Izzy's head. She steps up on a block below me so we can look eye to eye, her hair teased out in a ponytail, her face sprinkled with golden glitter.

"That was seriously the best game we've ever had!"

Her red lips stretch into an enormous grin, and her eyes are vibrant, almost twinkling like the gold on her skin. She talks rapidly, her hands moving with every word.

"Oh my God, Reagan. Seriously…I thought we were going to lose, and then no…Nico just says *no,* and it's like awesome, and he almost gets tackled and then he doesn't and then he throws the ball. I mean, that was far, right? So far!"

I giggle the more she talks, and eventually she smacks my bare knees playfully.

"Don't make fun of me. I'm excited!" she says.

"I'm not," I say through laughter. "It's just...I watched the game, too. You don't need to give me the play-by-play."

"Right," she says, nodding with a short breath, lips closed in a tight smile. I hold her gaze for a second, and then roll my eyes.

"Go ahead," I say.

"Oh, thank God. I just can't quit talking about it. That was seriously the best thing I've ever seen. And Sasha is so fast! And Nico...oh my God, Nico! Reagan, he is so freaking hot!"

I force the same look on my face, but the second she shifts from being excited about the game to being excited about Nico, my body does the strangest thing. My skin goes numb, and there's a rush through my veins that feels like morphine—tingling until my stomach drops and clenches. She's talking so fast that I hope she doesn't notice the small flinch that I can't control. I blink it away.

He's hot. She thinks he's hot. It's nothing. It's just the game. The excitement.

I preach to myself over and over, but my friend mentions Nico one more time before she's done. And I can't lie to myself this time.

"I am so into him, Reagan. He better be going to Charlie's for after-game," she says, and I get to my feet, letting my eyes focus on the rail I hold, on getting my feet back under my body, on the crowd exiting behind and around me. I turn so I face them, and I keep my eyes down while my head begs "no!"

I'm not sure what that *no* means—no, Izzy cannot be interested in Nico, or no, I should not care. I think it's both.

"Hey, I'll meet you at Charlie's, okay? I have to go change!" my friend shouts from the field level. I raise my hand with a thumbs up, and I turn enough to see her grab her pom-poms and weave through the stream of friends and family all making their way out to the field.

The stands empty quickly, and I give a polite nod to Coach O'Donahue as we pass on my way back into the press box to get my camera.

"Hell of a game," he says.

"Sure was," I say, turning to watch his back as he takes the steps down one at a time. He's faking, too. I recognize it, because that's the way I walked away from Izzy—like everything's fine. He wanted Nico to fail, and he's going to want that every single Friday until it happens.

I get back to the press box rooftop and my hands grip my camera, turning it to power it down and begin packing up, but my sideways glance also catches a glimpse of Nico...and Izzy. I leave the camera running and point it on my surveillance targets, every piece of me feeling childish, just not enough to stop. I look through the lens, but can only tell Nico is smiling and Izzy's head is bopping up and down, her hands still wild and her hair vibrating with every word she says.

I almost quit watching, but then Alyssa comes running up, and Nico bends down, sweeping his niece into his arms, holding her on his hip and nuzzling noses with her. He looks to Izzy and says something, and Izzy hands Alyssa one of her pom-poms, which she grips and shakes against her chest. The sick feeling rushes back, so I drop my camera lower and power off, promising myself not to look again.

I keep the promise, packing and carrying my equipment to the film room, dropping most of my things in the locker in my father's office so I can keep them safe while I go to Charlie's. I'll pick them up again over the weekend. I keep the small handheld camera out, holding it in my lap while I shuffle to the training table in the back of the room, sliding into my familiar seat, my legs stretched out in front of me and my father's favorite assistant and trainer, Bob Melch, by my side.

"Hey, Reagan. You get that dandy of a game on film?" Bob asks.

I smile and nod.

"Sure did," I say.

He places his large, wrinkled hand on my shoulder and pats down twice. Probably even more than my dad, Bob is excited about the film

I'm making. He's been the trainer here for two decades, and this year—it's his last. While most of the members of the coaching staff fall into that football-coach stereotype, Bob bucks the trend. He has sixteen grandkids, and not a single one of them plays football. I asked him about it once, and he told me he'd rather they got into the arts—or took up film, like me.

"This right here? It's just a game. What matters are the relationships inside of it," he told me.

I was maybe thirteen when we had that talk, and I've never forgotten those words. I hope I never do. I wish my brother heard them. I'm not sure he would understand, though. Noah's programmed to win, and the rest doesn't really matter much to him.

It's almost twenty minutes before everyone is showered and sitting on the rows of benches in front of my dad. His arms are folded, the playbook still tucked under his forearm. He hasn't changed positions since he entered this room several minutes ago, looking up only slightly to congratulate certain players on specific plays he thinks they went above and beyond on. His mouth is a hard line, and his players begin to quiet as they nudge each other until the room becomes so still that I hesitate to breathe.

"Congratulations," my dad says.

Several seconds pass without a response. He doesn't want one. They know. No shouts, no "hoorahs" right now. They look him in the eyes and he nods, taking in the young, naïve faces in front of him.

My head falls forward to check my camera view, and I zoom in tighter on my dad.

He lets his arms move to his sides, the playbook clutched in his right hand where he taps it against his thigh.

"You're not celebrating. That's…that's good. I was afraid this would be harder, but I'm glad to see that you recognize what this really is…what…*tonight*…really was."

I register a few swallows by players in the row closest to me. Nico is at the front, nearest to my dad, his head down and eyes at the place where my father's shoes hit the floor.

"Defense," my dad begins, pausing to breathe in deeply through his nose. "Boys, tonight was pitiful. I'd like you all to line up here right now. Come on. Line up. Up front. On your feet!"

Players look around the room, staring in one another's faces, as members of our defensive squad get to their feet and amble toward the front of the room, standing in a line facing my father, their backs to the rest of us.

"Gentleman," my dad says. My heart is beating with the power of a sports car's engine as I wait for his voice to rise, for the shouting to begin. I knew my dad would not be happy with just winning. Winning—that closely—is still failing in a lot of eyes around here, and even though Coach O'Donahue is his point on defense, the responsibility falls squarely on my dad's shoulders.

"Turn around," my dad says, his voice sterner, but still in control.

I zoom out to capture the entire line of juniors and seniors, many of the faces those I grew up with, all standing bulky shoulder to shoulder, freshly showered, but still showing the red, purple and blue cuts and bruises from the field.

"I'd like you each to shake Nico's hand. One at a time. And I want you to thank him," my dad says, the words coming out through gritted teeth. "You thank him for saving your sorry asses! For turning around your shit performance and somehow pulling something out of his ass with less than a minute in the game! You apologize for putting him in that position, for putting us in danger, and then you get your shit, go home, and show up here again at five in the morning and prepare to work!"

"Yes sir!"

The response is in unison, and the handshakes commence, each more awkward and full of fear than the last. Nico doesn't respond, and his jaw flexes with every new grip, his eyes flitting from face to face, and his mouth growing tighter every time.

As soon as the final shake is done, the defensive squad, minus Sasha, who my father had play both ways, slips through the side door into the locker room. My father waits as the door shuts, walking close to the door to listen, to see if anyone dares to speak when they think they're safe. Satisfied that they don't, he turns to face the rest of the room.

"Nico," he says.

Nico nods, his eyes still on the closed door behind the line of guys my father just shamed.

"Game ball," my dad says, catching the toss from one of his assistant coaches and pitching it to Nico's hands. "You earned it. It doesn't mean shit, because now we look to next week."

"Yes, sir," Nico says.

Their eyes freeze on one another in a short standoff until my dad looks out around the room.

"Go home," my dad says, leaving without another word, his office door slamming shut behind him.

I let my camera roll while everyone's slow to move at first, eventually grabbing their bags or belongings and standing. I close my camera and slide from the table, passing by Colton, Travis, and my brother who are lingering outside my father's door.

"I wouldn't go in there," my brother laughs.

I meet his eyes, and for the first time I can remember, I see something unkind in them. He's almost reveling in the spiral, loving that things weren't quite perfect without him. And there's something a little menacing in his stare, too. I don't respond, instead opening my father's door and letting it close behind me. I don't speak, moving right to the locker and placing my small camera in the bag with my other things, clicking the door closed and fastening the lock.

"You can pick it up Saturday. I'll be here early," my dad says, his eyes down at the paperwork in his hands which are resting in the fakest pose ever on his desk. He's looking at spreadsheets, and I know he's not *really* looking at anything.

"Okay," I say, moving back to the door.

"Are you going to Charlie's tonight?" he asks. I pause with my hand on the door handle and nod.

"I was thinking about it," I say, my answer honest. I'd planned on going with Izzy until my stomach twisted seeing her talk to Nico. Now I kind of want to go home and sit in the shower until the hot water disappears and my body can't stand the cold.

"Nico going?" my dad asks, his eyes raising slightly from the papers, but not fully to me. His question catches me off guard, and I shift my weight.

"I…I don't know," I say.

He nods a few times, then glances up at me through raised brows.

"I don't want you giving him a ride home," he says, and he waits for my response.

My brow pinches, and I let out a short breath through my nose, but nod in agreement.

"Okay," I say, turning my full attention to the door and leaving.

My brother and Travis are gone, probably already on their way to Charlie's. The parking lot gets full fast, with families and players crowding in for the free ice cream the owners give out after wins. We always pack the lot until midnight, until the neon lights are shut off, and sometimes well past then.

And tonight is the first one ever that Nico Medina will be there for any of it.

I snag the last spot in the lot. It's near the alley, and it isn't really a parking spot, but I know nobody is picking up the trash this late on a Friday night. I have to slide against the metal garbage bin to get out because I have to park so close. I'm sure I've smudged some dirt on my white shirt, but I brush the front and worry less about the back as I get closer to the party.

A few girls I recognize say hi, but I don't stop until I get to my favorite picnic table closest to the building. Izzy is already sitting on the table, the straw from her chocolate shake lodged between her teeth as she tugs it free from her cup with her mouth then pokes it back in for a new position.

"Hands free, huh?" I tease as I sit next to her.

"My hands get cold, so I leave all the work up to my mouth," she says, just loud enough that Travis hears and stops at our table to comment.

"I can give your pretty mouth a work out, Izz. Whataya say?" Travis reaches into his pants as if he's really going to do anything. Izzy waits him out, not even blushing with embarrassment, and eventually he has to push his hands in his pockets and laugh to avoid feeling foolish.

"My mouth will never touch any part of *any* of you, Travis Wickersham," my friend says, her lips wrapping over her straw then slowly stretching into a closed-mouth grin. She sucks in a taste of chocolate while Travis looks on, and he holds his hand over his chest.

"You break my heart, Izzy. But I'll get over it," he laughs.

"She just won't give in because my sister is in love with you," my brother says, his voice behind me and instantly sending my head three years into the past and my temper a dozen levels hotter.

"Noah!" I shout, twisting in my seat to look him in the eyes, only to notice Nico is just over his shoulder, hearing everything.

"Awe, there's enough of me to go around, Reagan, but I don't think your brother will approve," Travis chuckles.

My eyes flare and dart from person to person, in quick panic. All I want is for this to stop, for my brother and Travis to move on, for the subject to change. This friendly banter—or *not-so-friendly* at the moment—is typical Prescott-twin activity. My brother and I have been pushing each other's buttons since the days of long car rides to our grandparents' lake house in the summer. We've always been competitive—even though our skills don't match. I'm the one who gets straight *As* and takes first prize at the science fair, and Noah hits the ball over the fence in Little League. We fight over shelf space, over whose trophy, medal, certificate—whatever symbol of our achievement—gets to take up more real estate and is placed in the very center of the mantle.

But there's something in my brother's tone tonight—an edge that's just a little different. Something…bitter. When I step in closer, mostly to keep my brother's voice down, I realize he's also working on a pretty nice buzz, the smell of whiskey from our dad's favorite stash, strong. I've gotten used to this smell over the last year, too. It's on him when he crawls into the house from parties—it was on him the night he crashed the car, too.

"You're on pain meds, Noah. Don't be an idiot; what are you thinking," I say, doing my best to keep my voice a whisper, but gritting the words through my teeth so he can see how serious I am—how disappointed I am.

I can almost see it coming before I'm hit with it, but I'm not fast enough. My brother's hand grabs my shoulder, and he pushes me out of his face.

"You're not my fucking babysitter, Reagan! You have such an enormous stick up your ass. Always Miss Perfect. *Oh, look at me, Daddy. I'm making a movie. Can I make a movie about you?* Guess what, Reagan? Nobody gives a shit about your dumb-ass documentary—not even Dad! He just wants you to be busy, and he's always complaining about how you get in the way out on the field. The coaches fucking *hate* that you're in the press box. What are you going to do when you go to college and realize that the only people who think you're talented at all are fucking related to you?"

My fingers tingling, my face red, I glance around to see dozens of eyes on me—including Nico's. I clench my jaw to keep my emotions as even as I can, and I stand, but the little girl who doesn't want to let her brother get away with it gets the best of me, and I let my shoulder fall just enough into my brother as I pass that I nudge his arm from his crutch, causing him to hop.

"Asshole," I say under my breath.

"Bitch," he says back without pause. His word comes out crisp and loud, and it stabs like a knife. I stop in my tracks instantly, my hand swelling with blood. I've never wanted to hit him. I've never hated him so much.

My eyes tear up, and I spin to let my hand fly at his face, but before I can, Nico's stepped up to him, their faces only inches apart.

"Apologize," Nico says.

His eyes don't blink. He's the boy who's always right, and he's delivered my brother one single expectation. As much as I should be honored, instead I'm mortified. My brother doesn't call me names. Sometimes we don't talk, and lately he's been distant. We haven't talked in days, really. But we don't go to dark places with each other. We compete, but at the end of the day, I'm always in his corner.

Always.

My head tilts, and I look to him, his eyes hard on Nico's, his posture rigid—not wanting to say he's sorry, but only because he doesn't want to give Nico the satisfaction. Well, what about me? Who gives a shit about his pissing match with Nico. This is about me!

"I hate you!"

My lips quiver when the words fall away, and my hand covers my mouth quickly, my breath a short tremble and my eyes stinging with the red I know has filled them up.

"Reagan," Travis says, stepping closer to me, his voice suddenly sweet. Decorum matters now, because I got my feelings hurt. *Now* they'll be kind.

Travis reaches for my arm, and Izzy tosses what's left of her shake at him, the lid popping free and light brown frozen sugar spilling in heavy drops across Travis's neck, chest, and arms.

"Shit, Izz!" he says, looking down with his arms stretched out.

My eyes grow wide while my young crush and brother's best friend wipes away large swipes of milk-chocolate shake, letting it fling from his fingertips to the ground. I begin to giggle, and Izzy looks at me.

"Izzy, I love you," I say, my laughter somewhere between the kind that precedes crying and genuine giddiness.

"I love you, too, Reagan. What do you say we leave the boys in the sandbox?"

My friend loops her arm with mine, tugging me along the main walkway into the small restaurant and through the throngs of people in line, waiting to place their order. She drags me all the way to the bathroom, and I laugh the entire way until we make it to the large stall in the end of the ladies' room, where I fall into her hug and weep heavy tears against her chest.

I cry for a solid ten minutes, and my friend strokes my hair, which I kept down because Nico said it looked nicer that way. She doesn't ask questions, and when I'm finally able to breathe, she walks me to the sink and runs cold water, dampening paper towels and wiping away any remains on my face that I was ever sad at all. When she's done, she looks me in the eyes and smiles until I can't help but do it back.

"Your brother didn't mean it," she says, and I nod lightly, not so sure, but wanting to believe it. "He's upset. His identity has been shaken, and he just doesn't know how to cope with it all. He took it out on you, and he shouldn't have."

"You're right," I sigh, my throat sore and my body a little tired from the instant emotional drain.

"And Travis…he's just an asshole," she says, her mouth twisted into a disgusted expression that makes me laugh. "Seriously, Reagan. I hope you're over him, because that guy's a loser. Oh my God you deserve someone so much better."

"I've been over him for years, Izzy. You know that," I say.

"Yeah, but I just want to be sure," she says, holding a pinky out for me to link with my own. We lock fingers and shake once, our *forever* promise that we save for things we really need to mean and believe in.

"Good," she says. "You should like a guy like Nico. When he stood up for you, Reagan? Oh my God…"

My mouth hangs open, my soul desperate for it to form the words— *I do like Nico.* Instead, I watch my best friend hold her hand over her heart, smitten by a guy she never noticed before, a guy who stood up to defend *my* honor, a boy *I* talked into taking this risk. A boy I never noticed this way either, except for the years he was pushing my buttons and making me angry—making me *think*. Nico was always there, but I never knew him.

"You take as much time as you need. If your brother asks, I'm going to probably tell him to fuck off, if that's okay," my friend says, leaving me by the mirror as she steps closer to the door. Another girl walks through, one I don't really know very well, so I grow shy and my heart flutters.

I don't want strangers to think I cry.

"Yeah, I'll tell him, too," I say through forced laughter. I plaster a smile on my face, and Izzy blows me a kiss, flinging the door open and disappearing—probably to find my hero, who I don't really know all that well either, but know better than she does.

The door comes to a close, and the intruder in the bathroom shuts her stall, so I let my smile slip away, my mouth tired of pretending. I turn the water on and fill my hands with soap, to give myself a reason to be here. I don't carry a purse. The only things on me are my phone and small wallet stuffed in the back pocket of my jean shorts. I take in my reflection, looking for that confidence—some sign that says I'm a girl that's going to walk out of here and turn heads. My hair is straight and flat, tucked behind my ears on both sides, a small sweeping of bangs that are too short to fit into a ponytail anyhow stick to my forehead.

I rinse my hands free of soap, and pat them dry on my legs and white T-shirt because there are never paper towels in this bathroom. I head to the exit the second the only other girl in here with me opens her stall door. I'm gone before she can see me.

The small hallway by the restrooms is quiet, but just four steps away, into the main part of the restaurant, people are packed in, standing room only. It's always this way when we win. My family came here, to Charlie's, after the big loss. We were the only people in the joint. My father wanted to come because it was ironic. It was the first time the owner didn't tell him "good game." My dad hasn't been back since.

I don't really like crowds. My circle of friends is small—it's Izzy, really. I know people, but I don't know anybody well, so I usually stand off to a side until I can slip away unnoticed, back to the dark of my room with my computer and camera equipment.

I want to escape now, but I don't want people to think it's because of what happened with my brother. I wonder who else saw? I hate that Travis did. I hate that he was a jerk. Travis has always been nice to me, but maybe that was before—when we were kids. Things are different now that we all graduate in a few months. It's like we had to choose a side—a type—that we were going to be. My type falls on the outside and my brother and Travis—they live in the center.

My thumbnail lodged between my teeth, I scan through the windows as best I can, but am unable to find my friend. I know she wouldn't wait in line. Izzy doesn't have to—people deliver her things. I bet someone handed her the chocolate shake the minute she walked up.

Giving up, I walk through a side exit and make my way back to my favorite picnic table, drips of chocolate still there as evidence of everything that went down. I step up on the bench and sit on the tabletop, taking in a long breath and brushing my hair from my bare arms, the humidity making everything feel sticky. I tap my feet in a haphazard rhythm, my feet hot in my white shoes. I wish I'd worn socks.

When a heavy black Nike kicks one foot out of place, I jerk my head up, ready to be defensive, tired of being pushed around tonight by my brother and his friends, but Sasha's smile disarms me. He steps up on the seat, and I move over a few inches to make room so he can sit next to me. When I look him in the eyes, I see a boy just as out of place as I am.

"So are these things always this crowded?" he asks, leaning back and looking out at the sea of people gathered in bunches around the parking lot. Car doors hang open to play music. People sit on the backs of pickup trucks. Girls giggle while boys try to throw ice at them. Guys play catch with a football while family cars try to make their way into the drive-thru line.

"Yeah, pretty much. It's been like this here since I was a kid…after game night," I say, thinking about the times I came here in the back seat of my parents' car, my face pressed to the window wanting—waiting—for *my* time to come. And here I am. My time.

What a disappointment.

"We have things like this…in West End." Sasha looks up at me with one brow cocked.

"I thought you didn't live there anymore?" I ask.

"Psshhh, I don't. I hate that place, yo. But…I don't know. Not all of it, ya know? It has good parts. And when I got my license, I started going back to visit," he says, a smile playing out over his lips while he speaks, his eyes flitting up to the night sky. "Ah damn, so many people are exactly the same. It's crazy. We have this mini-mart kind of place, and that's what this reminds me of. On Sundays, after church, that parking lot is crazy full. The food there is so good, and everyone races out of service to get in line. And the drinks are always colder there. I don't know how, but they just are."

"You go there for church then?"

Sasha nods.

"My mom goes to a place by our apartment, near St. Augustine's, and I went there with her after we moved. But as soon as I could drive, I started going with the Medinas," he says, his eyes coming to me briefly before falling to his hands on his knees. He's nervous, and it's sweet. When he's with Nico and their friends, Sasha is the loud one.

"You must love his family," I say, inviting his eyes back to mine. When our gazes meet, he smiles, his lip raising higher on one side.

"I do," he says. "Nico…he's…"

He stops without finishing, and after a few seconds, his eyes move from mine back out to the crowd. He doesn't have to say the word. There really isn't a single one that fits everything Nico Medina is.

Special.

Loyal.

Smart.

Mysterious.

Important.

My stomach sinks again at the thought of trying to define him. I want more words for him. I need to know more of his story, but right now, my best friend is laughing at his jokes, both of their backs to me while they talk with Colton and a few other members of the team. I could walk over there and insert myself. My friend would welcome me. Nico would involve me. But I'm still not so sure I belong—not right there.

Not right now.

This isn't my shot. And our stories are too different.

CHAPTER 9

I pull up to the stoplight above the freeway right before crossing over into West End, my camera equipment piled in the seat next to me, covered by my pink-flannel shirt. My mom used to tell me stories about people getting carjacked in West End, but now that I'm older, and watch the news and read the paper, I never hear of it *really* happening. I think she made it up—a fear tactic—to keep me from driving into an "bad neighborhood." But that thought crept in about a block ago, so I pulled my shirt from around my waist, and spread it over my things as if that actually conceals everything.

My father held an early-morning practice today, just as he promised the guys he would. And he worked the team hard. By the time I arrived, everyone was accounted for. Everyone, but my brother. I suppose he wasn't expected, but after the speech he made—about how he would support the team in his new role—I would have thought he would have shown up. Noah actually never came home. He told my mom he was staying at Travis's for the night. Neither he, nor Travis—who lives next door—came home, though. My mom was aware of this when I came home at eleven. She was aware of it when I was still awake and creeping down to the fridge for a glass of milk at two o'clock, and she was aware of it this morning, when she sat at the breakfast table with her head barely held up on her arm, the coffee in her cup cold long ago.

My mom is a worrier. She also has terrible anxiety. She medicates—upping the dosage against doctor's orders—and my brother's self-destructive behavior is not helping things. I knew I didn't want to be around when he showed up. Not that my mom would discipline him. She'll do just the opposite, actually, because that's what we do with problems in the Prescott family—we cover them up in happy paint, put on sunshine smiles and pretend everything is fine. When boosters started writing op-ed pieces in the local newspaper calling for my dad's resignation after last year's season, my mom began forcing our family to go to the art shows and plays in the city. We needed to be "more well-rounded" she said.

More like we needed to show off how upscale and pedigreed we were, why even though he lost, my father was still the right coach for Cornwall, because he attended theater. This is also why the PTA would never find a more perfect and qualified president for their social committee than my mom. Sometimes, I wonder about all of the work that happens in her head, the strain she puts on herself to make sure everything in our lives looks perfect. I catch her talking to herself sometimes. Other times, she falls apart. I don't see the tears, only the remnants. She always has an excuse—"allergies" or "something in my eye."

I pretend, too, I suppose. I pretend I don't notice, or that I believe her. We're a house of flipping posers.

When I left her at the kitchen table, the sun barely up, she was already pulling out her calendar to plan the next function. By the time I get home, I'm sure some major fall dinner party will be planned for our house—all coordinated on zero hours of sleep and a nice cocktail of chardonnay and Xanax.

My dad fixes things the opposite way. He dives head first into the problem, but burrows himself so far in that he becomes manic, losing control. That was evident at this morning's practice when his unrealistic expectations left three players with heat exhaustion and a handful of others on the verge of pulling muscles. When he called practice for the day, the sun high above everyone's head, hunger in their bellies if they weren't sick, he didn't bother to stay behind while the team cleared the field. If he had, he would have seen one player do an extra set of everything.

Nico.

I watched from my car. In fact, I didn't bother to film a thing. At the time, I told myself I was just tired—giving myself a break. Every few minutes, I'd convince myself that I was going to go home soon, to help my mom, to go back to bed—to *get the enormous stick out of my ass.*

My brother's cruel words were locked in my head, and every time I shut my eyes to sleep last night, they popped right back open at the thought that I was wasting my time with this film business.

Nico changed my mind about that, too, though. I watched him run one more set of bleachers, and then count out on his own for a solid minute of up-downs, his legs weak and barely able to carry him, but his will fighting to make them work just a little longer.

Seeing him want something so badly was beautiful. That's how I feel about film.

I should have offered to take him home, but instead I let him hitch a ride with Sasha, and then I sat in my car for an extra hour, giving him a head start so I didn't look like I just followed him.

I realize now exactly how little good that did. His eyes narrow on my windshield as I pull into his driveway. His niece is in the front yard, skipping through a sprinkler, while he sits on the porch in a plastic chair. He's still wearing the gray T-shirt he wore during practice. In fact, the only difference from the version of him I saw an hour ago is that his shoes are unlaced, and the sweat has dried a little.

He cocks his head to the side and raises a brow, so I raise a hand, curling my fingers up and down in the weirdest wave of my life.

"Nico, come play with me!" Alyssa yells from the yard, her arms swinging wildly through the stream of water, trying to fling it toward me. She's giggling, and I can tell she's trying to get me wet.

"Maybe in a little bit. Why don't you come in; let me make you some lunch?"

Nico stands while he talks to his niece, but he keeps his curious eyes on me. I had no real reason to come here. This is the most impulsive thing I've ever done, and I'm rapidly understanding why I'm not the kind of person who makes impulsive decisions. My palms are sweaty, so I wipe them on my denim-covered thighs before tugging the fold on the end of my shorts down my legs so I can exit the car.

"But I don't want to stop. Nico, please? Five more minutes?"

Alyssa giggles while she twists, her hands flinging stronger now, a few droplets hitting my arm. I smile at her and wink.

"Oh no, I'm all wet!" I say.

Her giggling picks up, and she cups her hands now, filling them—albeit poorly—with water before skipping closer to me and throwing it at me. I don't feel a thing from it, but I pretend again while Nico walks closer to us both.

"Ah, you got me wet again…oh no!"

I cover my cheeks and pretend I'm scared, shielding myself from the water. While I'm acting, Nico sneaks up behind her in the yard, and just as she turns around, he lifts her over his shoulder.

"Ah, I've got her. She won't get away with this!" he teases, running in tight circles around the sprinkler in the middle of their small grassy area.

His niece's hair falls heavy toward the ground while he dangles her upside down, his strong arms holding her easily, swinging her head through the streams of water while the air fills up with the sweet sound of her laughter. I laugh with them, the sound so infectious. And when her cheeks turn pink, he flips her upright again, holding her to his chest while he sits in the damp grass, the water spraying both of their faces and soaking their clothes.

"I'm sorry, Nico!" she giggles. "I'll dry your friend off. Just let me ess…ess….ex-cape," she says, the word getting trapped between her tongue and the tooth she's missing in the front. I want to hear that word said just like that from now on. I think I need to start every day with a water fight with Alyssa. I think I understand why Nico is so strong.

"Okay, if you promise you'll dry her off," he says, letting her out of his arms.

I have no time to react before Alyssa wraps her arms around me, hugging my legs with her shivering wet body, her wet hair sticking to me and making me wetter than I would have been had I joined them and skipped through the sprinkler, too.

"Thanks," I mouth to Nico, who steps closer to the driveway from the grass.

He winks at me, then laughs.

"You better run in and put dry clothes on before Nana gets home," he says, patting his niece on the butt as she sprints by. His eyes watch her until she makes her way into the house, and the smile on his face is something I haven't seen him wear before, except maybe at the pep rally, when he talked about the meaning of *family*.

I watch his face glow with love until he turns his eyes to me and catches me. For the first time ever, I don't look away, though. I'm not afraid of being caught.

"What?" he says, after a few seconds pass. He speaks through a crooked smile, and the earnestness with which he does just about everything hits me hard.

"I like watching you with your family. You're like that with Sasha, too," I say.

"Oh, you've seen me spin Sasha around on my back through the sprinkler?" he jokes.

"No," I say, laughing and looking down at his wet shoes, socks, and soaking cotton shorts. The material clings to his thighs, and he shakes them loose with his fingers. "I…" My tongue stumbles as my eye follow his hands up the length of his arms as he pulls off his soaking wet T-shirt, wringing it out by twisting it in front of him. It's not the water falling away from the shirt; it's not the water at all. It's how his stomach chisels, his abs curve individually and how his chest grows broader until I realize I'm staring and not talking at all.

"I just mean that you seem like family with Sasha. That's all," I say, only glancing up enough to see his face looking at me sideways, one eye squinting, and his lip tugged up in a smile. I turn away the moment our eyes meet, and I wait at least three seconds before looking up again. I know, because I count in my head. His eyes are still waiting for me, his head cocked in the same position. His lip raises higher this time, and a small, breathy laugh escapes.

My shoulders fall as I exhale and turn my head to match his, leaning to the side and putting one hand on my hip.

"What?"

His lips press together tightly, and curl slowly on the sides, until both cheeks are dimpled with his suppressed laugh. I'm amusing him, and I don't know why. I hold my hands out to my sides and raise my shoulders and eyebrows, and finally his lips break their hold and his laughter escapes.

He never answers me, instead looking to the wet shirt in his hands, which he slings up and down a few times, then lies flat on the hood of my car.

"Uhm…"

I point at it as he passes me, walking up his driveway toward the house.

"Your engine is hot. It will dry faster there," he says.

I glance back at it over my shoulder, the wet cotton dripping down the front of my hood over my headlights. When I turn back, I run into Nico's chest, not realizing I was as close to his porch as I was and that he had turned to wait for me. His hand wraps around my upper arm and my face touches his bare shoulder, my eyes closing while my skin heats up in instant blush.

"Oh, sorry…I wasn't looking," I stumble.

His hand still on my arm, he squeezes, an *almost* hug.

"It's okay," he says. "Come on in."

Nico holds the screen door open, and I step inside, walking past him. He gestures toward the kitchen, where Alyssa is already sitting in a wooden chair at the head of a giant butcher-block table. The little girl is wearing an oversized T-shirt—clearly her uncle's—and a pair of unicorn leggings. He rustles her hair as he walks by, stopping to scoop the length of it up and twist it into a temporary ponytail on her back.

"Nana told me not to let you get too wet outside. You're going to get me in so much trouble," he laughs, bending forward and touching her nose with his. She scrunches her face and moves her nose back and forth against his.

"You're the one that made me get this wet!" she says, her voice loud and confident. I smile because she's so much like her uncle.

"Well played, Miss Medina," Nico says, squeezing her cheeks in his hands and kissing the top of her head. His eyes move to me while he does, and he winks just before he turns to move toward the counter.

"We have corn tortillas, some of Nana's carnitas left and…nope. We're out of cheese. You okay with cheeseless soft tacos?" Nico asks, his eyes shifting between me and his niece. I look to her for a response, and she grins with an open mouth and an overexaggerated nod.

Nico leans into the counter and begins opening up a small plastic bag of tortillas.

"I figured you would be okay with that. You don't *like* cheese. But I was more asking for our guest," he says, shifting his focus to me.

"Oh, no…it's…it's okay, really. I'm not that hungry," I say, not wanting to intrude on something that was probably supposed to be just for the two of them.

"Stop it. I hear your stomach growling. And my mom's carnitas is the shit," he says, spinning on his feet and opening a cupboard behind him, pulling out three plates and quickly fashioning a soft taco on each.

He slides a plate in front of me, then turns back to the counter to grab his and Alyssa's, urging me to sit in the chair at the table. I smile and slink into the seat, tugging my plate closer while I whisper, "Thanks."

He and Alyssa both pull their food into the palms of their hands, taking large bites and smiling at each other with full mouths. I pick a small piece of the meat from mine and taste it, and the flavor is so powerfully delicious that my mouth waters at the first touch. I follow their lead, folding the tortilla tightly and biting into the end.

"It's really good," I say.

Nico nods. The three of us eat in silence, but he watches me through every bite, his mouth hovering in this sort of *almost* smile that keeps me off guard and makes me aware of every grind of my teeth, swallow of food, and shift of my fingers in holding my food. I try not to meet his gaze, but it's almost magnetic in the way it calls to me, and every time my eyes meet his, I grow warmer.

"What?" I ask finally, putting the last piece of tortilla down on my plate just long enough to pick up the small paper napkin he sat down with it to wipe aimlessly on my chin in fear that I'm wearing food.

Nico lunges forward, grabbing my discarded bite and popping it in his mouth, and all I can do is look at him, stunned.

"That's what," he says, chewing through a closed-mouth grin as he stands, picking up all of our plates and walking away from me backward.

"Hey! I wasn't done with that," I protest, standing and following him toward the sink while his niece pushes in her chair and runs to the front room, flipping on a television.

"Only a little bit of TV, then you need to do something else, okay?" Nico says loudly, leaning forward so she can see him around the corner. She nods, then settles into the softness of the sofa.

"You limit her TV?"

Nico's brow pinches, and I realize my question might have sounded judgmental.

"Sorry, I just meant…it's nice. Or, it's not something I'm used to…I don't know. I'm just going to shut up now," I stammer, my hands busying themselves with the grooves of the tiled countertop, my fingers tracing the squares one at a time.

"All this time, and *that's* what shuts you up? Gah! I could have won so many debates in class just by flummoxing you with the novel approach of limiting the amount of TV kids watch," Nico teases. I look up at him with pursed lips, my eyes narrowed and my mouth twisted.

"Kidding," he chuckles.

"Sorta," he adds after a few seconds.

I pick up a dish towel near me and throw it at his head. He catches it swiftly and throws it back, and we both freeze with our eyes on one another. I want to look away, but I force myself not to. The pep talk happening inside my head is comical, but it works, and I end up seeing his gaze through. He doesn't break either, but his cheek dimples, and his lashes sweep in slow blinks—his expression that of a guy who's become strangely comfortable looking at me.

"I try not to let her be a couch potato is all. We have a lot of kids in the neighborhood, and when it's light out, I like to try to encourage them to go out and play. The boys all want to play video games, but that's okay because Alyssa doesn't want to play with them anyways. She's into dolls and hopscotch and…you know…girl stuff, I guess," he says, leaning forward and pulling the towel across the counter, rubbing it in large circles and eventually draping it over the edge of the sink.

"My dad didn't really like us watching TV either," I say. My words must intrigue him, because he pulls himself up to sit on the counter across from me, and his head shifts to the side.

"Did he give you guys limits?" Nico asks.

"Not…really. But if he got irritated with us, or just, like…thought we had watched enough for the day, he would walk by and unplug it," I say. Nico laughs instantly at the image I conjure, and as I think back on the scenes from our childhood, I begin to laugh, too. "Yeah, I guess subtle was never really part of Chad Prescott's tool kit."

"Doesn't sound like it," Nico chuckles, his laughter filling the space between us for a few seconds until it subsides, and once again we're left with our eyes meeting, and my brain searching for words and courage to let him look at me like this for just a little while longer.

"I…uh…I was wondering if I could interview you?" I finally interject, breaking the silence and killing the smile that was on Nico's face for so long. His brow wrinkles. "For my film? That's…that's why I came."

It's completely *not* why I came, but it's the excuse I gave myself. It's the lie I concocted while I sat in the school parking lot. It's the ruse for getting to spend more time with him, for getting to ask him questions and learn more of his story.

Nico pushes free from the counter, and I move to the archway between the kitchen and living room, hoping he'll follow. His hand cupped behind his neck, he stretches to look out the open screen door before his eyes come back to me.

"Yeah, I guess so," he says. "Where do you want to do it? Maybe…front porch?"

"That's great," I smile, hating that we're moving back outside, closer to my car—closer to me *leaving*. I do need to get my things, though. "I'll get my stuff, and set up. Do you…want to get different clothes on?"

My eyes have been working hard not to ogle, and now that he's standing again, that task is proving to be more impossible. As if he can read my mind, Nico reaches up so his fingertips touch the top of the archway, stretching enough to flex the line of muscles that fall down his sides, into his shorts and…*oh God.*

"Yeah, I'll meet you out there," he says as I turn away and move toward the screen door.

I mumble out a "sounds good," and pass between his niece and her view of the television on my way out the door, marching quickly to my car and unlocking it to pull open the passenger door. I grab my shirt and tie it around my waist, then slide the large camera bag over my shoulder so I can carry the tripod in my hands.

It takes me only a few minutes to set up a good shot on Nico's porch. By the time I have the shot framed on the plastic chair—I've positioned just in front of a vine growing up a section of lattice—Nico steps through the door wearing a pair of faded jeans and a black T-shirt with a gray *X* painted over the center, only slightly to the left.

Nico sinks into the seat, but straightens his posture quickly. I adjust the height of my camera, and look at his face through the lens, giving myself the gift of a few extra seconds to study his features. His teeth are almost perfectly straight, and I wonder if he's ever had braces? His jaw is strong, and his eyes have the ability to reflect whatever color is around them—right now his brown mixing with the green grass in front of us and the bright blue of the sky. It's so much easier to see him through the lens.

It's so much easier to *let* myself.

I don't take advantage too much, though, not wanting him to grow impatient, and when I have him framed just right, I press the record button and sit back on my heels.

"I have an extra chair, if you need it," he says.

I hold up my hand in protest.

"I'm good. I'll just sit on the ground. I like sitting this way, really," I say, falling back to sit comfortably and pulling my legs in tight.

I reach up to tilt the viewer on my camera so I can see, but stop on Nico's face. He smirks. Dimple deep and eyes shadowed by his dark lashes, he's the devastating kind of handsome.

"I like your shirt," I gesture, not wanting to linger on the fact that, once again, *he* was looking at *me*. "Does it mean something?"

Nico glances down, then holds his hand over the gray *X*, his palm resting flat, covering it whole.

"*X* marks the spot," he says with a slight chuckle. My lip tugs up, smiling on one side of my mouth. "My brother gave it to me. I was too little to wear it at the time, but now that I've grown into it..."

His eyes twinkle when he looks back up at me. I've often thought the twinkle was something made up, a thing that only happened in cartoons and fairytales, but I was wrong, because Nico's eyes dance, *and they twinkle*. I bet they do a lot of things.

"You and your brother..." I start, pausing to think through my words, not wanting to hit on something that's a sore spot. Or at least not without entering into it delicately. "Are you...close with your brother?"

Nico's smile stays in place for a few seconds, but slips into less of one as he leans back and folds his hands behind his neck.

"Vincent…is…" He stops, his eyes lost to the sky behind me as his head shakes slightly and his lips pull in tight. When his gaze lands on me again, I sit up higher, lifting myself to a large garden stone so it doesn't look like Nico's staring down during the whole video.

"Vincent has made a lot of mistakes," Nico says, finally, and as much as he's content to leave things there, my curiosity kicks swiftly.

"What kind of mistakes?" I ask, my brow pulling in. I wrap my arms around my knees and force myself to listen quietly, my ears also testing to make sure the TV is still on behind the now-closed front door of his home.

Nico looks up again, his teeth holding on to the tip of his tongue, his eyes just over my shoulder. His mouth opens with a breath, but his chest falls soon after, and he sucks in his top lip, looking back to me. His eyes close and he shakes his head just enough to signal that this line—it's off limits.

"Okay," I say, the breeze picking up and blowing strands of my hair over my face. I left it down again today. I haven't put it up again since Nico said he liked it this way.

I glance at the screen for my camera, our eyes meeting this way—in black and white. Nico blinks slowly, eventually shifting his weight and looping one arm over the side of the chair, sitting with one of his legs pulled in. I notice he's still only wearing socks, and the sweetness of it makes me smile. He's at home here.

With me.

"How about we talk about football?" I ask.

"That sounds good," he grins.

"Who taught you how to play? I can tell…you…what you do, rather. It isn't just street ball," I say. "Where did you hone your skills?"

Nico leans forward, rubbing his hands together with a smile.

"My uncles," he says, through a chuckle. "My dad…he was never really around. I don't even remember him, really. But my mom's brothers more than made up for it. They had a ball in my hands from the time I was a tiny kid. We had a team in West End, like…Pop Warner or whatever. We held carwashes for uniforms and all of that. I played until I was ten or eleven, and then my Uncle Joe had a heart attack. I kind of lost interest after that. So did Uncle Danny. I played for fun...ya know...with Sasha and the boys? But...I was done with the real thing."

"Until now..." I say, my smile pulling up on one side.

Nico's expression mirrors mine, and he settles back into his chair again.

"Well, there's this girl..." he starts, and my heart doubles its rhythm. "She can be kind of...persuasive."

"Ha!" My laugh comes out automatically. "I wish I could persuade you. Nico Medina, arguing with you has been the bane of my high school existence."

His smirk lingers, and his eyes close in on me.

"You *love* arguing with me...and you know it," he says, his tongue pushing out the side of his mouth, just below his lower lip. I bite the inside of my cheek and stare him down, eventually shaking my head with a sigh.

"So your Uncle...Danny?" I glance back up to confirm I have his name right. Nico lets me loose from his stare and nods, looking down at his hands again, pressing his fingertips against one another and flexing. "Did he come to your game?"

Nico's smile grows fast.

"He's coming Friday. He lives up near Metahill, up north. My mom's going to pick him up and bring him," he says, his cheeks colored with a hint of pink. I think he might be nervous about having his uncle watch him.

"He's going to be so impressed," I say, and Nico shrugs my compliment off, twisting uncomfortably in his seat. I'm starting to learn that as comfortable and confident as he is with his academic talent, he's exactly the opposite with athletics. Maybe it's just because he's out of practice. I know it's not because he's lacking on the field. As smart as he is in the classroom, he's twice as smart out there.

Nico leans forward, and all my camera is capturing is the top of his head. I can tell he's starting to feel less comfortable in the hot seat, so I stand and turn the camera off.

"I'd like to meet him," I say, unsnapping the camera from the tripod and folding up my equipment. Nico glances up at me with one eyebrow raised and a half smile that I'm starting to fall for…*a lot.*

"I'd like you to meet him, too," he says.

Our eyes lock again in that space we've grown used to. I wonder if it makes Nico feel the same? I wonder if he's wishing I'd look away, or if he's hoping I don't. I swallow from the intensity, and he blinks a few times, his focus falling to the camera and equipment in my hands.

"You need me to help you with that?" he asks.

I lift it up and down a few times to show how light it is, then chuckle.

"I'm not that weak," I say.

"Oh, I know you're not. I've carried your school bag," he laughs, standing and stretching toward the rooftop gutters. His fingers grip the edge lightly, and his shirt raises enough that his stomach shows. I turn to face my car quickly.

"I should probably go," I say, not wanting to leave at all, but very much out of excuses to stay. "Tell your mom I said hi."

"I will," he says, following me to my car. "She'll be bummed she missed you. She wants to get to know you more. Mom likes to keep up on all of my stalkers."

My eyes flash wide, and I laugh awkwardly.

"I'm sorry. Next time I'll ask before I come," I say, glancing in his direction, my eyes not making it all the way.

I fumble with my keys and unlock the car, dropping my equipment in the seat. I reach to unwrap my shirt from my waist, but instead of covering things, I just toss it on top, not wanting Nico to see me have such a low opinion of his neighborhood. When I turn to face him again, his hands are in his pockets, and his eyes are down.

"Do you want my number?" he asks, gazing up with a brow raised.

"Yes," I answer quickly, my chest expanding fast and my inner voice reminding me to be cool. "That'd be nice."

I pull out my phone and swipe it on to type, but Nico reaches and takes it from me, typing in his contact info. He hands it back, but doesn't meet my eyes.

"Your friend...Izzy..." he says, and my heart sinks. "She said something about some dance or something? Right after next week's home game."

"Homecoming," I say. The word comes out flat—like I said a password.

"Yeah, that. I've never been...*you?*" He brings his hand to his neck, rubbing the back of it, and eventually bringing it over his face.

"I went last year..." I say, remembering how Travis took me out of pity. My brother put him up to it, and Izzy encouraged it. I was really over him by then, and the entire night felt like a forced babysitting event. I didn't even like my dress.

"You think you'll go again? Like...with your friends or whatever?" he asks. His hands have fallen deeper in his pockets, and he looks up at me in short glances.

My friends.

My...*friend.*

He wants to know if Izzy will go.

"I don't know, maybe. I'll have to talk to Izzy about it," I say, positioning my key in my hand so I'm ready to leave.

I step around my car, and Nico backs up a few steps to give me space.

"Well...let me know...if you guys go. Maybe I'll make Sasha come," he says.

"Yeah, sure," I say, pulling my door open wide.

My fingers automatically pick at the dry skin on the side of my thumb, a nervous habit I've had since I was a small child, and I look at it, knowing that I'm doing this because I want out of this trap—I don't want to set Nico up with Izzy, and if he dances with her, I don't want to watch. I open my mouth to give myself an out, to lie and say I probably won't go because of something I have to do, and I probably won't be back in time. I'm instantly distracted though by the heavy thumping from a car stereo, and both Nico and I turn to see a dark red car stop at the end of the driveway.

Nico steps a little closer to me as a guy gets out, a black flat-brimmed hat shadowing his eyes and a long-sleeved black shirt hanging low enough to meet the line where his jeans sag, far below the waist.

"Hey, Nicooooo," he says, dragging the name out long and slow. His eyes are heavy, and his expression is amused. He flicks a lit butt onto the driveway and steps on it. It looks like a joint.

Nico walks over toward him, meeting him near the back of my car.

"Pick your shit up. You know my mom doesn't want to see that stuff," Nico says, meeting the guy's gaze. His visitor laughs through clenched teeth.

"Fuck that. You pick it up," he says, his lips snarled to carry his threat. Nico doesn't flinch, and I shift closer to my car, one foot inside, my keys in my hand.

After a few seconds, Nico walks to the butt on the ground and snags it between two fingers, walking over to his friend and holding it out. The man in the hat only continues to laugh, and eventually Nico lets his hand fall down to his side.

The man's eyes move to me, and his lip raises again as he nods to acknowledge me. He's in his thirties, maybe a little older, and his hands are covered in black symbol tattoos.

"You get yourself a white girl?"

My balance gives a little, and my heartbeat picks up fast. I look to Nico, who glances from me back to his visitor.

"What do you want, Cruz?"

Nico doesn't even acknowledge his question about me.

The guy's eyes linger on me for a few seconds, but eventually he turns his focus back to Nico, leaning forward and spitting on the ground between them.

"Your brother around?" he asks.

"No," Nico's response comes fast.

The two stare into each other for several seconds, until the man Nico called Cruz leans forward to spit one more time. He nods when his face comes back up and his eyes meet Nico's, then he glances to me and back to his car.

"Vincent's been gone a long time. You see him, you tell him I'm looking for him," Cruz says, running the back of his palm over his chin as he takes a few steps backward.

Nico never agrees, but he nods enough to let the man know he heard him. Cruz walks back to his car, the engine still running and the music pounding so hard that it's drawn Alyssa's attention to the screen door. My eyes move to the little girl, and I want to tell her to say inside. I don't have to, though. She stops with her hands flat on the screen, watching.

"White girl's pretty," Cruz says over the roof of his car. "Hey, baby. Don't waste your time with a punk bitch."

He stares at me for a beat, and though it's only a second or two, it feels longer. Eventually, his attention moves back to Nico, who still doesn't give him any reaction at all other than the hard line his mouth has been in for the last minute.

Cruz's mouth curves again, and his chest shakes with a sinister laugh as he climbs back into his car and drives away.

I wait while Nico looks on, as if he's making sure his visitor is gone, and then he turns and walks back up his driveway, stopping next to me, but never meeting me in the eyes.

"You should go," he says, looking down at the joint held in his fingers. He gazes up to see his niece at the door. "Alyssa, get inside," he says, his tone stern as he walks toward the house. The little girl disappears, and Nico pulls the screen open, steps inside and lets it fall to a close behind him.

I wait for a few seconds, wondering if I should go back inside and offer to help, though I don't know what with. I wonder about that man—who he is. My stomach twitches with the beating of my heart, a rhythm that hasn't stopped since the moment that man looked at me like I was his to take.

Eventually, I get in my car and do what Nico asked. I drive home, running through stop signs and turning right instead of waiting at the stop light on the way out of West End. I go two miles out of my way on the freeway just to leave faster. And when I get home, I bring my things inside, ignoring my mom and her party book at the table on my way. My brother's room is still empty.

I collapse on my bed and let my equipment rest at my feet, then I pull my phone from my pocket and stare at Nico's name, still up on the contact screen. My finger runs over the CALL icon, hovering without touching, until I let the phone slip from my hold completely, watching the screen while it fades and Nico's name goes away.

CHAPTER 10

I let my film consume me for the rest of the weekend; I even convinced myself there were too many shots in the can I needed to work on editing for me to spend time at practice today.

I was avoiding Nico, was the honest truth.

We'd sparred in class, which was nothing unusual, but for some reason, I couldn't seem to pause long enough to even hear his perspective out. I resorted to name-calling.

I got kicked out of class.

That...that's the real reason I am at home. My mother will never hear about it, unless someone whispers to someone else in a long chain of socialite telephone. Even then, the likelihood that each link in the chain would get the story right is incredibly low. I'll take that gamble. My father, however, has probably already heard that his daughter called his new star quarterback an ego-driven dickhead.

Dickhead.

That's the word. I probably could have said just about anything else and been all right. In fact, I *have* said just about everything in Mr. Huffman's class before. I've pushed the boundaries, and he's never even flinched. Dickhead is the line, I guess.

It just slipped out.

It started when I saw Nico talking to Izzy when I walked into class. I acknowledged that my gut was sinking, and that I was being petty by pretending not to hear my friend say "hi" when I walked in and sat at my desk near her. I pulled out a notebook and began manically flipping pages, as if I was looking for something that I needed quickly, which therefore *must* be why I didn't hear her. I flipped pages until Mr. Huffman began taking attendance, and I didn't look up until he started talking about the last reading we did from an excerpt of Plato's *Republic*.

I was content to do nothing but listen today. The reading wasn't anything earth-shattering. Of Plato's concept of a perfect world, the idea that those with the highest intellect and understanding of thought should lead isn't really controversial. Frankly, it's sound judgment. But then Nico argued that Plato was right to believe the philosophers of the world should lead and be kings. I dug in to take the opposite side, no other reason than the fact that every word out of Nico's mouth was exactly the point of view I had written out in my notes. Behind the scenes—*in my head*—I agreed with him. Out loud—different story. He said everything first. And then everyone looked to me—waiting…expecting me to have some amazing counterpoint.

After a few starts, eventually my arguments fell thin.

I had nothing.

I rattled on about how the philosophers lacked specialization and focus, a bunch of crap I'd read in the counter-opinions at the back of our book, and Nico called me out on it by the time I was done.

That's when *dickhead* happened.

The closer I get to home, the more embarrassed I am about getting kicked out. I know it looks like I ran away, on top of it. I *did* run away.

My phone buzzes in my back pocket, but I don't pull it out until I park in our driveway, my car lined up directly behind my brother's. He can't drive in his condition, so the car has sat unused for two weeks. He wasn't in school either, a fact that my father noted, but in the midst of pressure to win this week's matchup against the giant Division I school Metahill, my brother playing hooky sort of fell off the radar.

I yank my bag over my shoulder and leave my equipment in my car, pulling my phone out from my pocket while I march up my driveway. It's a message from Izzy, asking if I'm okay. I write back that I am, just embarrassed, and consider adding that I have cramps to give myself an excuse, but she types a response too quickly.

IZZY: *Nico was asking about you. I think he feels badly that he pushed you so much.*

He didn't push me. Not comparatively. I've had three and a half years of classes with Nico, and we've gone rounds before. Today was mild in comparison, at least on his part. I push on the handle for my front door and let my back fall against it to close it, my phone gripped in my hand while I think before typing.

ME: *He didn't do anything wrong. I'm just having a bad day. Noah ditched today, and things with my brother have just been weird.*

It's not entirely a lie, but it's also not the reason for my behavior. I use Noah and his crap as an excuse. When my best friend sends me back a heart, I sigh in relief and head to my room, grateful that my brother's drama can buy me this. I let my bag fall to the floor when I enter the hallway, and I'm dragging it behind me when I catch a scent that I instantly recognize.

My brother's door is closed, but I can tell his light is on. I rest my ear against the wood paneling, waiting for some clue that doesn't come. My mom's car is gone, so I know we're home alone, which is the only reason I break the boundary rule Noah and I set for each other. We're supposed to knock, but the second I push down on the door handle to his room and meet the resistance of a lock, I know that what I smell is marijuana.

"One second," he says, and I hear a shuffling sound on the other side of the door.

"Don't bother. It's just me," I say.

A few seconds pass before my brother opens his door, balanced on one leg in the small space between the frame to block me from seeing more in his room. I don't need to see more, and I don't know why he thinks he'll get away with this.

"What are you thinking?" I lean my head to the side, my eyes meeting his glazed and red ones.

Noah's lids flutter, and he laughs once.

"Why don't you go back to your books and movies and computers and whatever other shit you do," he says in a tone that I'm sure is meant to intimidate me. All it does is incite.

"How many times do you think you can fuck up and dad will make it go away, Noah? Jesus…Mom is totally going to know you're smoking that shit in here," I say, pushing his door open from his loose grip. When I do, I see Travis sitting on my brother's bed, his eyes just as puffy and red. "Oh, and you're going to fuck his life up, too?"

"Get out of my room, Reagan. And don't tell Dad," my brother says, gripping my arm tightly and pushing me backward the few steps I took into his room. I try to fight back, jerking free and forcing my arm against my brother's chest, but high or not, he's still a lot stronger than me. Even in a cast, balanced on a crutch. In a blink, my feet are back out in the hallway, and my brother is pushing his door closed in my face.

"Dad's going to cut you from the team if he finds out, Travis. You'll lose scholarships," I argue, trying to reason with my brother's friend.

I can't see his face to read his reaction, and he doesn't speak. My brother's pushing the door harder, and my window inside is shrinking.

"You're going to play ball again, Noah. Think about next year…think about college," I say, working myself up to continue to argue and give him reasons not to turn himself into a stoned loser, when his pushback stops, and my hand falls forward as the door slings open again. I stumble on my feet a bit, but right myself quickly. When I look up, my brother's standing with his arms crossed, and as red as his eyes are from smoking, they're also lit with something else…something angry.

"I'm not going to Cal," he says.

I shake my head and scrunch my eyes, not understanding.

"Okay, so…you didn't even really *want* to go to Cal. You were looking at Florida, and Texas, and…"

"Dad took a call from Cal," he interrupts me.

My mouth hangs open mid-sentence, and I tilt my head, still not following his train of thought. He chuckles, and the sound stays in his chest while his eyes haze with the effects from his joint.

"He took the call and told them about Nico," Noah says, emphasizing the name, the word crossing his lips with spite and vile, his mouth sneered with bitterness.

"Maybe he's just trying to help. I know Nico has a lot of academic options, so…"

Noah cuts me off with more laughter, falling a few steps back and then leveling me again with his gaze.

"He's played one fucking game, Reagan. One game, and Dad's feeding him to Cal," Noah says, his brow pulled in.

One game is a bit of a gamble; I agree. And I can tell by my brother's expression that he doesn't think Nico deserves my father taking a risk like that. But I've also seen the potential that I know my father sees, too.

"Maybe there's more to the story, Noah. You don't know; maybe Dad promised him he'd make some connections…or give him an opening. They do things like that all the time to get players into Cornwall. They *lure* them," I begin to explain.

"They *had* a quarterback, Reagan. They didn't need to go reward some scholarship kid with my position. We had Brandon," Noah says.

"Noah, don't pretend you don't understand what putting Brandon at QB would mean. You know he's Jimmy's nephew, you know what Dad's up against. You know they would have had Dad replaced by midseason," I say.

My brother exhales heavily, and his eyes fade off into something beyond me, a nothingness that has his attention. I wave my hand in his sightline, but it doesn't make a difference, so after a few seconds, I turn to walk back to my room.

"I would have always been better, though," he says, and I stop in my tracks. When I turn, Noah's eyes meet mine. "I will always be a better quarterback than Brandon Skaggs."

My mind works to make sense of his words. I don't want to think them, but no matter how I take what he just said, it always comes out the same. My brother is jealous of Nico's talent, and he'd rather my dad lose his job than not go out as the best.

"What about Dad?" I whisper, not wanting this to continue to play out in front of Travis.

Noah doesn't respond, though. He doesn't blink, and his mouth falls into a hard line, his eyes holding mine hostage while his own ego takes over his heart and mind. I fight against accepting it, but eventually I don't have a choice. I sigh, letting my eyes sag with hurt, letting my brother see my disappointment, hoping he feels how sad his choices are making me.

"What's your deal with that guy, anyway?" he says, choking my emotions and putting the rest of my thoughts on hold, my muscles tensing. "You know there's no way in hell Dad is going to let you go out with a guy from West End, right? And Mom would flip her shit if you brought home a Mexican."

My hand flies at my brother's face, hitting him so fast that my eyes barely register it. The only thing to see is the red mark left in the wake of my slap. My brother's head is tilted to the side, and he brings his own palm to cover his cheek, spitting on his floor, then slamming his door closed in my face.

I stand still, my eyes looking at the grain of the wood for several seconds. My heart races, and my fingertips tinge with the power of just having hit someone. If I let myself, I could cry right now—*hard.* I'm not sure why, exactly. My chest is swimming with so many feelings, and I sway from disgust to fear to heartbreak to anger with every beat of my heart.

There's a part of me that wants to keep fighting with Noah, to hit him again…and again. Then there's a part of me that is scared because he knows I feel something for Nico. I'm scared because Noah sees it, and I'm even more terrified that he's right about my family. And I'm sad because what if that means I can't like Nico the way my heart is desperate to?

And what does that say about me if I let all of that stand in my way?

My mouth closed and my lips quivering, I draw in a long breath through my nose before taking careful steps down the rest of the hall to my room. When I get inside, I shut the door, and I don't come out for anyone or anything until I wake up for school the next morning.

CHAPTER 11

I pull into the school parking lot just as the bell is ringing. I normally leave early in the mornings, just after my dad. I like to spend time in the lab, editing on the equipment at our school. It's nicer and I can do a lot of the nuanced things, like fix the sound from my shitty mic and add notes to my editing file for shots I think I still need. I skipped that all today. I missed doing something I love because my brother has made me dread things.

I see Nico in the mornings. He gets to school early, too. In fact, Nico Medina is almost always the first person to arrive at Cornwall, even though it takes him probably an hour to push his way there on his skateboard. In the winter, he rides in darkness. Even now, fall weather beginning to settle in, Nico's morning trek is likely cold and dim. Still, he's always first.

I'm sure he was first today. I'm sure he was also looking for me to pass by his favorite table in the library on my way to the video lab, so he could question me about the whole *dickhead* thing. But I never passed by. Instead, I waited at home for minutes to tick by until I knew I could sneak into school unnoticed because talking to Nico might mean admitting I feel something for Nico, and that might lead to me wanting things—wanting to *be* things…with Nico.

For three years I've passed by that table in the library, glanced at the board under his feet, sneered at the memory of something he said in class, and then I went about my business, my mind moving right along from Nico Medina to whatever the next thing was I saw. Lately, though…my thoughts are kind of stuck. On him.

On his story.

His voice.

His…eyes.

I've never had a *real* boyfriend. I've had dates for dances and guys I've gone out with to go to the movies with Izzy. There was the guy who worked at the water park over the summer who made out with me in the cabana during his break, twice, but I was not the girl he took to the summer parties. I pined after Travis for a few years, and then I settled for awkward first kisses with boys I thought were *cute enough*. Not once did I ever call someone my boyfriend, though. I had my focus—graduate at the top of my class, perfect my visual-arts skills, get into Prestige, win an Emmy or a Globe. It was a list that would take time, but I would do it.

I haven't thought about Prestige in days. When I watch the video I've captured at night, I don't think about my film. There's a story I want to tell, yes, but more than putting together a great story, I'm obsessed with getting its pieces, because I want to know more about the boy who has catapulted into the starring role.

I want to know Nico's story. I want to hold his hand.

I want that kiss from my dream to be real.

None of this matters because Nico likes Izzy. It doesn't mean I don't still want him to want me instead. Sometime during my sleepless night last night I decided that all of those things my brother said wouldn't matter at all if Nico liked me back—as in *liked me* liked me.

I also decided that I would spend today avoiding all of it, because no matter what Nico Medina felt or didn't feel, worrying about it was starting to mess with my head.

With my equipment bags slung over my shoulder, I walk through the main doors of the school to the sound of the final *ding*. I don't like being late, so I jog down the main corridor toward my ancient civilization class, my arms weighed down with my things. Two doors away from my destination, something tugs my bag loose from my right shoulder, and I stumble on my feet, trying to recover it. When I realize someone is tugging against me, I spin to look behind me.

Nico's expression is caught somewhere between amused and hesitant. I stare at him feeling the same way, with a touch of anxiety because I *do not like* being late.

"I need to get to class!" I say, jerking from his hold.

His lips purse, and his head falls to the side as he takes a step back and pushes his hands into his pockets. He's smug. I breathe out once, hard, through my nose, and he chuckles lightly under his breath.

"What?" My word echoes in the hallway, and I turn to my left and right to confirm it's now empty. Shit! I'm late.

"You called me a dickhead," Nico says, pulling my attention screaming back to him.

I breathe a little harder, my heart starting to pound with this nightmare. Confrontation is so much more enjoyable when it's in a class, over some line in a book. This kind sucks ass.

I knew I'd run into him eventually, have to answer to my behavior, but I expected a little more time. My mind races through my options, and I keep my mouth shut while I think, my eyes on his, taking in the hint of a smirk while he waits for my excuse. Then it hits me. I don't really *have* an excuse. I have stupid girl emotions, and a brother who is trying to take me down with him, but none of it is an excuse for how I'm treating Nico. I sure as hell don't want to tell him that, though, so instead, I cross my arms over my chest and sway once to adjust the weight of my bags while I stare him down in that position.

Nico runs his hand over his mouth, and after a few seconds I can tell he's laughing behind it.

"You think I'm being funny?" I ask.

"Oh, I think you're being hilarious," he says, letting his hand fall away and relaxing against the wall behind him. He's so comfortable, even though he's late for class, too.

"We're going to be late," I say, rolling my eyes.

"So," he quips.

A laugh punches out from my chest.

"So, he says," I mumble to myself.

"Yeah," he says, drawing my eyes back to his. "So."

I meet his stare again, and we both battle through this standoff. I'm clearly losing, and my arms start to quake with the weight they're carrying. I shake my head at him and begin to walk away, but his hand wraps around the strap of my bag again, this time pulling me closer to him.

"Nico, I'm late for class. My things are heavy. Just…tell me what you want?"

I push my lips together tight, but can feel them twitch. I'm nervous, and I want to go back to fighting with him over ancient philosophies and the foundation of religious beliefs. That…*that*…is actually easier than standing here and feeling like this.

Feeling…*vulnerable.*

"You missed practice yesterday," he says.

"It's allowed to happen without me there," I respond back quickly.

My tongue passes over my bottom lip, a move I don't even realize I'm making until Nico's eyes catch it. He looks at my mouth in a split second, and his chest moves with his breath. It makes my mouth dry again, and my heart beat even faster. I can feel every twitch of my nerves vibrate through my body, so I shift my weight and let my bags drop to the floor so I can flex my tired fingers. Nico grabs them in his.

I don't meet his eyes. Instead, I stare at the way his hands are holding mine hostage. His grip is strong, a suggestion I shouldn't try to pull away, but not so strong that I couldn't if I wanted to. My instincts tell me I should, but I don't.

"You're mad at me," he says, his fingers sliding to mine, his thumb covering the top of my knuckles while the rest of his hands hold my palms.

"I'm not mad at you, Nico. I was busy. I have things that don't have anything to do with you," I say, still fighting.

He chuckles.

"You're still mad at me," he says, and I glance up just enough to see his smile, all lopsided and perfect, the dimple that he gets when he's right in its place. I hate him so much.

"Why would I be made at you," I sigh, acting as best as I can while my mind races through all of the reasons I *am* mad at Nico Medina—not a single one of them really his fault.

I meet his challenge, staring back at him, forcing the stern expression to remain on my face, while he looks back at me with perfect lips curved up a hint on one side and unfair eyes that act as target sights. I'm caught in them, and they will not let go.

"You're mad because you think I want to go to that homecoming dance thing with Izzy," he says, and I laugh once because…fuck!

"Admit it," he smirks.

"Nico," I begin, finding it hard to even say his name. "I could care less who you want to go to some stupid school dance with."

"*Couldn't* care less," he says quickly. I tilt my head and pinch my brow. "You said you could care less, but really…you mean you couldn't."

I jerk my hands away and huff.

"Could you?" he says, his hands back in his pockets, his head tilted, angled so I can't ignore it.

I push my tongue in my cheek and shake my head, glancing away, but always coming back to his gaze. His stupid, perfect, eyes and face that I want to put my hand on. The damned lock of his hair that falls forward when his head leans forward, his tongue caught in his teeth. His kissable lips that I felt in a dream and watched speak in class. His arrogance. His confidence.

"Gah!" I exhale, shaking my head and focusing on the bricked wall behind him. He stands there with one foot against the wall, his back leaning into it, so comfortable seeing me so uncomfortable.

"You make me so mad!" My eyes slide to his, and his lip ticks higher.

"I knew you were mad at me," he nods.

I stretch my arms out wide, my eyes wider, and I stare up to the ceiling with another shake of my head.

"Fine!" I shout. "Yes, you got me. I'm mad at you! Can I go do class now, please?"

Nico snickers, and I cross my arms over my chest. He pushes forward from the wall, taking a few steps toward me. On instinct, I take one back, but not far enough from his reach. He reaches for my hand again, and I hug myself tighter, tucking my fingers under each arm for protection. I'm throwing a fit now, but I'm this far in, there really isn't any way to undo it.

Nico holds my elbows when he's unable to get to my hands, and realizing how ridiculous I would look spinning out of his hold, I give in and let him. His touch is gentle and warm, and I wish I could just get over myself and take his hands back in mine. But I'm scared. My bottom lip shakes with nerves. Nico's eyes glance at it, so I pull it into my teeth. I want to hide every weakness from him, but eventually I'll have to curl up inside myself. I have too many.

"Why are you mad at me, Reagan?"

He says my name, and the word falls from his lips soft and sweet. No judgment, no challenge. My lip falls loose from the hold of my teeth and my eyes flutter shut for a long blink. I open again to find him waiting, still looking at me.

"I don't know," I say, with a small shake of my head.

"But you are," he says, and I nod with the same slight movement, sucking in my bottom lip and breathing through my nose.

"Yeah," I say, my lip falling away and my eyes only able to look at his cheek.

"Would you still go to that dance with me?" he asks, and my eyes crinkle with the short laugh that escapes me, my face tingling, my arms held hostage in this strange cradle because that's all I was willing to give him. "Even though you're mad at me, which...I'm willing to get to the bottom of, will you let me take you to a dance?"

I pause, holding my breath, my mind racing through every aspect of what this means—Izzy, my father, Noah…*Nico.*

"Yeah," I say, my eyes trailing back up to meet his.

I'm holding myself tighter than I ever have, my fingers actually digging into my sides, my nails rough against my skin through the fabric of my gray Cornwall sweatshirt. Nico doesn't flinch once. His eyes stay on mine when I give in, and his expression doesn't shift from the gentle, sweet one he's held.

His right hand lets go of my elbow, moving to the few strands of hair resting against my forehead, falling over one eye. Nico takes them with his thumbs, moving them behind my ears, his eyes watching his movement then settling back on mine.

"You've worn your hair down ever since I said I liked it," he says.

I breathe in long and deep, letting myself feel this moment—all of it. I *have* worn my hair down. I did it hoping he would touch it, but never once actually thinking he would.

"That's how I knew," he says, and my forehead crinkles. He smiles on one side, repeating the gesture and moving the long wave of blonde hair from my face again. "That's how I knew I was more than just some guy you wanted on your dad's football team."

My pulse drums against my ribs. I don't respond. I don't need to. Nico is right. He's more than some guy. He's more than a great story. I swallow under the intensity of his stare, and my lips grow numb in anticipation. I want to be kissed right now, out here in the high school hallway. I want the clichéd moment in my mental scrapbook, and the more breaths I take, the surer I am I'm going to get it.

Nico steps back quickly, and I linger in my bliss, oblivious until he speaks.

"She's coming, Mr. Vernon. Her bag slipped, and we were just picking up her equipment," Nico says. I blink once, then glance to my left where my ancient civilization teacher is hanging from the doorway, a clipboard propped against his stomach with one hand.

"All right then," he says. "I figured it must be something like that. I'll write you a note, Nico, for helping."

I chortle a laugh to myself, and Nico nudges his foot against mine.

"You liar," I whisper.

"I believe you mean *dickhead,*" Nico says, leaning into me. I flush and wince all at once, but regardless of my crush being out in the open, I'm never letting Nico Medina completely get the best of me.

"That, too," I say in return, which only makes him laugh.

"You like me," he says, winking as he steps by me, my bag held in his hand, his forearm flexed. I take it from him as he reaches for the late slip from Mr. Vernon. "Thanks, Mr. V."

"Anytime, Nico," our teacher says.

Nico's dimple is the last feature I take in before his eyes slip from their hold on me and he heads toward the other end of the hallway, hands in his pockets and nothing on his back. I'm not sure where his stuff is, but I know that he planned on waiting me out. I could have shown up an hour late and Nico would have been there. Because he wants to take me to the dance. Not Izzy. *Me.* And that feels...

CHAPTER 12

"So are you going to tell me he asked you to the dance? Or are you just planning on showing up with him and bobbing between me and your hot new boyfriend all night, hoping I won't put things together?" Izzy asks.

I'm trying out a new lens on my still camera outside the gym. I asked Izzy to pose for me, so I could use her as my test subject. She's meeting the rest of the cheerleaders here so they can all pile into the van for the game tonight on the north side of town. Her question comes out of the blue. Izzy and I haven't talked much this week, and I haven't seen Nico other than at practice or in class, so I haven't had to contend with the two of them being in the same place yet. I was going to tell her, but I was also afraid.

"Uhm," I say, my eye still flat against the viewer while my fingers delicately twist the lens in and out, repeatedly bringing the paint smudges on my friend's arm in and out of focus.

"Nico told me," she says, looking at me through the lens, her eyes direct. I suck in my lips and back away, looking at her for real. My chest thumps wildly. If I'm this nervous talking about Nico with Izzy, I'm pretty sure I'll vomit when I have to tell my dad.

"Reagan?" she says, standing then sitting close to me, no longer in my camera's view. I unclip it, giving up and putting it away.

"I was afraid you'd be mad," I admit.

Izzy laughs, but when she realizes I'm not kidding, the sound falls away and her mouth slopes into a look of sympathy.

"Reagan, I think a lot of boys are cute. I don't run around putting MINE stamps on them. If you liked him, which…clearly you do! You could have just said something," she says, leaning into me while I pull the camera bag to my lap, sliding the mini tripod in place and pushing in the various camera parts.

"Yeah, but you never dated Travis, and I felt kind of like a hypocrite, so…"

"First of all, I never went out with Travis because he's an immature ass-head without a plan," she says, her mouth a hard line that eventually twists into a grimace while her eyes look off to the side. "He is hot, though, so it wasn't easy. Still…loser. No plan!"

I giggle, feeling some of the pressure I put on myself this week leave my shoulders.

"I'm sorry. And it's just the dance. He'll probably go with me and realize what a boring wallflower I am, especially when I'm more interested in how the guy lines up the tracks for the music than actually *dancing* with Nico," I say, laughing at myself. I'm a terrible dancer, even when it's nothing more than slow swaying in a circular pattern. My feet find the tops of other people's.

"He asked me about you," she says, and I look from my lap to her in an instant. "Yeah, I thought that would get you. I knew he wasn't into me. That night at Charlie's, after I left you in the bathroom, I ran into Nico. His very first question was if you were all right."

"He was probably just worried because Noah was being…*Noah*," I say, still not ready to admit that Nico feels remotely the same way for me as I do for him.

"He asked about you several times, Reagan. And when he saw you talking to Sasha? On that bench? He did not like that…*at all!*"

I smile with her last few words, looking down at my hands, which are nervously zipping and unzipping the camera bag, then looking back at my friend, meeting her eyes.

"He didn't?" I bite my lip.

"Nope," she says, pushing up straight and wiggling her head in a triumphant display.

"Are you still going to the dance?" I ask, hoping that my friend will be there. I can't rely on Nico alone. I need allies, people to stand awkwardly with me on the sidelines, to dance badly to pop songs and to sneak out balloons meant to be decorations. This is what Izzy and I did at last year's homecoming. I was looking forward to the repeat, and I don't want a boy to get in the way.

"Of course I'm going. Uhm, hello...someone gets a crown!" I roll my eyes because Izzy won't win, but every time there's a dance with pretend royalty, she acts like she has it all sewn up. My brother and his girlfriend Katie were the frontrunners, last I heard, but I haven't seen them together in days. I'm not sure if that matters to the voting student body, but maybe...just *maybe* it will play in Izzy's favor.

I chew at the inside of my cheek and glance from my friend to my lap a few times before squinting and looking up at her again.

"He really asked about me?"

She closes her eyes and laughs.

"Yes, he *really* asked about you," she says, grinning through her words, but cocking her head to the side the second she finishes, her smile falling. "But...what's his deal today?"

"What do you mean?" I ask, my brow pinched.

"He wasn't here at all. He missed the entire day, and word on the street is Brandon might get the start tonight," my friend says.

I pull my phone from my pocket, hoping for some message. There isn't one, though. I haven't given Nico my number yet, and the only person who ever calls me is sitting next to me right now.

"I knew he missed humanities, but I just figured he was excused, or maybe left early with the team," I say, looking around the quickly-emptying student lot. Sasha's car is in its place, and Travis's Jeep is here, which means they're accounted for. I stand, lifting my camera bag with me, and I start to wonder if Nico made it on the bus or not.

"I guess we'll find out. You're going to the game, right?"

I nod in response, my mind now lost to wondering where Nico is and if he's okay. A few of the other cheerleaders walk up, nodding hello to me, so I excuse myself and walk to the film room to tug on the door. It opens easily; I step inside, my eyes adjusting to the darkness until I can find the switch to flip on the lights.

"Hello? Anyone still here?"

My voice echoes, and I don't expect anyone to respond. My dad travels with the team, and most of his coaching staff does, too. I yell out a few more times, testing the room before walking to my dad's office near the back. My dad doesn't keep secrets in this building, so I know it's safe to inspect his office. The only clue I get is the list of ineligibles on his desk, and there's only one name listed under truancy—Noah Prescott.

Maybe Izzy's wrong. Or maybe she only has half the story. I decide the latter is probably the most likely, and I close up the office and film room, flipping down the lights as I exit the building just in time to see the cheer squad pulling out of the lot.

I walk to my car with a little more speed than normal, anxious to get to Metahill to see if Nico's warming up or Brandon. When my hand hits my car door handle, I pause, something catching my eye on Sasha's silver car parked only a few spaces away. I let go of the handle of my car and move to his, realizing the closer I get that the blue thing flapping against his window is actually paper.

Pulling up the windshield wiper, I tug the paper clear and unfold it so I can read whatever message is scribed on it in black marker.

Your boy ain't playing tonight. And you're going to get your ass flattened.

I look in both directions, the lot empty and the building behind me now completely quiet. I crumple the note up, knowing Sasha probably never saw it before the bus left, and not wanting to leave it behind for him to find later. I drop it in a trash bin near one of the parking lot light poles between our two cars, and I get into mine, backing out so quickly my tires squeal. I pull away from the school fast, and by the time I make it to Metahill, my dad and his team are just taking the field for warm-ups.

My mother came along with Linda, Travis's mom. They almost always ride together. Travis's parents are divorced, but his mom kept the house. Our mothers grew close when that happened, and they both serve on the booster board together. Sometimes, I wonder if Mom talks to her about leaving Dad. Football, when it's played like this? It has a way of tearing up families.

I pared my equipment down for tonight's game. I have my small video camera that I'll set up on top of the press box, but I left the heavier one that I use for interviews at home. Tonight, I want to focus on still photos. Bob, the team trainer, set me up with one of the state certified press passes, so I should be able to get on the field—at least for a little while.

I stop at the front of the bleachers, where my mom is setting up her bleacher pad along with Travis's mom. My mom and I aren't close. It's not that we fight or that I resent her or harbor any angst. We just aren't close. I've always been more interested in the things my dad does. My mom has always been more interested in doting after Noah. My father rides Noah hard, and he's soft and sweet with me. Such is the Prescott family circle, I suppose.

"You planning to take some nice shots of the team tonight sweetheart?"

My mom is probably pointing out my access to the field to show off to the few other parents who are setting up their seats around her. Travis's mom is used to it, and she smiles at me amiably then busies herself with her phone. A few of the others *oooh and ahhh* at my camera, asking me questions about my project, my plans after high school, and what my angle for the film will be.

"I needed some still shots to fill in some of the voiceover, and I just kind of like the effect," I say, my mom's smile outlined with bright-red lipstick and wide eyes. Her ears didn't hear a single thing I just said.

"Sure hope this film has a happy ending, unlike last season," one of the older men, sitting a few rows up, says.

My mom's eyes flinch, and her smile shifts at his words, but she keeps her appearance up—as always. Coach's wife is the ultimate cheerleader. She's also the ultimate liar.

"Oh, now…last season was old news. I think this year is shaping up to be pretty exciting. Chad says the boys are really gelling," my mom lies. I know it's a lie, and most of the people listening do, too, but nobody seems to want to call her on it. Or at least, I don't think they do, until I lean forward to hug my mom and hear the same older man contradict her.

"That's not what I'm hearing," he says. My mom's hands grab at my sides, so I squeeze back, then rub my hand in a circle on her shoulder, signaling that I heard him, too.

"I hear that new kid from West End is a show boat. That's what my grandson says, anyway. Such a shame Noah got hurt the way he did. I bet he really could have used a good season to prove last year wasn't all his fault," the old man says, clearing his throat with a harsh cough that rattles something deep in his chest. He chuckles to himself while he stands and pulls a pack of cigarettes from his back pocket. "Hell, I bet you *all* could have used Noah to have a good run. But maybe this will end up working out. What do I know. I'm gonna go get a smoke. You wanna come, Bern?"

The old man nods to the heavier man sitting next to him, but he just waves him on, uninterested. My mom's smile has shifted to the restrained kind, and she responds only with shrugs and head tilts. It's her way of dealing with it, pretending she doesn't understand the intricacies of the game. I know better. Lauren Prescott was a University of Alabama cheerleader, which is where she met my father. He was a receiver—second string. When I was little, she was very involved in my dad's game-day plan. It was the talk of the dinner table, and I loved every second of it. Somewhere along the way, though, an invisible line was drawn, and our dinner table became quiet—except for bitter quips and digs about alienating us from the boosters or planning expensive parties to ignore real problems.

"Well, I know Chad's really excited to see what Nicolas can do," my mom says. Nobody is really listening any more, but I have to correct her anyway.

"He goes by Nico," I say.

"Oh, like a nickname. How nice," she says.

Yes. How nice. And you'll get to meet him, after he takes me to the dance next Friday, and you can pretend you knew his name all along, or worse—be all of those things that Noah says you are. Be…racist.

I did not inherit my mom's ability to pretend, so I leave before I have to, excusing myself to the press box where I set up my camera and begin to scan the field in search of Nico's profile. I find him quickly—up front—between Sasha and Colton. I'm not sure what happened to him today, or where he went, but he seems to be cleared to play. At the very least, he was allowed to dress.

Once my video camera is set, I power it down to save space for the game film, then take the bleachers two steps at a time until I get to the field. The air is crisp tonight, the slight breeze enough to turn my fingers pink. I tug my Cornwall sweatshirt from around my waist and slip it on over my long-sleeved black T-shirt that hangs below the sweatshirt's bottom. I'm grateful for the extra fabric when the wind picks up, cutting through my thin leggings and sending shivers over my body despite my attempt to dress warm.

I decide to move around the field to get my heartrate up, so I jog to the far end and lie on the grass, taking shots of the team stretching, of my father talking with his staff—of him having a more private and stern conversation with Coach O'Donahue. I zoom in, thinking I might just be able to read their lips, but my view isn't clear enough. My father holds up a hand, turning his back on Coach O'Donahue, who stands still for several long seconds before shaking his head and slipping out a swear word on his way to the sidelines.

When the cheerleaders begin to trail onto the track, I walk the long way around the field up to Izzy, nodding toward Nico so she sees he's here.

"Huh, he must have had a really good excuse for missing," she says, shrugging it off.

"Yeah," I say, pulling the camera up to my eye, focusing on Nico's face while the team gathers in two halves—defense and offense.

My father and Nico talk, and it's off-to-the-side and quiet, away from the others. There's a moment where my dad puts his hand on Nico's shoulder, their heads coming in close—a beautiful display of mutual respect. My brother never had that.

My brother never had that.

I scan the sidelines, finally seeing Noah. He's alone, balanced on his crutches, a water bottle in his hands, his eyes watching Nico take his place. My brother is so broken and bitter. I would be, too. If only he knew Nico more, I think it would help. I think he would root for him. But then...maybe not.

The crowd is beginning to fill in empty spaces, so I leave Izzy and the others and climb back to my corner on the roof of the press box. Coach O'Donahue is already standing on the other end, his headset on and his own camera filming the team. His head turns while I step up the final rung of the ladder and position myself behind my camera.

I feel his eyes on me for several seconds before he speaks.

"You going to be filming every single one of these games?" he asks.

I keep my eyes on my viewfinder, pretending to tune the focus.

"Yeah, I plan on it," I say.

His eyes are still watching me. I can sense it—see from my periphery that he's studying me—and eventually I can't pretend I have anything to do other than look back at him. I smile when I do, but it's the careful kind I give someone I don't trust.

"I could just give you my film. No sense in two of us being up here," he says. It doesn't come out as a kind gesture at all, or maybe I read it that way.

"It wouldn't match. My camera films in HD. But...thanks," I say, taking pleasure in the fact that his eyes fall a tick in disappointment.

"All right then," he says, after a few seconds pass. He flips a toothpick around in his mouth, and his eyebrows lift as he shifts his focus back out to the field.

The entire first half passes without another word from him to me, only his chatter to the coaching staff below, reading the other team and trying to predict for defense. While we don't talk, though, I catch him watching me every few minutes. It's usually after he says something in the radio, or when he criticizes Nico, or a passing play. I never once react physically to his words, but I do pull my phone out and text Izzy when his comments become almost unbearable.

ME: *I don't think Brandon's uncle is a big fan of Nico.*

Izzy usually has her phone in her bag, so I know she'll get my message at some point. I just need someone to commiserate with, and I hope she sees what I'm seeing.

Nico is struggling. He just can't seem to find time, to get his footing right. He can throw, but the coverage is too tight. Sasha can't break free, and Travis...*he isn't trying.* Nico's been sacked three times, and had the ball stripped once, and the scoreboard is proof that something is wrong. We're down twenty-one to seven, but we're making a good run right now. It's almost halftime, and somehow—through a fifteen-yard run on his own and one pass that manages to find Sasha's hands—Nico has us twenty yards out.

We need this touchdown.

He needs this touchdown.

I move to the field, leaving Coach O'Donahue and my camera behind. I slip through the railing on the bleachers near Izzy, sitting on the small bench behind the cheer squad while they hold their hands linked as they stand behind the sidelines, urging the rest of the crowd to follow and have faith that the Tradition will score. I glance behind me to see my mother standing, but no one else from her camp. Most of the students are up on their feet, but the rest of the stands are a group divided.

They want him to fail.

"Come on, Nico. You can do this!" I shout, my voice raspy, I scream the words so loudly. I move to the edge of the field, making use of my pass, and when one of the coaches looks at me suspiciously, I hold the pass up like a shield. He rolls his eyes, but I don't care.

I sit on the corner, near the other team's end zone, and I zoom in with my camera, snapping shots of Nico waiting for the ball. He's calling the count—he's shifting the offense.

They're out of place, but Colton snaps on signal as he's told, and Nico has to fight. Colton holds the middle, but the line crumbles around him, and Nico has to run. He leaps over one defender, only to find another waiting for him. Completely exposed, the clock ticking down to the last two seconds, Nico makes one final push.

He's hit so hard that his helmet flies off. Whistles blare as I stand to my feet, my chest heaving in panicked breath. The referees run in, hands waving, and Bob sprints to the middle of the field with water and his medical bag tugged against his side.

He makes it to Nico, pushing people away to give him room, but before he can tell Nico to lie flat, he's on his feet, charging toward Travis and a guy named Zach, who was supposed to protect his left side. Zach's a three-time all-state left tackle. He doesn't miss, though he's frequently called with penalties—for holding. He didn't hold anyone during that last play. He let them right through.

Chaos settles in fast, Nico's hands flying to Zach's chest, shoving, while Travis grabs Nico's pads. The rivalries make themselves apparent quickly, Colton sticking up for Nico and Sasha, Travis and several of the other guys shoving to get into the circle, pushing and throwing punches. The referees start tugging on collars, pulling players apart, and my father and his staff do the same. Eventually, my dad is standing between Travis and Nico, one hand on each of them, his clipboard at his feet and his face burning red in anger and frustration.

"Get your asses in that locker room…now!"

My father's voice carries over the hushed field and stadium. It takes the team several seconds, but eventually they all relax their tense muscles and begin to file toward the end of the field, to the visitor's locker room, in a straight line.

I snap a few photos as they walk past me, Nico's face hard and his eyes set on the guy in front of him. He doesn't even notice I'm here.

I pull my feet in as the rest of the team passes, a few of them glancing at me, but only briefly. The coaches walk by, and I begin to trail behind everyone, when my father stops me, his hand heavy on my shoulder, urging me to stay put.

"Sit this one out, Reagan," he says. My eyes meet his briefly, and I nod with a tiny movement.

I watch them all disappear behind the heavy doors, and I imagine the words being said the moment they close. My father always has something to say—the *right* thing to say. I don't know what that could possibly be now, though.

I walk back to my mom, who is talking with Travis's mom and a few of the others. There are whispers about changing to Brandon, about how something isn't right. A few women tell my mom they're worried for her husband. "This must be so hard on Chad," they say. My mom smiles and thanks them, assuring them he can handle it.

He *can* handle it. But can she? The crack in her armor shows, and I think others can see it in the small slant of worry in her eyes, the constant repetition of "it's going to be okay."

Is it?

When I notice Izzy walking over to the cheer bench with a small bag of chips and a soda, I walk over to sit with her, wanting to avoid the chatter happening amongst the boosters. She tears the bag open and tilts it toward me, so I grab three or four chips and begin nibbling on them.

"That was bad," she says after a few minutes of silence. The band has started to play, which drowns out a lot of the chatter I still feel like I can hear from the people in the stands.

"Yeah," I agree. I pop an entire chip in my mouth and let the crunching sound drown out my thoughts. It works for a few seconds, but when I'm done chewing, my mind is thinking about the note I found again.

"It's like there are spies, or defectors or…I don't know, I can't think of a really good war analogy, but it's clear that not everyone is on Nico's team," she says, turning her gaze to me and holding the soda out. I grab it and take a drink, swallowing slowly.

"Someone left Sasha a note," I say, turning to meet her eyes again. She tilts her head. "I found it, right before I came here. It was kind of threatening, and it basically said all of this was going to happen."

"Shit, Reagan. Like, they're bullying Nico?"

I shrug my shoulders, and Izzy shakes her head.

We both stare at the field, watching the other school's band form shapes and blare their horns for about six minutes, playing to the home stands on the other side. When they begin the fight song, Izzy stands, knowing that our team—in whatever form that might be right now—is about to come out for the second half.

"Boys are stupid," she says, not looking at me as she walks away.

I chuckle to myself, but not for long. I pull my legs up and finish my friend's chips, rolling the bag into a ball and tucking it in my back pocket, noticing my phone. I pull it out to find a message from her, replying to the one I sent earlier.

IZZY: *I think they're trying to push Nico out. I heard one of the coaches tell your dad it's time to pull him.*

I read her words a few times, sighing heavily each time I finish. Nico is better than all of them, but believing in him is going to ruin my dad.

When the quarter starts, I climb back to the top of the press box, and I don't allow myself to look at Coach O'Donahue, even though I feel him staring at me.

Nico's face is the same hardened one that marched to the locker room. It matches the expression on everyone's face. The only person who seems to be fired up is Sasha. He's moving from player to player, patting their backs and helmets, trying to rile them up, to get them to come alive. He's getting absolutely no response, though, and the more I watch, the more worried I become.

We start with the ball, and just like the last half, our side goes three and out. Nico doesn't get sacked, but despite how hard he scrambles, he just isn't able to make that ball move ten yards. Our kicker moves the ball far, so I hold onto hope that our defense will be able to hold the other team, to give us a fighting chance.

"It's time, Chad," I hear Coach O'Donahue say. I don't look at him. I don't want him to know I'm really listening. There are four or five of us up here now, but his voice still carries. "The kid isn't getting it done. Let's let Brandon take a shot, maybe a different approach will work."

I watch the field as our defense slips, letting the Metahill team move to midfield. They're almost in field goal range at the very least.

"Chad, you need to let this go! Get over your goddamned failed experiment, would you?"

Coach O'Donahue is turning to face the parking lot behind us, trying to be more discreet, whispering through clenched teeth into his headpiece. "Come on, Chad. If you can't make this call, people are going to want more things to change...not just what's on the field."

My jaw grows rigid, and I grind my back teeth together hard while my hands clutch the metal of my tripod.

"Shit!"

I glance to the side enough to see Coach O'Donahue pull his headset from his ears. He's running his hand over his face, fuming. I turn my attention back to the field before he catches me watching.

Another play by the other team gains six or seven yards, and my father holds up his clipboard, smacking it with his hand over his head repeatedly, trying to get someone's attention. I watch the disarray, his players not really knowing where to go or what to do, and my dad finally calls a time out.

The defense comes to the side slowly, but my dad meets them several yards onto the field. He urges the players on the sideline to come out with him, and he pulls everyone in close. I zoom in to see his hands moving wildly, more smacking of the clipboard until eventually it cracks in half. My father drops the pieces to the ground and holds his hands out, his eyebrows lifted high.

He breaks the team and sends the defense back out, only this time, I notice that Nico *and* Sasha are both out there. Nico...his quarterback.

I lean forward to look at the crowd, seeing the whispers I expected to see. My mother gets to her feet, her hands clutched in front of her. I don't need to see her face to know what expression she's making.

The play goes off, and our defense battles, Nico breaking through on the right, Sasha on the left. Their quarterback stumbles, and Sasha capitalizes, gripping the guy's arm, dragging him to the ground, the ball popping loose into Nico's hands.

It's sixty yards, and the people in his way seem too numerous, but he takes them one at a time, sprinting to the middle, spinning loose, twisting. The only person trailing Nico down the field is Sasha, running just as fast, diving, and tripping up the only other player on the Metahill team that possibly had a shot at catching them. The crowd in the stands starts to hum, the sound of anticipation growing to screams and chants of "go" the closer Nico gets to the end zone, until his feet are finally inside.

He takes a few more long strides through the middle, holding the ball in one hand and jogging through the end zone to the referee, handing him the ball, then running to the sidelines where my father waits to smack his helmet and shout "good job!"

Nico heads to the water, guzzling while our kicking team takes the field. My father comes over again and stares at him, talking to him, encouraging him to breathe—to rest.

"That was amazing," I say, turning to Coach O'Donahue. His headpiece is still off, and his fingers are pinching the bridge of his nose. He pauses to look at me, his eyes barely open, just enough to show his disgust.

"That was a goddamned circus trick; that's what that was," he says, slipping his gear back in place and adjusting his posture, as if he just hit some reset button and is ready to go again.

"Well, it beats quitting," I say, meaning that in every single way a person could take it.

He doesn't look at me again.

The Tradition wins twenty-eight to twenty-one, and Nico ends up playing both ways for several plays. Another interception from Sasha helps tie the game, then Nico runs in the final play with a few minutes left on the clock. Our defense holds them to win.

The walk to the bus is quiet. I film it, but stop, because it makes me sad. We just won a tough game, and nobody is celebrating. They aren't celebrating because their egos are mad about petty shit that doesn't matter. I don't even know *why* half of them have decided to work against Nico, but I know the reason can't possibly be rational. It's spiteful, and it's built up on rumors and lies, I'm sure.

Near the end of the bus, I hear a woman squeal a happy sound, so I turn and see Nico being embraced by his mother, Alyssa wrapped around his leg. A man who looks a lot like him, only many years older, stands with his hand on Nico's shoulder, facing him and nodding silently. Nico glances in my direction, and I smile, lifting my hand for a subtle wave. I didn't want to interrupt his family, but he jogs over to me, gripping my hand in his and urging me toward them.

"I want you to meet my Uncle Danny," he says, grinning at me bashfully, looking up at me from the side then back down at his feet. I notice his mom spot our hands as we walk up, and she pinches her lips into a tight smile, raising her eyebrows at her son.

"Danny, this is the girl I was telling you about. This is Reagan," Nico says.

My insides drop and my head feels light hearing him admit to talking about me to a man I know he admires. I turn to Nico, who's once again looking at his feet, then give my attention to his uncle, reaching out to take his hand.

"It is so nice to meet you," I say.

"The pleasure is mine, Reagan," Danny says, covering the top of my hand with his other. He squeezes once, then lets my hand go, pushing his own into his pockets, just like his nephew always does.

"Some game, huh?" I say, and Nico laughs once next to me, lifting his head to look at the bus, and the few players still walking up from the field. He shakes his head and breathes in deeply, so I brush my arm into his to let him know I understand.

"It sure was," Danny says. "I never thought I'd see this kid play again. He was always the best player on our team. Thank you for getting him back out there."

"Oh, I don't think I did anything," I say.

"That's not what I hear?" Danny says with a wink.

"I gotta go. I'll see you at home, Mom," Nico says, cutting the conversation short. My face is burning at his uncle's teasing, and I'm sure his is worse.

"Thanks for inviting me out, Nico. I'll head over to Cornwall next week. I want to see you take that field," his uncle says, pulling Nico under his arm. They break apart and tap their knuckles, and Nico glances to me briefly, showing a hint of his embarrassment as he turns to head to the steps for the bus. I catch my father waiting for him at the entry, his eyes moving to me after Nico passes by. I raise a hand to wave, but my father ignores it, getting on the bus with his team.

"I have to drive back, too. It was really nice meeting you," I say, shaking Danny's hand again, then moving on to Nico's mom. She pulls me in surprisingly for a hug, tilting my face and kissing my cheek, and I smile at her gesture.

I feel warm and loved all the way to my car, and I drive home in silence, not wanting even my favorite music to break my momentary bliss. It all ends the second I pull into the school lot, the bus arriving right before me, and Sasha and Travis shoving one another under the orange glow of the parking lights.

More players tag along, and pretty soon, fists are flying and blood is spilling. I catch Noah standing near the exit of the bus, and I walk over to him.

"What's happening?" I say, my head shaking while the coaches all struggle to stop one brawl while another starts.

"They're falling apart," Noah says. I nod to agree with him, but when I look to his face, I see the smile spreading along his lips.

"Noah!" I shout.

He flits his eyes to me, but doesn't try to mask his expression.

"He shouldn't have played tonight, Reagan. Quit trying to act like he's so perfect. He ditched school today. I told Coach O'Donahue. Dad's the only one that wanted to start him…"

"You told Coach O'Donahue? Are you insane?" I interrupt, my face falling at my brother's confession.

"They wouldn't have played me," he says.

"You don't know that. You don't know why Nico was missing today. Jesus, Noah. Are you trying to get Dad fired? You can't play, so what…Dad should lose his job, too?" I'm shouting, but the words seem to run right through my brother. He shakes my temper off and pushes forward on his crutches, moving to a few of the players on the other side of the crowd.

The buzzing sound is loud and impossible to ignore. It blares three or four times until everyone turns to see my dad standing in the center of the fight, a bullhorn in his hands, his finger pressing on a red button. He holds it the final time for several seconds, the shrill sound echoing off the bus, school, and neighboring houses.

Eventually, fists stop and bodies shift, every player and coach standing to face my dad, even the ones who I know aren't in his corner.

My dad spins in a slow circle, looking every single person in the eyes, including me.

"I have coached for two decades. I've assisted before this, and I sat there on the sidelines, like many of you, on a team that had a lot of integrity and reputation for greatness. I wore Crimson in Alabama, and I wore blue and gold here. I understood what an honor it was just to put on that goddamned uniform every Friday or Saturday night."

My father's nostrils flare with his breath, and I can feel him struggling to remain composed—as much as he can—in the middle of his team's self-destruction.

"What did I tell you at halftime?"

It's silent, and my dad waits for almost a full minute before someone finally steps forward to speak. When I realize it's Travis, I hold my breath, worried that he's only going to make this worse.

"You said nobody's job out here was guaranteed, sir," Travis says.

"Damn right," my father responds, loud and quick.

He begins to pace, and I lean against the bus, my eyes moving from him to Nico, who is watching my father quietly and respectfully. His face is bruised, and he is finally showing the wear from tonight's game.

"Monday, we begin again. We…start over. I'm going to post a list. If you're on that list, then you are on the team. The rest of you better show up ready to try out. Nobody is guaranteed, and I don't give two shits who your dad or uncle is!" My father shouts his ultimatum, and a few of the coaches flinch at his choice of words. Jimmy O'Donahue snickers to himself and looks away.

"I suppose Nico gets to be on that list?" Travis says, stepping forward more, backing up his opinion. I think he was expecting others to join him, and when they don't, he starts to sway on his feet and look around.

"You all can probably guess the few names that will be on that list. And if you think they're going to be there, then guess what?" My dad stares into Travis's eyes, moving closer until there are only inches between them. "That means *you* know who's really playing with their heart and who's doggin' it. Quit pretending you don't. And quit being an embarrassment to this program. You embarrass me, your parents, and yourselves."

My dad holds Travis's gaze until my brother's best friend blinks and his eyes fall down to his feet. He knows my dad's right, and he knows he's acting like a child. I don't know why he's taking over for acting out on my brother's aggression, but it's not winning him any points in anyone's eyes but Noah's.

"I don't want to be on that list," Nico says, breaking the silence. Heads shift and my father turns to look at him quickly, his brow pulled in. Nico steps forward. "That's part of the problem, Coach. I know you mean to reward hard work, but that's just not how it comes across."

Nico turns to look down the line of players, most of them the guys who gave up on him tonight and let him struggle.

"You all think I'm getting some sort of special treatment. I'm not stupid. I hear the shit you say—sorry Coach, no disrespect with the language," Nico says quickly, holding up his hand. "I hear you, though. I know I'm the scholarship kid. I know that Sasha and I, and maybe Jason and Malachi over there, are the only people with brown skin on this damned team. We feel it. You don't have to say anything guys, if you don't want to, but you know…you *all* know. We feel it. You whisper about it, even when you don't think you are. We must be getting favors. We must be here to make sure Cornwall isn't *too white*. Why the hell couldn't it be because…we're good. Maybe we're just…good."

Nobody speaks. Mouths are shut, and consciences are evaluating the words Nico just said. He isn't wrong, and even though I feel some of the guys wanting to protest, they won't—they can't. They would be liars.

"So keep me off that list. I'm going to earn my way just like the rest of you. But you better be willing to prove your skills, because I'm done holding back, and I'm done not beating other teams by thirty or forty points," Nico says, turning so he faces Travis, stepping forward until they stand only feet apart. "And I'm done pretending I don't hear the things you say."

Travis swallows, his eyes meeting Nico's. The standoff is short, and it ends in Travis giving Nico a slight nod, a silent pact between the two of them.

I wait by the bus, watching as the team slowly breaks away, some not even bothering to head to the locker room at all. My brother walks away with Travis, but the bond that was there for years feels different between them. When Noah starts to talk, Travis doesn't engage. That might change the minute they get in the car and drive home, but the fact that Nico put those thoughts out there in the open has done something to everyone—even my dad.

After several minutes, I'm standing in the parking lot alone. My father's car is the last one besides mine in the lot. Nico left with Sasha, not bothering to stop to talk to me. I didn't expect him to, but I felt slighted somehow still. Izzy tried to talk me into going to Charlie's, mostly because she likes drama and wants to see how many people still decide to show up.

I want to go home, and maybe for the same reason Izzy wants to go to the ice cream shop. I want to see how tonight affected my mom. I want to see if Travis drove home, and if my brother and he parted ways. I want to ask my brother what he was thinking. I want to shake him, and scream at him.

I want him to apologize to me—for being a goddamned asshole!

And I want the adults to quit plotting for ways to take my father down. They're not so different from the students, and Nico said it all. I hear them, too. They think I can't...they think my mom can't. We all hear them.

The streets are quiet on the way home, and I purposely don't drive near Charlie's, so I'm not tempted to stop. I head directly home, pulling into my driveway, feeling a sense of comfort when I see Travis's Jeep in his driveway. My mom's car is still not home, though, and when I unlock the front door, the house is quiet and dark. My brother's door is wide open, his lights off, and his bed the same unkempt mess it's been for days.

His leg may heal soon, but the rest of him—the other parts he's slowly destroying—I don't hold out much hope.

CHAPTER 13

"Mom? I can't find my nice shoes!"

On my knees, I burrow into my closet, tossing loose clothing from the floor. It's picture day at school, and I have one pair of nice shoes—the ones I wear to church.

Church!

I leap to my feet, remembering taking my shoes off on Sunday on the ride home. I'm sure they're still in the back seat. I sprint down the hallway, sliding in my socks. I stop hard when I see Vincent standing in the front doorway, close to Momma.

"Vincent!" I shout, running to my brother.

"Shhhh," my mom says, twisting to face me with a finger over her lips. She's holding a tiny baby, bouncing lightly, and there are tears in her eyes.

Whose baby is this?

"Nico? I'd like you to meet your niece...Alyssa," Momma says.

I step closer to see the tiniest person I've ever seen. She's wrapped in a pink blanket, her mouth moving like a fish's, her hand struggling to pull loose from the blanket.

"She's hungry," Momma says. She looks up at Vincent. "Do you have a bottle for her?"

My brother is shaking. He balls his fists and pushes them into his eyes.

"I don't know. I...I don't know how to do any of this. And she just left. This morning, I got up, and she was gone. And I don't know how to do any of this," Vincent says.

He lets his hands fall and his eyes dart from me to our mom to the tiny baby, and his chest begins to shake. My brother starts to cry, and he covers his mouth with his hand while our mom bounces the baby lightly and whispers softly in the tiny girl's face.

"It's okay, isn't it Alyssa?" she says.

The baby...my niece...starts to make more noise, almost like hard hiccups. And in a second, her face turns red and her lips curl down as she begins to cry.

"Vincent, bring the bag. I'll show you," my mom says.

She carries the baby into the kitchen and tells my brother to sit in a chair. She hands him the baby—his baby—and he holds her close to his chest, his eyes almost frozen open. The little girl looks so breakable in his giant arms and against his chest. His arms are covered in grease marks, and the number tattoos he had before are marked over with designs and pictures.

"What happened to those?" I ask.

My brother glances to me quickly, then looks back at his child. My mom begins shaking a bottle, spilling a small amount on her arm. She wipes the drops off on the front of her shirt then hands the bottle to my brother, guiding his hand as they both work the tiny tip into Alyssa's mouth. She starts to suck on it instantly, her cheeks pushing in and out, and the look of it makes me giggle.

"It's pretty cute when she eats, isn't it, Nico?" my mom says.

"Yeah," I say, dragging my chair closer so I can watch.

We're all silent for more than a minute, and then Alyssa makes a suckling sound that makes me laugh again. Vincent laughs with me, and he looks up, into my eyes.

"She's amazing," he says.

"I love her," I say, bending forward and pressing my lips on her tiny warm forehead.

"I love her, too," my brother says, his eyes back on his daughter.

"We'll figure this out, Mijo. Come home," my mom says.

My brother watches Alyssa in his arms, adjusting his feet under the chair and moving her even closer to his body. He nods.

"Okay," he says. "Okay."

CHAPTER 14

There are some sounds that simply never happen in the Prescott house on a Saturday morning. We don't hear a lot of pots and pans, for example, so when I catch the first few clanks, my eyes pop open instantly as if to alert the rest of my body that a foreign intruder has broken into the house.

Clank-clank-clank!

I jolt to a sitting position at the sound of a heavy pan careening off the counter onto the floor. At least, that's what I *think* that sound is. It goes quiet, and I wait for another sign, but nothing happens until my nose recognizes the most magnificent scent.

Bacon.

I slide out of bed and crack open my door, leaning forward to listen closer. Then I hear something even *more* foreign.

Whistling.

I rub my hands over my eyes and yawn, letting my feet slide down the hallway, pausing at my brother's door. I touch it with my fingers, relieved that it's closed. He must be inside. He came home.

Quietly, I slide the rest of the way down the hall to the very front of the house, the blinds all still shut. I squint, looking at the clock over the refrigerator—five o'clock. My dad has four pans going—one on each burner—and he has something crackling in each. I was right about the

169

bacon, but he also has some peppers and onions, sausage and eggs. The smell is surprisingly amazing, and I take a seat at the breakfast bar, letting my chin fall into my hands while my feet kick at the rail underneath.

"Whatcha doin?" I ask, and my dad jumps, his back to me. His eyes are red, and I doubt he slept at all last night.

"Do you know that I used to want to be a chef?" he says.

I bunch my lips and furrow my brow.

"I'm being serious. In college, when I met your mom. I had this dream that we would graduate Alabama, and then I'd head to culinary school," my dad says, picking up the pan with eggs and rolling it from side-to-side with his wrist before giving it the perfect flick, folding the egg in half. He chuckles at it and grins. "Still got it."

"Why didn't you?" I ask, leaning back at the sound of my parents' bedroom door opening at the end of the hall. I smile when my mom's weary eyes meet mine, and when her expression looks questioning, I jerk my head toward Dad.

"I got the job at Cornwall. And I don't know...I just couldn't say *no*," my dad says.

"Honey, what in the hell are you doing? It's...Saturday. Aren't you going in to watch films?" My mom shuffles over to the coffeemaker, pulling the water container out and filling it at the sink. My dad leans into her, kissing her cheek, and she raises an eyebrow at him.

"I am. But, film can wait...for breakfast," my dad says. "Omelet?"

He holds the pan forward for me to see, and I take in the perfect egg speckled with cheese, peppers, bacon, and onion.

"Wow. Yes, please," I say, sniffing one last time before he pulls the pan away and slides the perfect breakfast creation onto a plate.

"You want one, Lauren?" my dad asks my mom. She stands still, the water container for the coffeemaker now full in her hands, and she stares at my dad with an expression of disbelief.

"Uh...sure," she says, her lip curling on one side.

"Cheese?" my dad asks as he cracks two eggs.

"Yes," my mom says, her brow still bunched. She turns to me, and I shrug, pushing my fork into my breakfast and lifting a steaming bite to my lips. I blow for a second or two, but shovel it in quickly—unable to stave off the desire any longer, because the smell is just so damned tempting.

"Holy crap!" I say, the delicious flavors melting around my tongue. My breakfast is usually a granola bar, and the only other times we've had food prepared in our kitchen, it was from a caterer making mini-somethings for a party.

"Glad you like it," my dad says, sliding a napkin toward my plate.

"I'm planning the homecoming barbecue today with Linda. She's coming over at noon, which is in…seven weeks," my mom says, her lips blowing the steam from her cup of coffee while she holds it between her fingers under her mouth. My dad twists to the side and lowers his head, looking at her with pursed lips, and my mom's mouth bends into a smirk. "What?"

"It's not *that* early," my dad says.

"Chad, I haven't been awake this early in…"

My dad interrupts her with a kiss on her lips, and my eyes are frozen on my parents. The moment is unnatural, but sweet nonetheless. My mom's mood shifts from surprised to shy, her cheeks red and her eyelashes fluttering. It's been so long since I've seen my parents look like love. All it takes is a single phone call to end it.

The machine picks up after the second ring. The only reason we even have a home phone is for all of my mom's party planning. But that's not who's calling at this hour. They won't leave a name—they never do. My father's voice on the recording clicks in.

"You've reached the Prescott home. We are unable to take your call right now, so please leave a message. Thank you."

I stare at my plate, only four bites gone, but my appetite no more. The beep follows.

"You're a disgrace to this program, and if you think we're going to let you continue to make a mockery of this team, you're sadly mistaken!

Last night was unacceptable. Do you hear me? Your days are numbered, Coach Prescott. We want change! We want results!"

The woman hangs up.

Our kitchen is silent.

My dad leans back, clutching the handle on the oven while he bends, leaning his head forward and shutting his eyes. He can make all of the omelets he wants, but the fact of the matter remains—my dad isn't a chef. He's the coach of The Tradition. And with that great honor comes great sacrifice.

"I'm going in," my dad says, the light gone from his eyes.

He flips the dials on the stove forcefully, and grabs two of the pans, stepping on the lever for the trash and tipping them over so the food— freshly made—slides in. He drops the pans in the sink heavily, and my mom steps to the stove, grabbing the final two pans with him, their hands overlapping.

"I'll get these," she says.

I watch them stare into each other, so goddamned helpless. After a few seconds, my dad nods, leaving her to finish what he started. He grabs his keys from the counter and pushes his Cornwall hat down on his head, the brim low enough to hide his eyes from view.

"I'll be late," he says, flipping the door open and shut without another word.

I'm no longer hungry, so I stand and move to the trash, sliding my uneaten breakfast in, then moving to the sink to help my mom rinse dishes. I hear her pull out her bottle of pills behind me, the rattling sound as she shakes them into her hand. I glance over my shoulder, relieved only to see one in her palm. She puts it between her lips, then turns to find her coffee, taking a sip and tilting her head back while she shuts her eyes.

"Sometimes it all just doesn't feel worth it," she sighs. When her eyes open on me, they seem sadder than they have in months.

I turn the water off on the sink and dry my hands on the towel, stepping close to my mom and wrapping my arm around her waist. Her eyelids tremble closed as she leans into me.

"Hoorah," I whisper.

It takes her a second, but eventually, my mom's body quivers with her laughter. It's quiet, but it's not crying, and that's all I can ask for.

"Hoorah," she says back, raising her arm over her head in a fist. She looks around the kitchen, nodding, her mouth curving into an even bigger smile, until she laughs louder.

"What a goddamned mess!" she says. "You go on; I'll finish this up."

"You sure?" I ask.

She nods, then takes the towel from my hands, urging me to head back down the hallway. I do as she says, gathering fresh clothes, showering, and then piling my equipment into my backpack, ready to go by six.

By the time I leave my room, the kitchen is shining and the house is once again quiet. My mom's door is open, so I look out the front window to the driveway, noticing that her car is gone. My brother's door is still closed, so I leave a note on the counter that I went to the lab room at school. Nobody will see it to care, but just in case.

The streets are empty, and the sun is barely up over the horizon. I pull into the closest spot to the lab, squinting when I look to the bottom of the hill, noticing my dad's car in its usual spot. He'll be here alone for several hours. The rest of the staff won't show up until nine or ten.

With my heavy bags slung over my arm, I tug on the main door for the school, relieved when it opens. Cornwall encourages students to come in on weekends. Usually, it's the arts programs, or the music and dance studio rooms that are being used. The media lab is always empty, so I don't think twice when I flip on all of the lights as I enter the first room on the left.

Nico jumps from a chair, his hands cupping the headphones on his ears as he spins and glares at me with wide eyes. I drop my bags and fall flat against the door, gripping my chest.

"Shit!" I say.

Nico pulls the headphones down so they hang around his neck, then presses his palm into his left eye, looking at me through his other.

"What the hell are you doing here?" I ask.

He glances behind him at the editing desk, then swings his focus back to me.

"I...this place is open, right? Like...anyone can use it. Or...do you have to check it out, or sign up? I'm sorry. I..."

"It's open. No, it's fine. It's just...I'm the only one who ever comes in this room," I say, feeling finally making its way back down my arms and legs.

I bend down and grab my things, and Nico steps over the chair he was straddling clumsily, his leg caught in the cord of his headphones. He hops on one leg until he frees himself, meeting me a few steps inside the door.

"Here, I got it," he says, taking my bags from me and carrying them to the main work area. I walk slowly to catch up.

"You're always carrying my shit for me," I say.

"It's how I court girls," he says back, glancing to me with half a smile. I blush.

"Oh," I say, pulling my lips in tight.

"I didn't expect your shit to always be so heavy, though," he winks.

"I'm filling my bags with rocks. I just want to see how far you're willing to go," I tease.

He stands tall and turns to face me, the chair he was just sitting in now the only barrier between us.

"The distance," he says.

I wrinkle my forehead.

"I'm willing to go the distance," he repeats. "No matter how far that is."

My lips twitch, and I bend to their will, smiling while he looks at me. My pulse picks up speed, too.

Nervous, I reach for the chair between us and slide it out so I can sit. Nico takes a step back, making room for me. He leans forward to pull his headphones from the jack on the side of the computer, and loud music fills the room from the computer's speakers.

"Sorry, I was kind of cranking it up," he says, his arm brushing mine as he bends forward and clicks the volume down. He looks at me as he stands back up, and for a second, I think he might kiss me. He doesn't, but I sort of think he wants to. Our eyes meet, and we both laugh lightly, Nico turning to rest on the desk next to me while I tuck my hands under my legs. I'm wearing the same sweatshirt I wore last night, along with my skinny jeans instead of my leggings, my hair still damp and twisted over my shoulder. I notice Nico's eyes follow the length of it down my arm where the ends are dripping, so I pick them up and comb my fingers through.

"I took a shower before I came here," I say.

He nods, and his eyes stay on mine. I wish we had something to argue about right now. Arguing with him was always so easy. This—*this* is hard. The quiet. It's too honest.

"So what are you working on?" I ask, shifting in the chair and reaching to the mouse to bring the dark screen back to life.

I see Alyssa paused in a video timeline. She's making a face, her hands pressed on her cheeks, which she has puffed out with air. It's silly, and I laugh before I look at Nico with a smile. He stares at his niece's image and runs his hand on the back of his neck, sighing.

"Actually," he says, kneeling down so his eyes are on my level.

He holds the front of the desk inches away from me as he bends, and my eyes take a moment to notice the muscles of his forearms, the size of his hands and the way his nails are cut short, but not to the skin. He breathes, and I feel it against my arm—I tense, giving my focus back to the screen.

"I kind of don't know what I'm doing," he says, clicking the PLAY button and letting the video clip play on.

Alyssa blows out, her lips making a raspberry noise, and her giggles soon taking over. She waves close to the camera, then covers her mouth with both hands before blowing a huge kiss.

"I love you, Daddy!" she yells, and hearing her voice—so high, so loud, so proud—causes my eyes to tear.

Nico rests on his hands, his chin against them as they lay on the desktop. He lets his head fall to the side, and I watch his eyes dance over the joy playing out on the screen. The way she loves her daddy is the same way Nico looks at her.

"I want to make Vincent a video," he says, stopping short, his tongue pinched between his teeth until he breathes out a short laugh, and his lips curl into a smile that dents his cheek. The video ends, and I click STOP just as Alyssa runs off the screen. Nico blinks at the visual slowly, his face frozen in the same expression, like he's afraid to tell me the rest.

"I can help you," I say. His eyes flit to mine, and his smile grows.

"Thanks," he says.

"Sure," I say.

Our eyes stare into each other for a few beats, until I can't take it, and look back at the screen, dragging the player back to the beginning. Nico grabs a chair from the other end of the room, sliding it up next to mine so close that the metal touches. I feel his body against mine when he sits, a series of barely-there grazes that fire off a million sensations down the length of my body. I shift in my seat, moving just enough to the left that I can't feel him any longer, though somehow, even through inches of nothingness, I can still feel his heat.

"So, do you just want me to cut all of these clips together?" I ask.

"I have some photos too. Here," Nico says, pulling his phone from his back pocket. I take it, our fingertips touching on the exchange, and I know I don't imagine the way Nico's thumb runs softly along my knuckles.

"Th…thanks," I stutter, laying his phone flat on the table in front of the keyboard.

I lean to my other side and pull out a cord, connecting his phone to the back. It takes me a few seconds to navigate to his photos, and I flip through them quickly, seeing pictures of him and Sasha, him with his family, his uncles, a few of the guys I recognize from that night at the football game, before Nico joined The Tradition. I stop when I see one of me, from the side, sitting at my desk in humanities, flipping through pages of a notebook, my hair down and draped over my shoulder.

"I like your hair down," he says. I glance at him, knowing I'm blushing, and he leans to the side, his arm pressing into mine just enough to tell me it's okay, his smile bashful and showing me he's embarrassed, too.

"So…photos, yeah," I say, turning my attention back to the screen, blinking and scrolling back to the beginning of his photo gallery, pausing on ones of Alyssa and him. "You want me to just…"

"Reagan."

I know he's looking at me. I can feel him, and I'm so unsure what to do. My foot is wiggling side-to-side along the floor, and my knee is moving in the chair, the nerves traveling rapidly up my leg. Nico's hand touches me, his finger sprawling over my knee with just enough pressure that I stop. I suck in air, and my lips tingle. I feel him turn to face me, his hand sliding from its hold on my knee until it lets go, his fingers finding my face next, the same light pressure urging me to turn my head. My eyes trail behind the movement, clinging to the view on the computer screen, my hand gripping the computer mouse until I give in and shift to his gaze.

His eyes soften the moment we meet, the gold and brown blurring under the heaviness of his dark lashes. His lips aren't smiling, but the straight line is more reverent than anything else, and as his thumb sweeps across my cheek, I gasp, letting go of the breath I didn't realize I'd been holding.

"I like your eyes, too," he says, and I become instantly aware of how heavy my eyelids are.

"And your freckles," he says, running his fingertips down my cheek, to my chin. My face flushes from that attention next.

"And your…lips," he says, brushing his knuckles slowly across my mouth, his eyes low and staring at my upper lip. My breath hitches against his touch. His eyes come back to mine, wrinkling at the sides with his smile.

"And your temper," he says, his mouth pulled up on one side, the dimple there. "And your voice. And the way you argue. How you work so hard. How you look over your shoulder when you're late. How you distract yourself with doodles when you're early. The way you look at me…"

My eyes flash wider, and I take a sharp breath through my nose.

"Just don't ever stop looking at me," he says, scooting closer, his knees touching my leg, his hand bringing my face to his. Nico's nose brushes against mine, and my eyes fall shut, my lips parting, almost reaching for him.

"Look at me like you expect more. Look at me like it isn't going to be easy." Nico breathes the words against my lips, pausing when his bottom lip connects with my top, the faintness of the touch so much better than any other real kiss I've had. "Make me earn it," he says, pausing again to take my top lip between both of his. "I'll earn it. I'll never stop trying to earn it…to earn you."

"Nico," I whimper, my lips trembling against his. He presses his forehead to mine and brings his hands to my cheeks, his fingertips sliding into my hair, the wet strands sticking to my neck and shoulders, wrapping around his wrists like golden shackles.

"You push me, Reagan. You…" he chuckles. "Damn, do you push me. You push my buttons sometimes, and then…you show up to my house all clumsy, with your camera and this crazy film thing. I wanted to kiss you then."

His lips pass over mine again, softly, and I open my mouth to feel him just as much, my tongue touching his lightly at first, his lips quickly capturing mine with more force as his fingers slide further into my hair. Nico begins to stand, his lips still on mine, my head tilted up as he moves over me until I stand to meet him. He kicks my chair to the side, never letting our lips part.

"I wasn't going to kiss you, I swear, it's just," he chuckles against my mouth, towering over me, the front of his hair falling forward and tickling my face. "I did, and now…I can't stop."

My hands reach up to cup his face before sliding down his chest, my fingers clutching his gray T-shirt, and Nico begins to take steps forward, walking me back until I feel my legs hit the supply cabinet on the far wall. His hands slide down my sides, reaching around my thighs and lifting me so I'm sitting on the counter as he steps between my knees, his mouth even harder on mine now.

He pauses for breath, his chest rising and falling fast while he sweeps his lips over mine, as if he's afraid to leave them untouched.

"I wanted you to kiss me," I say, my eyes closed until Nico's fingers find my chin, tilting it up so I can open and look him in the eyes.

"Yeah?" he asks, the gold flecks so bright, his smile so perfect.

"I had a dream you did," I admit, letting my head fall forward into his chest. His arms wrap around my head, and his lips kiss the top. "Oh my God, I'm so embarrassed."

"Don't be," he whispers into my ear. "I dreamt about you, too."

"You did?" I ask, my voice echoing against his body.

"No, not really. I was just trying to make you feel better," he says, the rumble of his laughter vibrating where my face hits his chest.

"Oh my God," I say, squeezing my eyes shut.

Nico steps back and lifts my chin again, his fingers sliding strands of wet hair from my face. I blink open to see him looking at me carefully, studying each hair and putting it back in its place until his eyes come to rest on mine. His mouth tugs up, the familiar curve in his cheek that I love there. I breathe deeply through my nose, and he leans forward to kiss the tip of it.

"I like the way you blush, too," he says.

"I do that a lot," I say.

"Yeah…but still…" He smiles. "I like it all the same."

Nico leans forward again, and I let my head fall back completely, looking up at him, so warm against his chest, my mouth smiling against his as we fall into one more long and tender kiss. Minutes pass as his mouth works over mine, closing over every inch of my top lip first, then my bottom, tasting me in long strokes of his tongue, his hands never leaving from their home on either side of my face.

Home.

Nico is so much like home; like no home I have ever known.

When he steps away the final time, his hand runs down my arm until our fingertips link, and he gently tugs me to my feet and back toward the chair in front of the computer. He pauses to kiss me lightly one more time before I sit, when I finally do, he leaves his hand on my knee, his thumb drawing gentle circles that send shivers throughout my body and leave me constantly on edge and quite out of focus.

I flip through photos with him, dropping ones he likes into a folder on the desktop before moving back to the video and running through his favorite parts. Nico points to the screen sometimes, and his hand covers mine, stopping me when I click, teasing me. His comfort in touching my body makes my heart race every single time.

Every. Single. Time.

When I look at the clock, I realize that the sun has long since risen in the sky. More than that, it's noon. We've managed to string together dozens of his favorite shots, and Nico has actually learned things…things that *I* taught him. I added effects and suggested spots to trim his video, to splice sections together, to let Alyssa's words run in the background.

We watch the end result, and he pulls my hand into both of his, his fingers kneading mine, feeling each individually, almost as if he's constantly testing to make sure I'm real. His touch both keeps me grounded and sends me floating, like a push and pull, the rhythm in sync with my heart's. I force myself to pay attention to the screen, letting the sound of Alyssa's laughter fill my ears, my chest, my heart—she fills everything.

"Where's your brother, Nico?"

I let the question linger, and I'm patient for his answer. I'm almost ashamed of what I expect. Even more when he finally speaks.

"Afghanistan," he says.

I let his fingers play over mine, and we sit quietly taking in his niece's sweet face in front of us.

"He left, three years ago. He..." Nico swallows, and I squeeze his hand in mine, looking down at how our fingers fit, wishing there was a way I could feel his touch more. I want to—I want to make every touch feel like more, so I can hold onto it when I'm alone.

"Vincent got mixed up with the fifty-seven," he says, and I nod slowly, not really sure what that means. "They're like...a pretty bad gang. There used to be a few drug houses in West End, but the cops busted them, moved them out. It doesn't mean that the gang goes away. It just means...it means they move, the same problems, slightly different address."

"Your brother...he...sold drugs?" I ask.

Nico shrugs and shifts his weight, his focus more intent on my hand in his.

"Not totally, but he was...he was around for a lot of things when they went down. He was the low man on the totem pole, I guess you could say?"

I nod.

"Then...Alyssa came along," he says, and I glance up to see his crooked smile, his eyes moving to the screen then to me. "Her mom bailed when she was days old. She was pretty hooked on some bad shit."

I breathe in deeply, not wanting to show how unnerved his words are making me.

"That guy...that day at your house," I say, and Nico grimaces, looking down again.

"He comes around sometimes. He's smalltime, selling at playgrounds and shit like that," Nico says, laughing through a serious face. "He's actually the narc who got the houses in our hood busted. He needed to save his own ass. He's been dealing in West End since I was a kid, though. Fucking asshole used to chase me home from school."

"Oh my God!" I say, unable to hide the wince that paints my face.

Nico raises a shoulder.

"It's not really that bad," he says, looking up at me through his flickering eyelids. "It's a flawed system, sort of. Like…like the Axis and the Allies, World War Two. Only, instead of countries, it's groups of punk-ass losers looking to make a quick buck. These guys hook up with the ones on the next street so they have someone to watch their backs, then the ones they bully make friends to watch *their* backs, and then you mix drugs in, and money and territory, and then all of a sudden you have a war."

"War, huh?" I ask.

"Feels like it sometimes," he says, shaking his head and smirking.

I reach up and touch the lock of hair falling into his eyes, giggling when he goes cross-eyed watching me. "Only you would make such a nerdy analogy for gangland warfare," I say.

"I'm pretty sure we decided that you, Miss Prescott," he says, touching my nose, "are by *far* the bigger nerd."

I narrow my gaze on him and pout, which makes him laugh.

"So why is your brother in the Middle East?" I ask.

"Marines," Nico says, confirming what I thought. "He got his act together, and talked to a recruiter. Probably lied a little about drugs and shit to get through the process, and his past didn't really do him many favors. But he wanted to do something big with his life, step up and be the dad she deserves."

I watch him look at Alyssa's image again as he leans forward and clicks to save the file we made.

"He sounds like a pretty great brother," I say.

Nico's mouth forms a tight smile.

"I've always thought my brother was the greatest man in the world, even when he probably didn't deserve me thinking so," he says.

"We do that for our brothers," I say, thinking of my own, how lost he is and how my heart aches for the time when he was just my bratty twin who I secretly adored.

"Yeah, we do," Nico says, slipping his hand loose from mine, and scooting closer to the computer to email the final video file to himself. "That's why I missed school Friday. He gets video calls every now and then, and one came Friday. We have to go to the community center to log into their computers, and sometimes the Internet is too damn slow. We got to talk to him Friday, though. He looked so much older."

"How old is he?" I ask.

"Twenty-five," he says, chewing at the inside of his mouth while his lips slide into a proud grin. "He said he missed Alyssa, seeing her face. He looked so goddamned sad, and I just thought—"

Nico reaches up with his arm, sliding it along his right eye, wiping away the tear I see forming.

"I think he'll love the video," I say. "If you want, I can send it to him. We both can. Maybe you can come over one night, after practice."

Nico looks up at me from the side, his mouth quirking up in a faint smile.

"Yeah?" he says.

"Yeah," I repeat.

I lean in, my lips twitching with the need to feel his again, but just before I reach him, the door slides open, and we both twist in our seats to see my father standing in the doorway along with Jimmy O'Donahue. I let go of Nico's hand quickly, and stumble to a stand so I'm facing him.

"Dad, hey," I say, my body beat-red with guilt, my palms sweating and my heart thumping wildly while my dad's eyes shift from Nico to me.

"I saw your car. I'm getting pizza," he says, nothing about his tone warm or fuzzy or happy in the least. "Nico," he says, his name coming out clipped, smothered in a hint of a threat, perhaps.

"Coach," Nico says, standing next to me. I scoot to the right, giving us distance, and I feel Nico glance to me.

I swing my arm against my side, my mind spinning, unsure what to do, what to say—what to confess to. My eyes are wide, and the Western standoff we've all found ourselves in only grows more uncomfortable when Jimmy O'Donahue clears his throat, drawing my dad's attention to him, his face looking to the ground, to his feet, away from me and Nico.

"Got it," Nico says through a soft and unhappy chuckle.

My lips quiver, and I want to apologize immediately, but I don't. Nico holds up his phone and leans in.

"Thanks for the video lesson, Reagan. That sure was…swell of you," he says, speaking slowly and pointed.

"You're welcome," I say, glancing to meet his gaze for a breath, his eyes hazed with disappointment. I widen mine with a plea—I just need time. He nods slowly.

"Yeah, I sure am," he says, bending down to grab his backpack, slinging it over his shoulder and moving toward his coaches—my father—and reaching out to shake their hands.

My dad holds the door open, his eyes on nothing in particular, but most definitely not on me. I gather my things and log off the computer, only looking him in the eyes a second at a time while I pass through the door.

"I'd love pizza," I say, knowing in my gut that sitting in a booth with my dad and the guy trying to steal his job is the last place on earth I want to be. I want to be with Nico, but I fucked that up, too.

"We should pick up Noah," I say, if only to take the heat and attention off me.

"Good idea. I'll call him," my dad says, quick to agree.

We both need the ally.

CHAPTER 15

"Fairy tales…"

Mr. Huffman writes the word on the board, the chalk breaking with the force with which he scribbles the final letters. He tosses the half still in his fingers onto the metal lip below the board, clapping his hands together and turning to face our class.

The irony of today's class discussion is not lost on me. I doubt it's lost on Nico, either. We read a selection of the original Grimm tales in preparation for today, and Mr. Huffman challenged us to consider how they evolved into the now-famous versions with happier endings. The Grimm tales, as they were intended, are bleak and without promise. They are reflections of the time—stories of hunger, desperation…*war*.

Nico and I may very well be a Grimm fairy tale.

After another night without sleep, and a Sunday of exchanging snide comments with my brother while we both moped around the house, I finally sucked it up and sent Nico a text.

I'm sorry.

I typed paragraphs upon paragraphs, more words in a text form than I think I have typed to Izzy ever, and then I deleted them. I spent an hour crafting the perfect thing to say—building the perfect excuse. I spent an hour typing out lies.

My dad is strict.

I'm afraid he won't want me dating one of his players.

I was worried he saw me kissing you, and I got embarrassed.

Some of those things were slightly true, but mostly…not.

I deleted them all, and when it came down to it, I was just sorry. Sorry that I was afraid of showing my dad how much I like a boy from West End—a boy whose neighborhood my parents don't want me to go to; a boy whose last name is different from ours. And then I felt ashamed, because when I showed up at Nico's house, unannounced, his mom welcomed me inside. She kissed my cheek and hugged me. She didn't see a girl who was different from her son, and if she did, she didn't care enough to show it.

I came to school early, hoping Nico would be sitting in his favorite spot in the library, but he wasn't. I looked for him at lunch, but he was nowhere to be found. I'd seen him pass by through the halls, dozens of moving bodies between us and his thoughts and eyes always somewhere else. I knew he was here. I knew I'd see him. But now that I'm sitting here in this seat, staring at the boy a few rows over and a few chairs ahead, his hands gripping his desk at the top while his long legs fold underneath, I fear I've fallen back in time—to a place where Nico Medina hates me.

"You all did your reading, I assume?"

Mr. Huffman's question brings our eyes to the front. He tilts his head, feeling us out, then nods.

"Good," he says, moving to his desk at the front, folding his arms over his chest and leaning his weight back. "So what did you think? How do Grimm's tales compare?"

"They don't," Nico says, taking the lead right out of the gate.

I sink back in my chair, not wanting to catch his periphery. His jaw is working, and his eyes flit up to our teacher briefly before coming back to his hands, his knuckles bent with his hard grip around the front of his desk.

"Beyond the obvious, Nico…what do you mean?" Mr. Huffman asks.

Nico breathes in deeply through his nose, pushing his mouth into a hard line.

"Grimm's stories aren't really fairy tales. They're more like...folk tales. They're allegories, reflections of how terrible things were for the common and poor at the time. You can draw more comparisons to the front page of the Daily Press than you can to the typical fairy tales. I mean, like today, the news has this story about two bodies found sixty miles away from the nearest highway, buried in shallow graves by drug lords who weren't paid what they were owed. That..." Nico pauses to laugh out once, a punctuated sound that matches the way his head lifts and his shoulders raise. "Stories like that are Grimm stories. Fairy tales, though—those are like the way people *want* to think the world works."

"It's true," Mr. Huffman adds. "If you look at the evolution of the stories, each edition becomes more mystical, religious undertones are added and good always wins in the end."

"Good *never* wins in a Grimm tale," Nico says. "They just...they just are what they are. Life happens, and people make choices, and then life goes on."

I hold my breath because he tilts his head enough that his eyes find mine and his hair slides forward. The disappointment in his expression levels me, and I'm reminded that all I could say was "I'm sorry."

"But we *want* the prince and the princess, and maybe wanting something better is enough," I say, not realizing I've interjected myself until my first words leave my mouth. I lean forward and hold Nico's gaze, but I feel the rest of the classroom's eyes on me. I turn slightly to see Izzy's face, and she smiles faintly, knowing enough of the hole I've dug for myself to understand that this is me, trying to claw my way out of it.

"You can be a toad in love with a beautiful girl all you want, but in the end, you're still a toad. That's how everyone is going to see you, and you know what? That's how the beautiful girl sees you, too—when other people are looking," Nico says.

My lips part to protest, but another student interjects, moving the topic to class systems and comparing fairy tales to Plato's *Republic*, which is probably what Mr. Huffman really wants to hear from us today. I let him talk, but I keep my eyes on Nico's. He looks at me for nearly a minute, and his sad expression hurts my chest. It hurts to watch him think, to know every word he just said was about me—about *us*. I see him, but I see everyone else's prejudices, too.

When the bell rings, Nico grabs his bag and board in a swift movement, slipping through the door the second it opens. I fumble with my things, perhaps not really wanting to catch him just yet. All this time, and I still haven't worked out the right things to say.

"Your dad...not real hip on you going out with Nico?" Izzy asks, hooking her arm through one of my bags and carrying it for me.

"We really haven't discussed it," I say.

"Even after you and I talked? You said your dad walked in and saw you guys *almost* kissing. That's not so bad," she says, and I twist my head and mash my lips. "Yeah, well...maybe it's bad. But more like *awkward* bad."

"My dad didn't say a single word to me at dinner. He actually talked to my brother, which—I'll admit—it was nice to see them talking, but then we drove home, and he went right into his room, and he acted like I was invisible Sunday."

Izzy nods in understanding, and we push through the main doors toward the locker rooms and parking lot. My friend slides my bag back to my arm, then squeezes her fingers around my wrist.

"I'm about to quote my mother, and I don't like that I'm doing this," she says, and I laugh lightly through my nose.

"Okay," I say.

"Sometimes, Reagan, you just need to rip off the damn Band-Aid," she says. "And it always hurts more when you do it slow."

"That's...I'm pretty sure your mother didn't come up with that," I say, squinting one eye and smiling on one side of my mouth.

"Yeah, I know. She repeats a lot of things like that. But still...she says it, and it's a good saying. Kinda applies here," she says, jiggling my hand in her hold.

I nod in agreement.

"Yeah, it does. Rip it, huh?" I say.

"Give it a good rip! Like, pull out the hair and shit," my friend says, and I wince at the color she adds to the visual. "Girl, your arms are hairy. That Band-Aid's gonna leave a mark."

I laugh as she walks away and rub my arm instinctively.

I don't bother going to my father's office. I know he won't talk to me, and I'm not ready to do the ripping just yet. But soon—I'll rip soon. I move out toward the field where the team is stretching, and I set up my things on the bench the cheer squad usually takes up during games. They practice inside during the week.

My eyes work to find Nico while my hands begin to unpack my equipment. It doesn't take me long to catch his familiar frame. He has a certain profile that I gravitate to, and he stands an inch or two taller than everyone else. I sit down with my tripod standing between my knees, pulling down the legs to click them in place.

"Seat taken?"

I heard my brother's familiar new gait scraping along the track. He's gotten faster on his crutches, and he's begun to put pressure on his cast from time to time. I'm not really glad he's come close to me. We haven't spoken much since our blowout. I am glad he's at practice, though. I look for positive signs in everything. This…it's a positive sign…*I think*.

"You thinking of joining the cheer squad, too?" I say, squinting as I look up to Noah, the sun bright behind him. I'm trying to be normal with him, even though I don't really want to.

"I do think I could probably up their game in the dance department," my brother says, pushing his tongue in his cheek and ultimately chuckling.

"They are pretty awful, aren't they," I say, sliding my bag closer to my hip so my brother has a place to sit.

"Nobody cares if cheerleaders can dance, Reagan. We watch them because their skirts are short and we like to look at their asses," he says, leaning his crutches along the metal bench and sliding down to sit, working to keep his leg straight.

"Keep it classy, Noah," I say.

"Always do," he says back quickly. He leans forward and pulls a bag of sunflower seeds from his pocket, pouring a handful into his palm and tipping his head back to dump them in his mouth. He holds the bag out for me, and I scrunch my nose at it.

"You've got something against sunflower seeds now, too?"

"I just don't like spitting," I say.

Noah leans forward and spits out three or four shell pieces at once, sending them to the ground like darts.

"That's the best part," my brother says, leaning back with his arms stretched out on either side. Even injured, my brother is larger than life. His build came with little effort, probably thanks to our dad's genetics. He's broad-chested and his arms have always bulged with muscles, from the time he hit puberty. He looks like a college man now, even if his maturity level says otherwise.

My dad walks through the center of the field, and his eyes settle on me and my brother, his mouth a hard line under the shadow cast by the brim of his hat. We both sit up a little straighter, holding our positions until he looks away.

"I hate it when you can't see his eyes," my brother says.

I chuckle, then turn my attention to my camera, focusing and recording some basic footage I might be able to use for B-roll. I fight my instincts to zoom in on Nico, spending extra time on Sasha and Zach and a few of the other guys until one of the coaches whistles for the players to pair up. I'm focusing on Travis when that happens, and I follow him through my lens as he stands up and walks to the other end of the field—to Nico.

"Wha…" I begin to say, catching myself, my mouth hanging open. I glance over to Noah, but he's still sitting in his upright position, maybe a little forward so he can spit out more shells. His eyes see it, too, though. I follow his line of sight, and I know he's watching them as they eventually shake hands. Nico lies down first, and Travis takes his leg and walks it forward in a stretch. I no longer care about the B-roll—I've moved on to voyeurism. I watch it all through my lens, and I see their mouths move, Travis smiling, maybe even laughing.

"Nico tell you that A&M is sending people out to watch homecoming?" Noah says, pouring a new handful of seeds into his palm, tilting, then chewing.

"No," I say.

"They are," Noah says, spitting again before leaning back into a relaxed position. He pulls his sunglasses from his hat and slides them over his eyes. "Specifically to watch those two."

Noah points his finger to the field, to the far end, where my camera is focused. I look into my lens, watching Travis help Nico to stand and trading positions with him.

"Is that why Travis is playing nice?" I ask, my stomach sinking because what a second ago I found hopeful has soured into pretend.

"Sorta," Noah says with a shrug.

My shoulders sag as my breath leaves my chest and I deflate. I blink slowly, taking in the view of my father walking over to the two boys, talking to them. Travis responds while Nico looks out in the distance. My dad stares at him, stepping in closer until Nico turns to make eye contact, finally nodding. The grudge, or chip, or whatever it is—it's still there.

"Why sorta?" I say finally.

Noah's quiet and doesn't answer for almost a minute. When he speaks, I think he's changing the subject.

"Mom found my pot," he says.

I burst out a laugh, then stop the recording on my camera.

"I'm pretty sure you don't want that on my video," I say.

"Whatever," Noah shrugs.

"I'll delete it," I say, glaring at him until he turns to look at me. I can't see his eyes, only my reflection in his sunglasses, but he gives me a nod of thanks.

He turns his gaze back to the field, and there's more chewing and spitting, and I start to think that's all he's going to tell me. I form my question in my head, dying to know how Mom found out, when Noah begins to share.

"I made Travis take me Saturday night. We buy from this guy in West End, and I guess he lives near Nico or whatever. I don't know; we always meet him at this small park on one of the corners. Anyhow, we walk up to the car, and the guy rolls down the window, and I give him my money, but he holds his hand out like he's waiting for more," Noah says.

His voice is even, and his eyes remain out on the field—the story coming out emotionless. My arms start to tingle with anxiety, so I tuck my thumbs in my fists and press them against my hips, frozen and rapt, hanging on his breath and waiting for the next word.

"I was like, 'dude, that's what I always pay you,' and the guy went on about how prices are going up, and he did me a favor last time. He said I owed him that from before, and he wasn't going to give me the bag. I started to get a little pissed off, but I could tell Travis was getting nervous, so I didn't get physical or nothing. I just sort of...maybe yelled at the guy a bit, called him a few names. He rolled the window down more, and I saw the piece sitting on the seat next to him."

"Jesus, Noah..." I hum, my lips tingling and my mind picturing every word he says.

"Yeah, I know," he says, glancing to me, but only briefly. "The guy was high on something. I could tell, and I don't think he was going to let us go without getting way more than we gave him. Especially since I'm on crutches; it's not like I could make a break for it."

"Oh my God, Noah. Why didn't you tell me about this? We need to file a police report, or do something, or..."

Noah chuckles and pulls his glasses down, turning to look me in the eyes.

"Reagan, I don't need to file a public document that says I was out buying drugs in West End," Noah says, his mouth set in a hard, serious

192

line.

I pull my lips in on one side and nod.

"Yeah, I guess you're right. I just…Noah, if Mom knew all of this…"

"Nico saw us," he interrupts.

I look up to find my brother's eyes still waiting for me, his expression unchanged.

"He…saw you?" I hold my breath, pushing my hands into my thighs harder, my shoulder tense and arms flexed.

"He walked up and got in the middle of shit that was going down. He told the guy that we were connected to someone that could bust him, third strike or something like that. The guy stared at him for a long time, and I was waiting for him to call bullshit, but eventually he just nodded and threw a bag at me. That's how Mom found it…"

"I don't understand," I say, my focus on him intense.

"I was so freaked out, I left it in Travis's Jeep. His mom got the call from your dad, about A&M, last night. He came over to tell me, and grabbed it on his way. He didn't want any of it near him, kind of freaked out about testing or shit I guess, and then I got distracted with his news, and then Dad came in to tell me that Texas was pulling their interest in me…"

"Wait," I say, holding up a hand. "Texas is pulling out?"

"Yeah, well…it's not like I'm putting up numbers this year, and other guys are so…"

"Noah," I say, my face falling in sympathy.

"Don't," he says, pushing his glasses back up and looking back out to the field. He spits the final few seeds from his mouth. "It sucks enough without you pitying me about it."

"You'll go somewhere else," I say.

"Maybe," he sighs.

I look back out at the field and watch the squads break out to run drills, Nico working with Travis. His movements are rigid, and he's throwing angrily—forcing the ball instead of letting it work naturally.

That's my fault.

"How'd Mom find your pot then?" I ask, greedily, wanting my brother's screwup for a distraction.

"I left it on the middle of my goddamned desk. Which, ha…I mean come on, I never have homework out on that thing or anything. I might as well have just tossed it to her," he says, laughing at himself.

"She probably would have just smoked it," I deadpan.

Noah snorts out a laugh.

"True statement," he says. "She said she's not going to tell Dad, so who knows. Maybe she'll keep it for herself."

I chuckle, but eventually my laughter fades. We both sit silently together watching The Tradition run drills. I quit filming several minutes ago, so I lean the tripod and camera back, hugging it to my chest, resting my chin on the top of it. It looks like any other practice, only that our practices never look ordinary. Things are off. The field is quiet, and players look tense. You can see it in their eyes—my dad's ultimatum. You can see it on my dad, too—the way he walks, hesitates, guards his words. He's snapping at players and coaches, but without the backup material he usually unleashes on them. Chad Prescott is known for calling players out on their weaknesses, but then he spends thirty minutes teaching them why and how to fix them. Today, he's just hurling insults.

"They all hate him," I say, not really expecting a response.

"Dad? Or Nico?" Noah responds. I turn and meet his gaze.

"Both of them," I shrug.

My brother looks at me and pulls his lips in tight, filling his chest with a long inhale. He turns to look back out on the field, and eventually pulls his crutches in his hands, lifting himself to stand.

"They don't hate Nico," he says, taking a few strides toward the field before stopping to talk to me over his shoulder. "They resent him. He's better than they are."

My brother swings his cast in long bounds on his crutches, crossing the track and eventually meeting Dad at the sidelines. They stand next to one another and watch the plays happen in front of them. Every time, my dad yells something. My brother doesn't react. He doesn't know what to say, how to fix things for Dad. He can't even make the right decisions for himself, but somehow I feel like maybe…maybe he's trying.

I watch as the frustration level grows, evident in my father's face—the red color it turns, the wrinkles deepening on his forehead, the tantrum he throws with his hat and clipboard. It isn't that any of the guys are making mistakes, it's just that they aren't playing with passion.

The same plays happen over and over, and players take turns running to the water station, drinking and rushing back to the field, almost as if they're afraid to take a break. Sasha gets too ill to continue eventually, Bob calling my dad over to tell him that he has to let him rest. My dad looks at Sasha, knowing that he isn't one of the ones he needs to motivate. Sasha will play for Nico, no matter what. My dad's hand comes down on Sasha's shoulder, and I watch as he grabs his gear and makes his way to the locker room and eventually his car, pulling out while the rest of the team keeps pushing on.

Nothing changes, no matter how many times they run through drills. An hour turns into two, and soon the sun is setting, and the field lights are buzzing above our heads—the bulbs warming. This practice is going to happen well into the night. My dad intends to keep them here until he sees a change. I don't know that he's going to get one.

And Nico—he's going to have to ride his board home eleven miles, in the dark.

My legs tired from sitting in the same position, I take my camera in my hands and stand, stretching them out and walking onto the field. Coach O'Donahue eyes me, and I acknowledge him with a wave, not wanting him to think he has any power to intimidate me. He doesn't wave back, but he does look away.

I move near my dad, behind the line where Nico is taking snap after snap from Colton while Travis sprints down the field, trying to catch up to his ball. Nico's overthrowing, and even though his arm should be dead tired, somehow his passes seem to get farther and farther out of reach.

"You know, Coach," Bob says, leaning in close to my father. I stand quietly between them, my camera rolling, my ears listening. "There's this saying they have about experiments, how if you repeat the same thing over and over again and get the same result, that maybe it's a sign you should move on and try something else."

"You think I should start Brandon, Bob?" my dad asks, his voice coming out clipped and his tone irritable.

Bob puts his hand on my father's back and pats it twice, leaving it in place while they both look out on another failed play in front of them.

"I think maybe you're coaching with something hot on your mind, and those boys—they can tell. I think maybe you can run them into the ground tonight all you want; won't change how they show up to play for you tomorrow. I've got no opinion on who you start at QB, Chad. I *do* have some thoughts on the man I see standing right here, though," he says, patting my father one more time before putting his hands in the front pocket of his sweatshirt and rolling his shoulders. "This ain't you, Chad. I know the boys disappointed you, and I know they're struggling, but this way? This has never been how you get things done. Besides, you keep this up, I'll be taping every single one of your players up just so they can make practice."

Bob spins and our eyes meet, his giving me a small wink. I smile at him on one side of my mouth, but don't turn when he walks back to the training bench. I keep my focus on my dad, the way he looks to the side and ruminates on the words Bob just said. My dad chews at the inside of his mouth, just like my brother always does—like Nico—and eventually pushes his whistle between his lips.

"All right, bring it in," he says.

His tired players fall in line, forming a half circle around him, each of them taking a knee, some of them pulling their jerseys off, taking off their pads, their bodies drenched despite the frosty air coming from their mouths. Fingers are pink with cold, and faces are red with heat. My father simply looks exhausted, the stands behind him dotted with boosters watching it all play out.

Everyone is on display.

Everyone is judging someone else.

"You worked hard today," my dad says, shaking his head, warding off saying the wrong thing. "We didn't get great results, but that...that's partly my fault." He rests his hand flat on his chest.

A few heads turn up to look at him, but most of his players are looking down. Nico is staring straight ahead, to the empty lot and the dark field he probably wishes he never left. I stare at him and let my body fill with regret. My eyes go directly to his lips, to the mouth that whispered the sweetest things against mine. I let my gaze travel to his chest and arms, to the way he kneels, balancing his weight on his helmet on the ground. His shoes are scuffed, and wrapped with tape, holding them to his feet. His body, so strong, is sheer exhaustion. Even so, I know if my father asked him to, Nico would stay out here until midnight—until the sun came up—throwing that pass again and again. He would throw until he got it right. And then, he'd keep going.

When I move back to his face, I flinch. His eyes are waiting for me, and I don't know how long they were. He stares at me, not blinking, and I look back into him. My father's voice fades to the background, and all I hear is the sound of his breath, despite being several feet away. Nico's chest rises and falls in slow, calculated draws, his face blurred periodically by the frost from the air escaping him. I never break my hold on his eyes though, and neither does he.

Were our tale one of the Grimms', it would end right here and right now. The earth would open up to swallow him whole in front of me. Fire would rain from the sky and burn us all, scorching and marring our skin. That man in the car in West End would kill my brother, and nobody would be able to stop him.

But Nico did.

Nico is the twist in the tale. He's the element of good. He's what humanity should be—the lesson to be learned. He is hope.

Nico stands, his eyes leaving mine, and I startle, realizing that everyone is breaking for the night. They all move to the center, and I fold my tripod up, and hug my camera again. My brother hops to the center with them, and my dad looks to Noah, urging him to send them all off.

"Whose house is this?" Noah shouts.

As broken as they are, as beaten and disheartened and filled with doubt, The Tradition answers.

"Our house!"

The chant plays out, and I find Nico's eyes in the sea of faces, his mouth screaming with just as much passion as it did the first time he chanted those words in the gym.

They don't hate you. They resent you, because you're better than they are.
You're better than us all.

The players all begin to step back, and before it's too late, I move into the crowd.

"Nico!" I shout. When he doesn't turn, I yell again. "Nico!"

I shout four times, Travis finally hearing me and nudging Nico on the arm. My hero turns toward me, but doesn't come. He's waiting…waiting for me to do something I should have done a long time ago, something I should have done Saturday, when my dad found us.

He's waiting for me to be proud to be his.

My eyes dart around the field, my heart pounding so hard I feel it in my fingertips. My body shivers from the cold, and I catch my father's eyes on me, just as I'm about to speak. I make a choice—this time, I choose differently. I rip the Band-Aid off.

"I'll wait for you right outside the locker room. Let me take you home," I say, my eyes pleading for him to say "okay." His lip quirks, just enough, and my lungs fill fast.

"Get a ride home with one of the guys," my dad interrupts, stepping closer to me.

I turn to look at my dad, his eyes on Nico, his expression one of authority.

"Dad, I can take him home. It's fine," I say.

"I'd rather you didn't, Reagan. It's late," my dad says, still not bothering to look at me while he speaks.

"It's not that late, Dad. And it's only eleven miles. I'll drive carefully, and…"

"Reagan!" my dad shouts, looking down, his chin at his shoulder, but his eyes still not on me. "That's enough. Go home. Don't worry, someone will give Nico a ride."

My body vibrates with my pulse, and every piece of me grows tense. Others are watching us now, watching me be scolded—watching my father want to protect me from this *at-risk boy*.

"I am not a child, Dad. If I want to give my boyfriend a ride home, I'm going to," I say, mentally lining up the next part of my argument. *I'll start buying my own gas. I'll save up and get my own car. I'll talk to Mom and see what she thinks. I'll make Noah come with us.*

"Nico, go on, get changed. I'm sure you understand," my dad says, his nostrils flaring. My face flushes red. I'm mortified, and I'm heartbroken. I open my mouth, ready to protest, but stop the moment he speaks.

"Yeah…I get it," Nico says, stepping into the space between me and my father, his head down until he stops right in front of my dad, lifts his chin and looks my father in the eyes. "I'm good enough to throw the ball for you, but I'm not good enough for your daughter."

"That's not it," my dad says, stopping short, shaking his head *no*, but lost for the words to go along with it. He has nowhere to go from there.

"Sure it is. You might not think that's what you mean, but…I bet you wouldn't have a problem with her driving up north, to Metahill. I just live eleven miles in the wrong direction."

"Nico…" my dad says, his weight shifts, his voice a little less urgent—less sure.

"Coach."

Nico stares my father in the eyes, not to intimidate, but to challenge, certainly. Several of his teammates are still around, including Colton and Travis, who both look on, their eyes fixed on the field between Nico and my father. It becomes clear soon that my dad isn't going to have a miraculous change of heart.

"It's okay, Reagan," Nico says, still facing my dad. "I can ride my board."

"I'll take you," Travis says.

"Thanks, yeah. See…it's fine, Travis will take me," he says, sucking his lip in and glancing down from my father, the disappointment evident to me…to everyone. "Hey," he says, turning and taking a few humble steps in my direction, his eyes soft over me, his mouth curling in the faintest smile. I start to shake my head *no*, no because I'm not willing to let this go. Nico nods *yes,* though, and reaches for my fingers, glancing down and smiling at our touch. "I'll call you when I get home."

He looks back up, staring into my eyes, and his dimple shows, though faint.

"You texted me, so I finally have your number," he says.

My eyes feel heavy, my brow drawn in as his hand slips away. He walks slowly to the locker room with Travis and Colton. Eventually, the rest of the team follows along, the coaches long gone, in their cars and on the road already. I'm left under the bright floodlights with my father and my brother, and all I can think about is how different the three of us are for people who share the same DNA.

"Reagan…" my father starts, and I cut him off, recognizing the tone. He's going to lecture me, explain how he knows best, how the neighborhood isn't safe, how this isn't about Nico at all, but I just can't hear it. I just can't, because that boy did nothing wrong, and neither did I. And I'm embarrassed.

"Don't," I say, closing my eyes.

"It's just that it's late, and you're only eighteen, and…"

"I said *don't*, Dad. Please, just…" I stop, and open my gaze on my father, his mouth set in a firm line.

The three of us stand silent, and I tug my equipment bag up my arm and fix my grip on the tripod, thankful when my father's phone rings. I look to my brother, who actually seems sympathetic, raising his shoulder in a slight shrug. "Could have gone worse," he whispers.

"I'm sorry…she…she's what?"

My dad pushes a finger in his open ear and holds the phone tight to his head, turning slightly away from me and my brother.

"Right…I see. Yes…I'll be right there," my dad responds, ending the call and staring at his phone screen, his body rigid, and his eyes not blinking.

"Dad? What is it?" I ask.

"Your mom," he says, and my pulse picks up as the blood leaves my head. I feel faint. My dad's eyes flit to me. "She drove the car through the garage…into the house."

"Oh my God!" I shout, holding my hand to my chest.

"Linda heard the noise and ran next door. She says Mom's high off her ass on marijuana. Where the hell would she get that?"

My dad looks back at his phone, as if it's going to give him any answers. My eyes grow wide, and I feel the earth pull me down as my blood rushes back through my body. My mouth is frozen open and dry as hell. I tell myself repeatedly not to say a word, when my brother falls on the sword that's been waiting for him for weeks…probably months.

"Fuuuuuccckkk," he breathes, his eyes closing and his head tilting to the sky.

Noah Prescott may as well get used to those crutches, because in less than an hour, I'm pretty sure our father is going to break his other leg.

CHAPTER 16

"So, let me get this straight," Izzy says, her phone cutting in and out while she moves around her house. "Your brother...has to pee in a cup."

"Yep."

When Noah and I got home from practice last night, chaos does not even begin to describe the scene we walked into. It seems the good ladies of the social committee for the Cornwall boosters decided to organize a coup—meeting at Jimmy O'Donahue's house with his wife, Tori. After an hour, Tori had sold the other women on her idea: Lauren Prescott was not the best fit for the new direction The Tradition social committee needed to go in. According to Travis's mom Linda, the women were concerned that my mom had too much on her plate with Noah's injury and "recent challenges." What they meant was my brother was becoming a slacker, druggie asshole, and it was a convenient excuse to push my mom out.

Linda got to my mom first, just after quitting the committee herself. She told us my mom was quiet, but seemed to take the news all right, saying that it was almost a relief, and that it would give her time to maybe focus on her own health. Then, when Linda went home, my mom tore into Noah's pot and smoked herself into a fit of paranoia. She drove through the garage thinking the car was in reverse. When Linda found her, she was giggling hysterically.

"How's your mom?" Izzy asks.

I tuck my phone in the crook of my neck so I can slip my Vans on my feet.

"She's…okay, I guess. I haven't really talked to her. She's still sleeping, and Dad left already. I mean, I guess it's like nothing happened really, only…there's a big-ass hole in our house covered up with plywood and plastic, and my brother isn't allowed to have a door. I mean, for real—Dad removed it," I say, grabbing my bags and looking over my shoulder at the gaping doorway that leads to Noah's room.

He went to school early with my dad—another thing he'll be doing until my dad decides to let him off the extremely-short leash.

"I can't believe no one got arrested," Izzy says.

"I know, but really, it was more about the insurance claim and fixing the garage," I say, stopping outside our front door to slip my key in and lock up. When I turn around, I startle to see Nico leaning against a car, parked at the curb in front of my house. "Hey, Izz. I gotta go."

I don't even bother to wait for her goodbye. I hang up, slip my phone in my pocket and walk up to my boyfriend. He waits for me to get close before pushing off the brown, four-door, boxy contraption he drove here in. There's a dent in the back side-passenger door, and a bungie cord wrapped around the front bumper, holding it up.

"Whatcha got here?" I ask, my heart fluttering—*actually fluttering*—when he reaches down and grabs my hand in his without hesitation. He pulls it to his mouth and kisses my knuckles, grinning against them.

"It's just a loaner…for now. My uncle says if I can fix it up enough, I can keep it. He got a new car, and this one's not really worth enough to sell," Nico says, turning to nudge the tire with his toe. "This sucker's twenty-seven years old, two-hundred-thousand miles and counting."

"Wow, I don't think we've ever had a car hit six digits," I say.

"Anything will last if you give it enough love," he says, shooting me a quick, crooked smile.

"You're corny," I say.

Nico swings the passenger door open, then steps close enough to me that his lips find my neck. I get a peek at the smirk on his face as he slides his mouth closer, eventually dusting my skin with a soft kiss while he tucks my hair out of the way.

"Just this once," he says.

He pulls back, and our eyes meet, my arms dotted with goosebumps and my neck and chest warm from his touch.

"I wanted to take you to school. If that's all right," he says.

I peer over his shoulder and squint, studying the seat, then bring my hand to my chin, as if I'm considering my options. He tilts his head to the side and sighs, so I give in.

"My chariot awaits," I say.

"Well, it'll be chariot-worthy one day, but for now, it's a Toyota Camry without a working heater," he says, grimacing.

I pull the hoodie up from my sweatshirt and show him my hands inside my sleeves.

"I think I'll be fine," I say.

Nico smiles crooked, then takes my bags and puts them in the back seat while I slide into the front. He gets in with me, and we drive to school in a tense sort of quiet. His radio isn't on, so I'm assuming it probably doesn't work, and the heater does work—periodically—the blowers blasting air one second and completely cutting out the next. We idle at the last light before school, and Nico leans between us, touching the vent in the middle, and just as his finger reaches it, it sends a shot of air into his face that blows the hair from his eyes.

I suck in my lips trying not to laugh, but when he turns to face me, his hair spread haphazardly around his forehead, until he blows it out of his way, I lose it and laugh hard and loud.

"All chariots have glitches," he says.

I smile, and he moves his hand into mine, threading our fingers. I look at them, locked together, for the last block to school. Nico pulls into an open space in the last row for visitors, and I kick myself for not grabbing my parking pass for him to use.

"I'm sorry you have to park so far; I didn't think…"

Nico stops me, leaning forward and pressing his lips to mine. He pulls away, and his lips stretch into a wide grin.

"I wanted to park down here. I need to talk to your dad," he says, and for some reason, he's still smiling instead of scowling.

"You…want to talk to my dad?" I repeat it like a question.

"Uh huh," he says, pushing his door open with his foot, hopping out and jogging around the front before I have a chance to open my side.

"You…I don't know…want me to come with you?" I ask. My stomach twists. I'm still reeling from ripping the first Band-Aid off. I'm not so sure I'm keen to go ripping again so early.

"Nah, I got this. I'll see you at lunch, okay?"

Taking my hand, he lifts me up to him, his fingers catching my chin softly and his head falling against mine.

"Mmmmm, okay," I say, letting my eyes fall closed.

We stand like this for a few seconds, until I feel him take a deep breath and step away. I load up my bags on my arms and give him one last glance, my eyebrow raised on one side in question. He nods with a smile and squeezes his eyes shut, letting me know he's sure and it will be okay. I believe him for about ten seconds. I start to worry again when I get to the main door for the school, and I turn around just in time to see him standing in front of the film-room door. He's jumping and swiveling his head from side to side, like a boxer about to get the shit kicked out of him by the heavyweight champion of the world.

When I was a freshman here at Cornwall, there was a girl—a senior—whose parents went through a very public, and very hostile divorce. It wasn't the kind of separation that played out behind closed doors, or in courtrooms. It was the kind where cars were spray-painted with words like BITCH or MANWHORE when they were left unattended in the school parking lot for any longer than a minute. The girl, Jill, ended up dropping out over the holiday break, unable to cope with the whispers and stares from the rest of the student body.

My mother drove her car through our house.

I have become Jill.

I was ready for it, for the most part. I navigated the questions from curious people in my first period. With Izzy's help, we managed to answer all of the inquiries from the rest of the cheerleaders without ever divulging that my mom was high and that it was because of my brother's pot. Third period is advanced chemistry, and the people in that class with me are so hardcore about academics, they couldn't give a rip about the gossip I stirred.

By noon, I'd made it through the first half of the day with only a few things shouted in the hallway and some laughs behind my back. I was head and shoulders above Jill, and so far ahead of my brother, who was now also forced to eat lunch with our father in his office—daily.

For the first time in days, maybe even weeks, I was feeling comfortable...almost relaxed. I think that's why I didn't see it coming.

I entered the cafeteria and slid into line easily, spotting Nico at a table in the center, waiting for me. I balanced my tray carefully in one hand, gripping the side while my arm shook with the weight of it and my equipment bag. I held my tripod under my other arm, and was nearly through the line and on my way to Nico when a girl with long brown hair flipped my tray into my chest. She pounded the tray with her palm so hard that I lost my balance and fell back hard on my ass. The impact forced the air from my lungs, and I let out a gasp, catching the attention of anyone who may have possibly missed what went down.

I had no idea who the girl was, but she called me a bitch and told me to stay away from Nico. All I could do was sit there and blink. I'm still blinking, but now my arms are tingling with anger and my mind is racing through all of the things I should have said.

"I can't believe I didn't hit her back," I say to Izzy.

She's holding my shirt out over the sink, soaking it with water from a wad of paper towels. I spilled pizza and Coke down the front of my favorite T-shirt—a white V-neck with lyrics from my favorite song written on the front. My brother bought it for me two Christmases ago, and I know he had it made special, because my favorite band isn't big, and they most definitely don't have swag items.

"Hold still," Izzy says, jerking my shirt forward more.

"You're going to stretch it out," I huff.

She stops scrubbing and puts her hand on her hip, her lips pursed while she looks at me.

"Your shirt is covered in today's lunch special. Do you really think a little stretching is going to be the worst thing left behind?"

"Sorry," I shrug.

She rolls her eyes and continues scrubbing, and after a few minutes, I notice the smirk on her face.

"What's so funny?" I ask.

"You…Nico," she says.

"We're funny?"

"Yeah…kind of."

I stare at her eyelids while she looks down at my shirt, her fingers working away the last remnants of the stain. She flits her eyes to mine eventually, then tosses the wet towel into the trash and takes a step back.

"That's as good as it's going to get," she says.

"Thanks," I say, standing and straightening my shirt with one hand and rubbing my tailbone with the other. I catch my friend's reflection in the mirror, and raise my eyebrows at her when I notice she's still smirking.

"You know what that girl said when she marched out of the cafeteria with her friends behind her?" Izzy says.

"No, what?" I ask, not sure I really want to know.

"She said she couldn't believe Nico Medina was hitting it with some skinny white girl," Izzy says, laughing out the last three words.

My brow pinched, I turn my attention back to my reflection, my hands around my waist, measuring. I guess I'm skinny. And I know I'm white. I'm practically freaking clear, my arms and legs are so pale.

"Quit judging yourself, Reagan. That's not why I told you that," she says, and I glance back to her in the mirror. She shakes her head and breathes out a small laugh. "It just made me think. There is always going to be someone who doesn't like the idea of two people together. Black, white, Latino, gay, rich, poor—it's all just shit we make a big deal out of, Reagan. Shit...I don't like the idea of your brother dating Katie Loftgrin."

My eyebrows shoot up to my forehead because—my brother? Izzy?

"Yeah, well...so what. I have a crush on your brother. I don't *really* want to date him, but it doesn't mean I want someone like Katie dating him," she says, her eyes darting around the bathroom as she realizes just how much her voice echoes in here. Her cheeks redden.

"Izzy?" I whisper, turning to face her for real.

"I've kind of liked him since we were kids. And maybe that's the only reason, really. And it's stupid, my beef with Katie, but you know what? I don't think your brother should be with a girl whose family is so rich that they *literally* own a jet. I don't think he should date a girl who has no concept of the game of football."

"Izzy, you don't really understand football..."

"Oh, I understand it enough!" she interrupts me.

I pull my lips in tight and try not to laugh at her, at how ridiculous she's being, but I can't hold it in, and when I finally do laugh, she rolls her eyes and starts to pick up her things.

"I didn't tell you so you'd make fun of me," she says.

I grab her arm to stop her.

"I'm sorry," I say, still smirking, but slowly regaining control. "I know...I know you didn't. Why did you tell me?"

"I told you because people are prejudiced for a lot of stupid reasons. That girl? Her name is Lexie, and she thinks you're too white to deserve the boy she likes. She's from West End. *He's* from West End. You're...not. How could you even begin to get their world?" my friend says.

"I know..." I begin, set to agree with her, but she shakes her head, cutting me off.

"No, that's not it. Reagan, your world...Nico's world...same fuckin' world. You come from different parts, but who cares? You meet in the middle. You meet here, this place—we're all going to Cornwall. Nico came here from West End. You're here because your dad's the coach. I'm here because my parents went here. We all have our own stories, and they part and intersect in many different places. It's what makes us individuals. And no matter who we decide to tie our story to, there is always going to be someone who thinks they know the secret about why someone fits or doesn't fit."

My friend reaches forward, taking the hem of my shirt in both of her hands and pulling it out to study it, to see if the stain is gone. She says the rest with her eyes down.

"Some people are racist. Some people are jealous. Some people are just fucking ignorant," she says, her eyes coming up to meet mine as her fingers let go of my shirt. "Don't let someone else dictate how your heart feels about someone. I will never say a word to Katie Loftgrin, no matter how...*jealous*...I am of her relationship with Noah. I won't, because all of those reasons I make up to hate her? I know I've made them up without really knowing her story. And I know it isn't fair. I strive to be better than that."

"You may just be the best human at Cornwall," I say to my friend.

She chuckles as she steps closer to the mirror, pulling her lip gloss from her purse and touching up the pink, dragging her nail along the corner of her mouth to make sure the line is perfect.

"Yeah, well...you tell your brother any of this and I'll cut you," she says with a straight face. I laugh at first, but stop when she isn't. Her eyes dart to me in the mirror, and a few seconds pass before she winks. I laugh then, but still am not certain she was kidding about her threat.

I follow Izzy out of the bathroom, and Nico jumps up from the floor where he's been sitting with his back against the wall.

"Hey, you okay?"

His eyes are lowered, and his brow is pulled in.

"My shirt smells like pizza and cheap powdered soap. Other than that, I'm good," I say.

He tugs both of my wrists forward, my body following until my head falls against his chest.

"I'm sorry about that. I went out with Lexie our freshman year, and I was immature and maybe didn't end things well. She's been a little possessive of me ever since, and…"

"And I'm a stupid white girl," I say, going for self-deprecating, but when I hear the words out loud, I realize how ridiculous they are.

"One, you are not stupid," Nico says, pulling me forward and kissing my forehead softly. I blush when I notice a few girls walking by in the corridor spot us and whisper to each other with a giggle. "And two, I wouldn't care if you were green. Me liking you…you liking me. That's kind of *our* deal, and that's all that matters, okay?"

He slides his hands up to either side of my face, his forehead rolling against mine. The hallways are beginning to fill up with the rush after lunch while students hurry to class, and I know people are looking at us. I've never really been affectionate with someone in public, especially here at school. Maybe being coach's daughter has *always* put me off limits in some way, but standing here, being held like this by Nico— being adored…

My face reddens from the attention I know we're getting, but my tummy warms because for once, it's me standing in the hallway like this with a boy. It isn't some girl with Travis, my brother and Katie, or some other girl he's been dating, Izzy, one of the cheerleaders—*it's me*. The blush is good.

"You like me," I tease, biting my bottom lip.

Nico chuckles.

"Yeah, I *more* than like you, Reagan. I asked your dad if I could take you to homecoming, and we were all alone," Nico says, and my breath stops with his confession. That's what he was doing this morning.

"Oh my God…" I say, my eyes falling shut, the blush growing hotter. "What…what did he say?"

The warning bell sounds, and the flurry of activity grows louder as students begin to rush to the next period. Nico steps back, and I worry when I look at his face that his expression isn't going to be very positive. I'm almost shocked when I see the dimple.

"There was a lot of silent staring, which was…well…let's just say I lost my first staring competition," Nico chuckles.

I cringe.

"No, no…" he says, lifting my chin. "He gave me a bit of a lecture. He wanted to know what car I planned on driving, and I took him out to the lot, to see my ride. He kicked the tires. He flipped the hood up and pulled on a few things, then sat in the driver's seat."

"That's…okay, I guess…that's good?" I say, hopeful.

"I think it was good. He told me if I wanted to ever throw a football again, that the seats better stay in the upright position, which made me want to die a little," he says.

"I think I just did…die I mean," I say, my brow pulled in so far it's practically folded.

Nico takes a step or two back, his backpack over one shoulder and his eyes on me as he winks. "You just worry about making sure that you wear comfortable shoes and a dress. I plan on admiring you in my arms all night—so no sitting in the dark corner and hiding at a table. You and I are going to dance to every shitty song that gets played."

I swallow, because…dancing. But I also grin. It hurts my cheeks, and when I turn around, not a single person cares about any of it.

Practice had a certain air to it today. I want to think that it's just the old adage *what a difference a day makes,* but I think maybe it's something more. Players seem to be responding to not just Nico, but my dad. The same drills that were nothing but disastrous yesterday, seem effortless today. I'm about to chalk it all up to the flu or a miracle when Noah takes the bench next to me again and points out the *real* reason.

"You see 'em?"

He gestures to the far corner of the field on the away side, four men all dressed in maroon and white sweatshirts and polos sitting with sunglasses gleaming the sun from their faces.

"A&M?" I ask.

"Yup," Noah says, adjusting his position next to me, jutting his leg out.

I watch the four men, and while they talk to one another, they don't talk often. Their conversations stop the moment Nico has the ball. There are a few seconds of phones coming out, notes perhaps being typed, but other than that, their presence is subtle.

Subtle, but felt like the goddamned Goodyear blimp.

"Thank God everyone's got their shit together today…so far," I say, holding my breath while Nico steps back and pumps the ball once before releasing it deep to Travis. The catch is effortless; the throw is perfect. The reaction is…*restrained.*

"We had a little team meeting, before they came out to stretch," Noah says, leaning to the side and spitting out fragments of seeds.

"Why are you obsessed with seeds lately?" I ask, and he turns to me, pulling his sunglasses down and glaring. "Exactly how much pot were you smoking?"

Noah presses his lips into a hard line.

"Oh," I say.

He turns back to the field, and I do, too, at first, but then his words from before catch up to me.

"You…had a team meeting?"

I glance at him, but he isn't engaging me, so I keep my eyes on the field, my stomach muscles relaxing a little every time a play hits the mark on the field. I let my question linger out there, hoping he'll answer…eventually.

"Part of my penance," Noah says finally, and I give in and look at him again. He won't look at me, but he doesn't pause. "Dad said he was losing the team, losing their respect. He knows Nico's the only way they're going to have a shot at anything this year."

My brother spits out the rest of his seed shells and works his tongue over his teeth. It's gross when he does this, and I worry that my brother is going to turn into a chewer. His ability to form habits comes so naturally.

"What do you think?" I ask.

He's quiet for several seconds, but I can tell he's thinking...maybe even hesitating a little. Honesty hurts him. It always has.

"I think Nico's the best quarterback we've ever had," he says, pulling the bag from his pocket and tossing it to the ground with disgust when he sees it's empty. "I fuckin' hate him for it."

"But that's not his fault," I defend.

"I know," Noah says. "Doesn't mean I don't anyway."

I breathe in slowly, letting my shoulders rise while my chest expands, my attention moving back to the four men in the bleachers, one of them now on the phone.

"He treat you right?" Noah asks.

I pinch my brow, wondering why he cares. I decide that I want my brother to care, and I also want to quit hating him a little, too.

"He does," I say, unable to prevent the smile that sneaks in on my lips. I pull my sleeve over my palm and chew at the edges.

"Good," Noah says.

It's quiet between us as we both let the action on the field take over our conversation for most of the time. When the players break though, that gap that still exists—the one left after my brother embarrassed me, after we fought, after this week and all that's happened—it begins to feel like a bleeding wound.

It was time we sucked it up and closed it.

"I still haven't interviewed you...for my *film*," I say, adding a little tinge to the final word—bringing him back to that night in the parking lot, when he took cheap shots at me to make himself feel better.

Noah doesn't answer immediately, but I can see from my sideways glance that I hit a nerve. His jaw works in and out, and I know from years of sleeping one room away from him that he's grinding his back teeth together because I've made him uncomfortable.

"Wanna do it now?" he says finally.

I'm a little surprised. I expected my defensive brother. I was anticipating him to say something to the effect of "look, I'm sorry, all right?"

I was waiting for excuses.

"I'd love to," I say, pulling my gear out and setting up a shot of him here on the bench. I frame just enough of the action behind him to blur it to the background, and Noah glances over his shoulder while I finish getting ready.

"Is that your way of getting back at me?" he asks.

I pause and glance up, my mouth quirked on one side in question.

"Me here, all broken and busted, and the game I love behind me," he says.

I stare at him, blinking slowly.

"I'm just giving the shot context. I don't do things to be cruel," I say, realizing as I speak that that…what I just said? I said it to be cruel. My brother leaves his eyes on me, and they narrow while he works his lips, mashing them with perhaps his internal thoughts of exactly how mean he has been to me. I plan on asking him about it, in three, two…

"Let's talk a little bit about your injury. Since you broke your leg, you've been distant…maybe even…harsh…to those you love. Talk about the struggle," I say, pushing my face to the camera, my eye on the viewer. I don't want to make eye contact with him right now; I want to shoot for honesty, and I can't risk having him intimidate me.

Noah shakes with a silent laugh, then looks down at his hands while he cracks his knuckles. His head falls from one side to the other with his thought, and then he glances to the side as a whistle sounds in the background. A slow smile plays on his lips.

"Do you know what it's like to love something so much that it's the only thing you can see in your future?"

I take in Noah's question, and wait for his gaze to swing back to the camera.

"Yes. I do believe I know what that's like," I say, moving my head up enough to let my eyes hit his briefly. I keep my mouth in a hard line, and I connect with him just long enough for him to breathe out another laugh and blink to look down.

"Yeah, I guess you do," he says.

I wait, letting the silence sink in and keep my camera tight on Noah's face, his passion playing out behind him, obscured but recognizable.

"You know what the doctor said when they set my leg?" Noah asks.

"No…what?" I respond.

He chews at the inside of his mouth and then looks up, but not quite to the camera.

"He said my break was nothing more than just dumb luck," he says.

He doesn't smile or laugh. His mouth falls, and his lips curve down slightly. His eyes make their way back to me through the lens.

"Dumb luck," he repeats, his mouth held open, as if he's working out the words that follow. "I am losing the future I thought I had. I'm going to end up playing for some school that has no shot in hell of being seen by anyone, and then I'm going to graduate with some degree I don't even know how to use because football, Reagan? It's the only goddamned thing I know. What does that mean for me? Why am I even bothering? There's a part of me that just…hell…"

I swallow, because I know. I've watched him give in. I've watched him quit. He's given up.

"You're too good to give up," I say.

"Am I?" he asks.

I nod, not speaking.

"Tell me why you love this game, and being a part of The Tradition?" I ask.

Noah shifts his weight and looks out to the right. The team is breaking for water behind him, and our father is walking across the field slowly in our direction, just out of the camera's view.

"When I started? I wanted to make Dad proud," Noah says. My father is too far to hear it, and I know it's why he said it now.

"Okay, but why keep going?" I ask, pushing him for more.

He leans forward, his leg stretched out in the only position it can rest, his hands on his knees, his fingers flexing around the caps.

"Because being the son of a man who had a legacy, though not big…it puts thoughts in your head. You start to think you can beat that legacy. You start to think people expect you to at least meet it. And then, there's this weird life we have because this team…it's so important to people. And the way they look at Dad when he wins? The way they treat us when we lose? It's fucked up, Reagan…"

He pauses, and holds up a hand to apologize for swearing.

"It's okay. It's a documentary. Speak like you really do," I say.

"Fine, well…yeah, then. It's fucked up," he says, his eyes low again, his lids blinking. I feel our father's presence behind me. That's why Noah isn't talking, and I start to tell him we can finish this up later, but he looks right into the lens and doesn't give me the chance.

"As screwed up as it is to live your lives for a game, I still wouldn't trade it for anything in the world. Getting to lead these guys, getting to have them look up at me…have the alumni look up to me, the boosters…*Dad*—well, I imagine that's what it's like for people that get voted into seats in Congress or get to run major corporations. It's such an unbelievable privilege. And I lost it, because of…*dumb luck.*"

Noah glances over my shoulder, and I know he's looking at our dad.

"Doesn't mean I don't still want to see them win, see Dad win. Doesn't mean I don't believe in them…without me. I just hate it. It hurts more than anything I've ever known," Noah says.

"You'll get it back," our father says, his voice carrying from over my shoulder. I don't turn, instead keeping my focus on my brother's face. He chuckles to himself quietly, but keeps his eyes on our dad's.

"You think so?" he asks.

"I know so," Dad says. "Dumb luck be damned. It hasn't seen the spirit of a Prescott boy pissed off at the world."

Noah's lips twist as he tries to keep his smile in check. The right side finally lifts high enough that he gives in and smiles, nodding.

"True story," he says.

"True story," my father echoes.

I cut the camera off, and step away.

"We're going to see if we can work on a few of the blitz plays, teach Nico how to read them and avoid them. Think you're up for helping?"

My father stands with his hand out for my brother, and after a second, Noah takes it and lets my dad help him up to a stand. He pulls his crutches under his arms and swings a step or two away from the bench.

"I'd love to," he says.

I wish I'd gotten that on film. But maybe…maybe some things are meant to be private.

I watch them both begin to walk away, but before my brother gets too far, he stops, urging my dad to keep walking. Noah takes a few swinging strides back in my direction, stopping, his weight propped up on his crutches.

"Your video isn't stupid," he says.

"I know," I say, proud that I had that response ready.

Noah smirks, looking down at his feet and nodding.

"I was a dick to say that the other night," he says.

"I know," I say again, twice as proud this time.

Noah laughs.

"I deserve that," he says.

"Yes, you do," I say.

"We good then?" he asks.

"Not even close," I say. His eyes flash to mine, and I let my lip curl the tiniest bit on the right side, just to ease his conscience enough that he can get through today. I don't want him off the hook, but I do want my brother back.

"A'right then," he says, smiling enough that I know he knows I love him, and that I'm still pretty mad. He ambles toward the team—still very much his team, and he moves in next to our dad, trying to find his place now…whatever that is.

CHAPTER 17

The evening air is unusually warm, and I'm thankful. Cornwall always holds the homecoming dance directly after the game. It's one of the few incredibly typical things that we have here, but even still, it's always made into something bigger than it really is or needs to be.

Paper decorations go up around the gym walls, and bleachers are pushed in to make room. Lights are off, special kinds brought in to set the mood. We hire a deejay. All of that is fairly normal, but then expectations are placed on everyone and everything. Dresses are the best. Couples are judged, while whispers begin to pick up the week before about who is going with whom, why they broke up with someone else, or if they're going to *hook up* after the dance.

My dress is three years old. It's white, eyelet style—the hem falling just above my knees. The sleeves are straps, and I left my sweater in my car since the weather was so nice. However, now all I can think about are my bare, freckled shoulders. The skirt is an A-line because those are the only types of dresses that don't make me think about my hips. I wore it last year, when I came with Travis, but spent most of my time with Izzy. While this afternoon, when I slipped it on during my dash home before the game, I told myself I was fine with wearing the same thing two years in a row, now—sitting on the first row of bleachers with my mom and Travis's mom, Linda—I feel like maybe I should have tried harder.

"What is Katie wearing," my mom asks, almost a whisper.

My brother's girlfriend will be wearing something designer and new. She does for everything. So will Izzy.

So will every other girl going to the dance.

"I don't know," I say, my attention on the field.

There are five minutes left in the fourth quarter, and we are up 38-14. Nico has had a spectacular game, running the ball in twice on his own and connecting with both Travis and Sasha for twenty-plus yard passes in the end zone. I've been splitting my time focusing on his game and the booth filled with maroon-and-white shirts up above. I left my camera recording on its own for the night on top of the box, but I amped up the mic, just in case it might be able to pick up their conversation. Now, though, I doubt I'll even listen. Nico has been so impressive, there's no way they don't want him.

"I would have taken you shopping," my mom says next to me.

I turn to respond, but see she's still looking out on the field. I think her feelings are hurt that I didn't ask. She's just been so erratic the last few days that I didn't want to push things with her. I wasn't sure what version of my mom I would get—the one who says she's fine with being off the social committee, who says she hates those women and can't wait to see how great her life is without them, or the one who not-so-secretly cries about it all in the bathroom.

"I just really like this dress," I settle on saying.

My mom looks over and runs her hand down the fabric, folding it over my knee and patting my leg.

"You look beautiful," she says, and I can tell she means it. It warms my chest.

"Thanks, Mom," I say, placing my hand on hers, threading our fingers, and squeezing.

The game clock is ticking down quickly now. St. Augustine isn't a very strong squad, and we've run them ragged. My dad lets Brandon take the final set of downs, and Nico joins Colton and several of the other guys—including my brother—near the middle of the field on the sidelines. Helmets off, they all seem light and happy, a different mood from the one that has dominated practices this week. They've worked hard, and tonight...it showed.

With only a few seconds on the clock, I stand and begin to straighten out my dress, suddenly even more aware of my curled hair, my lack of lipstick, my self-applied eyeshadow and blush. I can't see my reflection, but in my imagination, I look like an ill-prepared clown. I start to fidget with my hands when I glance around the stands and see the other moms and booster parents—the crowd that just last week sat down here, with my mom.

I glance to my mom and see she's looking at them, too.

"You're better off without them," I say.

She looks to me and smiles, but it doesn't quite reach her eyes.

"I told them I was stepping down, too, but they made me promise to finish this godforsaken barbecue tomorrow," Linda says.

"You don't have to step down; I told you that," my mom tells her friend—maybe her *only* friend.

"Lauren, I hate those women. I've been dying to be done with this. Way I see it, you've given me six extra weeks of my life back," she says.

My mom smiles bigger now.

The clock hits zero, and the cheers aren't as loud as normal with most of the fans already leaving, rushing toward the gym doors or to the field exit to take photos with their sons and boyfriends. I make eye contact with Nico, and he bunches his hand in a wave. His mom had a church event tonight. She made him promise her he would take photos of the two of us. I know my mom won't leave without snapping a few of her own, so I'll make sure she takes some with our phones.

I watch as Nico talks to Colton, and I see my father walk up next to him, along with my brother—the four of them making their way slowly through the crowd, up the walkway to the locker rooms, until they disappear into the darkness.

"I'm really looking forward to meeting him," my mom says.

I smile at her, but let it slip a little when I turn away. I'm nervous about them meeting, because my mom has been so odd about it, almost like she's overcompensating for her questions she has. She's asked me about Nico's family, his home, his brother, his niece, his car, his grades, his voice, his height, his looks—it was a piecemealed interrogation of sorts to get a picture in her head of what this boy from West End is like. I went on a double date with Izzy over the summer, and I don't even think my mom asked the boy's name. He was a friend of Izzy's family, and that was good enough.

I joked, finally, telling my mom that we didn't live in *West Side Story*, and we weren't the Jets and Sharks. She rolled her eyes at me, but her constant questioning still came.

I lead her to the walkway outside the locker rooms, and I wait nervously while more people gather around us. My white dress begins to feel less and less formal as girls walk up in sequins and silk. Hair is done up in twists, and one girl has diamonds embedded into a braid that wraps around her head.

"That's lovely," my mom says, pointing it out to me. I smile and nod, all the while feeling my stomach grow tighter. My hair is straight, but curled on the ends. I thought I was really going the extravagant route by blowing it out.

My eyes fall to my feet, to the only fancy thing I have on—a pair of wrap-up wedges that zigzag around the top of my feet and crawl halfway up my calves. I take refuge in the fact that at least my feet look like they belong here.

Several of the players are starting to exit, and there are squeals and flashes from cameras as girls meet their boys. My eyes dart around, and I offer fake smiles to anyone I make eye contact with, concealing the rolling nerves playing out in my stomach and chest.

My father finally walks through the metal door, and when he spots us, he raises his lip on one side and runs his hand over his face while he walks over. He stops a few steps shy and holds his hand over his mouth, nodding.

"She looks nice, doesn't she?" my mom says, reaching out and touching the skirt of my dress again, making it sway briefly along my legs.

My dad lets his hand fall, and his eyes focus on my waist for a long while, his expression something foreign. He begins to nod again as his eyes make their way to mine, and he steps in closer, pulling a small box from his front pocket. I glance to my mom, whose lips are still in a tight smile, and then back to my dad. His fingers tremble while he works open the small, beaten-up box, and he pulls out a thin, silver chain with a star on the end made out of stone.

"I'm not real good with jewelry and stuff, but your mom said I picked all right," he says, unhinging the clasp and nodding for me to lift my hair and turn. I do as he says, and he loops the necklace around my neck, the weight of the star comforting against my collarbone. I hold it between my fingers as I spin back into him.

"Daddy," I say, my head falling to the side, and my eyes matching his. I understand that look now, and it's the kind that can only be explained by the special bond between a girl and her father.

My dad clears his throat, and takes a step back, his eyes falling to his feet and his hands going to his pockets. I pinch my brow, but quickly realize what he's reacting to. I turn to see Nico, his hair wet and combed back, and his equipment bag stuffed with pads and clothes at his side. He's wearing a dark-gray button-down, a black tie, and black slacks. His shoes are shiny, like a patent leather, and in his other hand is a plastic box with a deep-blue flower and ribbon. He follows my gaze to his hand and lifts it up.

"Oh, I…I brought a corsage. It's a little wilted…I left it in my locker during the game," he says, his eyes meeting mine in brief snapshots, his lips caught in a forever kind of smirk that is pushing his dimples deep into his cheeks.

"Here," my dad says, reaching for Nico's bag. "I'll take your things home. You can get them when you drop Reagan off tonight."

"Oh, thanks," Nico says, handing his bag to my father. They don't

222

make eye contact, and the awkward exchange is somewhat amusing.

"Yeah, well, I'm holding your things hostage until I get her, and if you're a minute late…" My dad lets his words trail off as he pushes his tongue into his cheek. Nico blinks a few times, then chuckles.

"Yes, sir," he says.

"I'm not kidding," my dad says.

"Oh, I know," Nico responds.

He takes my hand in his, and his eyes flit to mine, words perched on his lips. He doesn't speak, but I can tell he wants to, and the look on his face makes me blush. He holds the cluster of flowers to the top of my wrist, turning my hand and tying the ribbon on the underside, just above my palm. The soft material dusts along my skin, and tickles, but I leave it as he tied it, grateful for the reminder that it's there. Blue flowers have fast become my favorites.

"Well, Nico," my mom says, shooting my father a glance that warns him. He raises his brows and takes a step back so my mom can move in closer. "It is such a pleasure to meet you."

My stomach is pattering heavily with butterflies, and I wait for something to go wrong as my mom takes Nico's hand. I've run through the dozens of embarrassing things she could say, based on the questions she asked about him, including what country he was from.

"*This* one," was what I told her. She responded with a surprised "oh," and that was the last question she asked.

"Nice to meet you, too, Mrs. Prescott. Thank you for coming to our game," Nico says.

My mom's head tilts to one side, and she keeps his hand in hers. Her gaze comes to me, and I smile tightly, widening my eyes, mentally begging her to let go of his hand. She finally does, but looks back to him.

"I don't miss a single game, Nico. Haven't in years," she says. "I have to say, you've given our family a reason to be hopeful this season."

"Noah's shoes are hard to fill," Nico says. Without my coaching, he says the absolute best thing he could ever have said to my mom, and I can tell he's won her for good by the look in her eyes.

"Well, yes…but you bring some pretty nice shoes of your own out there. It's been a long time since I've seen someone run the hard count out on that field," she says, and I chuckle lightly to myself when I see Nico's head tilt in surprise. "Honey, I've taken in a lot of football games in my lifetime. Pretty sure there isn't a single thing you can do out on that field that I won't recognize."

"Yes, ma'am," he says, laughing lightly.

"Lauren is fine. *Ma'am*…that's too old, and my hair color is too good for you to think I'm old," she says, giggling.

My eyes flash wide and meet my brother's, who has walked up to join my dad. My mom is falling into flirty behavior now, so I step in before it becomes embarrassing.

"Mom, can you take our picture? I promised his mom we would send her one," I say, handing my mom my phone and Nico's. She smiles and nods, obliging and taking several photos of both of us, and then some of me with my dad and brother. Noah is wearing his best gray suit, the pant leg pulled down taut over his cast. It takes me a few minutes and photos to realize that Katie hasn't shown up to take pictures with us, and before I can ask, my mom does the honors.

"Is she meeting you here?"

My brother's brow lowers and his mouth grows rigid as he blinks a few times.

"Katie and I aren't together anymore," he says, and instantly my mind goes to my best friend. This is Izzy's chance!

"Oh, honey…" my mom says, falling into her doting habit.

"I broke it off; it's okay. We just…I don't know, she's like *really* into clothes and shoes and shopping. We're too different."

"So you're coming…alone?" I ask, my head leaning to one side as I ask.

"Uh…yeah…why?" my brother asks.

"No reason," I respond quickly, my answer clipped. He pinches his brow, and I wink, now wanting to sprint to the gym, to find Izzy and tell her the good news.

I kiss my parents on their cheeks, leaving them with my brother while I take Nico's arm and walk toward the gym. I drown in his scent, a mixture of soap and cologne, and something else that is always so distinctly him. I've come to recognize it, noticing when he's near and missing it when he's gone. It feels silly to love the way someone smells so much, but I do with him.

He stops me at the corner of the building, taking both of my hands in his, lifting the one with the corsage slightly higher.

"I hope it's okay…the flower. My mom insisted I give you one, and she said blue would match your eyes," he says, laughing out the last few words and shaking his head, embarrassed. When he looks back up at me, he bites his lip. The silence is unsettling, but in the best possible way.

"What?" I ask.

"You look really pretty," he says.

I suck in my bottom lip and stare back at him.

"Thank you," I say, the words coming out in a whisper.

Nico looks over his shoulder as a rush of couples walk by, a few saying "excuse me," and causing him to step in closer to me to let them pass. He takes advantage of the nearness, sweeping my hair back on one side and leaning in to press his lips just below my ear.

The feel of his hand sliding down my arm grounds me, and when his fingers meet mine, I flex them open, everything falling into place when his knuckles glide against mine and fit where they just belong.

We walk side by side to the gym, Nico handing a pass to the students at the table, guiding me through an archway made of balloons, and bypassing a row of tables near the entrance, leading me straight to the middle of the floor. Nobody has started to dance yet, but a slow song is playing. It's country, and I don't recognize it, but I can barely hear it over the thumping of my pulse rattling my entire body.

I can feel eyes on us, people watching to see who is moving to the dance floor first. I was hoping we'd sit for a while, maybe work our way up to a slow dance or two, but then I remember Nico's warning—that

I'd spend the night here with him, in the middle of the floor where everyone can see us.

"They're all looking at us," I giggle nervously in his ear, and he draws me close. His hands rest on my hips, and I link mine around his neck, our cheeks close while my eyes snap around the room, tallying up where people are, who's watching, and deciphering if anyone really cares.

"They're all looking at *you*," Nico says.

I pull back and tuck my chin, glaring at him.

"Not being corny. Just being honest," he says.

My lip ticks up on one side into a half smile, and I move back in against him. I let my eyes wander around the room, and while a lot of people are looking, I think they mostly see us as a couple they don't recognize. A few of them might be wondering why the new quarterback is with the coach's daughter—even fewer probably thinking our pairing has something to do with his position. But mostly, people seem to move on with their own dates, their own insecurities, their own crushes, jealousies, gossip-fests and more. Nico and I make slow circles in silence, under glittering lights installed just hours ago, and with every pass of the eyes that were moments ago watching us, fewer look up, until at last—we're alone.

Nico doesn't let me go for four songs, and we talk very little. I pay close attention to the feel of his fingertips on my waist, to where they move, how far up my back they travel, how they graze my arms and move my hair. I note every touch and shiver with the feel of it. I've forgotten about my repurposed dress, about the eyes around the room—I've forgotten about anything that was before there was a me and Nico, and then I start to laugh.

I try to hold it in at first, but he can feel my chest moving, my shoulders raising with each chuckle. Finally, he steps back enough so we can look at one another, and I fail at trying to hide my laugh.

"What's so funny?" he asks.

"Do you know how much I used to hate you?" I say.

His eyes flash wide, and his mouth falls open. I realize instantly how my sentence sounded, but there's no other way to say it, so I shake my head slightly and simply own it.

"Wow...*hate,* huh?" he asks, lifting his brow when he says the *h* word.

"Yeah...I...did, but maybe...maybe not really," I stammer.

"Not...really...hate," Nico says, boiling it down to three words. He laughs once, but narrows his gaze on me, waiting for me to explain.

"Our freshman year, we exchanged papers," I start, and he tilts his head back and laughs.

"I gave you a *B!*" he remembers, his chest raspy with his laughter. I purse my lips, and when he looks back to my face, he only laughs harder. "Oh...my God, you were so pissed!"

"Umm, yeah!" I say, stopping our swaying, my hands moving to my hips.

Nico moves one hand to his neck, rubbing, but he continues to chuckle at my expense.

"You had all of these notes for me, and I didn't read them, but I saw them on your paper when it was sitting on top of your desk during attendance. I hadn't written anything on yours. I thought we were just going to talk about them. I had no idea how Cornwall worked. Up until that day, I'd only really been in public school in West End, where you raced through assignments so you could get to recess fast."

Nico moves in closer and takes my elbows gently, scooting me into him, moving his hands to either side of my face, his eyes meeting mine with a jolt—the brown turns gold under the yellow hue of the dance-floor lights. My bravado melts a little, and I move my hands to feel the buttons on his shirt, my fingers roaming along his hard chest.

"You had written so many things that I was so sure you hated my paper, and it pissed me off because I worked so hard on it, and I knew it was good. I just figured you were being a snob from the city, so I wrote a B on yours even though it was totally an A. It was probably the smartest thing I'd ever read," he says, his head leaning slightly to the side. My eyes match his, and I fall a little more for him.

"I was so mad at you over that. And you *always* battle me in class. You have…every year. And debate…"

Nico steps into me, catching my bottom lip between both of his, halting my words and holding me hostage in a soft kiss. His hands cup my face, and I tremble at the sound of his breath against mine while his tongue takes a slow and deliberate swipe against my lip. We remain shielded between the couples who have slowly filled the dance floor, and when his lips leave mine, the feel of him lingers. I tuck my lip in my mouth and taste where he was, smiling.

"You're the smartest girl I've ever met, and…I had no idea how to handle you. When you walked over to our field that night," Nico begins, but never finishes, his teeth holding on to his top lip. He doesn't need to say any more. His eyes move around my face, as if he's memorizing everything about me and locking the details away for safe keeping.

"I'm glad I came over to watch…*your real game,*" I say, repeating the words just like Sasha had said them weeks ago.

Nico laughs softly and pulls me against him again, and I fall back into place, letting him hold me through fast and slow songs while couples come and go on the floor. At one point, I see Noah standing next to Izzy, both of them drinking glasses of punch, their eyes moving around the room as they point at people and whisper and laugh. When Izzy catches me watching them, she turns to Noah, then back to me, pressing her finger to her lips, her face serious, reminding me to keep my word.

I would have broken it if I needed to. The moment Noah said he had ended things with Katie, I thought of Izzy, of what she confessed. But seeing them now, in their natural comfort with one another, I realize how much I would ruin if I meddled with that. Izzy likes my brother— as in *likes* likes him. And he may very well like her, too. If so, then nature will have to intervene, because they both also like moments like the one they are living in right now, and how shameful it would be if I robbed them of more of those by making things uncomfortable.

I hold up my finger around Nico's neck, and press it to my lips. Izzy winks, and I nestle in closer, breathing in the musky smell on him. I let my hands push up into his hair near the base of his neck, and I love the thickness of it. It's still damp, though mostly dry from his shower, and just touching him makes me think of his game.

"You played so great tonight. You all did," I say.

Nico hums a response, and I relish how his hands adjust their grip, falling to the small of my back.

"My brother help you guys at all? I know…I know Dad had him out on the field a lot this week," I say.

"I don't know about the other guys, but me? Yeah. Your brother has been a lifesaver," he says, and I jolt a little in surprise.

Nico chuckles.

"What's funny?" he asks.

"Nothing, just…surprised to hear you call my brother that," I say.

"You mean since he hates me and all?" he responds.

I pinch my brow and push back to look him in the eye. He chuckles and cups my head, bringing me close enough to kiss the top.

"It's just his way of dealing. He made a joke out of it, actually. He would say 'I hate you' after everything good I did. Eventually, we'd slap hands twice and he'd say 'I hate you' and I'd say 'good' after every tackle I broke or pass I nailed. He's fronting, and I let him. It works for us. I grew up in a neighborhood full of guys who had to put on big chests and hard faces. Noah's no different," Nico says.

No, I suppose he isn't.

"The A&M guys say anything?" I ask.

Nico's muscles get rigid, and I squeeze his arms, sliding my hands up around his neck.

"I saw them there, and Noah told me," I say.

"I don't like to think about it. I just…I guess I don't want to get my hopes up for anything and then have it all come crashing down," he says, and my heart sinks that he thinks so little of the attention he's garnering.

"They're watching you because you're *that good*," I say, nuzzling against his neck. I allow myself a kiss, and he stills at my touch. I step back enough to look at him, but before I speak, his eyes meet mine and the look in them is so raw and thankful that I decide to leave it at that.

"Can I take you somewhere? Before...before I have to take you home? I swear, it's safe, and I don't have any funny ideas. I just don't want to be late, because I promised your dad. But there's somewhere...just somewhere I really want you to see."

I hold his stare for a few seconds, then nod. His hand falls to mine, and our fingers tangle as he leads me through the crowd and out the door, a little more than an hour remaining before he has to have me home.

Nico pulls up hard on the car door handle for his work-in-progress Toyota. I slide in, sitting on a new seat covering that's soft and fuzzy. I let my fingers pet the fabric, and I grin at Nico as he pushes the door closed. I pull my buckle on as he walks around the car.

"I like the new seats," I say, reaching over and running my hands along his as he gets in.

"First of many upgrades," he chuckles. "So far, this...and some oil...are the only things I could afford to do."

"You'll get there," I say.

"Yeah, well, I'm starting after church on Sundays at the Hungry Hill right by the highway. Sasha works there, and he makes decent money," Nico says, adjusting his mirrors and looking over his shoulder as he pulls out of his space.

"Isn't that a trucker stop?" I ask, vaguely recalling the red sign beaming on the other side of the freeway.

"Why do you think it's such good money?" Nico says, pushing his tongue in his cheek. It takes me a few seconds to get his innuendo, and when I do, I smack him on the arm.

"You are not going to sell *favors* to truckers," I say.

"Oh my God, Reagan. I can't believe you're so dirty. I meant that I was going to sell popsicles on the side. Jeeze, you're a dirty girl."

I blush hard and tilt my head, shooting him an incredulous expression. He laughs at me, then turns his focus to the road. I look away, too, but I keep thinking about how he called me a *dirty girl,* and my thoughts slip from sweet and naïve to…

I clear my throat, shaking off the heat trailing down my body and up my chest.

"Where are we going?" I ask, taking glances at his profile, the way it's lit up by each streetlight, his hair less slick than before when it was still wet from his shower. I love the way the front falls over one eye. It makes him almost from another time.

"It's not far. It's just a place I go, sometimes. And, I don't know…it's silly, but…I want to take you there," he says.

"Okay," I smile, letting my eyes linger on him a little longer. He can tell I'm watching, and his lip quirks up on the side closest to me.

"You make that face in class…when you're right, or when you know you're about to kill everyone with some smart thing you're about to say."

He turns to me, and his grin grows. The dimple is at its deepest.

"I do?" he asks, his eyes wrinkled at the sides. He looks back to the road.

"You do. It's how I know I'm about to lose," I say.

"You never lose," he says quickly.

I chuckle and speak at the same time.

"Oh…I lose. Trust me," I say.

"Nah," he says, his words again swift.

My brow is low as I watch him suspiciously. I know I lose, and I know that he's the strongest debater I've ever come up against. I'm more likely to win an argument with my father than Nico Medina, but I let it go for now, because even with this…he's probably right.

We pull to a stop before he crosses the highway, parking the car in a small neighborhood just on the other side of West End from the freeway. Nico jogs around to my side, helping me open the door, and taking my hand as I climb out, his eyes shifting to my bare knees then grazing up my body until they meet my waiting stare.

"You caught me," he says, and I let my lashes sweep a slow blink.

"I'm flattered," I say.

Nico leans against the door to shove it closed after manually pushing the lock in on the inside.

"I wasn't sure what to wear, and my dress is kinda old," I say, flaring the skirt out to the side, letting the fabric slip through my fingers.

Nico grabs my hand and leads me down the brightly-lit sidewalk, down a dip to a walkway that seems to be leading to an overpass bridge for pedestrians to cross the highway.

"I wear these pants to church every Sunday," he says, smirking. "Your dress is far more impressive than my slacks."

I push my lips into a tight smile, and when he turns away, I giggle.

"What's funny?" he asks.

"You said *slacks*. It's such a…grandpa kinda word," I say through laughter.

"Is not," he says, pushing me with his hip. I push back, and he reaches around me to bring me to him, poking me in the side to tickle me. I squirm, but secretly love being held so close.

"It is," I laugh as we walk up a small slant and step out over the rushing cars of the interstate. "You talk like an old man."

"It's just because I'm more mature than you are," Nico says, leading me by my hand now out to the center of the bridge where we stop. He turns to face me. "When is your birthday anyhow?"

"September," I say.

"October," he says, his mouth grimacing.

"Ha!" I poke his chest with my finger. "I'm older! Your excuse fails, Nico Medina. Your use of the word *slacks* is just weird."

"Fine," he says, the bend in his mouth a sexy kind of smile that draws me close. "You win the first argument against me ever. How does it feel?"

"It feels like maybe you gave in because you wanted me to be happy, which, as you pointed out once, isn't really selfless at all," I tease.

"This is true," Nico says, pulling me close, his nose brushing against mine. "I take pleasure in seeing you happy."

The breeze blows my skirt about my knees, and my hair flies wild around my shoulders as Nico pushes his hands into my hair on either side of my head, his forehead resting on mine briefly until he tilts my chin up enough to dust his lips across mine. I want more, to feel his lips stronger against mine, but he gives me this small taste and pulls away. He doesn't let go of my hand, but he turns, his other hand gripping the metal grate that walls us in and protects us from the cars and trucks speeding beneath us.

"So this is your place, huh?" I ask, watching the lights blur below.

Nico sighs, his weight sinking into the bridge wall as he rests his arm in front and leans his head into it.

"I used to come here with Sasha, on our bikes. There's a cool park over there," he says, gesturing to the neighborhood we parked in.

"I know that park!" I say, pulling myself up to stand tall, leaning into the gate. I can just see the lights over the trees in the distance. "My brother played football there."

I look back to Nico and catch him smiling at the same view.

"So did we…but…not on the same field of course," he smirks.

"Off to the side, in the dark, I presume," I chuckle.

Nico nods slowly, his head rolling and his eyes hitting mine.

"They don't really have lighted parks in West End, and in the summer, it was too hot to play out in the day, so we'd grab our bikes and pedal over this bridge to play where the light was barely enough," he says. "We did that for three summers in a row, until Sasha moved, and my bike was stolen. I walked a few times, but my mom didn't really like me out late on foot. I didn't like it either. We stuck to the streets then, until the shootings got everyone freaked out."

"Shootings?" My stomach tightens.

Nico nods, shuffling his feet and turning to lean his shoulder against the metal, reaching to take both of my hands. He plays with my fingers, working his around mine. It's sweet how he's both comfortable and familiar.

"There were a few, when the gangs got kinda bad. It was really only a couple incidents, but there were some drive-bys—before the drug houses got busted. Everyone got really freaked out, and a lot of people moved. Mom made sure we were always inside before dark," he says.

"Your brother, too?" I ask, my instincts telling me before Nico.

"Not always. He was older, so he...he would hang out. It was mostly the money that enticed him. I think he wanted to help out Mom, maybe buy some nice things. It got outta hand, though. The danger...the violence. I don't think my brother ever expected the violence, and I know it scared him."

I lean into him, snuggling against his chest, then moving my arms around his neck, my chin resting on his shoulder as I look out over the other side of the bridge.

"It's two different worlds," I say, noticing how quickly the landscape becomes dark on the other side. A block or two of businesses have lights, and then it's nothing. Only, I've driven there—I know it's not the case.

"I still came here. Sometimes, I'd sneak out—my mom only caught me once. I would always ride my board back before she was awake, but I'd just come here to sit. I liked to watch the traffic," he says, glancing down at our feet as he kicks the grating near his heel. "I would sit on that side and stare through this one, watching. I wanted to know what life was like...over there."

I pull back to look at him, our eyes meeting instantly. His mouth falls into line, and I can tell he hates to admit that out loud—that he wishes sometimes that he were somewhere else.

"Life wasn't so grand over here, either," I say, though I know that the weight in my world is far lighter than that carried on Nico's side of the highway. "Your side sells the drugs; my side...we buy them."

Nico's head falls, and his eyes get softer. We've talked about Noah, about how he stepped in. Nico played it off, but I think that was for my benefit—I don't think he wants me to have a visual of how bad that night probably really was, how close to danger Noah had come.

"It's one fucked-up ecosystem, isn't it?" Nico says, and I laugh out a breath, reaching my fingers through the fence next to me and looking down at the rush of traffic.

"Yeah…it is," I say.

He looks on with me, and we stand together while a few cars honk as they pass below us, each driver probably thinking he's clever or disrupting our intimacy. What's strange, though, is how incredibly intimate it is right here. We're on display for most of the city, at least the portion on the road at this time of the night, yet we're so alone.

"So why this place?" I ask him finally. "You wanted to bring me here…why?"

Nico's expression slips into an excited one, and he reaches into his pocket, grinning at me. He holds a lock out in his palm then reaches into the opposite pocket for a pen, showing it to me.

"We're going to plan our next bike ride and you want to be prepared so you…brought a lock?" I shake my head as I stare at the lock in his hand, my lips pulled in on one side. "Sorry…I don't get it," I say, giving up and shrugging.

"Come here," Nico says, leading me farther across the bridge.

I start to notice metal pieces attached to the fence as we move closer to the West End side, and when we're right upon one of them, I stop, pulling it in my hand and tugging. Dozens upon dozens of locks, some key and some combination, are hooked onto the bridge, some dangling from dangerous locations. Each lock has something either written on it in ink or scratched into it. Most of the messages are love notes—a girl loves a boy, a boy loves a girl, and then the date. A few of them are clumped together with dates spread a year apart, and I can tell they mark an anniversary. Some of the anniversaries are happy, some are hopeful. Others…*tragic.*

"These are amazing," I say, running my fingers over some of the larger locks.

"They just started showing up here one day. Sasha and I were riding our bikes across, and he stopped, thinking someone had left their lock there. He tried to break the code at first, but I noticed the writing, and I got him to stop. The next day, a few more locks were here. The collection grew two or three at a time over several months, and now…"

"There must be hundreds," I say, my eyes focusing and realizing just how many speckle the fence that stretches to the other side of the highway.

"The city or state or whoever owns the bridge has cleaned them off before, but they always come back. I think they just gave up eventually, and now they're like this organic art kind of thing. They're people's stories, and I thought…"

"You want to put our story up here, too," I finish for him.

He nods, and his bashful smile dents his cheek.

"What do we write?" I ask, my heart picking up and my nerves surprising me. I haven't felt this uneasy rush with Nico in a while, and it's unsettling, mostly because I'm scared. I think maybe he means a lot to me, and maybe I want to tell him, but what if…what if he's somewhere different with us?

"I had an idea," he starts, putting the cap of the marker in his mouth and pulling the pen free. He speaks with the lid in his mouth, and it makes him talk crooked. It's adorable, and I can't help but giggle. "I'll write on one side, and you write on the other," he mumbles, shooting me a glare when I laugh at his speech. He spits the cap to the ground. "I only have two hands, you bully."

"You're right; I'm sorry," I say, bending down and picking the cap up.

Nico holds the lock in his hands, tilting it from my view, and he writes out a short note that only takes him seconds. His eyes flit to mine a few times before he declares that he's done, then hands the pen to me.

"Okay," I say, exhaling harder than I mean, too.

"Don't make it so hard. Just write…whatever you want to say. Whatever's on your mind and you're willing to put here permanently," he says. "Oh…and preferably about me, because otherwise my side is going to sound really stupid."

I bite my lip and look at him while my mind searches for courage. A dozen adjectives, and as many words for feelings dart around my head, the phrases coming and going fast. After a few seconds, I feel like I'm playing a game of Scrabble, searching for the best word to score the most points.

"You're making this hard," he says.

"Okay, okay…just…give me a minute!" I scold him, my eyes intense on the lock in my hand, my fingers squeezing the pen hard.

There's one thought—one thing I could write—that I keep thinking. This one sentence plays on repeat, and it scares me and tempts me to look at the other side. I feel my fingers twitch to spin the lock in my palm, but I won't cheat. I would never. My eyes move up to Nico's, which are waiting for me. The smirk on his lips is almost like a poker player's bluff, and I don't know if I should call it. I look back down to the lock, my teeth sawing at my lip, and I hold my breath as I write.

The words are short and sweet. I put the pen back in the cap when I'm done, and hold the lock between my fingers—Nico's message on the other side.

"So do we…turn it? Or…how does this work?" I ask.

Nico takes the lock from me, then tugs it loose, like a hook. He leans his head toward the fence, and I realize he's asking me to pick a spot. I find one that's at both of our height, and it's a place where the metal is melted into an odd thickness—the only place where the latticework is uneven. I like that it isn't perfect, and if I'm tethering myself to something, I think it should look a little amiss. There's comfort in imperfection.

"Okay then," he says, looping the lock in place and pushing it in until it clicks, his thumb rubbing along the bottom until the combination is scrambled.

"Do you know how to take it off?" I ask.

"No idea. I threw the combination away," he says, his eyes never once leaving mine while I continue to look from him to the lock, nervously. "Go on…read it," he says, finally, and I practically lunge at it, twisting it upside down so I can read what Nico wrote on his side.

Me, too.

I let my thumb run over the words, the ink now dry, and my lips curve up as I do. His note...it couldn't be any more perfect.

"What'd you say?" he says, his hand sliding around my waist and along my stomach, his chin resting on my shoulder as he holds me from behind.

"I said..." I pause, my mouth suddenly dry. My eyes fall closed and I let go of the lock, turning in his arms until my back is against the bridge's wall, next to our lock, and Nico has me caged between his arms. "I said, 'I'm falling for you.'"

His mouth curves as mine did, and his forehead tilts until it rests against mine.

"You are, huh?" he says, the words tickling my lips. I love it when he speaks against my mouth. I wish we could have all conversations just like this.

"I am," I say, stopping to take his bottom lip into my mouth.

"Kiss me," he demands. "You take charge, kissing me like you want. I want to know what you want from me, how you feel. Show me," he says, his expression not arrogant or cocky, but rather desperate perhaps, like he needs to know what I want and feel.

Though my nerves fire up, I do as he asks, because I've never wanted to kiss him more. My hands slide up both sides of his face, and I step up on my tippy-toes, turning my head just enough that we fit together perfectly, my mouth opening to take his, to taste him. I kiss his top lip first, letting my teeth graze over him, then I nibble at his bottom. When he smiles against me, I do the same, letting my right hand move into his hair, feeling it soft and thick between my fingers.

I begin to kiss him harder, my tongue entering his mouth and meeting the resistance of his quickly. It's with this touch that Nico can no longer be passive. His hands slide behind my back and he pulls me into him, turning me away from the gate and walking me backward to the large concrete pillar at the center of the bridge. My back against the coolness of it, Nico moves forward until he has one foot resting on either side of both of mine, his body pressed against me, his hands sliding down my hips, inching slowly until they finally grip my ass.

My breath hitches as his fingers clutch at the fabric of my dress, bringing it up only an inch or two with the raw hunger of his need. He lets go, sliding his hands up my sides, his thumbs running over the curves of my breasts, coming close to places I've never been touched, but suddenly desperately want to be. His fingers trace along my bare shoulder, and his head dips down, his mouth taking my neck, tasting my collar bone, the rough edge of his teeth scratching against my bare skin. His hands trail lower, along my arms, until he reaches my wrists, and he grabs them in his hands, lifting them and holding them above my head against the concrete as he leans into me and kisses my mouth raw. He holds me there for a few seconds before letting go and moving to cup my face again, letting me free from the wall and pulling me to him until we're standing in the center of the bridge, the only light from the cars below and the sliver of moon above.

When he releases me, I'm dizzy and breathless, and I let my head rest against his chest.

"I have never been kissed like that," I say.

"Me neither," Nico says, his mouth coming down to the top of my head.

Somehow, I didn't believe that to be true, but I let him get away with it. I let him because it makes him happy to make me happy, and that thought—the idea that I'm his girl, *the* girl for him? That makes me deliriously happy.

CHAPTER 18

We pull onto my street with exactly eight minutes to spare. I think Nico was watching the clock all along to be sure he delivered me home early. He confirms my suspicion when his car clears over the hump of the curb and he shifts it into park, turning to me and says, "Brownie points."

My smile meets his, and for a moment, we sit in the quiet of my driveway staring at one another—nothing but a night full of football, dancing, and kisses between us. Tonight...it was a perfect fairy tale. But all tales have villains. Ours is ruined the moment my eyes realize the other cars in our driveway—two parked on the street. The cars...they're familiar.

"Did your parents have a party or something?" Nico asks, twisting in his seat and looking around us.

"It's the board," I say.

I slump back into my seat. I don't want to go inside, because I know.

I know.

"Like, for Cornwall?"

Nico still pivots where he sits, glancing from the two cars in front of us to the few parked near my favorite tree. I take in a deep breath, and as I exhale, I let my eyes fall shut, remembering all that was good tonight—before everything fell apart.

"Why would they be here?" Nico asks. I open my eyes on him, the wrinkle of confusion set deep in his brow.

"You have the fifty-seven…we live with the board," I say, and his head cocks to the side. I watch as realization washes over him, his expression shifting from confusion to understanding in a breath, his eyes moving toward defiant.

"Why would they want to meet with your dad now?" Nico says, his hand on his door. He's out of the car before I can answer, running to my side to open my door for me.

"I don't know," I say, even though in the pit of my stomach, I have a suspicion. The board doesn't make house calls unless they want to take care of something they perceive as a *problem*. Noah's indiscretions perhaps. My mom has already been let go of her post. The only other thing would be my father.

Nico grips my hand as I step up from the car, and we take a few steps toward my front door just as it swings open. Men and women—all dressed as if they're heading to Sunday school—spill from my home. A few of them laugh together, as if they've just left a business retreat and are excited to be heading to the bar. The others behind them have more somber faces. I recognize Thomas Loftgrin, my brother's now *ex-*girlfriend's father; he makes eye contact with me.

I know.

Nico steps to the side while nearly a dozen people leave my home, and as they head to their cars, we look toward the open front door they left behind. My parents didn't see them out.

I swallow as we walk up to the house, and when we step inside, my mom is standing behind her sitting-chair by the fireplace, her hands on the high back as if she's using it to protect herself from something bad. My dad sits across from her, his head in his hands, elbows on his knees. He's still wearing his deep-blue polo short, still tucked in to his khaki pants, his belt still tight. I bet he had just gotten home from reviewing the game, from talking with his coaching staff.

I bet they were here, waiting for him.

My mom's mouth falls open, and she begins to greet Nico and me, but her words never come. She pulls her mouth into a fake, tight smile, tears threatening to fall from her eyes. She's trembling, and I know she is near falling apart.

"Dad?" I ask, needing someone to confirm it—to say it out loud.

He lifts his head from his hands, his face serious, his eyes narrow and angry. Chad Prescott doesn't get emotional, but he does get pissed. Whatever this is, it's moved beyond that.

My dad's eyes meet mine, and he works his lips, sucking in the top one and letting it go with a slow nod.

"It's done," he says.

My mom gasps and covers her mouth.

"What's done?" Nico asks.

Shifting his focus to his young quarterback, my dad stares at Nico hard. He doesn't blink and he doesn't speak.

"Coach, what...what happened here?" Nico asks.

My dad's head falls slightly to the side as he exhales through his nose, his mouth still a hard line.

"It isn't *Coach* anymore, Nico. On Monday, you'll be playing for Jimmy O'Donahue. Don't worry, though. You...you'll be all right," my father says.

Nico's feet shift where he stands, and his hand grips mine harder.

"I don't understand. We...we won. We're winning," Nico says.

"It wasn't going to matter, Nico. This...it isn't your fault," my dad says.

"It's nobody's fault," my mom pipes in, her words coming out raw, through a stifled cry. "And it isn't fair. I hate this place! I hate their rules! You lose once...*once!* They hold it against you forever. I...I need to go talk to Noah."

"Noah was here?" I ask, my mom holds up a hand, covering her mouth with the other one as she excuses herself down the hallway. I turn my attention back to the room.

"He was. He had just come in, left the dance early—just like we asked him to. He pulled up right before Jimmy," my dad says, shaking his head as his eyes move toward the still-open door. My father stands and walks toward us, continuing on to the door so he can push it closed. As soon as it clicks in place, his fist comes down against the panels hard, rattling the door, frame, and wall that surround it. "Those goddamned assholes!"

I move my touch to Nico's arm, gripping it and holding him close to me, but he pulls loose, looking at me and holding up a finger. Nico walks to my father and puts his hand on my dad's shoulder, and that small touch pushes my father over the edge, his head falling forward into his palm, his body sinking into the door before silently quaking. Nico leans into him, resting his forehead on the place where his hand rests on my father, and I stand alone, watching.

"I'll quit sir," Nico says.

My dad straightens instantly, turning to face Nico as he runs his thumbs under his damp eyes.

"No," my dad says, shaking his head. "No. Absolutely no, you will not."

"I won't play for someone else," Nico says.

My father takes in a deep breath, his eyes at Nico's feet at first, then gliding up to look his prodigy in the eyes. My dad lifts his hand and rests it on Nico's shoulder, squeezing and forcing a hint of a smile to cross his lips.

"Nico, you play for you. You…you have never played for anyone but you. And…Jesus Christ, son, you frustrate me. *Frustrated* me, but hell if it didn't work. It was the right way to coach you. To let you fly. You play for you, and you will continue to play for you. You've got six games— *six!* You win that championship, and you go play for some big school that you deserve. And then you give those fuckers the middle finger, because they'll still be right here. Without you, Nico? They've got nothin'."

Nico's silent, and I can read him more than I've ever been able to before. His jaw works, and his brow pulls in as he stares at my father, breathing in and out through his nose until he finally nods.

"I'll play, Coach. But I can't be quiet out there. I can't just pretend any of this is okay. I'll play, but I won't keep my mouth shut," he says.

"I wouldn't expect you to, son. I wouldn't expect you to," my dad says, his mouth curving a hint more, this smile born from pride.

My father's eyes move to me, and he holds them there for a beat before they drift back to the ground, his hand falling limp at his side.

"Reagan, go check on your mom and brother, would you? I'm..." he chuckles. "I'm going to go have a drink. A hard one. A *few* hard ones."

"Dad," I start, but he holds up a hand.

"Alone," he says. "I'm all right, and I'll figure this out, but right now, I just need to go be mad as hell, all right?"

I pull my lips in tight and my eyes flit to Nico. He nods to me, but I can tell from his face that he's still processing, too.

"All right," I say.

My dad moves into the kitchen, and I hear the back sliding door open and close a second or two later. He likes to sit at the edge of our property, where it's dark and he can hide. It's where he goes when he loses, usually. At least, after he's done stewing in his office...which...isn't *his* office anymore.

I'm hit with dozens of tiny realizations. My dad's office, his job, his life and identity—*gone.* I turn to Nico, and he steps toward me, pulling me in his arms and pressing his lips on the top of my head. He's still dressed in his perfect shirt, his collar loosened, but only a little, his tie the same. I hold it in my hand, righting the knot to face the front.

"I'm going to go talk to Noah. You...you don't have to stay. Really, it's..."

"I want to," Nico says, cutting me off. His eyes level me, and I breathe in and out hard.

"I can't believe they fired him," I say.

Nico shakes his head, his gaze never leaving mine alone.

I lead him down the hallway, and we step cautiously through my brother's doorway. He's sitting on the edge of his bed, his leg out in front of him, his crutches on the floor. My mom is sitting next to him rubbing circles in his back. He's twice her size, yet she's still Mom, and he's still a little boy, all of eighteen.

His head is in his hands, his fingers pushing deep into his forehead. My mom steps up, running her thumbs under her eyes as she stands.

"Where's your dad?" she asks. Noah looks up, his eyes taking in me and Nico.

"He's in his spot," I say, looking from her to my brother.

She nods, then steps past me.

"I'll go join him," she says.

"He said he wants to be alone," I say as she leaves the room.

"He always says that. Stubborn man has been wanting to be alone for years," she says, her voice trailing off. I hear her open the fridge in the distance, the sound of a bottle clanking into glass, and I chuckle.

"Back to the wine, it seems," my brother says. I look him in the eyes and offer a pathetic smile. "I ruined her pot access," he chuckles.

I move to sit next to him, and we both lean forward with our elbows on our hands. We used to sit like this when we were kids and both were in trouble. I can remember every time—the spaghetti we stuck on the ceiling...the Kool-Aid we poured on the white carpet...the dog we tried to keep hidden in Noah's closet...the party we tried to throw our sophomore year.

"I won homecoming king," Noah says, reaching toward his pillow. He picks up a plastic crown and tosses it to Nico. "Here you go, man."

Nico rolls it in his hands and lifts a brow at my brother.

"Just figured you usually end up with everything that's mine," my brother says.

"Noah!" I scold him.

"I'm kidding," my brother says, but I think part of him still isn't.

"Don't be a prick. Not now," I say.

"Sorry," he says, looking up to Nico and holding up a hand. "For real, man. I'm sorry."

"It's all right," Nico says, spinning the crown in his hand and placing it on his head. His eyes look up at it, and I chuckle because he looks ridiculous. "Hey, maybe I can wear this at the Hungry Hill."

"You working there?" my brother asks.

Nico tosses his crown back to him.

"Yeah, on Sundays," he says.

"Isn't that place, like…where truckers get blow jobs and stuff?" Noah says, and Nico and I both laugh at the inside joke.

"That's," Nico pauses, pushing his laughter down, "that's not what I'll be doing."

Noah nods, then joins our quiet laughter. Soon, it's silent again in his room. We all stare at the space on the floor between us. I'm searching my mind for something to say, something that will make the last few hours disappear, only leaving behind the good parts with Nico. But I can't. I can't just have the good and leave out the bad in life. I have to take it all, for what it's worth. It's how people learn, I guess. Those bad things, they teach us stuff. My dad's job, and the loss of it? That taught me a hell of a lot about people, and the kind of people I want to be around.

"If Cornwall were in West End, they wouldn't treat people like this," I say.

My brother and Nico are quiet for a few seconds, then Nico breaks the silence with a laugh.

"If Cornwall were in West End, *you* wouldn't go there," he says.

"Not true," I lie.

Nico tilts his head and purses his lips.

"Fine, but still. You know what I mean," I say.

"Yeah, I know what you mean. People are allowed to make mistakes where I'm from. We have forgiveness," he says.

I hear Noah swallow next to me, so I move my hand over to his leg, nudging him.

"You all right?" I ask.

He's looking down, his hands folded over his knees. His face is more somber than I've ever seen it.

"It's my fault," he says, pulling his top lip in and sucking, letting it snap free with a pop before looking me in the eyes. "All of this…Dad's job? It's all my fault. If I hadn't fucked up. If I wasn't so damn angry that I was blind to what was really going on. Reagan, this is *all* my fault."

"Noah, no. It's not," I say, grabbing his arm. "Your problems…they don't bleed into the school's politics. The board didn't look at you having a hard time and decide to fire Dad because of it."

"No? You really think they didn't look at Chad Prescott's fucked-up son and make a judgment on him? You think Mom crashing her car through our house…because of something *I* did…didn't reflect on Dad? They were worried his fucked-up personal life was going to bleed out onto the field."

"Noah, you don't believe that," I say, standing in front of him and pulling his chin up, forcing him to look at me. "They've been dying to fire Dad the second Jimmy O'Donahue said he was interested in the job. And it's not about Brandon, because we all know he's a shit quarterback, Noah. It's about Jimmy, and Jimmy's pedigree, and the fact that his family name is on a dozen gold plates at the front of the school. The O'Donahues may as well have built Cornwall, Noah. It's about money. You cut them and they bleed goddamned gold! Dad didn't have a shot in hell."

Nico's head falls back against the wall and he sighs. I turn to face him, and his head comes up enough to look at me.

"You know I'm right," I say. "Tell him it's not his fault, Nico."

Our eyes meet and agree, and I can tell Nico believes every word I just said. He knows it to be true.

"Your sister *is* right, man. It's how that place operates. The cream rises to the top with dollars for stairs," he says. "The rest of us…shit, man. We have to grip and claw and fight and battle. And it ain't right. None of it. But I need this school. I can't come out of West End and get somewhere—somewhere *better*—without it. And as much as I want to quit on principle, your dad's right, Reagan. I can't do that either. I can't quit because the only person who would care is me, and the only person

I would hurt is me. It wouldn't teach them anything. It would be removing a problem for them, because me, and my scholarship, and my background…it makes problems."

Noah and I look at Nico, his gaze lost somewhere over our heads, his eyes serious—the reflection of someone who is driven to make his point.

"You are not a problem," I say.

He lowers his gaze to meet mine, his lip ticking up just enough to dent his cheek.

"No?" he says.

I shake my head to confirm it.

"What do you think happens when some kid from the Barrio lifts up the state championship trophy at the most prestigious school in the state?" he asks.

"It makes headlines," my brother answers, a little more confidence in his words, more strength.

"It. Makes. Headlines," Nico says, his smirk growing. "And it means *more* kids from my neighborhood, and neighborhoods like mine, start to think they can do it, too."

"And that makes people like the ones who came here to fire my dad nervous," Noah says, lifting himself to his feet and dragging himself toward Nico on one leg.

"It sure does," Nico smiles. "Nothing fucks with legacies like opening up the talent pool to competition."

"Suck it, Jimmy O'Donahue!" Noah shouts.

I watch them both slap hands, holding onto one another for a few seconds, their forearms both flexing with their renewed passion. They're both on the same side, finally. United in the injustice that took out my dad, and while seeing that feels good in my chest, my heart is also breaking because just outside, my father's is lost and broken.

CHAPTER 19

The disorder on the field all week was evident now. The Tradition found themselves down by a touchdown—against a team, that under normal circumstances, they should trounce. I was kept out of practice on Monday, told my filming privileges were now relegated to the press box only, and field access was not allowed.

I fought it. I went to the principal, asked Bob to try to help, pleaded with Mrs. O'Donahue, the new chair of the social committee—I asked and begged anyone who would listen. They all said *no*.

There was no real reason given. Coach O'Donahue made reference to some theory that I was becoming a distraction, but I knew that was bullshit. The only person I was distracting was him. But I had run into a wall. My film has hundreds of hours of footage and B-roll already; I know I can make something great from what I already have, but I need the last games of the season on tape, so I can't risk losing the press box, too.

I got to the game early, watching warm-ups play out on the field while I set up my camera on the roof of the box. I decided to sit by my mom for the game, so I staked out our spots near the front of the bleachers, laying down an extra cushion in case my dad decided to come. He flip-flopped on the decision all week, sometimes hell-bent on proving to them they didn't break him, then surrendering to the fact that they really had.

My father was now nothing more than a physical education teacher at Cornwall. His lifting classes were taken over by Jimmy. He went in on Sunday to pile up his things from the office under the watchful eye of Robert O'Donahue, Jimmy's uncle—the board member who started these dominoes by pushing the first one over a year ago when he forced the board to hire his nephew.

My dad was able to sneak a few important books out without them getting their hands on them, and I showed him how to log into his computer system remotely so he could extract and delete things that might be helpful to Jimmy's success. My dad also saved all of Nico's game-play clips. His new mission was to act as Nico's agent, voluntarily, of course, and make sure the A&Ms and Ohio States and Brown Universities—all interested in the quarterback from West End—continued to be.

Of course, if the rest of the season played out like tonight's game, those opportunities might dry up on their own.

My dad showed up at halftime, and I felt the stare from most of the people in the stands instantly. Even now, minutes left in the game, I can feel them looking at us. Some of them are waiting for my dad to do something, to fix what's happening down on the field. But that…that isn't his job any more.

He's reminded me of that every few seconds all night long. Nico gets hit on the blind side; my dad mumbles about Zach's blown coverage, poor positioning. Sasha misses a catch; my dad mutters out something about play calling, and not reading the defense correctly. Every word from him, though, has been under his breath, until now.

Nico misses another pass, throwing the ball deep, just out of Travis's reach. As he runs in, the punting team heading out, Coach O'Donahue pulls on Nico's face mask, jerking his head square with his, his finger pointing in his quarterback's face, his large body able to overpower Nico's. Eventually, Nico pushes himself free and throws his hands out, fighting back.

"You do not touch your players like that!" my dad yells, getting to his feet quickly. Within a blink, my dad has hopped over the front of the bleachers, his feet landing in a crunch on the track below, and he's on the field.

"Oh…shit," my mom says next to me. I look at her, her eyes wide and her hands clutching her purse against her chest. "We better get ready to go."

"He has to do something, Mom. That…you saw that, right?" I say.

"I did, but Reagan, I don't know. Oh God, oh God, oh God," my mom begins to mumble. She's uncomfortable with the attention, and I get it. My mom doesn't like to be the one who isn't liked, and right now—for whatever reason—we aren't.

On the field, my dad has reached Coach O'Donahue, and both of their hands are flying in all directions. I hear faint swear words from the distance, and the referees are whistling, calling their own timeout to sort the scene now unfolding on the field.

"I can't believe he's doing this," I say, a smile spreading on my face. My mom's face, meanwhile, grows more worried.

The other team has taken a knee, as if someone on our side has been injured, which I sort of feel is seconds away from happening. My dad is turning red—the kind of red I used to see when he would yell at my brother for being out too late…for smashing the side door of his Jeep into our dad's car…for smoking pot. Jimmy O'Donahue takes steps backward, and one of the referees steps between them both, grabbing the collar of my father's shirt. There are *boos* coming from the stands, and my mom keeps glancing over her shoulder, as if they could be happening for any reason other than the spectacle her husband just made.

She turns back to the field to watch my dad talk—more rationally— with the referee, a guy named Jeff Munds. We've known Jeff for years. He handles most of the big games in the state, and ends up doing a lot of ours because of that. My father seems to calm down thanks to Jeff, and as he starts to walk with him to the exit from the field, I watch my mom carefully, her nails in between her teeth and her eyes not blinking, but never focusing in one place for too long. She flits from the exit, to the field, to the score, to my knees, to the place down the bleachers where my brother is sitting with a few friends. It's like I can read her mind, and the way it's working out what every person here must be thinking about her.

And then, with a few words, everything about her shifts.

"What's the matter, Lauren? Can't handle the spotlight? Thinking of driving the car through Jimmy's house now?"

I don't even know where the shouting is coming from, but the words ring through clear, and my mother hears them. I watch her demeanor change, her chest fills with air slowly and her shoulders rise.

"Just ignore them," I say, my hand finding her arm. My mom reaches into her purse, probably for her keys, ready to leave. I assume she's going to go find my dad and make him go home. Her hand pauses, though, with one more shout from behind us.

"Tori O'Donahue's parties are better than yours ever were!" the voice shouts.

Of everything that's ever been thrown at us as a family, the one thing that has always been off limits is Lauren Prescott's ability to put together an event of any kind. My mother's degree is in hospitality, and before my father was making good money, my mom ran a five-star resort. Her events are perfection—always on time, always under budget, and enjoyed by all. To throw stones at her over that, especially now, is a bigger insult than I think anyone could ever realize.

My mom turns to me, and when our eyes meet, I see a glimpse of the woman she used to be before the stress of being the coach's wife started to tear her down. Her pupils dilate, just enough, and her head tilts a fraction. I imagine the sound of her neck cracking, though I think perhaps it really did. She stands, delicately folding the sweater that was keeping her lap warm, laying it down on her seat pad and walking, her arm looped through her purse, up the steps to the place where the voice came from.

I turn in my seat, leaving the chaos still being sorted out on the field and watch as my mom questions the rows of boosters sitting near the press box until a woman finally stands up and puts her hands on her hips, yelling more at my mother—probably about her party planning.

My mom's expression remains staid, and as her hater continues to yell, pointing and gesturing toward me first, then Noah, my mom calmly opens the snap on her purse and reaches in, pulling out the thin, silver bottle of leftover party paint she had in her purse from when she and Linda met to make posters for the first game. Without a second of warning, my mom takes one step forward and sprays it at the Tiger logo embroidered on the center of the woman's sweater, causing her to fall backward and scream.

"Oh...shit!" I say, scrambling up the steps, leaving our things and reaching my mom just as others around her are holding her down, several calling the police.

"Let her go!" I yell, trying to pry their grip from my mom's arm.

"That's assault! That...that was assault!" one woman yells.

My mom doesn't fight them, eventually sitting down calmly on the edge of the bleacher row and waiting. I sit next to her while clutching her purse in my arms to protect it from the circling booster wolves. The sounds of their yelling, their disparaging comments and cruel names— they're careful not to call my mom a bitch, but they come as close as they can without doing so—it all fades to background noise. They keep bickering, pointing and accusing, even when the police officer working the game comes up to take everyone's statement.

My mom calmly watches the field, her eyes transfixed on the scoreboard as the clock ticks down. She looks on as our defense completely falls apart under someone else's direction, Nico never getting a chance to touch the ball again. She watches The Tradition lose, and then a slow smile creeps across her face, and her eyes shift to mine before the officer kneels in front of her to get her version of the story.

"I suppose spray-painting a pair of fake tits looks better on your record than smoking pot and driving through the garage," she says to me, not whispering enough.

The cop, thankfully, doesn't seem to care all that much. He likely has to deal with yuppie, ticky-tack reports all day, working around Cornwall. How petty and stupid his report must look when turned in next to the guy from West End.

Dad had been escorted from the field, and waited for us on one of the few picnic tables in the grassy area between the football field and the locker rooms. I find him, after the woman—Penny Schmidtt, a friend of Tori O'Donahue's—decides not to press charges against Mom. Linda caught the entire thing on video with her phone, including the part where Penny called my mom some torrid names and tried to conceal the vodka she snuck in her enormous snakeskin purse.

"What was that all about?" he asks, gesturing to the stands, where my mom still weaves her way down through the crowd. I'm still holding her purse, which no longer conceals the can of paint. The police officer *did* take that off her hands.

"Mom sort of..." I stop, wanting to rephrase this. "She stood up for herself."

"She did, huh?" my dad says, looking from me back to the metal steps where my mom climbs down and tugs down her shirt, straightening her sleeves and pants to make sure she looks as if nothing happened at all. Polished and perfect—the Lauren Prescott way.

Her eyes meet my father's as she walks up to join us, and there's a slight sway to her hips, her own feminine brand of swagger. Her lips are puckered in a smile, and I'm sure if she could get away with it at night, she'd slide her enormous round sunglasses on just to prove how little she's bothered by everyone else right now. I know most of it is all an act, but the fact that my mother is finally acting like she doesn't give a shit is downright refreshing.

"You have a little...something happen up there?" my father asks, his right brow about two inches higher than his left.

My mom's lip ticks up to match it. She opens her mouth to speak, but stops at the cackling sound of the women walking down the steps a dozen feet behind us, one pulling a sweater out from her chest, some of the paint on her arms and hands.

"Those women are real bitches, Chad. What did I ever see in them?" she says, leaving her gaze on the ladies as they march to the center of the parking lot to the large Cadillac Escalade with a plate that reads JIMSGAL.

While my mother looks on, my dad's eyes never leave his wife, his mouth curving up sinisterly. My mom looks back to catch his stare.

"What?" she says.

"Absolutely nothing," my dad says slowly, shaking his head, stepping toward her and kissing her hard on the mouth, just like he did that morning in the kitchen.

In an instant, our attention is swung to the locker-room entrance on the other side of us. Valerie Medina has stopped Coach O'Donahue right outside the locker room. She timed it perfectly, letting all of the players filter in first and cutting him off just after his coaching staff stepped inside to safety. She isn't touching him, but with the way he's backed off into the dark corner, one would think she was wielding a sword and fists of fury.

"You will apologize sir, right now. You will apologize to me. To my family. And most importantly, you will apologize to my son. You *do not* touch him like that!"

We can only hear bits and pieces of her rampage, but that part rings out clear. My father hears and steps up to join her, crossing his arms just as her brother, Nico's uncle, has, which only inflames Coach O'Donahue more.

"Oh, come on! What the hell...did you put her up to this, Prescott?" I hear him say as my dad moves in closer.

My father only shakes his head. I draw in when I see my brother walking out from the locker room along with Travis and Colton.

"Listen...ma'am," Coach O'Donahue begins. His reference to her only makes her grow more stiff, and I can tell he's not scoring any points.

"It's clear you don't understand how things work out here. This sport is a tough sport, and I need these young men to be able to stand up to a lot of things. Now, if he can't handle me being tough with him, then maybe this team isn't for your boy…"

The underlying smile as he speaks says volumes. Jimmy O'Donahue *needs* Nico Medina to be anywhere close to successful for the rest of the season. But if Nico quits? If his mom pulls him? Well, that's out of his hands.

What he didn't bargain on, however, was Valerie Medina's spirt—and her coaching brother. And the rest of us, who remain here, all watching.

Valerie steps in close, her hair still flawless from her day at work, her blouse an exact match to her silky pants, her purse gripped tightly at the straps in her hand at her side. Her heels click against the concrete as she steps toward him, and she holds her finger in front of his face. Her words are so soft they're kept between her and the coach who tried to strong-arm her son. But he never speaks back when she's done. She backs away slowly, leaning in to say something to my dad, then turning to her brother and nodding for him to join her as they both move to the parking lot at a steady pace, her feet pounding into the ground with force in every step.

I move up and slide my hand under my dad's arm; Jimmy O'Donahue cracks his neck, spits on the ground, and steps into the locker room barking at Travis and Colton, "Get your asses in there," as the door closes behind him. The boys do, leaving my brother with me and my father.

"What did she say?" I ask my dad.

"She told him…he had a lot to learn about being a human, and that if he ever belittled her again—assuming she didn't understand football or the law—she would have her brother shove a helmet on his head so she could jerk his neck around and see how he liked it," my dad says, blinking, almost in amazement.

"Wow," I say, the word slow and round as it escapes.

"Then she told him she planned on getting the game tape, and she's still not sure if she wants to send it to the media or not," my dad says.

His words spark my urgency in an instant. I squeeze his arm and dash off to the bleachers, rushing up the steps to the press box, tripping on the last few metal rows and racking my knee against the corner so hard that I'm sure it's bleeding under my jeans. The press box door is still open, but the lights inside are off. I feel my way to the ladder and push up on the ceiling hatch to climb out onto the roof.

My camera is lying on its side, and I know before I even get to it that it's likely turned off. I pull it into my hands and switch it on, then sink back, my body resting against the small half wall that lines the roof. The film was turned off after three minutes. I filmed nothing more than a few warm-ups. Those bastards thought of everything.

I sulk back to my parents, my camera packed away in the bag, and my father nods to me as I get closer, questioning if I got it on film without really asking. I shake my head *no*, and his eyes close slowly, his arm stretching out for me to fall into his side.

My dad eventually sends my mom home with Noah, and he stays with me while every player leaves the locker room. One by one, they walk up to him and shake his hand. It wasn't something planned, which makes it all the more beautiful. My father's eyes tear at one point, when players that rarely get a chance to even step on the field walk up, some of them hugging him and telling him they'll always be playing for him, even if they're not.

Jimmy O'Donahue's coaching staff exits, too, but they stand against the far wall together, watching the display of affection for the man that should still be at the helm. My father was the victim of gross private-school politics, and they know it could happen to them at any moment. I don't fault them for holding on to their jobs. I know as they stand there together—away from Jimmy, who still hides inside—they feel the same as every player giving Chad Prescott their allegiance.

Nico is the last to step out, and he walks up to my father without even wavering, his gear slung over his back, his board tucked under his arm. My father takes his bag from him without exchanging words, then puts his arm around him just as silently.

"I told your mom I would take you home," he says, surprising me, because I didn't know that was part of their exchange.

"Yes, sir," Nico says.

"It's just *Chad* now, son. Just Chad," my dad says.

"Yes, sir," Nico says again.

My father chuckles, and I follow them both a few steps behind. When we get to the car, my dad looks over to mine, then his eyes come to me.

"I'll bring you back to get your car when we're done. Come on," my dad says.

I climb inside, letting Nico take the front seat next to my father, and we drive the eleven miles to West End in silence, Nico only speaking after we cross the freeway and my dad needs directions. We pull up to the house, and Valerie is waiting just outside the door with a bouncing Alyssa at her side. Uncle Danny's car is still out front, so I'm sure he's still inside.

I linger in the back seat of the car as Nico steps out, and I watch as my father helps him with his bag, walking him up to his house, and shaking hands with Nico's mom. She grips my dad's hand in both of hers, and my father doesn't look up from their touch for the longest time while she just speaks. Nico turns in the doorway, his eyes meeting mine, and he pulls his phone from his pocket, waving it to let me know he'll call. I pull mine in my hands and climb to the front seat as my father walks back to the car.

He gets in and shifts the car into reverse, exhaling heavily and checking his mirrors before finally pulling out into the roadway. We get to the stoplight at the freeway, and I feel my phone buzz in my hands. I'm about to look when my dad finally speaks.

"That kid is something special, and I'm not going to let what happened to me ruin it for him, Reagan. You tell him I promise, okay?"

My dad's face is serious; the red glow shines over his skin at the light, reflected against the way his jaw works and his lips frown in frustration.

A few sprinkles hit the windshield, and as the signal switches to green, my dad flicks on the wipers, the car now filled with the low hum of some sports-radio station and the squeal of the rubber blade along the window. The sound is comforting and pulls a dozen memories to the front of my mind, remembering the smell, the feel, every little sensation that went along with so many games that I rode home from in this very seat with my dad. It makes me smile.

"Okay," I say, finally responding to his question.

"Okay, then," he says back, his heavy hand patting my knee twice.

His face seems to soften with our agreement, as if making this promise out loud to me somehow eases my dad's pain. Maybe it does.

When his attention is completely given back to the roadway, I flip my phone in my palm and swipe open the message from Nico. It's nothing more than a picture of a heart. I send the same thing back, and then I hold it tightly in my hands, and I believe that my father will do what he says.

CHAPTER 20

"Mom, really…your dress is fine," I say as my mom fusses with the tie belt around her waist, hiding behind my dad's car in Nico's driveway.

Valerie invited us over for Saturday lunch with her family. She insisted, and my father couldn't refuse. For the last fifteen hours, my mom has been panicking about making a good impression, and my father has been pouting over giving up his first free Saturday in years. Mostly, my dad doesn't like to be social. The parties were always my mom's thing, while dad had the built-in excuse to leave and go talk football in the backyard with the other coaches or with my brother. He avoided. But when she asked him to come today while he stood at her doorstep last night with her son, he couldn't refuse.

"I'm not sure why we have all of this food," my dad says, popping his trunk and pulling out a box with a crockpot and two trays of cookies, brownies, and whatever other baked good my mom could buy at the deli counter on her mad dash to the market this morning.

"What's in the pot?" I ask, taking it from my dad. I look down and see something boiling through the lid.

"I made pozole," my mom says through a beaming smile.

"Like…from scratch?" I ask, my brow pulled tight.

"She poured it in from a mix. I watched her," my brother says over my shoulder as he awkwardly climbs from the car with his crutches that were stretched across our laps for the ride here.

"Thank God," I say to him.

"I know, right?" he chuckles.

"Hush, both of you. I could cook if I wanted to," she says.

Our father lets her walk on to the door, but turns to face us with the trays of cookies in his hands and shakes his head to show how little he agrees with that statement.

Alyssa has the door held open by the time my mom reaches the porch, and she already has her eyes on the trays of cookies. The laughter spills out of the house, and I can tell from here that several people are inside. I see my family straighten their posture, my dad pausing, probably considering running back to the car. I step in front of them and press my hand on Alyssa's head, scrunching her hair with my fingers.

"Hi, princess," I say.

"Hi, Reagan," she says, a small lisp slipping out through the new hole in her top line of teeth.

"Hey, you lost another one!" I say.

"I did!" she says, stuffing her hand deep into the pocket of her jeans and pulling out a crumpled dollar. "Toof-fairy!"

"Awesome!" I say.

I step inside, urging my family to follow. Nico steps up from a seat at the kitchen table and rushes over to me.

"I didn't know you were here, sorry. I would have helped," he says, leaning in and kissing my cheek chastely, moving quickly to shake my father's hand.

"Here," he says, taking the heavy pot from me. He carries it to the kitchen where his mom clears a place for it, and she pulls the lid off and smells the aroma.

"Oh, it needs to be stirred," she says, pulling a large spoon from a door and stirring the soup a few times while my mother walks up next to her.

"It's pozole," my mom says proudly, as if she spent hours slaving over it.

"Yes, I recognize it. Thank you…you didn't have to bring anything," Valerie smiles.

My mom acts bashful, waving her hand as if what she did was nothing at all, which…it really wasn't. I notice a pot on her stove and I step close enough to look inside, where homemade soup is brewing. Valerie's eyes catch mine, and she winks. I smile. She's going to keep this secret, and it makes me like her even more to see her spare my mom's feelings.

Nico leads my father and brother around the table and into the backyard where more people are gathered, introducing them, always calling my father *Coach* and saying Noah is his son and a great quarterback. I'm sure Noah thinks this is all Nico kissing up, but I know better. It's respect, his way of showing it. By the time they're sitting near a fire pit on a small brick patio in the backyard with Nico's uncle and a few of the neighbors, I see my father's comfort level starting to settle in. My brother's, too. I leave them, staying at my mom's side and talking in the kitchen with Nico's mom and aunt and Mrs. Mendoza from across the street.

While conversation outside seems to have evolved into the easy topic of football and Nico's potential—inside is another story. The lulls are too many, and I can see my mom struggling to fill them. She's complimented the house, which I know she thinks is sparse and old, but she's bluffed well. She's also praised the scent pouring from the kitchen, not flinching when Mrs. Mendoza said it was the pozole. It's really coming from Valerie's soup, but my mom sat up a little taller thinking it was hers.

"Your yard is beautiful," I say to Mrs. Mendoza after another long moment of silence. She perks up at my approval, and Valerie and a few other women in the kitchen grumble.

"Why thank you, Reagan," she says, turning her head from side to side, looking at the others.

"Am I…missing something?" I ask.

262

"Ugh," says the woman at the far end of the table. "She was featured in the *Southwest Gardener* magazine last month and ever since, her head. Oh my God, I mean…I can't even."

"I have *not* had a big head," Mrs. Mendoza says, which only ignites a round of laughter from every woman in the kitchen other than her, me, and my mom. My mom eventually bites her lip and giggles because it's contagious.

"Let me just show you," Valerie says, pulling open a drawer and taking out something that looks like a poster. She walks over to the table and unrolls a laminated copy of the magazine spread, holding the ends down so it doesn't curl up. The main photo is of Mrs. Mendoza in her front yard with a pair of shears and a bright-green watering can. "Just look. It's laminated. She made one…for all of us!"

"I only thought you would be proud of your friend," Mrs. Mendoza says as she begins to get up. I can tell her feelings are a little genuinely hurt, but I also get the sense that she's not about to get great sympathy from this group.

"Oh, Maria…stop. Sit down and just autograph it for me already," Valerie says, holding out a marker, her other hand on her hip.

Mrs. Mendoza stops only a step or two away from her chair, her lips pursed and her perfect lipstick slightly smeared by her pouting.

"Are you just going to sell it?" she asks, holding a serious expression in her face-off with Valerie. The quiet lasts for a few seconds before they both finally break into a laugh.

"Absolutely," Valerie says. "I'll put it on eBay, become a millionaire, and hire my own damn gardener for my house in Malibu."

"Pssshhh, Malibu is overrated. You want to go to Santa Fe," Maria says, taking the marker and actually signing the copy of her magazine article. "That's where all of the *new* rich people are going."

Valerie takes it and pins it to the front of the refrigerator with four mismatched magnets.

"Reagan, have you heard about Nico and the roses?" Maria says, taking her seat again at the table.

"No," I smirk, my mouth twitching in curiosity. I scoot my chair closer to hear her better.

"When he was a little boy, he used to sneak into my front yard with his kiddie scissors, the kind that barely cut paper, you know?"

"Yeah, I know what you mean," I answer.

"Well, he would cut a rose on his way to school. Only, I didn't know he was doing this. And every morning I would inspect my roses, feeding them and watering them, and always there would be one or two missing, almost ripped from the bush. It was the ugliest cut, and the petals would be sprinkled around the yard. I thought maybe it was someone's puppy, or a cat. So one morning, I got up extra early, and I lay down by my back fence, real low so no one could see me. And here comes little Nico with his school bag over his shoulder. He pulls out his sad pair of scissors and cuts a red one from the bush, sawing at it and eventually ripping it free, and I jump out and scream, 'Aha!'"

I jump a little in my chair, and the women laugh at me.

"You know what he was doing?" she says.

"No," I smile, shaking my head.

She leans forward in her chair, her arms folded on the table.

"That little stinker was taking the flowers to school to give to some girl he liked. He would bring her one every day. Of course, after stuffing it in his backpack and dehydrating it for most of his trip to school, it was always sad and pathetic-looking by the time he handed it to the poor girl, I'm sure. But he still did it."

"That's…" I sit back. "That's…really sweet."

The rest of the women all have the same expression, even my mom.

"It is," she says, closing her eyes briefly at the memory. "I started meeting him out front every morning after that. I would cut the rose for him, trim it up and wrap the stem in a paper towel. He'd always say, 'Thank you, Mrs. Mendoza.' He'd head off to school with a flower to deliver. This went on for a few weeks, and then finally I had to ask him, 'Nico, what does your girl think of all these flowers? Is she your girlfriend yet?'"

She stands, pushing in her chair and moving toward the kitchen, and we all turn, engrossed by her story.

"You know what he told me?" she asks.

I shake my head *no* again.

"He said she told him she thought he was ugly, and he should stop bringing her flowers," she chuckles.

My mouth drops to a frown fast, and my mom gasps a sad noise.

"That's horrible," I say, imagining a heartbroken Nico being told he's ugly by a girl he liked enough to bring flowers to.

"I thought so, too. But then I thought, he's still taking the flowers. So, I asked him what he was doing with the flowers now, and he said he was bringing them to new girls. He said he was going to give a flower to a new girl every day instead, to make them feel nice. And we kept up our deal, every morning. He took flowers to teachers, to the woman that ran the cafeteria, to the principal, to girls in his class. It didn't matter who they were, he said. They all deserved flowers. And one day, there would be a girl that he thought deserved them all."

My breath is gone when she lifts a vase from the sink, blooms of purple, pink, orange, white and red stuffed inside, each hand-cut carefully, stuffed and fit together in a clear-blue vase with a ribbon tied around the center. My eyes mist as she brings the vase close to me, and I rub my thumbs to blot away the tears. My mom does the same.

"Thanks, Mrs. Mendoza," Nico says from behind me, his hands stuffed in his pockets, pushing them down deep, his shoulders hunched in a shrug, his smile crooked. The sweetest boy I've ever known.

"You're welcome, Mijo," she says. I stand and take them from her, breathing in their scent before turning slowly and walking over to him.

"You're something, you know that?" I say, shaking my head and setting my flowers down on the corner of the table. I push my hands beneath his arms, wrapping them around his waist until he finally lets his free from his pockets and pulls me close to him, squeezing me against his chest and kissing the top of my head.

"They're beautiful," I say.

"You're beautiful," he says, letting out a small breath with his shrug and crooked smile.

"What's going on in here?" my father asks, a little looser after what I'm guessing is his third beer. He steps in through the back door and Nico lets go of his hold on me out of habit.

"Not much, Chad. Your daughter's boyfriend is just raising the bar really high, making all you men look bad," my mom says.

My father's brow wrinkles, and the entire table of women laugh, some reaching across to high-five my mom.

My dad turns his focus to Nico next.

"I just gave her flowers sir," he shrugs, keeping his shoulders high like he's waiting for the punch.

My dad looks to the table, leaning forward to smell them, then stepping back.

"Flowers, huh?" he says.

He pulls one out from center, holding it out in a gesture as if to ask if he can have it. Nico nods with a smile, and my dad walks around the table and hands it to my mom. She takes it in her delicate hand, her head falling to the side as she looks up to meet my father's gaze.

"You romantic fool," she teases, moving to her feet and then her tiptoes as she kisses my dad softly on the lips, blushing under his gaze as she sits again.

"Awe." Nico's Uncle Danny puts on a feminine voice to break the mood and tease my dad, and soon the kitchen is buzzing with laughter and music.

Valerie begins serving food, handing plates around and encouraging everyone to come in from outside, inviting more neighbors over to eat. My brother has found a spot on the sofa next to Nico, and they're both sitting with plates on their laps and the USC game on the TV. I stay in the kitchen, watching them talk, and pound fists over good plays.

"I love their game," my brother says.

"Oh my God, I know. They never huddle. But everyone knows exactly what the play is, where to go, and they hit it—every freakin' time!" Nico says loudly.

"Nicolas Medina, your tongue!" Valerie shouts from the kitchen.

"I said *freakin'* Mom," he shouts.

"Yeah, don't act like I don't know what freakin' means. Beat your freakin' head next time you think you can use that word here," she says, moving her attention back to her plate, reaching for a pitcher of lemonade in the center of the table.

Nico laughs her off, chuckling with my brother, and the scene of them both seems so perfect, I don't know why it's taken so long to happen.

"You like Southern Cal then, huh?" my dad says from the easy chair he's commandeered on the opposite end of the living room.

"Hell yeah…I mean…*heck* yeah," Nico says, quieting down, but still getting a glare from his mom.

They all turn their attention back to the TV, and my brother pushes himself up to his feet awkwardly, having to use Nico's shoulder for a lift so he can stand, his arm pumping as he shouts, "Go, go, go!"

"Wooo whoo!" There's a collective scream from the living room, and Alyssa runs through waving a homemade golden pom-pom in her hand, doing her best to do a cartwheel in the small space between the living room and kitchen.

It quiets again after the celebration, and for some reason, my eyes move to my father. He's stopped eating, and eventually he leans forward enough to set his half-full plate on the small coffee table in the center of the room. He rests back in the chair again and rubs his hands together, his eyes eventually settling on Nico.

"They're interested," my dad says.

Nico glances to him briefly, but looks back at the television, not realizing what my father means. My eyes grow wide, and I step from my seat, moving to the living room. My quick movement catches Valerie's attention, and she slides up next to me, looking at me, about to ask if something's wrong, when my dad continues.

"Nico," he says, getting his attention. Nico's laughing at something with Noah, but he turns to my dad, quieting down. "USC…they're…they're interested."

The only sound now is the announcer on the TV. Nico reaches forward and clicks the mute button, dropping the remote back to the table and folding his arms over his knees, leaning toward my dad. He looks stunned, and maybe a little frightened.

"I'm sure there are more, but I don't get all of the calls now. USC called before I was fired, and I sent them game tape. They followed up last week, and they're coming. They didn't say for sure, but I'd be ready to have the game of your life Friday."

"You're serious," Nico says, his voice almost a panic.

"I don't joke about football, son," my dad says.

Nico lets out a heavy breath, his hands moving to his hair, pushing his hat from his head and letting it fall against the wall while his fingers thread through the dark-brown strands on his head. His eyebrows lift high, and his eyes are glued wide.

"Nico, baby," his mom says, moving to sit on the arm of the sofa. He twists and hugs her, and she kisses the top of his head, looking to my dad as she does, mouthing, "Thank you."

My father smiles and nods, a look of pride on his face, but also pain. He wants to guide him through it all, but he has walls in his way now. He hates that he can't hold his hand completely. My father—he loves Nico. Just like I thought he would.

The lunch party lasted well into the dinner hour with neighbors, church members, family, and friends dropping in and out of the Medina house until the sun began to fall. My parents left, my mom rounding up my drunken sleepy father by about six. Colton and Sasha ended up coming over, and my brother stood in the middle of the road throwing a child-size football to them and Nico while they all made bets over who could catch the best pass.

Watching them made me wish we'd all grown up together—more

than we already have.

Eventually, Sasha, Colton and my brother leave, each offering to give me a ride that I don't take because I want to stay here, with Nico. Our time alone is mostly non-existent. We see each other at school, under my dad's watchful eye, in busy hallways, or at Charlie's with the rest of the school. I think we've both been counting on the time when the sun went down, and as his mother sits at the kitchen table with her girlfriends playing cards, his niece asleep on the sofa, a cartoon on the TV, Nico takes my fingers in his, leading me down the hallway to his room.

He leaves his door open a crack at first, but it falls more and more closed each time he passes. He turns on his stereo, then pushes the door in more. He pulls his blinds closed, and nudges the door. He spreads his blanket out nicely over his rumpled bed; the door clicks to a close.

"You are a bad boy, Nico Medina," I say, suddenly very aware of the loose shirt I wore over my favorite leggings, my feet in only socks as I left my Vans by the front door. My hair, of course, is down.

His eyes narrow on me as his chin falls toward his chest, his back against his door, and he reaches his finger forward, hooking it in the neck of my shirt, tugging me toward him. My feet obey, my hands feeling the softness of his gray Tradition football T-shirt, the ridges of his abs hard underneath. I breathe in and out once quickly in anticipation, catching just enough of his scent, the mix of him and whatever it is he showers in. I dream that scent.

Nico shakes his head slowly, his eyes watching as his right hand slides my hair from my shoulder first, then his left does the same. He swallows hard, his finger again hooked in the collar of my shirt, above my shoulder. He drags it over the crest of my arm gently, his head falling forward until his lips rest on my bare skin. As he tilts his head up again, his finger traces the line of my black bra strap, and a shiver runs down my spine.

His gaze come to mine, and he steps into me, spinning me so my back is flush against his door and his chest is touching me, mine aching for more as his hands move from my shoulders to my neck until they cup my face. Nico leans slightly to the right, as do I, and our lips come together softly at first. I can feel his shake when he holds my bottom lip between his.

"You're nervous," I tease, breathing the words against his mouth.

"I am," he says.

I kiss him again, mine trembling, too, but I don't care, because I can't stop the reaction my body has with him.

"Why?" I ask, trailing kisses down his jaw to his neck.

Nico sweeps my hair in one hand, lifting it so he can do the same, kissing along my collar bone, up my jaw and finding my ear, his teeth dragging along my sensitive skin.

"Because I want to touch you," he whispers, his words buckling my knees.

He sucks the lobe of my ear and leans his weight into me more, his head dragging along mine until our lips meet to kiss again. We kiss without breathing for almost a minute, and when Nico finally breaks away to look at me, I'm panting.

"You can," I say, feeling the heat rush up my chest, choking me.

He shakes his head, leaning in just enough to touch his nose softly against mine.

"Please," I whisper, and he stops moving. "Touch me. If…only if you want to."

Nico takes a sharp breath, and his eyes close as his fingers run along my cheeks to my shoulders. His lids open and our eyes lock briefly before he nods, his gaze moving to my neck and then following the path of his hands as he slides them along my ribs, down to my hips, reaching the bottom of my shirt and gathering the material in his palms.

He looks to me for approval, and I nod slowly, biting my lip and listening nervously to the sounds on the other side of the door. The women still giggle at the table, the television still plays lightly— everything is the same. And for once, for a rare moment, Nico and I are alone.

His hands continue to gather my shirt until his fingertips find my skin, the edge of my bra against my ribs, my stomach clenched tight with my held breath. Nico continues to move upward, the back of his knuckles dragging over my breasts slowly, against the silk and lace, against my chest and neck until he lifts my shirt over my head, leaving my arms up against the door, bound by the fabric.

His right hand traces my face as he leans in to kiss me, his lips tasting mine while his left hand comes down now to join the other, both moving along my sides in sync, stopping when his thumbs find the edge of my bra. My body arches into him, aching for him to cross the boundary I know he's hesitating at. I can't seem to ask him, so I breathe in, arching again, my breath falling away in a stutter against his mouth.

Nico steps back enough to let his head fall against mine, his eyes looking down at the movement of his hands. I close mine, waiting—*anticipating*. He traces the lace edge of my bra, the only nice one I really own, slowly, passing several times before running once over each breast. His fingers trail behind, and each small meeting of his hand…*there*…leaves me wanting more until his thumbs slip under each cup and rub against the hardest parts.

"Ah," I let out a small pant, and Nico nips at my lips, his hands caressing me even more, fully cupping each breast and bringing his fingers together to put pressure where it feels so sweet.

Reaching up, he grabs my shirt, tossing it to the floor next to us, and when I look at him nervously, he holds his finger to his mouth, reminding me to stay silent—*grinning*.

My head falls back to rest on the door, and he slides my bra straps slowly down my arms until they fall loose around my biceps. His hands move back to my breasts again, slipping inside the material, wriggling it down as I pull my arms free until I'm completely exposed, my chest heaving with my quick breaths.

His kiss begins at my bottom lip, but trails lower without hesitation as he drags his mouth along my chin, his fingertips pushing gently, forcing my gaze up as he leaves small kisses along my neck, sucking over the rise of my right breast until he stops in the center, his tongue passing over my hard peak, his teeth closing with light pressure that makes me want to moan. I move my arms around him, squeezing his head against me as he sucks so hard it hurts. I only want more, though.

Nico moves to my other breast, doing the same, his hands running up the back of my legs until they hold me from behind, pulling me tight against him. I can feel his arousal, and my body pushes back, wanting to feel it more. Lifting me up, he turns the knob on his door, locking it, and I look at him, questioning.

"We won't stay in here long," he says, his voice still hushed. "I just...I want to kiss you alone a little longer. I've waited so long..."

"I know what you mean," I say, smiling against his lips.

Nico rests me on his bed, and I fall deep into the softness, his body coming down on top of mine. My knees bend up on instinct, making room for him to press into me, our most intimate parts touching, clothed and chaste, but so hungry.

"I've never..." I say.

"It's okay," he says, brushing a kiss over my lips. "I don't want that. Not until you're ready. I just..."

"I know," I say, my hands flat on his back, pulling him toward me, wanting him to press into me harder to relieve the ache.

Nico's hands slide up my waist, grazing against my breasts lightly and pushing up into my hair as he kisses me hard. My fingers work his shirt up over his head, as I boldly rush to feel his bare chest against my skin.

Everything about him is hot, his skin searing, and I cling to it, my fingers grabbing his shoulders tightly as he presses his weight into me, his hips rocking with his kiss, a faint moan escaping him. His hands slide behind me, pulling my hips into him as his body rests on mine, our lips locked together and the friction of where our bodies meet growing into an undeniable heat that I can't help but chase. Wanting him, more of him, I push up on one shoulder, rolling him to his back so I can straddle him, my hips moving in a steady rhythm while my hands lie flat on his chest and Nico looks at me, his eyes pleading for me not to stop.

I can't stop.

I won't stop.

I want to feel this just as much as he does. I've never…

Nico pulls me to him, his hands grabbing my ass, helping me to move against him until the pressure becomes so strong that I feel it fall over the edge inside me, my core clenching, my stomach tightening. My face falls to his neck, to his shoulder, and my teeth sink in lightly on his skin, and I whimper with each wave, Nico pulling me into him again. Again. Again. Until I feel him breathe rapidly against my neck, his mouth tasting me, his teeth leaving a mark.

He holds me tight when the motion stops. After several minutes, his hands fall away, but his fingers tickle against my arms, moving my hair from my face, kissing me softly. His eyes rake over me one last time before he sits up, stepping over to his door, lifting my shirt and handing it to me. He puts his on, and holds out a hand, helping me to stand.

"You should probably comb your hair," he smirks, and I blush hard.

He runs his fingers through a few times, but I do more as he steps to his drawer, pulling out a pair of shorts and boxers. I shut my eyes tightly, embarrassed, and he chuckles.

"Oh, now you're shy," he says.

"Just…just, oh my God, go change," I say, both hands quickly covering my face.

Nico steps up to me, pulling my hands away, his nose nuzzling mine, his dimple evidence of his smile.

"Don't cover your face. You're too beautiful," he says.

"Oh my God, corn—," I say, and he kisses me before the word can fully leave my lips.

"Corny," I finish when he's done. He winks, and slips out of his room, holding his thumb up to let me know the coast is clear, and nobody heard a thing.

I wait for Nico just inside his door, and he takes my hand, guiding me down the hallway to the back patio door, opening it to lead me outside. We sit by the fire pit with our feet up, tossing in bits of leftover food, and pieces of paper, watching them ignite and fly away as embers. There's laughter inside, and we both lean to look around the fire, his mom slamming her hands on the table with her heavy laughter, the other women joking, too.

"I wish my mom would have stayed," I say.

Nico looks to me, his brow low.

"She could use friends like these. That's all," I say, watching the scene in the kitchen fondly.

"My mom liked her; I could tell," he says.

I tilt my head to the side, letting it fall against my arm, pulling my leg up so I can look at him, the way he looks with the fire glowing and outlining his profile.

"I memorized your profile," I say, pulling my knee in closer. He flits his eyes to me, but looks back at the fire, his feet resting on the bricks of the pit. He pokes a stick into the flames, moving a chunk of wood and making it crackle.

"Yeah?" he asks.

"I did. Because you don't really make eye contact in class. You sort of go to your own little world when you think. I don't even think you look at our teacher," I say, squinting as I realize this fact.

Nico smirks and chuckles lightly, his lip raised on one side.

"I don't," he says.

I pull in my brow.

"Why?" I ask.

He takes in a long breath, eventually dropping the stick to the ground.

"At my old school...at Public? You sort of always got in trouble when you made eye contact," he says, laughing at his own answer.

"That feels strict. Like...don't even look the teachers in the eyes? Will their laser beams get you?" I joke.

"No," he chuckles. "Nothing like that. Just...there was always someone doing something wrong—talking in class, yelling something, or pushing someone around. Sometimes people would break things, or draw on the walls or whatever. The teachers could never catch the right person, so if you looked them in the eyes, they would just say 'You! Come here!' Then next thing you knew, you were against the wall at recess and all of the other kids were making fun of you."

"That's awful," I say.

He laughs, then reaches down for his stick again, breaking a piece off and tossing it into the fire.

"When I got older, though, it's like the teachers couldn't stand that I knew more than they did. If I looked them in the eye, they'd try to tell me I was wrong about something, or to be quiet and not ask the questions I was asking," he says, tilting his head to look at me. "I begged Mom to let me apply to Cornwall when I was in eighth grade. She said if I could get the scholarship, I could go."

"You and Sasha both got in," I smile.

He chuckles.

"Yeah, but he's here because he's fast. They wanted him for soccer and track," he says.

"You're the brainy one," I say.

"Don't you mean *nerd?*" He cocks his brow.

"Oh, now you want to be the nerd," I tease back.

Nico leans into me, poking his finger into my side and tickling me. I giggle and gasp for breath, reaching to try to tickle him back, when we both freeze, our eyes meeting Mrs. Mendoza's as she stands with one hand over her mouth in the center of the now-opened patio door.

"Maria?" Nico questions, his hands falling away from me. He gets to his feet quickly, rushing to her, her face ghosted, her eyes red, the tears falling nonstop. "What...what is it?"

He gets to her and holds her arm in his as she reaches for him, her balance off. She struggles to speak, nothing coming out but nonsense. Eventually she gestures inside, only able to say, "You need to go get your mom. The door...go..."

Nico's body goes rigid, and I see his breath leave his body in a blink before he sprints inside his house. I rush to my feet and move to Maria;

we embrace each other, both looking inside through the glass.

Nico's mom is on the floor, on her knees, sobbing with her hands pressed flat on the floor in front of her. At the door, two men dressed in full military uniforms stand solemnly. Nico has stopped in front of them, his hands gripping at his hair, his shoulders rising and falling with his rapid breath, until eventually he kneels to the floor, pulling his mother into his arms as he sits back, holding her while she cries through her worst nightmare.

"Alyssa!" I say, seeing the little girl stand next to the door, her hand holding the door frame, her small face looking up at the two men, not understanding. I rush inside to help, but before I'm there, Nico has called her over, and he's holding her in his arms, too, rocking them both and telling them it will be okay.

"It's going to be okay, baby girl," he whispers, his eyes wet and fixed on a dream in the distance. "Shhhh, Momma. He was brave. It's going to be okay."

The air outside, behind the Marines at the door, is quiet. West End is peaceful tonight, and the moon is full. But nothing is okay. A brother, father and son has fallen.

Nico's home—it will never be the same.

CHAPTER 21

My father came to pick me up from Nico's house. He ended up staying for three hours with me. In an instant, Nico had lost his light, and I could see it. He was so broken—*is* so broken. I don't know how to fix it any more now than I did days ago…when he held his mother, and all of the pieces she was breaking into, together as best he could on the cold concrete floor.

It's Friday, and Nico has missed practice the entire week. I've talked to my father about it a few times, and he thinks Jimmy O'Donahue is going to try to start Brandon in Nico's place. The board doesn't care—they're cold and heartless, and they don't want a distracted quarterback.

They want the win.

Tonight's game is important. If we win, we clinch a spot in the state playoffs. But more than that, USC is showing up tonight—they're coming to watch a few of our players, and they've sat in on a few practices this week, none of which Nico was at.

I've been banned from being on the field at practice, too, and despite Bob's best attempt to lie that I was his assistant and *he* needed me on the field to help with training, the wall put up between me and the coaching staff stayed strong. They know who I am, and as far as Jimmy's concerned, I'm the enemy.

I haven't talked to Nico, other than a few short conversations on the phone. I dropped off a stack of homework assignments by his front door yesterday. I set them amidst the flowers, notes, and pans of food that had been left for Nico, his mom, and Alyssa. I recognized the roses from Mrs. Mendoza's yard, and when I went home, I pulled several of the dying ones from my vase, drying them and sliding them into the pages of a dictionary to press them flat. They will forever be one of the most precious things I've ever been given.

I'm unfolding the blanket on the front row of the bleachers to save room for my family when a pair of hands slips into view, grabbing one end and helping me.

"I thought you could use company, since nobody wants to sit by us," my brother says, helping me shake the blanket out before laying it along the front row.

"Hey, no crutches!" I say, noticing he's in a modified type of cast cut below his knee.

My brother hops on his good leg a few times.

"I went today. Doc says it's healing incredibly fast. I still can't put pressure on it, though," he says.

"So you...hopped up here?" I scold him a little, knowing how my brother hates obeying any orders, even the ones from his doctor.

"Scooter," he says, turning to look over his shoulder. I look to the corner, by the bleacher ramp at the end, and I see it.

"Cute...why pink?" I ask, looking him in the eyes again.

"Mom's choice. She said she's still punishing me in little ways. I have a feeling that's going to last for years," he says.

"Yeah, you're probably right," I say.

We both sit on either end of the blanket, and my brother holds my various pieces of equipment as I set up my tripod, wanting to keep it in front of me to film tonight. I'm not taking any chances of it mysteriously getting turned off.

"Dad says USC is coming," my brother says, handing me my equipment bag when we're done so I can zip it closed.

"They are," I say, inhaling and holding it for a few seconds before blowing it out hard enough to move the few fine hairs around my face. "I hope they let Nico play."

"Oh…they will," Noah says, his eyes out on the field where the team of referees are arriving and inspecting the sidelines. I stare at him for several seconds until he turns to look at me. "What?"

"Why are you so confident, Noah Prescott?" I ask, my lip ticked up in suspicion.

"Let's just say Travis and Colton have a plan," my brother says, pulling his seed bag from his back pocket and tearing it open with his teeth.

I watch him and his smile slides up on one side, too, to match mine, and he winks.

"I hope they know what they're doing," I say.

"I think they've got it handled," he says, looking on again, pouring in a handful of seeds and relaxing back, his arms on the bleacher seat behind us.

My parents arrive a few minutes later, whispering about something that gets both Noah and me curious. I stare at them, leaning forward and showing my obvious interest until my mom finally acknowledges me with the tilt of her head.

"You two are whispering like teenagers and speaking in code. How would you like it if Noah and I did that," I tease, but I genuinely want them to stop.

My mom pulls her lips in tight and smiles with a nod.

"You're right. Chad? We should tell them," my mom says, turning to my father.

"Holy shit, you are *not* pregnant!" my brother says.

"Uh…" my mom laughs out once, hard and guttural. "No. That…that is *definitely* not what we are talking about. Good lord, we finally almost have you two out of the house."

"Gee, thanks," I say.

"Well, that one's kind of a handful," my mom says, pointing her thumb to my brother on the other side.

I laugh and he flips me off. My mom smacks his arm with the back of her hand.

"It's news about me, actually," my dad says, running his hand over his chin, his gaze swinging from my brother to me and then back to my mom. "I…got a job offer today."

"Oh my God, seriously? That's…that's amazing! What? Where?"

"Well, I've always thought your mother looked good in Crimson…" my dad begins, and my brother spits his seeds from his mouth in all directions, pushing up to look my dad in the eyes.

"No fucking way!" Noah shouts.

"Noah James, you watch your mouth!" my mom scolds.

"Sorry, but…Mom…is he serious? Are you…Dad, are you serious?" Noah asks, and I lean forward to watch my dad's face, too.

The smile is the proudest I've seen him wear in years.

"We're moving to Alabama?" I ask, my stomach sick with the mixture of excitement and worry because I don't want to move.

"Not until you graduate. I wouldn't start until next year, fulltime, but I'm going to be working part-time for the rest of this season on the West Coast. I'll be recruiting. I have games and practices I need to go to in California next week," my dad says, excited for the first time since I can't remember when. "Come fall, I'll be the assistant offensive coordinator. Pay's about the same as it is here, but it's a foot in the door. Who knows, I might just find myself in a head gig down the road."

"You will, oh my God, Daddy, I know you will!" I say, reaching over my mom's lap and hugging my dad.

My father's news forms an instant bubble around us, and even though I know there are people walking by, climbing to seats far away from us, not wanting to be associated with our family, I don't care because *they* are the ones who are fools. They're missing out on being a part of our celebration. I glance at the group of women my mom had her issues with last week, and I snicker to myself at the scowls on their faces, the way they try to give me the evil eye to prove a point. They are still stuck in their miserable world where one day someone is on top, and the next they're tossed to the side. It could happen to any one of them next, and I'm so glad my mom has already escaped, however ungraceful her exit was.

It doesn't dawn on me how close we are to game time until I hear the roar from the crowd on the other side of the field. We're playing North, a school with a record just as good as ours, and a quarterback who is being touted as one of the best in the state.

The team runs through a tunnel of cheerleaders, and usually by this time, The Tradition is huddled beyond the lights, chanting and getting pumped to take the field. I look over at the space just outside the entry gates, though, and the space is empty.

"Where are they?" I ask.

"I don't know…that's…strange," my dad says, standing to his feet and stretching to look beyond the darkness.

My eyes move from the clock ticking down the warm-up time, to the closed locker room door, and to the other team that has taken up the center of the field for their stretching. My knees start to shake, and my mom holds her hand on my right one.

"I don't get this. Where are they?" I ask.

"I don't know," she says.

I check the frame in my camera, and capture footage of the other team, showing the time on the clock and our empty side of the field, until we're down to two minutes.

"I see Jimmy…" my dad says, his head falling to the side as he slumps back down to sit. "He's walking out with the other coaches, but that's it."

"They're not coming out unless he starts Nico," Noah says, cracking a single seed shell between his teeth, almost satisfactorily.

My dad glances to Noah, and so do I. My brother looks at us and shrugs.

"I told you they had it handled," Noah smirks.

"Holy sh…" I stop when I see Nico's mom walk in front of us, stopping with her brother and Alyssa at her side.

"Valerie, hi. Please, come sit with us," my mom says, moving back behind me and giving the soft row lined with the blanket to Nico's mom.

"Thank you," she says, her voice raspy from lack of sleep.

She slips into the space next to me, Alyssa climbing to her lap and her brother moving to sit next to my father at the end.

"Nico says the scouts are here," Valerie says, and I can see her eyes fighting to stay strong, not to shed any more tears.

"They are. We saw them walk up. They're in the box," I say, looking over my shoulder.

Valerie turns my direction and looks up, too, staring for a few seconds, breathing slowly. When she turns back, she stops when her eyes meet mine, and she smiles, but the kind that's made from a broken heart. She squeezes my knee, and I cover her hand with mine. I don't have any words to say that will make this better, so I leave it at a simple embrace and a look. I can't fix her pain, and nothing will.

We turn back to the field as whistles begin to blow, and my eyes search for a clue. Coach O'Donahue is talking with the referees while one of his assistant coaches rushes back down the field, hopping the fence for the shortest route and sprinting to the locker room. The other team's four captains are holding hands, waiting in the center of the field for the coin flip, and I start to worry that Jimmy's not going to cave.

"They're going to forfeit," I whisper.

"Huh? Why? Why would they do that?" Nico's mom asks, scooting forward, her eye worried and searching.

"Nah…they won't," Noah says, leaning forward and winking just as the chant of "hoorah!" echoes from the dark behind him.

My chest fills with air and my body feels light, and I realize just how much my muscles have been clenching, on edge.

The team moves toward the field, and I see my friend holding a banner up while she sits on another cheerleader's shoulders, stretching the hand-painted paper, perhaps the ugliest looking drawing of a Tiger I've ever seen, across several feet to another pair of cheerleaders on the other side. The team huddles and disappears behind the banner, their "woofing" and chest-pounding growing like thunder until they break through the center, Nico and Colton at the front, Travis right behind them.

My family and Nico's stands and screams. I'm filled with adrenaline, and my nerves are out of control, my fingers tingling and my legs unable to stop moving. I apologize as I sit down next to Valerie, and she hugs me from the side.

"I can't stop moving, either. It's okay," she says.

With my camera set and propped next to me, I let myself watch kickoff with my own eyes. The North team is huge—in both numbers and size—and they manage to gain twenty yards on their initial run. They make the fifty, and I start to worry—my father and Nico's uncle both shouting the things they see wrong, agreeing and shouting louder.

In a blink, Sasha changes the course of the game. He pulls away from the line, shifting and staying with the targeted receiver, reading the pass perfectly and leaping in front at the right time. He's only able to bring the ball down before the North offense tackles him, but he jumps and pounds his chest as he makes his way to our side, tossing the ball to the ref.

Coach O'Donahue has his offense pulled off to the side, and he's holding up a hand to the ref, giving them instructions before yelling, "Break." When Nico rushes to the field, I get to my feet, not caring that it's only the first play. I'm so happy to see him out there, so proud and so relieved that Jimmy didn't ruin this, too; I have to stand. My mom stands with me, and before long, I've started a movement, and the entire right side of the bleachers is on their feet, screaming.

The hard count is a thing of beauty when it's done right. It requires trust. It thrives on surprise. It needs precision and a certain amount of faith. Rarely, if ever, have I seen a quarterback use it right out of the gate. My dad recognizes it, too, and I smile seeing the smirk on his face. Nico shouts his cadence, the rhythm different, his offense ready— North falls into their hands.

"Offsides!" the announcer says.

The head ref signals the five yards, and both teams move—our opponent now lit and flustered. This is where Nico wants them.

Off guard.

Before the defense is even set, Nico's calling the play, only enough time for them to make it to the line before he's backpedalling, Colton holding the line, Travis sprinting. Fifteen yards out, Nico's pass is a bullet to his chest, and the defense wraps him up. In no-huddle, hurry-up mode, The Tradition scrambles, and they do it again. And again. The same play, only slight variations. North has no answers, and in less than a minute, Nico hits Travis in the end zone, and we're up six to zero.

"That was unbelievable," my dad says, scratching at his chin while my mom grabs his arm in both of her hands, shaking it in her excitement.

"He's better than me," Noah says.

My mom starts in quickly with her "no, honeys" and "you're different," but Noah holds his hand up to stop her.

"He is. He's better than me, and it's okay, Mom. I'm in awe," Noah says, his eyes clear and wide, his head shaking at what just happened on the field.

Nico's Uncle Danny leans to high-five both my brother and my dad, while Nico's mom beams with pride, Alyssa clapping and screaming her uncle's name over and over again—*Nico, Nico, Nico!*

Our defense takes the field for kickoff, and I get an idea. I ask Valerie if Alyssa can come with me, and when she nods *yes,* I take the little girl's hand and tell her I'm going to show her something "very cool." I lead her down to the steps at the middle of the bleachers, and at a quick glance to check that the coast is clear, we climb down to the field level, but stay near the stands until we walk over to Izzy and the rest of the cheer squad.

I sit with Alyssa and watch both the game and my best friend cheer as The Tradition defense holds North to three downs, forcing them to punt. Izzy jogs over to me during the timeout.

"Hey, I remember you," she says. Izzy has always been good with kids, despite not having siblings of her own. She's bright and bubbly, and I'm sure in Alyssa's eyes she's a fairy princess.

"This is my friend Alyssa," I say, making eye contact with Izzy so she understands. She smiles at me softly before kneeling down to be on Alyssa's level.

"Hi, Alyssa. I'm Izzy. I met you after one of Nico's first games, and Reagan has told me a lot about you. She says that *you*...are quite the cheerleader," my friend says.

Alyssa tucks her face into my arm, but smiles when she tilts it to the side, nodding in big movements.

"You maybe want to cheer with me? For a little while?" Izzy asks.

Alyssa's eyes bulge, and Izzy jogs to the equipment box a few yards away, coming back with a set of golden pom-poms. Alyssa takes them in her hands, and as she stands to test them out, the other girls come over to meet her.

Within seconds, Alyssa is swept into the fantasy, the girls all working together to create a routine she can do. They teach it to her, while Nico leads the offense on the field to another six, this time with a forty-yard run of his own. In less than five minutes, we're up by two touchdowns.

Nico's play continues to be nothing short of miraculous. At one point, Coach O'Donahue begins to take credit, a certain swagger to his walk along the sidelines, as if any of this is his doing. As if *he's* the one who believed in Nico Medina all along.

And maybe that's the story the board will start to tell. Perhaps that's how they'll play this. It doesn't matter, because run after run, pass after pass, my father stands and high-fives Nico's uncle, he laughs and cheers with my brother—he hugs Nico's mom. The real motivation, the *real* faith—it's right here.

Alyssa performs with the cheerleaders during halftime, and Izzy lifts the little girl high on her shoulders, letting her rile up the crowd. The sight makes Valerie cry. When Alyssa climbs back up to join us in our seats, she keeps the pom-poms with her, showing each of us how to use them best. This little girl will never know her father, but his brother is playing for him out on that field—and I swear she can feel it.

We all feel it.

North has only managed a field goal, and with seconds to go, our team is on the fifty-yard line, and one more down before the lights go out and the history books on tonight are closed. I'm confident Nico is going to get a visit from the USC men in the booth. I'm certain they've already made phone calls, and I'm also sure that they'll walk down to the field and shake Jimmy O'Donahue's hand before they leave, asking for an introduction.

But Nico plays on. Just as hard. These few seconds…they aren't for scouts, or haters, or boosters or even his team. This moment—it's for Vincent.

Colton snaps the ball, and Nico moves with the grace of a panther on the hunt. His feet work in tandem, each knowing where to go, when to slide, when to push—when to run. He breaks a tackle and spins, bolting to the other side to give his best friend time to get in place. Sasha's running with all he has toward the end zone just as Nico arches back, his arm pumping, his chest letting out a grunt that I swear I can hear as he releases the ball. The spiral is perfect. The distance is there. Sasha is being trailed, but he won't be caught, and right as his feet cross the goal line, the ball is waiting to greet him, hitting his hands for the longest completed pass I've ever seen thrown on this field.

The stands erupt, and the band pumps out the fight song with enough verve that it shakes the metal floor beneath us.

"Oh my God," Valerie says, over and over, her hands wrapped around my mom's. Travis's mom rushes over to us, hugging my dad, then both my mom and Valerie. The men celebrate, reliving the play, and students start to rush the field as the announcer confirms that The Tradition, once again, is going to the State Playoffs.

There are balloons, and my best friend dances her horrible dance, throwing in a few cartwheels with some of the other cheerleaders. Alyssa breaks free and runs down to join them, while even more people spill out onto the field.

The players bump fists and chests, and they all surround their coach, moving like a swarm toward the end zone, taking pictures and celebrating. My eyes search for Nico, and when I find him, he's on his knees, his head in his hands and his helmet on the ground next to him, Sasha at his side. His shoulders shudder once, and my breath hitches with my cry.

"Daddy," I say, reaching for my father's arm.

"I see him. I see him," my dad says, stepping over the seat in front of him, leaping over the bar to the track and jogging out onto the field.

People have begun to quiet, and the team has started to look on, many of them taking their helmets off, taking a knee while the boy who owns my heart tries to mend his broken one on the fifty-yard line.

I hold Valerie's hand, and we squeeze each other hard as my dad rushes to Nico. He falls to his knees, too, Sasha standing behind him, and my dad holds his forehead to Nico's, his hands gripping his shoulders while Nico shakes with grief.

"I can't..." I say, letting go of Valerie and following my father's path, sprinting the minute my feet hit the turf until I'm at Sasha's side.

Nico's friend puts his arm around me, and I cling to him while Nico cries so hard that his voice is incoherent, nothing more than moaning wails as my father lifts him to his feet and brings him to his chest to hug him tightly.

"I know, son. I know," my dad says, his fingers flexed around the back of Nico's head. "You did good. You were so good. He would be proud. You made him proud."

My eyes burn with tears as Sasha's hand rubs my back. He fights to fall apart on his own. Nico's hands cling around my father, gripping his shirt, and he buries his face in my dad's chest, his body shaking with each heavy sob. My dad continues to hold him tight, praising him over and over again while the rest of our world looks on.

My eyes scan the crowd, and people are still—voices hushed, mouths closed. The Tradition is still, every guy on the team now on a knee, even the coaches. We all wait while Nico grieves. I wish I could take his pain away. I wish I could reverse time, to somehow change the course of history so his brother wasn't in the Humvee that was attacked by a rogue group of separatists. I wish Nico had more than the flag given to his mother, more than the golden star that is pinned to the sleeve of Nico's jersey. I wish he had his brother. I wish Alyssa had her father.

I wish. I wish. I wish.

The silence is heavy, and I can tell we're all beginning to feel it. Minutes pass with Nico in my father's arms until he finally steps from my father's hold, bending down to pick up his helmet. Nico runs his arm over his eyes, his focus on chalk paint of the fifty-yard line and the grass just a few steps ahead of him. He nods to himself slowly as the crowd begins to clap, and their support sends him to tears again, only this time he's ready for feeling it. Nico raises his helmet in one hand and tilts his face to the sky, turning in a slow circle, his other hand a fist against his mouth. He kisses it finally, letting it go and pointing to the stars, swaying and talking to his brother—talking to the heavens.

When he looks back down, his eyes find me, and I rush to him, falling into his arms, leaping and wrapping my legs around him while he drops his helmet and holds me tight, crying into my neck.

"I'm so proud of you. He would be so proud, Nico," I say. "He is. I know it."

Nico kisses my neck and holds me close, holding a hand up again to acknowledge the people still cheering for him. His hoarse voice whispers, "Thank you," in my ear, and I slide from his hold, but remain at his side while every single player and coach talks to him.

CHAPTER 22

Since my lips first touched his, perhaps even well before that, I knew in my heart that there was no winning a debate against Nico Medina. But since that time, in our days together, I've learned why.

He has simply lived too much for my small life to be able to compare.

"More's idea that we make thieves, and then we punish them, is the basis for so many modern moral tales," Nico says.

I watch him dizzily, awed by his speech on our reading of *Utopia*. When Mr. Huffman calls my name, I only startle.

"Huh? Oh, no...I...I actually agree with him on this. I've got nothing," I say.

Mr. Huffman's eyes narrow on me and his mouth forms a tiny tight smile, mocking me for giving in so easily to the boy I like.

But that's it. I don't just *like* Nico Medina. He has my heart, completely. In the weeks since his brother's death, I've watched Nico become even more of a man of his house, helping his mother through funeral arrangements, benefits for Alyssa, and now court hearings to ensure that his niece stays with them.

Vincent's ex, Alyssa's mom, is a mystery. She could very well be dead. All they know is her name was Moriah Keaton, and she had a severe addiction. Nico made calls every day after school until he found a lawyer willing to take their case. He helped his mom work through forms and file testimonies to strengthen their case to keep Alyssa home, where she belongs.

Mostly, though, I can't argue with Nico because he is the example—the exception. When Cornwall first met him, they labeled him. At-risk...*thief.* Turns out he's the philosopher king.

"It's why our system is broken," Nico continues, Mr. Huffman nodding, a smile on his face. "We failed to learn from the stories that warned us that if we create environments that perpetuate poverty, that force the people in them to beg and steal, then we're equally to blame for many of their outcomes."

"People have choices," Megan argues. I admire her will—now that I've stopped sparring, she's still willing to try to provide a counterpoint to Nico.

"Sure they do," Nico says. "But what you don't have, when you live in the golden palace, is such severe temptation. You have to choose between a career in law or art or media or...film."

He glances at me, smirking in apology. I glower a little, because I don't like being an example when he argues against the privileged.

"But in some places, the choice is between taking two jobs at once that together barely pay minimum-wage and offer no guarantee that they'll keep you employed, or something illegal that promises one-time riches, and guaranteed future opportunities if you're willing to stomach selling your soul. It's hard not to sell your soul when you grow up without food on the table."

Nico leans forward, gripping his desk, but a smile curves on his mouth and he relaxes, leaning back and looking at me. I chuckle to myself because he's proving that he doesn't have to always avoid eye contact.

"Then how do you draw the parallel to selling drugs, taking drugs?" Megan asks.

Before Nico can answer, I do.

"Drugs make the pain go away—real or perceived. And more often than not, the palace pays the money, the ghetto deals what they want. It's the perfect definition of supply and demand," I say, my eyes flitting around the room, to the many faces looking right back at me. "We pay a lot of money to make them criminals."

Megan scoots forward, her brow pulled in, ready to argue, and I twist in my chair, willing to offer up my own example—my *own* exception.

My family.

The bell rings before I need to, though, and Mr. Huffman writes our next reading selection on the board. I note it down, pulling my equipment bags from under my seat and meet Nico at the door. He holds it open for me, staring at me with a trace of a smile as I walk under his arm and through the door.

"You're going soft on me," he says.

"Am not," I say.

Am I?

Nico laughs lightly next to me, sliding my heaviest bag from my shoulder and carrying it to the lab for me.

"You are. You would have torn me up over that argument three months ago," he says, one eye squinted more than the other as he gives me a sideways glance.

"Not true," I say.

"You know, I could totally argue the other side right now," he says.

"Yeah, but you don't believe that," I say.

"Oh, but I *do!*" he says, his eyebrows lifting.

I stop at the lab door, tugging it open and dropping my things on the table just inside. I flick on the lights as Nico follows me in.

"It's more of a question of free will, if you ask me. It's easier not to fight the forces that work against you, to bend to your environment, but that doesn't mean it isn't possible," he says.

I lean against the computer table and fold my arms over my chest.

"Well of course," I sigh. "But in general…"

"In general…" he says, stepping up closer, his toes touching mine as his hands untangle my hands that are guarding my body. I stand up straighter, letting him pull my arms around him while he puts his over my shoulders. "In general, Reagan Marie Prescott, I'm so goddamned in love with you that I don't even care about being right anymore."

I open my mouth and close it just as promptly, my eyes pulling in, my heart starting to sound. "Shoot," I say, letting my head fall against his chest as I stare at our feet, my toe kicking at his. "Damn you, Nico Medina. That shut me up fast."

His lips come down on the top of my head as he wraps his arms around my head. I love life here in his small homemade cocoon.

"Good," he hums.

My skin tingles, and my heart races even faster. I'm nervous, something I haven't been with him in a long time.

"I love you, too," I say, my face buried into his chest, burrowing further.

Nico steps away enough that I can't hide, bending down and pulling my chin up, looking me in the eyes.

"Yeah?" he asks, his eyes hopeful and golden—so golden.

"Yeah," I say, my nod small, but my pounding heart heavy.

"You love me?" he asks again, quirking a brow to question, now teasing me. I push against his chest.

"Yes, you big nerd! I love you!"

His smirk grows, and his dimple deepens, so I push him again. This time, though, he catches my hands and pulls me into him, moving his hands to my face and kissing me softly, saying the words again against my mouth.

"I love you," he whispers, his mouth caught between kiss and smile.

My cheeks sore from smiling and my lips raw from kissing; I finally go to work on my film, wanting to make the deadline to deliver it to Prestige for consideration. Nico stays, pulling up a chair and sitting so one leg is behind me and one next to me. His kisses along my neck distract me at first, but once I get into my zone, I'm able to focus, even with my muse so close, tempting me.

Over the last few weeks, I've boiled down my footage to just enough.

I need twenty minutes, so I have more editing and trimming to do—especially if I want to add the state championship game into the storyline, which…I do.

The Tradition steamrolled over everyone, and Nico is poised to break the state's passing record in the championship game. He's a hundred and ten yards shy, and the team—*his* team—wants him to get there.

The offer from USC hasn't come yet, and I can tell it's weighing on him. I know he wants it, but he hasn't brought it up since the game the scouts were at. I think because that night is too painful to relive. I believe it's coming, though. I know it, just as much as I know I'm in love with him.

I'm running through close-up shots from some of the earlier practices and games, forwarding and rewinding, finding just the right clip to cut, when Nico slides his chair back from me, scratching along the tiled floor.

"Sorry," he winces.

"It's okay. I'm not picking up any sound in here. It's all…" I tap on the computer screen.

"Oh, yeah…right," he says.

He leans over and kisses me, then pulls his bag up his arm and kicks his board up to his hand from the ground.

"You have to leave already?" I ask, wanting him to stay, but knowing he can't.

"My chariot awaits new tires…and a radiator," he says.

Nico's been taking extra hours when he can at Hungry Hill. He's already fixed up his car quite a bit, but there are a few…*unexpected* expenses that have put off driving a little longer than he had hoped.

"Will you make it to Charlie's later? To celebrate?" I ask.

"Wouldn't miss it," he smiles, leaning in to kiss me one last time.

I watch the door, catching every last glimpse of his form the second the wheels of his board hit the hallway floor and he rolls down the hall. When the door falls closed completely, I stare at it a little while longer, smiling, because Nico loves me.

I never bothered to go home from the editing bay. It's our bye week before the championship, and Charlie's has a tradition of hosting our pep rallies during the playoffs. It's strange coming here without my dad, but he didn't want to make this night about him. He wanted this for the boys, because he said they earned the right to this memory.

Noah is coming. Despite Jimmy O'Donahue's complete lack of morals and empathy, he did do right by Noah. My brother has been on the field, on the sidelines, for every playoff game, and Jimmy told the team last night that he'd like Noah to lead them on the field for State. Everyone agreed.

I know that most of the players won't get here until late. That's the thing about the pep rally—they all pretend they're too cool for it, but they still really want to be here. They just think they should be in someone's basement, getting lit on cheap beer like they do in the movies. They'll do that, too—after they leave Charlie's. But for a few hours, around midnight, boys will be boys, and football will bring us all together, and we will just be a bunch of teenagers…living.

Izzy pulls into the spot next to mine, and I hand her a frozen hot chocolate as she steps up to our favorite table, sitting on the top with me, our feet on the bench.

"So Noah and Katie…they haven't gotten back together," I say, doing my best to sound nonchalant, failing at it miserably.

"Knock it off, Reagan. Seriously…me and Noah are fine. We're just what we are, and who knows, maybe," she says, stopping to take a long sip of her sugary drink.

"I know, but you like him, and I could totally hook you up…"

"Stop," she says, this time turning and raising a brow.

I huff and let my lips fall to my own straw, drinking my root beer float while I pout.

"Fine, but if you two end up getting married one day, and you regret missing out on all of these years you could have been a couple, I don't want to hear it," I say.

"Sounds good. Deal," Izzy says, her answer clipped.

I give up my matchmaking mission, and my friend pulls a bottle of gold nail polish from her purse, nodding to me to lay my hand flat on the table so she can paint my nails.

"Why would you bother doing that? You know I'm just going to peel it all off," I say.

She looks up at me, her hand poised with the brush above my knuckles, my hand still balled in a fist.

"Bitch, show some school spirit," she teases, her face mean, but pretend.

I purse my lips and roll my eyes, but flatten my hand for her, because she would end up winning anyway. I sip my drink while my best friend paints glitter on my fingertips, and when she's done, I spend the next ten minutes waving my hands, fingers sprawled, to make sure it all dries.

Colton shows up first, but Travis pulls in a second or two after with my brother. I show them my new manicure, and Noah laughs. "How long before you chew that shit off?" he asks, letting go of my hand after inspecting it.

"Careful, Noah. You're out of the house on good behavior," I say with a smirk.

"Pshh," he says, rolling his shoulders and walking away from me.

My brother's cast is off, and he's wearing a giant plastic boot device with a long splint until he gets stronger. He walks like the Frankenstein monster in it, but I won't make fun of him. He's healing about two weeks ahead of schedule, and he's hoping to make a few trips this week with our dad to some schools still interested in seeing what he can do. The scope of Noah's dreams has been narrowed, but when he found out some of them were still viable, he started to act a little more like himself. I can't take shots at something so important to him, no matter what kind of digs he's taken at me.

Noah's actually helped more with my film over the last weeks. He's taken my camera on the field for me, and he talked Jimmy O'Donahue into sitting down for an interview, which he did…reluctantly. I didn't pull any punches, and I asked him about working in an environment where everyone is always gunning for his job—especially since he took out my dad just to get the gig. He said it was a matter of knowing his enemies and keeping them happy. He's right.

I suppose my dad will be playing the same game in the fall, only on a bigger scale. At least he'll be the guy bucking for the job, for a little while, rather than the one fending off the attacks.

By about eleven, most of the team has showed up, and Charlie's parking lot is buzzing with a mix of music from competing car stereos, squeals from girls, laughter from guys, and a few quiet conversations tucked in corners. I sit back and watch it all, my phone turning over and over again in my hand anxiously. I'm waiting for my guy.

Nico texted about half an hour ago that he had gotten off work and was going to head home to change and have Sasha pick him up. I couldn't wait to see them both, actually. The night wouldn't feel right until then.

Somehow, Izzy has worked her magic and gotten another large shake, which I know she didn't pay for. She slides up to sit next to me again after making her rounds and talking with every group here.

"You're like the ultimate politician, I swear," I say, leaning into her.

"Yeah, except I'm only in it for the ice cream," she says, sliding the straw free and sucking out the milkshake from the bottom, her head tilted back. She shifts to look at me and winks while she slurps.

"You're like a milkshake hooker," I say, making her snort laugh.

"Oh my God, I am," she says, pausing briefly, then shrugging and diving back in to scoop out more.

I'm laughing at my friend, watching her try not to make a mess, and I don't see Sasha's car squeal into the parking lot. I don't see him park in the middle of the drive-thru, and I don't notice him kick the door open and leave his car running. I don't see anything at all until I follow Izzy's gaze and turn to meet his eyes.

He doesn't have to speak the second I do. I cover my mouth and run to the car with him, tears streaming down my face the second my foot lands inside his car.

Nico!

The blue car is always waiting. It's the only thing I'm afraid of. I'm not even sure I'm really afraid of the smoking man inside as much as I'm afraid of his car.

That car is on the corner now, and I don't have my bike. I should have waited for the other boys, should have walked home with Sasha and had his mom drive me here. I shouldn't be alone. But Momma needed me. She said she wanted me to help her shop for Vincent's birthday. Vincent is coming home for his birthday—he always does, and Momma wants to be ready, to make his favorite food and a cake.

My watch said four thirty. Momma's leaving at five. I had to go, even though my friends were staying to play more football. I always do as Momma says. Only…I wasn't supposed to go to the park that far away. It's my fault that he's here, my fault that I'm so far from home. If he gets me, it's because I was careless and didn't follow the rules.

I crouch behind the concrete block on the West End side of the bridge, and I watch the man in the blue car. His lips curl around a pipe, and his hands hold fire in his palms, burning the poison. His lips puff out white fog, and his head falls back against his seat. I have to go now. If I run now, he won't see me go, and I'll have a head start.

I'm faster than he is. I'm faster than his car. I'm not filled with poison.

My feet are numb, and I'm afraid my legs won't work, so I run in place for a second, watching the man to make sure his head is still back. I think his eyes are closed, and I know I have to go, but my body feels too weak.

I glance around, hoping to see someone I know, but the streets are all quiet and empty. The corner market is closed for the day. They don't stay open very late any more—not since the shootings started.

I hate that blue car. I hate the smoking man. I promised Vincent and Momma I would always run, and my brother is coming home. He's coming home for his birthday, and I need to help Momma make him a cake.

I take a deep breath and form fists, bending my elbows and pushing the back of my heel against the concrete to push off. I must be fast.

I count down, my eyes watching him the whole time. Three. His head is still back. Two. His car's engine is quiet. One…

My feet pound the pavement, and my legs work to turn what is normally one step into two, pushing fast and hard down the middle of the street, my head to the side, my eyes locked on my enemy as I run toward the houses, toward the alleyway that leads to my home. If I can make it there, he'll never see me. He just needs to keep his eyes closed.

Run faster, Nico. Run faster.

My heart is pounding, and my fists are turning red, I'm squeezing so hard. I grit my teeth and push harder, breathing out with my right foot, in with my left.

I can see the alleyway. I can see the shadow of the house on the corner. I'm almost there. I'm going to make it.

Run faster, Nico.

I look ahead, counting the steps. Maybe twenty. Maybe fifteen. Maybe ten.

I hear the engine. The car starts to move. I start to cry.

Run faster, Nico!

I don't want him to catch me. He'll never catch me. I will always be too fast for him.

Always…too fast.

CHAPTER 23

"Your portfolio of work is certainly impressive, Miss Prescott. I feel confident that you'll be getting a call from our admissions office."

Michael Buschwell is the dean of Prestige's Film Academy. When he called to set up my interview for his program last week, I promptly turned him down. He offered to come to my house, and so I agreed, not knowing how any of this would end. I mostly wanted to put it off, so I could deal with the day—survive it and get answers and see if they would destroy me or make me whole.

"This story...your documentary? It all feels unbelievable. But...I mean that as a compliment. What you captured—the backstabbing in private schools, the pressure of running a program like this, what it did to your family—*to Nico's.*" He stops there, pushing my laptop closed and sliding it back to me.

"It's people's lives. Sometimes, good people live in dangerous places, and selfish people live in safe havens. It's kind of messed up..." I say, not knowing what should come next. I tuck my hands under my legs, my pulse reminding me just how important this is.

"When we set this up, you mentioned in your email to me that your film...it isn't done," Michael says, his head slightly to the side. His eyes sweep from me to my computer as he pulls his hand away.

"It's not," I say, breathing in deeply through my nose, my back falling into the wood of our kitchen chair. "There's one more interview I need to do."

Michael nods, his eyes flitting to mine as he offers a courteous smile.

"Okay, then," he says, standing and pulling his jacket from the back of his chair. I stand, too, and wait for him to slip his arms through and straighten his tie. He reaches out a hand, and I shake it, hoping my palms aren't sweating too badly.

"I very much hope you'll share the final version with me then…when it's done?" His eyes look at me expectantly, and I nod quickly.

"Of course," I say.

He smiles.

"Good. Perhaps we can slip this in just in time for the winter awards ceremony then," he says over his shoulder as I follow him to our front door. My knees quake at his remark.

"That'd…be amazing," I say, managing to smile and remain calm.

"Wonderful," he says, as I open the door and hold it as he steps to our front walkway. "Well…I'll be in touch."

"I look forward to it," I say, battling in my own head as he walks toward his car, wondering just how long I need to leave the doorway open to look at him. I decide to close it before he reaches his door.

"Well?" my mom asks, sliding from her hiding spot around the corner.

She sat in the living room, quietly, while I talked with him. My brother and dad left early for the championship. I wished I could have shipped her off, too, because I just don't know about any of it. But now that she's here, I'm glad. I hug her and she pulls me in tight, her hands making soothing circles on my back.

"I think it went really well. I just…I don't know what to do now," I say.

"I know," she says, stepping back and squeezing my shoulder, her eyes meeting mine. "You'll do what's right for you, and you'll know when it hits you."

I nod.

I ride with my mom to the stadium, and she drops me off at the side entrance so I can carry in my camera and gear. I slip my press badge over my neck and show it to the security guard who pushes the door wide for me to rush through. There aren't many rooms open, so I quickly find the one where Valerie is waiting for me.

The stadium is starting to fill, but I know our seats are saved.

"Thank you for doing this, especially today," I say, pulling out the small mic and unraveling the cord. I plug it into my camera and hand it to Valerie to weave through her blouse and pin it near her neck.

"Anything for you, Reagan. Really," she says, her smile nervous.

I wait for her to finish clipping her mic and then squeeze her hand in mine, bringing her eyes to me.

"We can start over as many times as you'd like," I say. "Just…talk from your heart, and I'll edit it together."

She nods slightly, sitting up tall in her chair and brushing her soft curls over her shoulders.

"Tell me about your son," I say.

She laughs lightly to herself, letting her eyes fall closed and her red lips stretch into a proud smile. I watch her through the lens, letting her take her time. There's power in her silence.

"A mother should not outlive her children," she says. "When the marines came to our door, when they handed me the flag and told me that my oldest boy was gone from this world, I thought I would never recover."

"But you did," I say, leading her to keep going.

She smiles again, tilting her head slightly, one side of her mouth higher than the other as she stares right into the camera.

"I did," she says, "because of Nico."

I swallow, and force myself to hold my breath.

"When the police department called me and told me what my youngest son had done at that truck stop he worked at, my heart sank again. It was a stabbing pain, just like I had when I opened the door to two marines a few months ago. I only survived the first time because of

Nico…I didn't know how I was going to survive losing him."

She stops to pull the tissue from her lap and dab it on the corners of her eyes.

"I knew I'd need these," she chuckles. "Sorry."

"It's okay," I say, pushing my palms into my eyes behind the camera.

"What did the police tell you?" I ask, not wanting to hear the story again, but knowing I need it for the film. It's important, perhaps more than the outcome of the game tonight.

"I was getting ready for bed. Alyssa was asleep, and my phone rang. I knew Nico was coming home to change before Sasha came to pick him up, so I figured it was him, telling me he forgot his key. I knew something was wrong the second I heard a man's voice and not my sweet boy," she says, stopping to dab her eyes again. I reach forward and squeeze her hand. "He said my son had pushed a homeless man out of the way when a drunk driver was careening into the truck stop parking lot. Nico had apparently heard the car's tires and saw the man in its path, and he rushed to stand in the way. He was able to move the man, but Nico…wasn't fast enough. The car hit him, but the officer didn't know how bad. He had already been taken to the hospital before the officer was on scene."

"Sasha showed up while I was on the phone; I sent him to find out, so I could get Alyssa up and take her to my brother's. I sped so fast, and I kept practicing my speech to any police officer that might have pulled me over," she says, laughing lightly. "I felt like I could talk my way out of a ticket that day, you know?"

"I agree," I smile.

"When I got to the hospital, I just remember this feeling that hit me…" she says, stopping, her eyes drifting from the camera to something beyond my shoulder. Her mouth curves into a smile, and mine follows suit. "I felt Nico. In that hallway, leading up to the desk, to the room in the trauma center—there was this feeling that just embraced me."

"Like a miracle," I say.

She nods.

"Yes," she says. "Exactly like a miracle. I slowed down, and I walked past the desk, somehow not even needing to ask the nurse's station which room was my son's. I knew…my heart…it knew. I put my hand on the door and closed my eyes, and when I stepped inside…"

"I walked over to her and hugged her," Nico says from behind me.

I let my eyes water, watching his mom fight through her own tears through my lens.

"Yes, you did. You only had some scratches. They said you were fast, maybe the fastest, crazy kid they'd ever seen," she says, half laughing and half crying.

Nico walks into the frame, his legs covered in pads but his chest and arms still only wearing his Tradition T-shirt. His mom stands and moves her hands to his face, holding him and looking at him—admiring her brave boy.

"You're going to do great today," she says.

"You think so?" he asks, his mouth a lopsided smile, showing his youth despite his frame and muscles.

His mom straightens his shirt and pats her hands on his chest.

"I know so," she says. "And if that coach tells you to do something, and you think it's not right…" she glances at me, and I smirk, clicking my camera off. She leans in to her son, whispering loud enough that I hear. "You do what your gut tells you. It's never done you wrong."

"Okay, Momma," he says, bending down to kiss her cheek.

I move close to them both, helping Valerie to unclip the mic from her shirt, catching the cord as she lets it fall through the front of her blouse.

"I'll see you at our seats, Mija," she says, squeezing my arm.

I love her.

I nod okay.

The door falls closed, and for a moment, it's only Nico and me. He squares to me, and I move my hands to his shirt, gripping it and holding on. Our eyes meet, and he breathes in deep. I can see the weight of the world on his shoulders. I know this look—I've seen it on my dad.

"You're amazing," I say.

He breathes out a laugh and rolls his eyes, but I shake my hands where they hold his shirt, getting him to look at me again.

"No matter what happens, just remember that. Just know that you're amazing. You've done your very best, and this game—it does not define you," I say.

His mouth falls to a faint smile, and his chest rises as he takes my words in.

"Okay," he says.

"There...good," I say, reaching up on my toes and taking his bottom lip in between mine. It's soft and salty with sweat, and he smells like a boy who has been wearing the same shirt and pads on the field for hours every night. Yet, I don't care, because he's here. I can touch him.

We stand in silence for a few long seconds, and my hands slide down his arms until my fingers tangle in his. I follow my craving and look down to see our touch. Ever since I rushed with Sasha to the hospital, afraid Nico wasn't going to survive, I've been more aware of these simple moments between us. I hold onto them, wanting to store each and every memory because in life there are too many things one just never knows.

"How'd your interview go?" he asks.

I inhale quietly, my eyes studying the look of his hands as I think about his question.

"The dean...he liked me," I say.

"Of course he did," Nico says, his fingers still working around each of mine, his eyes low, too.

"I'm pretty sure they're going to offer me a spot," I say.

I feel Nico nod, and I know he's smiling. My eyes close, and I let myself feel his touch. Prestige is all I've wanted for so long. I've put in hours of my life, logged film in the dark, lost sleep listening to sound— my father had football, and I had this. But now it just seems so empty, my heart...it doesn't want it quite like it did.

And I think I know why.

"I'm going to go to Southern Cal, though," I say, and I feel Nico's fingers freeze against mine instantly. My heart doesn't pound, and my stomach doesn't sink. Instead…everything suddenly feels even. My lungs grow as I inhale and open my eyes, my mouth curving into a smile.

My mom said I would know. She said I would be able to choose what I really wanted when I really had to. I want to study film, but I don't need to do it at Prestige. I want to be near Nico. I want to see my brother play for San Diego, which is where he thinks he's going to go. I want to be near the boys that I love with all my heart, and I don't want to give them up because my plan has always been this one solitary thing.

"True story?" Nico asks, and I look up, laughing when my eyes meet his. His smile is crooked, and I move my hands back to his chest, shaking him.

"Oh my God, do not quote Noah. You're smarter than that," I say.

Nico bends down and meets my eyes, his wide and still waiting.

"Yes," I say. "Yes, *true story*. Yes, I want to go to USC. And not just for you. For me, because of Noah, and because that's what's right."

"But mostly me, right?" he says, his eyes hazing.

I push him, and he grabs me and pulls me in to kiss him.

I don't answer, because I've learned what pressure can do to people, and saying I'm making a choice mostly for him is pressure that both he and I don't need. But my heart feels stronger having made my choice. My head feels clear, and there's a renewed energy in my step. I'm pretty sure I know what that is, but I won't label it. I'm just going to enjoy it while it's here.

There's a pounding on the door, so I step up to kiss him one last time, letting his fingers slip free of mine as he jogs to the door, the sound of his cleats clicking on the concrete.

"All of West End is here to see you, you know," I say.

"I know," he says.

"Hey, Nico?" I stop him as he catches the door in his hand.

"Whose house is this?" I ask.

His lip quirks up.

"Hoorah!" he whispers.

The door falls closed behind him, and I sit back in the metal folding chair and simply breathe. We do things in life to make others happy. We make sacrifices because that feeling—the one I once thought was altruism, but have since learned is just love—it makes us feel good. We give, but it's never selfless. Nico has given so much. He's lost more than his share, and he's sacrificed beyond what is right.

Tonight—*tonight the universe gives back.*

It's not just customary.

It's tradition.

CHAPTER 24

"No, listen to me—this is the plan!"

I bring Sasha in close, putting my arm over his shoulder. Jacob and Thomas step in close, too.

The lights are going to shut off soon, and we all have to get home. Momma got me a new bike, so I can ride home fast with Thomas and Jacob. We have time for one more play, but it has to work. This is the only chance we have.

The sixth-grade boys always win. It really isn't fair that we divide teams by age. We're only ten, and they're so much taller than us. But my uncle says that the most important muscle you use in football is the one in your head. He says anyone can beat anyone if they just do that one right thing.

"Sasha, you know how I always have Thomas snap after green sixteen? This time, he's going to hold it, and I'm going to wait a tick before I say hike," I say.

"Nico, there's no refs out here. That hard count shit you see on TV doesn't work here, dude. Christian is just going to flatten Thomas's ass faster and knock you out. Don't give them that extra second," Sasha says.

I shake him with my hand on his back, and he flings my arm away.

"Listen, no…really. This will work, I swear. They won't be ready. It's like…it's like tripping them. Just, come on—try it just this one time. If it doesn't work, I swear to you guys we don't ever have to run this play again."

Sasha rolls his eyes and sighs, but pushes his hand into the center.

"Fine, whatever. Game's over anyhow," he says.

I smile and bite the tip of my tongue. I can't explain why, but I have this feeling—like I already know what's going to happen. Sasha is going to feel so stupid when I'm right.

I slap my hand on his, and Thomas and Jacob follow.

"Break!" we all shout, jogging to our positions on the line.

My knee finally quit bleeding from the touchdown I ran in myself when we started playing two hours ago. My legs are ready, and my body feels fast. But this sense in my gut, it's more than that. By the time I line up behind Thomas, I'm almost laughing—which only makes Christian, the biggest kid in our class and the one who always scores the winning touchdown out here, mad. His eyes lower on me, and he digs his foot into the dirt. If I'm wrong, he's going to hurt me when he tackles me to the ground.

I lick my fingertips and bend my knees, glancing down the line. Sasha and Jacob are lined up, their arms ready and bodies prepared to spring forward. They'll need to be fast, and I can't get caught. That single second—it's going to be the difference.

"Blue forty-two, blue forty-two," I shout, my eyes moving to Thomas's back then down the line, to Sasha. Our eyes meet, and my friend's mouth lifts on one side.

"Blue forty-two, green-sixteen…" I pause, and I count in my head that it's only a breath.

Christian lunges forward, but his brain tells him something's wrong, and his feet stumble, his fist hitting the ground, followed by his knee as he loses his balance.

"Hike!" I shout, picking my perfect moment.

Thomas shoves the ball into my hands, and I fall back two or three steps while Christian works to get to his feet. I've given myself room, and Thomas is holding Christian's brother, Angel, by the sleeves of his shirt. I know my friend can't hold two defenders for long, but I won't need more than a few seconds.

"Run, Sasha, run!" I shout, knowing that my friend is far faster than the two defenders tailing both him and Jacob.

Sasha can outrun anyone. I just can't miss.

I leap up on my feet with two side-steps, not sure if he's far enough yet, and I catch Christian coming at me. I twist, and his hand snags my shirt, ripping the threads from the bottom, but I break free, and I stay on my feet while his weight carries him too far, and he skids on his knee.

I rush to the other side while Christian gets up, and I know I have less time now. Sasha…he has to be far enough. This is our shot; it's the only one we have to win— so I take it.

My arm falls back and I thrust it forward, grunting as I send the ball down the field just as Christian reaches me and wraps me in his arms, pushing my face into the dry grass, my knee opening up again and bleeding as I skid along the hard ground.

None of it hurts. I don't feel a single thing. And I hold my breath as Christian pushes on my shoulder to lift himself up, satisfied that he has done enough. I don't move, other than lifting my head so my eyes can watch Sasha run. His legs stretch, and in those final beats, his stride seems to mature, giving him the two extra feet we need.

The ball hits his hands, and he keeps running until he crosses the goal line made of our extra hats and jackets. My friend never spikes the ball, but instead makes a wide turn, his speed still up as he runs back to me, his mouth an O shape with the scream he's belting.

I jump to my feet and brush away the grass from my chest just as his body hits mine, and he lifts me up and carries me several steps. I laugh as Jacob and Thomas run over to join us, and we take turns bumping our chests together and pounding our fists.

Sasha grabs my hand in one of his, then slams the ball down in my palm, lifting my hand up in the air in celebration.

"State champs, baby! State champs!" he screams. I join him, and we let our chant echo into the night while the sixth graders pick up their bikes and begin to pedal home.

"I will never not trust you again, Nico Medina! You're my boy, you hear that? You…me and you, Nico. Every time!"

I jump up on my friend's back and squeeze him, my palm pounding against his chest.

"One day, Sasha—we're going to win it all for real," I say in his ear. "I promise."

I have been standing with my mom and dad, Linda, Valerie, Alyssa, and Uncle Danny in the first row at the fifty-yard line for the entire second half. This game would have been a nightmare if my father were still the coach. The bracket just worked this way, but it also felt a little bit like karma was at play to line us up in the championship against Great Vista again—the school that knocked us out last year.

We ended the first half in a tie—seven to seven—but ever since The Tradition has come back out, they've been flat. Nico's runs aren't working. They're tying up Travis and Sasha. Our running game, which has never been strong, is losing yardage. We can't seem to get a break, and with less than a minute left, Great Vista is sitting on the thirty-yard line in need of nothing but a field goal.

I reach to both sides, grabbing my parents' hands, grateful for once to be free of my camera and with them through this. My press pass gave me access to the media booth, but not the field. I set my camera up to capture the game, but win or lose—it's the interview after that really matters to me. I won't need a press pass for that.

"Look at that," my mom says, nudging me and leaning her head to the left so I look down our row to Tori O'Donahue. The woman is holding her fists to her mouth, her thumbnails in her teeth, probably being gnawed to the bone. She's rocking on her feet, the rhythm picking up speed with every single tick of the clock.

My mom has been that woman. She was that woman only a few months ago. Since my dad was let go and she was kicked out of the social committee, her hair has started to look healthier, her skin full of color—the dark circles around her eyes requiring less concealer. And the wine, while she still likes it, seems to be lasting a little longer in our house.

"That poor woman; I feel so bad," she says, staring at Tori.

I open my mouth, about to tell her how big of her that is, when she blows it as only my mom can, turning and looking me right in the eyes. "I'm over it," she says, her mouth curving quickly. She's unable to disguise her malicious laugh.

"Mom," I say, my head falling to the side. My eyes scanning back to the boosters, to Tori and the women who were so awful when it was my mom in that position. "Nah, you're right. I'm over it, too."

We both laugh about it, giddy with ourselves and our catty behavior when suddenly the crowd begins to boo over a call on the field.

"Wait, what happened?" I ask my dad, the Great Vista team moving five yards closer from a penalty, and their top-notch kicker jogging onto the field with less than twenty seconds on the clock.

"They ran a hard count, and our boys jumped right-the-hell offsides!" my dad yells, tearing his hat from his head and throwing it down in front of him. You can take the coach out of his position, but you can't remove his spirit for the game—or love for the team.

"How? Of all teams, we should know how to anticipate that…how?" I ask, looking down the row to Nico's uncle.

"Your boy is pissed," Uncle Danny says, shaking his head.

I turn my attention back to the field, where Nico is running down the sideline, livid and on edge. He waves his arms, calling for the rest of the team to rush down the field with him, and they all shout and hold their helmets over their heads, trying to be a distraction as best they can from the sidelines.

It's no use. Great Vista's kicker is the best in the state. My dad knows the kid's name, Connor Pruitt, and while we watch his ball sail easily through the uprights, with another twenty yards to give if he needed it, the Cornwall crowd grows hushed.

"I hate him right now, but that kid—he's kicking for Alabama next year," my dad says, bending down and picking up his hat. He doesn't put it back on, instead rolling the brim and twisting the mesh in his hands. "I don't know…they can run two…maybe three plays. Even then, that Pruitt kid is going to push them back to at least the twenty, and we haven't gotten a run back yet."

Coach O'Donahue calls his special team over, my brother and Nico standing next to him, and I can see my brother looking up to the stands, his eyes scanning for my dad.

"Noah's looking for you. Dad…Dad!" I slap at his arm.

My dad waves his crumpled hat over his head, and my brother holds up both hands, and he begins to give my dad some kind of sign, circling his index fingers around each other. I've never seen him do this before, but my dad does it in return, and when I look down to the field, I notice that Jimmy O'Donahue is looking at my dad as well.

"What the hell are they doing?" I ask.

"They're trying something crazy," he says, his eyes wide and glued to his boys on the field.

"And they want your opinion?" I ask.

"Yep," my dad says, his lips falling shut tight, his eyes locked open.

The refs whistle, warning Jimmy to get his team to the field to receive, and the penalty clock kicks in. There's confusion, and a few players run on and off the field, almost as if they're not sure what the plan is, when it becomes incredibly clear.

"They're going to let Nico run it back," Uncle Danny says, and my eyes move to the field, finding Nico fast.

He's standing at the ten-yard-line, deep enough to give himself time, and he stretches each leg, pulling his knees to his chest then jumping up and down. Nico has always seemed tall; he's always looked strong—almost invincible against any opponent we've faced. Standing out in the middle of the field alone, eleven two-hundred-plus-pound, well-honed athletes gunning for him, the only word that I can think of is vulnerable.

"He can do this. I know he can. He's fast. Nico is so fast. Come on, baby!" Valerie cheers in front of us.

She's standing on her toes on the bleacher seat in front of us, her hands cupped at her face, and I know she's praying. I lock my fingers together in front of me and whisper a prayer, too.

The Great Vista crowd begins to drum and chant, their volume growing as their kicker lifts his hand, running toward the ball, his foot swift as it sends the ball end over end into the air. Nico reads it, stepping back first to gauge it, then waiting.

Waiting.

He glances at the line rushing at him.

His eyes find the ball.

Nico goes, getting three hard steps in before the ball hits him in his arms and chest, where he locks it safely in the crook of his right arm while his left pumps hard. He clears the first three defenders without a problem, turning in a full three-sixty to break a tackle at the forty-yard line and juking an oncoming attack, switching directions and heading to the opposite side of the field.

Our eyes work to do the math, watching every step while keeping the clock in our periphery, precious seconds being lost every time someone ties up Nico's legs and arms. He fights, pushing forward a few yards at a time, having to take long routes to the middle and back, just to not get caught, Coach shouting from the sides, counting down the time.

The clock is under ten, and the other side begins to count down with hope. As Nico makes a final push up the middle, they reach eight...then seven, then suddenly, their fatal error destroys both teams. Nico hears them. He has to—that's the only reason he would stop. He knows he can't make it all the way, but he also knows that The Tradition—it needs time. Nico is now wasting it.

His step slows just enough near the sideline, and the corner that's rushing at him manages to grab his arm, trying to strip him of the ball. Nico brings it into his body tightly, the defender pulling him down, swinging him by his arm and eventually flipping Nico like one of those old-school wrestlers pumped up with steroids and cocaine. His body falls with a heavy thud out of bounds.

Nico's down.

He stays down.

The ball is secure in his arms, but The Tradition is still thirty yards short of where they need to be.

The clock has stopped.

But Nico. He's down.

"Why won't he get up," Valerie says, her hand reaching out for her brother. Danny moves in front of my dad and puts his arm around her.

"He's fine. He just got the wind knocked out of him, that's all. He's okay," he says, but I can tell from his tone, he's not sure. My dad used that tone. I bet he used it with my brother, until he found out his leg was bent like an L.

"He's breathing. And he's moving his legs. He's okay," my dad says, assuring her.

My brother turns and waves at my dad, signaling something again.

"What's he saying?" I ask.

"I think...I think it's his arm. Noah can't tell those things, though. Let's wait. Bob's going out," my dad says.

The Great Vista band begins to play Seven Nation Army, and I want to run across the field and punch them all in the face. I begin to bounce on my toes, needing to see Nico stand, needing to know he's okay. The rest of The Tradition crowd needs it, too, because selfishly, they know we need Nico to win.

Bob gets him to his feet, and Valerie leans into me, breathing for the first time in almost a minute.

"Oh thank God," she says.

"It's his arm," my dad says. "He can't throw. Nico...he can't throw."

Seven seconds, and thirty yards, even Jimmy knows his nephew can't make that happen. He's not naïve enough to try, either. He knows that it would be perceived as playing "daddy ball" and doing his relative a favor. That only works if you win, and Brandon—he can't win. Not this. Only Nico can.

I turn to my right and find my dad is gone, and I look back to my left at my mom, and she's biting her nails—for once not nervous about losing a job or a position or points with some special society. She's just nervous about losing, period.

"Where did he go?" I ask.

"Press box," she says, and I turn behind me to see my dad sprinting up the steps two at a time, his hat still curved in his hand. I watch just long enough to see him standing on his toes, shouting through the open windows, then moving just far enough that the offensive coordinator inside can see the gestures with his hands. I don't know what any of it means, but someone does, because I watch Coach O'Donahue push his headset into his ear, cupping it while he paces until he stops in front of Nico, who is sitting on the bench, his helmet off and ice on his arm.

Nico gets to his feet and pushes his helmet on his head, my brother and several other teammates slapping his helmet while he runs out to the line of scrimmage just as my father makes it back down to stand by me.

"He can't throw," my dad says, eyes on the field, his mouth a hard line, his forehead creased with the wrinkle born from years of stress. Then suddenly, a smile creeps in, and his eyes shift to me. "But he can sure as shit catch."

"What?" I ask, turning to see Sasha lining up behind Colton.

Valerie begins screaming in front of me, leaning forward, looking to make eye contact with Sasha's mom. When she does, she claps, then crosses her fingers before looking out to the field.

It all happens in a blink, and if I didn't know who they were, I would have sworn that this was how they always played—that Sasha was the quarterback, and Nico was the one racing down the field.

Colton snaps the ball, and Sasha peddles back, the line working hard to give him time. He's not Nico, though, and his feet—they aren't as steady. The defense starts to penetrate, and Sasha panics, sprinting to the side—making his throw even farther.

But Nico runs. Nico just runs.

The clock times out when Sasha has no choice, the defense about to take him down as he releases the ball. We all hold our breath—both sides, the stadium filled with at least four thousand people. We could have heard a pin drop. My eyes follow the line, the ball on target, and Nico has managed to separate himself by two, maybe three steps. His right arm, the hurt one, tight against his side, he reaches out with his left, his fingers tipping the ball once, giving him just enough time to catch up to it in the air to bring it completely into his body.

If we thought Nico was fast before, he finds a new gear the second the ball is secure. His feet pound. My heart beats. Our mouths begin to chant. The crowd stomps on the metal stands. The Tradition players raise their helmets and rush down the sidelines, swinging their arms in circles, willing him to go.

Go!

Go!

Travis throws a last-minute block, tripping up the only player who has a shot at catching Nico, and I scream just as my boy's legs cross the goal line. He knew we had one shot.

My dad knew.

Nico was it. He was always it.

Travis rushes toward him, lifting him over his shoulder and carrying him into the rest of the rushing team—Coach O'Donahue throwing his clipboard down and rushing into the dogpile with them.

"Oh my God," Valerie says, turning into me and pulling me in for a tight hug. I rock with her, feeling her cry well-earned tears of joy; then I hug my parents and Nico's uncle, before I follow Valerie down to the field.

She pushes her way through bodies, stopping to bring Sasha into her arms, kissing him on the cheek, and leaving a pink stain from her lips. I hug Sasha, too, then let my dad congratulate him, finally pulling him in for a hug. My dad looks worn and relieved—gone is all bitterness. The feeling is freeing, and when I find my brother, his face is elated as if he were the one to make the throw himself.

He lifts me in a circle, spinning on his good leg, and I hug him tight.

"That was so bad-ass. Dad called that, did you know that? Dad called that!" he says, a boy proud of his father.

"I know," I say, scrunching my head against his and laughing. "Oh my God, that was amazing!"

I leave Noah and find my mom, holding her arm and smiling so hard my cheeks hurt. We both watch my father shake hands and congratulate Coach O'Donahue—the best satisfaction happening when he thanks my dad for congratulating him, without acknowledging the real gift my dad actually gave him. The second Jimmy turns around, my dad flips him off. The only other person to see it is Bob, and he winks at me and holds his finger to his lips.

My eyes scan the crowd, which only seems to be multiplying, searching for Nico. I let go of my mom's hand and begin to work my way through bodies, congratulating every player I run into, but only really caring about one.

I find him finally in the very center, cameras around him snapping photos, his uncle squeezing him at his side, Nico's arm is around his mother, and I wait patiently for them all to have this moment. When Nico's eyes find me, he excuses himself, and he steps right into me, pushing his left hand through my hair and resting his forehead on mine while he walks me several steps backward before kissing me with all of the adrenaline I know is still pumping through his veins.

"Are you okay?" I ask, my hands roaming up his arm, to his face, inspecting him.

"Dislocated," he says. "Bob snapped it back in. Said I'd be good as new…in about a week," he chuckles.

My smile comes hard and fast.

"Great. Just in time," I say through my laughter.

I hold his arm in both of mine until the crowd thins. I stay on the field with his family and my own while the state commissioner brings out the trophies, and I help him balance the MVP one in his hands so his mom can take a photo. Nico smiles and shakes hands, using his left and nursing his right, until we're the only ones left on the field. I leave him just long enough to get my camera from the press box, and even though he's exhausted and in pain, his arm wrapped in a plastic bag filled with ice, Nico gives me one more piece of him.

I sit him on the bench on his side of the field, his hair still slick with the sweat from the game, and I frame him in my camera, the field he just owned a blur behind him.

"Tell me about what went through your mind. Out there…those final few seconds. Did you think you were going to lose?"

I sit back while Nico's eyes haze in his thought. He's taking this seriously, and I love him for that. Finally shaking his head, he says, "No."

"You weren't worried?" I ask.

His lips pull into a tight smile, and he shakes his head again.

"No…well…maybe, when that guy had me over his head? That…that worried me," he chuckles, but leans to the side, his laughter fading. "But really? No…I wasn't worried."

"Because you knew you could do this?" I ask, my lip curled up on one side with pride.

Nico surprises me, though, shaking his head no.

"Not me," he says. "Us."

I sit back again, and exhale, considering his response.

"You know our trainer? Bob?" he asks.

I smile.

"Yeah. He's like an uncle to me," I say.

"That guy…he's really the one who should be coaching, you know? No offense to your dad," he says.

"None taken. In fact, I think my dad would tend to agree with you," I say.

"Well, he told me once, he said that the only thing that matters out here on the field, the only thing that really counts when that clock hits zero, are the people on my team," he says.

"That sounds like Bob," I grin.

"He's right. And these guys? Somewhere along the way I decided that they're my home. I'd put my body in their hands and trust them every second," he says.

"Yeah?" I question, but I can tell from his face he's serious.

"Absolutely," he says.

"So home, you say. What does winning MVP say about a boy from your home…from West End? What does it say for little boys in West Ends all around the country?"

Nico sits forward, his hands coming together. His eyes focus on them.

"It says the home doesn't make the boy—the family does. And my family, it's grown a lot lately," he says, looking up with a smirk. I hold his gaze, and I decide this last part—it's just for me, not the camera.

I push the power button and sit forward on my knees, pulling the mic free from his shirt. Nico takes it from my hands, kneeling and folding the cord up for me.

"I have one more question," I say, blushing.

"Go ahead," he says, his eyes on me, searing.

"All of that—running the ball in with your hurt arm, winning this game single-handedly but giving credit to your team, as if they really had anything to do with it," I say, my voice clearly denoting my sarcasm. "Taking a spot on my dad's team, helping my brother. All of that, just to make me happy. Tell me, Nico Medina…how did that make you feel?"

His lip ticks up, and his eyes narrow, his hair falling forward over one eye—my heart pounds at the sight of him.

"Terrible," he says, his lips fighting not to laugh. "I took absolutely zero pleasure from it. If I could go back, I would hide and avoid you like the plague."

His laughter breaks through, and I push into his chest, knocking him to sit on the grass. He pulls my legs around him, holding me tight.

"It made me feel like everything else I do for you does," he says.

The intensity of his stare and the closeness of him makes my skin tingle. I suck in my bottom lip and breathe in quickly through my nose.

"And how's that?" I ask, my head falling forward, my lips craving his—coming home.

"Alive," he says against me, his lips grazing mine with the sweetest words ever. "Loving you—it makes me feel alive."

EPILOGUE

Nico

The grass is cold.

It surprises me, because the last few weeks have been so warm. I've gone running every morning for the last month, and by the time I get back to my house after crossing the bridge and back, I'm dripping with sweat.

There's a chill in the air today.

I think that's Vincent...talking to me.

"Hey, bro," I say, pulling my shirt from my body and laying it on the grass, sitting on it and bending my legs in front of me.

I rest my palms on my knees, and spend the first several minutes just...feeling. It took a while before I could find the courage to talk out here. It took me a while to find my voice, I guess. My mom had Vincent buried in West Haven. It's on the other side of the freeway, and newer than the city cemetery closer to our house. She didn't want to see him surrounded by graffiti, she said. I'm glad he's here. He's close enough to home, but he also got out. My heart feels a stabbing pain every time I see his name etched in the small concrete slab buried in the ground, the green grass bordering it on all sides, the small metal vase perched on the corner—a rose, or something else, always inside.

I tip the vase back to check the level of the water and smirk when I see it's full. Momma and Maria don't miss a day. When the roses are out of season, the Mendozas plant something else.

"The women are still working hard to make sure you look good, Vincent. Your flowers are always the best," I smile, leaning back on my hands and tilting my chin to the sky, feeling a warm breeze brush my face while my fingers dig into the cool blades beneath them.

I breathe in deep, holding the air in my lungs. I need my brother today. I can't explain why exactly. I think it's just that this day was one I always pictured him being here for, and the fact that he's not? I feel it.

It hurts.

I sit up again, leaning forward and pulling the folded paper from my pocket. It's funny how easy it's always been for me to just speak. Last year, I argued both against *and for* the death penalty in front of the school board, a few legislators, and the two hundred people who attend the annual debate with St. Augustine. I didn't sweat. Nerves weren't even in the picture.

Today feels heavy, though. I'm not sure why. Maybe it's because it's the last time I get to be this version of me. I haven't felt like a kid since Alyssa moved into Vincent's room the day my brother shipped out, but I also haven't quite been *adult*. I've been…something else. Today, though…today, I become something *more*.

"I'm making a speech tonight," I say, unfolding the paper in my lap. "I know, I know—*of course I am. I never shut up*. You were always the first to tease me for being such a goody-goody."

I look up from the page, the breeze blowing the deep-green tips of grass around me. That's Vincent—*laughing*.

"I also know you were proud," I say. "You didn't have to say it. I felt it."

A car drives by slowly, so I lean forward and look into my lap. There's something personal about being in the cemetery. It's a place for secret conversations. Maybe that's just the way I feel, but I've noticed that other people that come out here—they like to be left alone, too. It's sort of an unspoken agreement. We don't stare, and we let people have their space and time. I glance up when the car disappears behind the thick trees.

"I was wondering if maybe I could just run this by you once? I know you never really liked to hear my speeches. You always said I was better when I didn't have something planned, but this one's important. There are a lot of people that show up for this thing, and I just want to make sure I get it right."

I clear my throat and look around to make sure I'm still alone. It's just me and the car—the woman driving was older, and she's too far for me to see now.

"Okay…here goes…"

I breathe in deep.

"I was afraid of you. I know that's not what you expect to hear from someone like me. I'm the kid from West End—I must be tough, I must be a thug, I must have a gun in my home, I must be in a gang…*I bet he's killed someone, I bet his brother's in prison.* You can see why I was afraid. I was so afraid that I would get here, and that's all you would see—a picture in your heads that was so far from the truth, but too impossible to overcome."

"I was afraid of discrimination. Of intolerance. Of ignorance. I remember the meetings the admissions board held when I was in junior high, the ones about getting rid of the scholarship program because it exposed good kids to at-risk youth. At. Risk. Youth. That phrase…it's too small. It's pejorative. It's not entirely wrong. Growing up in West End made me. That risk…it toughened me up. It made me fast. It made me fight. When I was a kid, I remember hiding on the floor of my room on Friday nights so stray bullets wouldn't harm me. I hated my home. I loved it. I would never choose it for someone—never wish for my child to feel the fear I did. I could never imagine growing up somewhere else. That fear made me. That fear is the reason I stand up here; the reason I pushed myself to learn, to question, to try—*to argue.* That fear was balanced out by faith."

"I was so afraid of you," I say, stopping and folding the paper, looking to the flat stone in front of me. These words...I know them by heart now. They're about Reagan and the friends I've made, but they're also about Vincent. "You made me, too. You lifted me. You pushed me. You believed in me. You saw the boy from West End. I surprised you. But you—*you surprised me, too.*"

"This life, our lives—they are colored by expectations. It's the surprises, though—how we deviate—that define us. Our time here at Cornwall, together...it's so very short. Today, we'll all stand on this field one final time and move a tassel on our caps to mark an end. We'll blink, and then we'll begin. We'll be afraid, but we'll fight. We'll push, and we'll remember who we were, what we thought we knew, what we know now, and how it's made us—and then we'll surprise. We'll shock. We'll amaze."

"When I was afraid, you challenged me. And now, I dare you. I defy you to be great. Do not just *be* tradition—*break* tradition. As only you can."

I fold the paper again and push it in my pocket, shaking my head as my mouth falls into its comfortable smirk.

"Do you have any idea how much you mean to me, brother?"

I know he won't answer, but I think he hears me anyhow. My brother could have died a dishonorable death. He didn't. His story is this blueprint for me, even the dark parts. I run my palm over my face, my eyes burning as I hold his memory close.

"I wish you could have met Reagan," I say, my smile growing, knowing how much my brother would tease me for falling for a girl so much like me despite our differences.

"She's so talented. The film she made is going to air on the public television station in California sometime in the fall. She had applied to USC as a backup, but she swears I'm not her only reason for wanting to go there."

"Truthfully, though?" I look down at my fidgeting hands, laughing to myself. "Vincent, I wouldn't care if I *was* the only reason. Is that bad?

323

It's bad, isn't it? It's selfish. I know it is. But this girl, Vincent."

I run my hand over my eyes again and move it to my open mouth then my chin, laughing into my palm.

"She has me so completely, and the only thing I can compare it to is the way you said Alyssa hit your heart. Like there's nothing too crazy, too far, too much..."

I stretch my legs out in front of me and rest back on my palms again, feeling my brother there with me. I don't speak any more. My nerves are calmed, and I know that when I step in front of my graduating class as their valedictorian in just a few hours, I'll be all right. I know when I pack everything I own—however slight those possessions may be—and pile into my barely-running car, that I'll make it all the way. I know that when I'm throwing the ball down the field, competing for the starting job at USC, that there's going to be a guy building up some young quarterback on the field in Alabama at the exact same time. And he'll be rooting for me. All because I surprised him.

I stand, shaking out the damp shirt I'd been sitting on and tucking it in the band of my shorts for the walk home. I bend down over Vincent's stone, balling my hand into a fist and resting it against the cool cement until I feel him tap back. My knuckles remain cold, and eventually I stand, pushing my hands into my pockets to begin the long walk home alone.

Alone, but not for long.

I love my home.

And I love what it made me.

ACKNOWLEDGEMENTS

This book is about more than just football. It's about family. And it's about the way people *see* other people. I grew up in a neighborhood much like West End. It wasn't always that way, but somewhere, during the years, shots rang closer, gangs took over, and people who called that place home for years, started to move away. Others stayed. And the horrible things that eventually happened on those streets—it wasn't their fault.

Drugs. The allure of a quick buck. Gangs, and a world that let kids grow up without parents and where money was thin but bills kept climbing, fostering desperation. Those were the circumstances. The people, though—they were *good.*

One of my first breaking news assignments for the first newspaper I worked for was a fatal shooting that took place in a carwash stall just a block away from my childhood home. When I walked the streets and talked to nearby residents, many of them were familiar. They'd been in their homes for forty years. Latino, white, black, or as Nico would say...*green*—that was never part of the conversation. My quotes were about the violence and the gangs, not about condemning groups of people based on their ethnicities or laying blame at their feet. But that conversation...it does happen. We hear it a lot. Subtle racism plays out couched under faulty reasoning and apologies, as if it makes it okay.

It doesn't.

It's not.

Ugly doesn't have a color. It lives among selfishness and hate. And as much as this story is about football...it's also about that.

But the football...the football is good, no?

Off my soapbox...I have to thank a lot of people for this story. Firstly, my parents and brother for giving me the greatest childhood a tomboy like me could ask for. I loved my home, and I love the people and families I grew up with.

To my beta readers—Ashley, Jen, Shelley and Bianca. Lost without you ladies. LOST!

To my hubs and son, my reason for anything and the ultimate support in all I do. My hubs also happens to be one hell of a beta reader.

Tina Scott and BilliJoy Carson—you make my words shine. You are my lifelines, and I write with confidence knowing I have you to catch me when I fall.

To dad, for making sure his little girl knew what a hard count was—and for loving that she also knows it's what makes Aaron Rogers special. (Note: I'm aware that there are a lot of things that make Aaron Rogers special.)

Angel Reyes—thank you so very much for becoming my Nico for the cover. You are a special human being, and I'm so glad that I've gotten to know you. You're going to do great things.

And Frank Rodriguez of DLRfoto…your photos leave me speechless. I will never stop dreaming up ideas just so I can talk you into shooting them for me. You're a gift, and a forever kind of friend.

I must also thank my amazing readers, bloggers and reviewers who without I know I would still be writing books that no one would see. You are the spotlight, and I'm forever grateful for the time and attention you give to me. I'm humbled by it. And Ninjas? You guys are the best. I meant what I said—better than the Fox Force Five.

I hope you enjoyed this story. If you did, I would deeply appreciate your review. It's often the only way indies like me are seen. And I welcome your email, too. You wouldn't believe the smile it will put on my face.

Whose house is this?

Our house.

Hoorah!

ABOUT THE AUTHOR

Ginger Scott is an Amazon-bestselling and Goodreads Choice Award-nominated author of several young and new adult romances, including Waiting on the Sidelines, Going Long, Blindness, How We Deal With Gravity, This Is Falling, You and Everything After, The Girl I Was Before, In Your Dreams, Wild Reckless, Wicked Restless and The Hard Count.

A sucker for a good romance, Ginger's other passion is sports, and she often blends the two in her stories. Ginger has been writing and editing for newspapers, magazines and blogs for...well...ever. She has told the stories of Olympians, politicians, actors, scientists, cowboys, criminals and towns. For more on her and her work, visit her website at http://www.littlemisswrite.com.

When she's not writing, the odds are high that she's somewhere near a baseball diamond, either watching her son field pop flies like Bryce Harper or cheering on her favorite baseball team, the Arizona Diamondbacks. Ginger lives in Arizona and is married to her college sweetheart whom she met at ASU (fork 'em, Devils).

Ginger Online

@TheGingerScott
www.facebook.com/GingerScottAuthor
www.littlemisswrite.com

BOOKS BY GINGER SCOTT

Read The Complete Falling Series
This Is Falling
You And Everything After
The Girl I Was Before
In Your Dreams (spin-off standalone)

The Waiting Series
Waiting on the Sidelines
Going Long

The Harper Boys
Wild Reckless
Wicked Restless

Standalones
Blindness
How We Deal With Gravity
The Hard Count

CPSIA information can be obtained
at www.ICGtesting.com
Printed in the USA
LVHW03s1453040918
589113LV00010B/908/P